T0354720

A SECOND LAYER OF
REALITY

A SECOND LAYER OF
REALITY

BRYCE BLANCHARD

iUniverse®

A SECOND LAYER OF REALITY

iUniverse books may be ordered through booksellers or by contacting:

iUniverse
1663 Liberty Drive
Bloomington, IN 47403
www.iuniverse.com
844-349-9409

ISBN: 978-1-6632-3219-9 (sc)
ISBN: 978-1-6632-6115-1 (hc)
ISBN: 978-1-6632-6116-8 (e)

Library of Congress Control Number: 2024907177

Print information available on the last page.

iUniverse rev. date: 09/10/2024

DEDICATION

To my mom, who motivates and cheers me on through everything.

To my friends, especially Tom and Vishnu,
who helped make this possible.

CONTENTS

PROLOGUE

Charles

I stumble through the door to the table, propelling myself forward with one hand grasping the edge while the other clutches my side from where the blade sliced into me. I grab the door and turn the handle, only to find it locked. I hear his dress shoes clacking against the wooden floor, getting tauntingly closer to my location.

"I know you know where he went."

The clacking draws closer as I fish my keys from my pocket, the jangling sounding like a chorus of cacophonic chimes, dull and disjointed.

"Trying to escape? We can't have that now, can we?"

I finally get the right key in the lock and quickly turn the handle to open the door, grabbing the war ax from the small shrine in front of the armor. As I do so, I hear the shoes stop at the door.

"All I want to know is where he is. Then I will go. You can spend whatever time you have left here without a bother from me."

I wheel around, brandishing my ax, to see the man in the doorway in his pristine suit, a smug grin accompanied by a piercing stare.

"Those are lies! Once I tell you, you will kill me!" I scream as I raise the ax, brace myself, and charge at him. His eyes glow as they did earlier, the sight replaying through my mind as I realize what will happen.

"Defying me does nothing but buy him time. It appears that you, too, are out of time."

Ten minutes earlier ...

I stroll into my house and turn the deadbolt. Stepping into the kitchen, I grab the milk and pour a glass for myself. As I do, I hear a knock at the door. Putting the carton back, I take a swig from the glass of milk before setting it down and reaching for the knife block, intentionally pulling the butcher's cleaver from it.

With the sweet swish of a clean blade ringing across the room, I turn to face the door. Another knock. I step up to the door and peer through the peephole, only to find a man in an exquisite suit standing in the hallway by himself, one hand lazily in his pocket. Giving off an air of superiority, the stranger looks up at the peephole as a grin crosses his face.

I reach over and unlock the door, leaving the hinge lock on as I do. I open it as far as I can to look through it.

"Can I help you?" I ask cautiously.

"Yes, all I will need is a moment of your time. I am looking for someone, and I think you might know where I should look," he says with his grin not quite reaching his eyes. I tighten my grip on the knife on the other side of the door.

"I am kind of new to the area. I don't really know anyone," I say dismissively, closing the door in his face and walking back to the kitchen. As I grasp the glass, I hear the door lock slide back open. I turn to see the door handle relocking before the chain bolt slides back off. I nervously take a step toward the center of the room, a bead of sweat rolling down my brow. The deadbolt keeps sliding to the open position before the door swings open, revealing the man, now with glowing green eyes, holding an old, ornate pocket watch with a hexagonal lid that covers the face. The lid has four golden bars that all converge on an emerald housed in the center. When looking at the face numerous gears all turn in the background. The hands each stand out due to a dark green edging that gives them an ethereal look.

"Let's get down to business, shall we? I have a schedule to keep, and I hate to be kept waiting, so let's make this quick."

I sprint at him while simultaneously raising the cleaver and start to bring it down. However, he unflinchingly raises his hand toward me and then, with a disinterested look, speaks in his stoic tone.

"Stop and listen."

Everything stops. I can only stare as he takes a step forward, his glowing green eyes betraying the malice in his calm demeanor. As he steps through the threshold, he takes the blade from my hands and calmly runs it across my side with a sigh. A searing pain erupts through my side as he carves the blade through.

"Did you know that time is what makes injuries so fatal? Without time, you cannot truly die from a smaller injury. Let's wrap this up before you run out of time."

He walks to the kitchen, pours himself a glass of my milk, takes a sip, and grimaces.

"I don't see what you like about that," he states as he drops the glass to the ground with disgust, letting it shatter. He steps over the broken shards of glass toward me and sits down on the barstool I keep by the counter.

"I have a question to ask, and the longer you take to answer, the more time you lose." He waves his hand, his eyes glowing green once more as I feel my body regain the ability to move.

"Now tell me, where is Solomon Helgen?"

CHAPTER 1

AN UNEXPECTED SITUATION

Solaire

"Can you believe that bitch? She sent me to the dean to ask her why we couldn't format the project with the information going down vertically rather than rolling horizontally. I made my point, and then suddenly, she said I yelled at her!"

He is a Hispanic transfer student with curly long black hair that frames a Casanova's face, with a pair of glasses that makes his defined chin and nose more appealing to the eye. He is wearing a black turtleneck with a camel-colored bomber jacket, accompanied by a pair of dark-wash jeans. I reach over and give him a pat on the back.

"It's all right, Bastian. She will get what's coming to her. Besides, it's time for the weekend. Don't worry about that kind of garbage."

My attire is a simple pair of jeans with a gray polo and a black coat over that. There are always a few locks of my dusty brown hair cascading into my view.

"Ms. Thessaler has always been a very strict teacher; I think you actually got off somewhat easily for the ridiculous situation you were put in," a voice to the right of Bastian retorts.

"Come on, Solomon. Are you trying to tell me you agree with her?" Bastian sighs exasperatingly. I glance over at Solomon and see his usual pristine appearance, his hair slicked back, one lock of it flowing off the side perfectly in order, his attire a set of black slacks and dress shoes and a black button-up with the collar popped. He is carrying his suit coat over his shoulder.

"Not entirely. I just like seeing you overreact to things like this. Though, I must admit, based upon your usual voice, that wasn't yelling."

"Hey!" I wince at Bastian's shriek as I see the ghost of a smile trace across Solomon's face.

"So, why do you always come to class all dressed up like that? Isn't it a bit strange?" I ask tentatively.

"Not really; they say dress for success, and I also like to look better than certain individuals who happen to irritate the teacher." Solomon discloses with a victorious glance at Bastian.

"Oh! It burns!" Bastian quips as he grabs his heart dramatically.

We reach the end of the corridor and shuffle into another classroom. I feel someone push me into the corner of the door. I turn around, sporting a fierce glare. I see Ray with a triumphant smirk walking to the door.

"Move out of the way, loser."

"The only thing I am losing is my patience with you, Ray," I say as I unruffle my coat and step through the door.

"Don't bother giving this wannabe gangster any attention. He has nothing going for him and no future," Solomon drawls.

"Why you ..."

Ray turns around, taking a step toward Solomon.

"That's enough out of everyone! Take your seats, please," comes a booming voice from the desk in the corner. I turn and see a larger teacher stand up, a heavyset man with a mustache and a tacky yellow shirt with a mismatching maroon tie. Julius Elliot, the history teacher.

With a scoff, Ray turns on his heel.

"You're lucky, Solomon. Mark my words: one of these days, the teacher won't be around to save you." I bristle, grinding my teeth and stepping forward, intent on showing Ray a thing or two, but a hand grips my arm, holding me back.

I turn to see Solomon's impassive look following Ray's back as he moves to his seat.

"He shouldn't get away with this, especially doing it to you," I snarl, and Solomon merely gazes at his retreating form.

"I appreciate you, Solaire, and despite your gratitude for how I cared for you after your family's accident, I can handle this."

"Anytime now, you three. Let's not wait for the grass to grow." Mr. Elliot sighs exasperatedly.

As we all take our seats, I hear Solomon get a text as an absurd jazz ringtone rings out. I turn to see him sit in his chair and lean into the back of it. Opening his phone to see the text, he raises an eyebrow. As Mr. Elliot starts slamming his lesson plan onto the desk, Solomon shoots forward in his seat, his face ashen as if he has seen a ghost.

"All right, class, today's lesson is on ..."

I cast a disturbed look to Solomon, who waves it off. I turn to Bastian to whisper to him as he leans carelessly on his elbow, gazing at the whiteboard. Then I hear the chair next to me go screeching back. Everyone turns their attention to Solomon as he starts striding for the door, transfixed by his phone.

"Mr. Helgen," Professor Elliot's voice booms out, catching Solomon's attention. All our attention is focused on him now. "Do you have somewhere more important to be than my class?"

Solomon stops, his hand resting upon the door handle, turning back to the class.

"He probably got a text from his momma to go home," Ray shouts from the other side of the class, causing a few of the students near him to giggle. This earns him a glare from Solomon, his teeth visibly grinding. Holding the door handle tightly, he turns as he opens the door. I hear Professor Elliot take a breath to speak when suddenly, the windows shatter. We all snap to see armed soldiers outfitted in black body armor, with black ski masks, diving into the classroom in pairs. Three sets follow, each soldier carrying a submachine gun. Fanning out around the classroom, each one stops at the edges around the room. Then, one more figure rappels in wearing the same body armor. Instead of a ski mask, he is wearing a black beret on his head with a symbol I have never seen before. The symbol in question is a gilded eagle, with its wings spread wide. Each wing is feathered and the gold highlights them perfectly so I can make out the image from where I stand. He has a nasty scar running through his left eye, robbing it of its color. On his back are swords sheathed, crisscrossing. He has a pistol holstered and a rifle in his hands, different from the submachine guns in the soldiers' hands.

His face is an unreadable steely mask, his gaze passing over each of us, stopping only on Solomon, who is still at the back of the room, his fear from earlier turning into a rebellious gaze, glaring right back at the new entry.

"Good afternoon, everyone. I am here for one thing and one thing alone. If I receive what I am looking for, I will not harm you." He pauses for a second, letting that sink in. "My employer wants me to find someone, and I was led to believe they would be in this room. I honestly don't care whether you live or die. All I want is to be paid. You have my word that if you give me who I want, you will all go free."

"Who are you looking for?" comes Mr. Elliot's voice, a shy whisper compared to his usual boom.

Without turning his head, he responds, "One who goes by the name Solomon Hel—"

Before he has even finished, Ray stands up, getting the attention of everyone in the room and training all guns on him, causing the fierce leader to draw a gun swiftly and aim it at him as well.

"Yes?" he prompts. Ray raises his hand, pointing in the direction of the doorway. I hear it swing open, followed by the crack of gunfire as one of the soldiers lets a few shots rake across the doorway.

"After him! Now!" the leader screams out as the soldiers follow after him. He takes a step forward and then pauses and turns. His soulless eye pierces me. As I stare into his lone eye, I start to see something inside it, a swirling that morphs into a beast-like creature. I take a deep breath and feel my mouth go dry.

"What is this man?"

"You. You may yet be beneficial to me."

He reaches out and drags me over the table. I see Mr. Elliot get up and take a step toward us, a sharp crack rings out, and then I see him stumble backward, collapsing across his table, sending the supplies everywhere. He grasps at his chest, and a red stain starts to pool out across his torso.

"All of you stay here. Do not move. If you chase us, this teacher will be the least of your worries," he states as he drags me to the door. My thrashing does not impede him in the least. He kicks the door open, sending it off its hinges, and turns to walk down the corridor. I see a trail of blood streaming down the hall, and I hear my captor chuckle.

"It seems they clipped him after all."

I struggled a little more, earning me a clubbing on my head from the soldier.

"Do not worry about your friend. You should be more worried about yourself." He grins down at me as I cradle my head. I hear synchronized steps and see the soldiers walking up the staircase, dragging an unconscious bleeding Solomon in tow.

"It seems everything is going to plan," he says with a smile. I hear footsteps, and I see Bastian around the corner, armed with two pairs of scissors. He rears back and lets one fly toward us. The leader ducks to dodge the lethal throw, pulls his pistol, and fires. As he does, a green wave flows through the hallway that stops the bullets in the air. A shocked expression crosses Bastian's face.

I hear footsteps come down the hallway, distant at first but steadily moving closer. The captain turns to his soldiers, holding Solomon.

"Take him now! We will follow as soon as we have bought you enough time."

I look up to the captain as he holsters his gun and pulls his swords. They gleam a strange light blue. Bastian readies his other pair of scissors as the two soldiers quickly dash back down the stairs with Solomon.

"You seek to buy time? How laughable. One cannot buy more time than they have—of that, I can assure you," a confident voice comes from down the hallway behind Bastian. Our attention focuses on the newcomer. The first thing I notice is his dark green tie, neatly tucked into his suit, and the matching handkerchief over his right breast. Upon it is a gothic-styled letter P. A set of matching cufflinks sit on his arms, his dark suit no doubt covering the others in his flawless appearance. His left hand is in his pocket as he advances forward, one step at a time.

"I believe you just sent your men off with someone I have been looking for. If you would be so kind as to have your men deliver him to me, I will be on my merry way," he states as he comes to a halt just in front of Bastian.

The captain takes a deep breath as a notable leathery stretch can be heard from his grip tightening around his swords.

"As much as I would love to entertain you, I don't even know your name," the captain growls out.

"How rude of me. My name is—"

"Alexander Crawford. Why are you here?" a voice rings out across the hallway, coming from seemingly nowhere.

An orange pulse comes from the direction of the voice.

What the hell is happening here? Then my mouth drops as the air starts to visibly crack apart, as if it is shattering into orange glass that slowly falls away to reveal a silhouette of a man, who steps from the bizarre distortion. I gasp as I recognize it to be the director of the school, from his dark skin to his bald head, clad in a gray suit with a dark tie, his reading glasses perched upon his perfect nose.

"Ah, it's been a while, Jeffery Durgess. Perhaps you can explain why, after all this time searching, I find that the one I was looking for was in your possession?" A sharp glare comes across Alexander's face, betraying his smug grin.

"Durgess?" the captain mumbles to himself, suddenly straightening and looking shocked at the newcomer. "As in the dimension shifter?"

A sigh comes from the director as he slowly shakes his head, as if this is amusing to him.

"Such an old moniker. I had thought it lost when I started teaching here, but seeing as you both know who I am, why don't you both take your leave and no one has to get hurt today. I do protest the use of violence within my school, after all," he lazily drawls, his carefree attitude contradicting his serious face and the strange orange glow that seems to surround his hand.

"I am here for the boys only. I want nothing else," the captain says as he straightens his posture, sheathing one of his swords while slightly lowering the other, extending a hand palm up as if offering a deal. "If you let me take them, you won't see me again," the man says, a smile on his face. The director seems to nod for a moment, then turns to address the captain. His gaze flicks to me for just a moment.

"Now, while I do despise the acts of conflict on the school's grounds, what right do you think you have to my students?" he drawls, raising his head, the orange glow starting to reach his eyes; his normally teal eyes glowing orange as the pressure increases within the hallway.

A shocked look crosses the captain's face. He scowls.

"Since we seem to be at an impasse, men, kill them! I will take our prize now."

The other two soldiers come running in front of the captain as he starts taking menacing steps toward me, each one covering a third of the distance. As loud gunfire starts behind him, the flashes from the soldiers' guns make it seem as if he is the only thing in the room.

"Stop," a single quiet word, and a green pulse flashes out from Alexander as he starts walking forward, the bullets all frozen in the air. The men pause as they direct all fire upon Alexander. His eyes glow an eerie green the entire time as the bullets all seem to stop in front of him. He keeps walking forward into them, letting them slide over his frame as if he is merely brushing them aside.

The captain grabs my coat and starts dragging me to the stairs to follow his soldiers. I wriggle out of my coat and stumble forward to the floor, only to see an orange portal open in front of me, allowing me to fall through it and land on the floor.

Groaning, I turn to see I am now *behind* the director.

How?

"How did I …?" I stutter in disbelief as I hear a rage-filled roar from the other side of the room and see the soldiers continuing to fire at Alexander. The distance is now drastically reduced to no more than three meters apart. The men frantically fire as fast as they can.

I hear a thud and a groan beside me as I turn to see Bastian, now lying underneath his own portal, which slowly closes. A sharp unsheathing sound comes from behind the soldiers as the captain starts advancing toward me, his eyes glowing with fury as he now has both swords brandished.

Just then, the gunfire stops as Alexander reaches the soldiers and thrusts both arms out, grabbing the soldiers by their necks and lifting them into the air. Their weapons fall to the ground, and time seems to stop as we all turn our attention to him. The eerie glow envelops his person as he takes a breath and mutters a single word.

"Consume."

With that, a green essence coalesces in front of the soldiers and streams down Alexander's arms.

"Aaaahhhhh!"

Both soldiers start screaming in agony as the orbs run down Alexander's arms and into the pocket watch that hangs from his side. As the last of it streams down, the soldiers grow stiff, and then everything—their bodies, their helmet, even their armor—turns to ash as they slowly crumble apart. Scattering across the floor, their separate forms are now indiscernible.

"Would you be so kind as to volunteer your time to me as well, mercenary?" Alexander hisses as time seems to start to flow again. A serious expression flows across the director's face as his arms start to glow orange.

The captain's swords glow blue as he steps toward Alexander. My sight is blocked as Director Durgess crouches down in front of the two of us.

"Listen to me carefully: Bastian, Solaire, you both have to find Solomon. Don't let anyone from Prometheus get to him first. Bastian, you will be his guide. I don't know how you are here, but frankly, there isn't any time to wonder about that." His arms, already orange, begin to change to a brighter color, almost blinding, as he slowly stands up.

"Go. Time is—"

A blade comes piercing through the director's chest, spraying blood over both Bastian and me. A look of shock comes over the director's face. A cough, and blood pours out of his mouth as Alexander's face appears over the director's shoulder.

"Time is up, Durgess. You should have joined Prometheus when you had the chance," he hisses into the director's ear.

An orange portal opens beneath both of us as the director grasps the blade emerging from his chest. As we fall through and hit the ground of a field, we catch a glimpse of the director as he stands between the portal and Alexander, his cruel green eyes glaring through the director at us.

"Do you really believe that by sending them somewhere else, you will buy them anything but time?" he mocks, twisting the knife. Durgess winces as a dribble of blood swims from between his lips.

With a growl, Durgess grasps the blade's edge, protruding from his chest, and a small portal forms in front of him. He leans forward, bringing the tip of the weapon into it. The portal shuts, and the blade falls into his outstretched hand.

Durgess throws his head back and spins, twisting with the blade in his hand. As he does, I catch a glimpse past him to see the smug smile across Alexander's face and a spray of blood suspended in the air around him, like a halo of death. He turns his head to the side, to where the captain is.

"It is quite unfortunate: mercenaries these days really aren't what they used to be. Unfortunately, I can't kill this one just yet. He knows where Solomon is."

A wet cough fills the air as Durgess hunches forward. The portal grows smaller still, until I can see only Durgess' back and head.

"I don't expect them ... *cough* ... to elude you forev ... *cough* ... just long enough to learn ... *cough* ... how to stop Prometheus."

"How do you think they will do that? You were once one of the few who could challenge us, and here you are now, groveling before me." I hear the victorious sneer. "Though I suppose I can give him a bit of motivation after you die. Perhaps I should rip the time from all your precious students."

I feel the blood drain from my face as I turn to Bastian, whose face betrays the rage he is feeling. I look back and see Durgess lunge forward, revealing Alexander, who has a nasty grin split across his face.

"Stop."

A lone word, so final and so very terrifying. His eyes glow as he focuses his gaze on me.

"Don't you worry, boy. I will kill Solomon. Then I will find you both and steal your time, simply because I can."

I gasp as I see the portal close, leaving the two of us in a field in the middle of nowhere, tall brown grass all around us. I take a breath, trying to calm myself down.

What the hell is happening? I have to be losing my mind.

I glance up at the sun and notice two things: First, the sun is blue. Second, there are two of them, one on either end of the horizon.

"Where the hell are we?" I scream.

CHAPTER 2

A BREACH OF TRUST

Solaire

I stand up, turning around, my calm facade quickly dissipating as I take in my new environment. The two suns are a great shock. As I turn around in the field, I see a gravel road. I follow it with my eyes to see that it leads to a medieval-looking city with strange protrusions in the distance. Branching out behind the city, a string of snow-capped mountains take up the right side of the horizon. Continuing my scan, I see a castle nuzzled within a bowl, seemingly carved out of the side of one of the mountains. A large spire lingers over the rest of the castle, a dark storm enveloping the sky above it. Starting from the end of the mountain, I see an endless stretch meeting a border of trees. It parts to reveal a large object suspended in the air, making it seem as if the trees are chained down to the ground. The forest then continues until it meets the icy mountains on the other side.

Upon turning around, I see Bastian sitting up. His demeanor seems deflated compared to the ferocity I saw while he was confronting the captain. His hand comes up to straighten his glasses as he looks up at me.

"We have to get moving. That only bought us so much time," he responds quietly. I stare at him incredulously as he rises.

"How can you be so calm? We have just been teleported to God-knows-where, by our principal, who was fighting mercenaries with magical powers and was then killed by someone else—who also just so

11

happened to have magical powers?" I shout, throwing up my arms with a dramatic flourish.

He flinches and raises one arm in a calming gesture, taking a small step toward me.

"Listen, we don't have a lot of time. We need to go. Once we get somewhere safe, I will—"

"Screw that! I have known you for ten years, Bastian. Ten years! Not once has anything supernatural ever come near me. For all I knew, you were normal, just like Solomon and just like the director." As he inches forward, I take a step back.

"Come on. The director gave us a chance by sending us here. We can save Solomon, but only if we go now," he hisses, his placating look becoming stern, matching his tone.

"How can I trust you? How many years did you keep this world from me?" In the space between my words, he looks down, his passion swapped for shame. Seeing his silence, I continue gazing downward, feeling my anger boiling under my skin. "Now, I don't care about you or what the director wants from me. All I care about is Solomon. He and his family have taken care of me for a long time." I grip my fist as I raise my head, glaring daggers at Bastian, who is still looking at his feet. He raises his head, steely resolve growing in his eyes. He puts a reassuring hand on my shoulder.

"The only way to save Solomon is for you to trust me."

I shake my head, unable to believe this nonsense. I throw his arm off me.

"Trust you? Whatever happened to those ten years I trusted you, huh? That's why we are here now! I trusted you, and now I don't even know who you are!" I shout.

He raises his hand. "Shhhh. Any louder and they will find us," he hisses. I shove him away from me.

"Who the hell are they? Tell me what I should be afraid of! Tell me what I need to do to save him!"

Bastian sighs, then takes a breath, which is cut short as a rustle in the brush causes him to glance to the side, immediately on guard. He steps closer to me, his arm brandishing scissors as he whispers, "You have to find a man named Charles Haplas. He should be able to help if we are separated." Another rustle from the tall grasses causes me to glance out across the grasses. A dry feeling flows over me, as if something is watching me.

"Wh-what do—"

A huge broadsword flashes out from the grasses. I stumble back as Bastian rushes in front of me, brandishing the scissors and knocking away the blade. The blade crashes into the ground, carving out a large crevasse. A gruff voice grumbles, "Look who we have here—a couple of trespassers. The only ones permitted here are the righteous."

I follow the voice and see a man with a large silver longsword with a crisscrossing leather grip. A centralized cross leads back to a pommel embedded with a topaz. The iron gauntlets lead up to a mountain of a man. He towers over me, higher than six feet, and his suit of armor bears a large orange cross adorning its front. His head is covered by a helmet that leaves his entire face visible. An intense yet playful gaze evaluates us, obscured only by a rogue strand of blond hair running down his neck, framing one side of his face. As he speaks, five soldiers, much shorter than he is, step out of the brush on either side of this behemoth, each donning the same armor but with swords and shields instead of a two-handed longsword.

"Run now!" Bastian yells as the giant sword erupts out of the ground toward Bastian, causing him to dive backward, the blade narrowly missing his face. I turn on my heel and sprint through the tall grass in the direction of the city. The fronds lash at my face as I barrel through them.

"After him!" a voice booms behind me. I run even faster, each step like trudging through water as I feel my heart racing. I can still hear the clash of steel behind me.

Bastian

"Run now!" I cry, lurching backward, barely dodging the huge blade that emerges from the ground.

I glance askance to see Solaire take off into the grasses. As I look back, the huge blade is thrusting forward to spear me. I wheel to the side, spinning on my heel, feeling the blade brush past my side.

"Interesting. You seem to be fast on your feet. However, I cannot just let him go. You two, after him!" he growls. The guards on the leader's right run after Solaire.

Intent on killing the huge soldier first, I lunge forward and raise my shears, rearing them back for a thrust as he turns his blade and raises it up from the ground, intending to bisect me.

I roll to the side and come out of the roll, thrusting with the shears. This catches the guard by surprise, and he drops his sword to grasp at the wound in his neck, blood spewing from between his hands. He stumbles to the side and falls into a crumpled heap. The other soldier thrusts forward with his sword. I bat it to the side and step closer to deliver another fatal blow as a shadow eclipses me.

I turn to see the broadsword slashing diagonally toward me. My eyes widen as I see the smirk on the giant's face. With no time to respond, I skip backward and feel a searing pain across my chest as the soldier is bisected by the massive blade.

I stumble back, one arm grasping my chest, the other holding the scissors in front of me defiantly, in shock that the soldier has been struck down by one of his own.

"After him!" the big man bellows, stepping in front of me. The two remaining guards are already scrambling to pursue Solaire.

"You are doing well considering you are alone and wielding a weapon so poorly," he grumbles, sneering as he steps to the side, walking around me in an arc to find an angle of attack.

"Glad to hear I am living up to your standards, sir giant, although you are leveling the playfield," I growl. I am now sandwiched between the soldier behind me and the one in front of me. Laughter rumbles from the big man's belly.

"I don't often give out compliments like that. You should just turn yourself over to me. I would hate to kill one as young and skilled as yourself." He lowers his sword. I let a smile grace my face but tense up again as the shorter soldier takes a step behind me.

"I don't even know who you are. How do I know you won't just kill me, like your soldier over there?" I reply with a merciless chuckle, gesturing at the corpse at his feet. The big man joins me in laughter.

"My name is Felgrand Tiang, Captain of Ashvale Fields. My duty is to keep the peace here. I cannot let people do as they please, especially those who fall through one of the dimension shifter's gates." He straightens his stance and relaxes his posture, his sword still at his side, and kicks the soldier's carcass. "As for this one, he was dead as soon as you got that close. Besides, dying in such a holy place is considered an honor," he says, somewhat sardonically. He smiles and shifts his gaze back to me. "You may as well give up now. You should be feeling the effects already."

My eyes widen, and then I finally feel it as I try to tighten my stance. My body feels as if it is … growing heavier?

"Wh-what did you do?" I ask, glaring at Felgrand, loathing the smirk that looms over me. I reach up sluggishly and touch my wound. "Poison?" I look up, shocked. "What member of the Church uses such a dastardly tactic? I thought they looked down upon it?"

"Oh, they do, but it is my duty to imprison those who are savable so they might have the chance to change their heathen ways," he replies with genuine passion.

I drop to one knee, hearing heavy footfalls behind me.

"Die scum!" the soldier behind me screams, charging forward.

"No, we are taking him alive! Stop now, soldier!" The big man strides forward, raising his sword. But he is too far, and he will not make it in time.

"Damn. Looks like I won't be meeting you, after all, Solaire."

I tighten my grasp on the scissors and whirl around to face this new adversary. My body protests all the way. A coursing pain runs through my body, and I lose feeling in the front of my chest. I let the scissors fly, sending them straight into the soldier behind me. His face contorts with bloodlust, and in the next moment, a look of shock as the scissors embed themselves to the handles in his head. The soldier's head cocks back, and his body slumps to the ground in front of me.

"It seems I didn't have to do anything after all." The big man chuckles once more. I fall backward, unable to keep myself upright any longer. I look up toward the big man, now standing over me, his eyes a fierce, steely blue. He glances at the fallen soldier and sneers.

"Can't even follow a single order. What good are you? Lie here and rot for your disobedience." I feel my eyes begin to grow heavier.

"There is no need to worry. You shall be reunited with your friend shortly within the walls of Ashvale." He pauses, then chuckles.

"The keep, that is." His chuckle rises to a booming laugh as he grabs my leg and drags me away. I feel my eyes finally shut.

Solaire

Have to keep running.

I am panting heavily as I finally break through the tall grass. I stop for a moment, resting my arms on my knees as I hunch over to collect a couple of breaths. I run forward to the gate to my left and peek inside. Seeing only migrant civilians walking around, I dart through the gate. As I do, I cannot help but notice an odd collaboration of medieval and new-age styles combining to form a most amazing sight. I stop and gaze out, taking it all in.

The streets are made of rectangular stones, perfectly set and extending all the way down the path. Vendor carts are leaning on the edges of the stone path, their patrons meandering and consorting with the merchants. The buildings include more modern designs, multistory with windows made from glass and intricate designs, each looking like a home from a suburban area. Myriad colors populate my view.

I hear the metal footfalls behind me. I look back to see two guards turn the corner and point at me.

"There he is!" one of them shouts. I turn around and take off down the road, dodging and weaving within the bustling crowd. I look back to see the guards shoving through the crowd as well. As I do, I come crashing into a waiter, sending the contents of his tray spilling over the two of us as I careen over the table, landing on the ground. I groan as I get up to dash off, only to feel a heavy boot land on my back, pinning me down.

Shit!

"Do you want me to kill this one, Stephen?"

The boot kicks my side, flipping me onto my back. The sharp hiss of steel rings out before I feel cold steel at the base of my neck. I close my eyes accepting my fate.

"Now, Darius, let's not be hasty."

My eyes slowly open to the sight of two figures over me. One is still seated while the other is standing over me, sword in hand. His swarthy grizzled face is darkened further by unkempt facial hair. Most of his body is clad in a cloak, cinched at the neck with a gold pin and held down by two dark leather spaulders on his shoulders. Where the cloak parts, I see a dark uniform underneath, fitted with a belt that holds various pouches and knives.

I turn to my savior, who is still seated, a calculating look on his well-kempt face. His attire is a cream-colored blazer with a fountain pen in the breast pocket. A white button-up underneath the blazer, the top button popped, suggests a carefree attitude, belied by the cold look on his face.

He reaches for the pen and clicks it purposefully, then writes down something on something I cannot see. I turn my attention back to the one named Darius, then see something that makes my heart sink. Upon the clasp at the neck of the cloak, there is a pin bearing a design—the same design as the insignia worn by the captain who attacked the school. My mouth runs dry, and I am unable to swallow.

"Won't you lower your sword? You are scaring the boy," the seated man rambles dully.

"He should be scared; he bowled into us in the middle of a meeting!" Darius growls. The metal footsteps of the soldiers arrive. Looking up, I see that the guards found friends while chasing me, as they now count six in total. One of the soldiers steps forward, one of the guards from the field.

"Hand over the one on the ground. He was caught trespassing in the Ashvale field. He is to be punished by the Church." Darius emits a grunt as he glances at the new arrivals. "Tsk. Not only did he wreck this meeting, but he also brought the guard to us." A look of disdain crosses his face as the grip on his sword tightens. I notice movement from Stephen, who sips from a teacup. Putting the glass down with his eyes closed, he seems to be casually ignoring the events around him as he savors his drink.

"Now, Darius, unforeseen circumstances tend to lead to rash decisions." Stephen's eyes snap open, glaring at Darius. "You, perhaps better than most, should know that."

A collective gasp runs through the guards at the mention of Darius's name.

"You there, remove your hood!" the guard orders. A frustrated sigh comes from Darius as a chuckle comes from Stephen.

"Darius, since they seem to be on to you, might you take care of the light work while I speak to our new guest?" Stephen says. A growl erupts from Darius as he turns and casts a dark glance my way.

"What about our meeting?"

A sigh from the table. I see Stephen toying with a pen.

"Always a one-track mind," he mumbles. "Due to our new guest and the guard, I believe this meeting is coming to an end."

"I can take care of them quickly. Then we can continue." Darius rushes out, a few voices of indignation coming from the guard.

"There is no reason you would take too long. Besides, I have grown bored with your presence. I feel our new guest will provide a better company. So, you can stay here and take care of them while I take our guest and get to know him. I will contact you later—after you have dealt with them," he says, standing and taking one last sip from his cup before closing his eyes. His other arm loosely holds an elaborate notebook at his side.

"Why, you little—" Darius says, stepping toward Stephen. A smug smile crosses Stephen's lips. As his eyes snap open, he sets down the teacup.

"Remember who you are dealing with, Darius Stajlet. I may not be the strongest, but I can still kill everyone here with extraordinarily little effort—you included," Darius growls. He turns to the guards. A few of them take a step back, while one steps forward, brandishing his sword.

"I knew I recognized him! That's Darius Stajlet, leader of the Thieves' Syndicate! You will be brought in—"

Before the guard can finish his sentence, a dagger is buried deep in his head, snapping it back as he falls. My attention goes back to Darius, who has his back to me, his arm now extended.

"Don't screw with me! I am in a particularly foul mood right now. None of you will be leaving here alive," he snarls, dashing into the soldiers—clangs and screams as guards start falling.

I feel a hand grasp my shoulder and flinch from seeing Stephen standing over me.

"Come, now. Let's leave him to it. Besides, I would like to get to know you better."

I scramble up, desperate to get away from Darius. I turn to see Stephen walking into a dark alley to the side of the café. Before I enter, I cast one last glare at Darius, who is still fighting.

I will get you to tell me where he is—once I have a way to force you to do so. I think as I step into the darkness.

Bastian
An unknown time later

Clink … clink … clink.

I startle awake to the unfamiliar sound of chains. Gasping, I bolt upright, my eyes darting around the unfamiliar location. I see bars and a stone floor, with a lone window across from the room, also barred shut. The corridor is lit with a torch, illuminating the empty cells around me. A sandy stone lines the floor, dust filling the cracks between the bricks. The faint flames give the room a golden cast. Scuff marks and scratches line the walls and floor. I pound my fist upon the floor.

"Damn. Guess Felgrand took me to Ashvale Keep then," I mumble to myself, glancing out the window, seeing many stories below me. I turn and face the bars. I grasp them and give them a tug to check for any weaknesses. No luck, so I listen to see if I can hear any guards nearby. The only sound is that of water dripping in the hallway.

They must not take care of this place, I think as I drop to the ground and grasp for the bottoms of my pants. Rolling them, I find my hidden

19

needle. I pull it out of its sheath. A six-inch weighted silver needle, perfect for throwing or picking a lock. I smile. Guess they don't know who they are messing with.

I reach through the bars of the cell, and a roaring scream echoes down the hallway. I hesitate, kneeling just within the cell. A bead of sweat runs down my brow.

What the hell was that?

The screaming stops. I involuntarily swallow, my throat feeling drier than ever. The only sound is the water dripping close by. I flinch as I feel a warm liquid brush against my knee. Prying my eyes from the end of the hallway, I look down to see a river of dark liquid running through the bars.

What ...?

My breath gets stuck in my throat as I push my empty hand into the liquid to feel a warm, sticky substance. I'm hoping it isn't what I think it is. I raise my hand toward the torchlight to see it reflect a crimson liquid, and my heart sinks.

What the hell happens in this prison?

My thoughts are interrupted by a strange squelching sound far down the corridor. I listen more intently, and my eyes widen. The sound continues, then, for a moment, everything goes quiet. The silence is pierced by a horrific scream.

"What the hell are you? You goddamn mons—aaaggghhh."

The screaming stops, and the squelching sound resumes. The bitter, acidic sting of bile rising in my throat springs me into action.

Whatever the hell that thing is, I don't want to be here when it gets here.

I shift my stance and reach through the bars to feel the lock with my crimson-covered hand. I scream as a bolt of electricity leaps from the corners of the cell, striking my protruding arm. I pull my arm back in and fall backward, sitting staring at the cell bars, horrified. Then I hear it, and I lose all hope; the squelching sound is now getting closer. I squeeze my eyes shut as I tighten my grip on the needle.

I can't die here! I think as I feel my teeth grind together. Then the squelching stops.

"Yo," a calm voice says from behind me. My eyes flash open, and

I wheel around, bringing my weapon in front of me to deter whatever newfound horror is behind me. My heart throbs harder, each second feeling like an hour.

I glance around the cell and see nothing. Then I notice a lack of light, and I look at the window. There, sitting with his legs coming through the bars, one hand braced on his knee lazily supporting his head, is a man. He is shrouded in a cloak. I can make out twin scabbards, one at each side of his body.

"You look like you could use a hand, Bastian."

A brief pause as my brain registers the figure in the window, trying to suss out his identity.

"Don't tell me you have forgotten who I am. After all ..." He pauses, throwing back his hood to reveal a dark-skinned man, cleanly sculpted short black hair that meets his goatee, neatly framing his face well. The light from the torch flickers off the glasses neatly squared upon his face. "I am the one who saved you from those monsters all those years ago." The breath I have been holding escapes my lips, and my muscles relax. I cannot believe he is here! The question of why is buried beneath relief that it isn't some monster.

"Strange, I seem to have a record for saving you in the presence of monsters." With a shrug, he lets his arm come through the window and rest on his knee. "Oh, well, you are just a lucky soul, I guess."

"Namar, what are you doing here, and what the hell is Ashvale Keep?" I mumble, dumbstruck. A grin stretches across his face.

"I wouldn't worry about that right now—unless you want to still be here when that thing gets here. I have come with the news. New orders have been assigned. Rather, a new contract has been set." My breath catches and I snarl at the prospect of going on another contract.

"A contract?" The bars give way as Namar slides into the room.

"Yes, Darius had an important meeting. Apparently, some fool decided to crash it. Darius decided to send a message. He wants this man dead." He reaches out, offering me his hand. I see the golden glint of the Syndicate pin on his cloak. I reach forward with a sigh.

"Just when I thought I got away from that life, it drags me back in.

However, after this, I need to ask you a favor," I respond dejectedly. Namar raises an eyebrow.

"A favor? Do you need my help? Fine, sure, as long as we get the bounty, I can help you. What kind of favor did you have in mind?" he inquires with a greedy smile.

"I need to find someone." Curiosity sparkles in his eye.

"Oh? That sounds easy enough, but first we need to collect the bounty." He flashes a maniacal grin.

"So, who is the unlucky bastard?" I ask. I see the smile run away from his face. Seeing I am annoyed at his avoidance of my question, he tempers his emotions.

"There is no name, only a description. That should not matter, though. We will find him. He was last seen within Ashvale, so once we get out, we can get right to it."

CHAPTER 3

NOT WHO THEY SEEM

Solaire

Stepping into the alley's darkness, I turn my attention back to the man in front of me. The cream-colored blazer turns darker in the shadows. He is holding a neatly folded suit jacket under his arm, clutching his journal to his side. He moves as if it is natural to hold his coat like that. He pauses and turns back, glancing over his shoulder when he reaches the mouth of the alleyway. I am so engrossed with studying my savior's appearance I fail to notice the bustling crowd and people walking past. I am so shocked by the rabble, I stop and can't help but stare. People of all different kinds are walking past. Trading stands, lined up and down the road, are attracting these people of all different statures. The social elite are donning fancy tunics and cloaks, each of which looks to be made of the finest of furs or the greatest of silks, whereas in between these bob the heads of the poor. The worst off among them stand out easily, their heads held high as they move through the bustling crowd with tattered clothing.

The stands themselves appear to be tents attached to carts, each one holding things from medieval items to modern ones. A person catches my eye as they walk past me. He has the face of a cat. His face is partially covered with fur, and thin black whiskers protrude from the cheeks of his face to the side. I eye the rest of the bustling crowd, seeing dozens of exquisite people within it—people with green skin, beings with pointed ears, some with scales covering their skin.

Then my eyes drift to an interesting sight. I see a small group of three people walking through the droves of commonfolk. They are dressed in scarlet cowls, all of which have tatters around the edges as they move through the crowd in an arrow-like formation. They stop in the center of the crowd, and one of them looks back and forth. It looks in my direction and starts moving through the crowd—to me.

My mouth drops open as they move closer. I get a look underneath one of their cloaks. It has light teal skin with dark highlights covering its face. Its eyes are large orange orbs, and in the center of them sit slitted pupils, similar to those of a cat. I sense Stephen's pause as he turns to me, my face one of pure shock.

"You appear surprised by the city of Ashvale. Evidently, you have not been here, despite this being a huge meeting ground for the different peoples of the Second Reality. And they seem interested in you."

I take a breath.

"Second Reality? And who are they?" I question tentatively. This catches Stephen slightly off guard, as a look of surprise crosses his face before he schools it into a small grin.

"You really have no idea where this place is, do you?"

I shake my head as he puts his palm to his.

"You must be from the First Reality—that is the only explanation for your oblivious nature." I feel my eyebrows scrunch together. "We try to keep it a secret from all who don't know about the other. What I mean to say is that the people of one reality have no business knowing about the other—unless, of course, they happen to fall into the other by accident." He looks back to the crowd of people, focusing on the scarlet-clad beings.

"None of these people have any clue about where you have come from, and you should not try to convince the people of this reality that there is another reality either, lest those people within the scarlet cloaks pursue you." I look toward the people in the cloaks as they advance toward us. With their terrifying gazes, each step feels like a countdown as they approach. The crowd parts like a sea before them, horror passing over the people whom these creatures walk past. Most of the citizens avert their gazes to avoid looking at them. As soon as they pass, the people scuttle forward, attempting to get as far from these creatures as possible. As if sensing my nervous stance, Stephen puts a hand on my shoulder. I flinch, stepping away from him.

"Do not be afraid. They will not harm you as of yet. They are known as Watchers, beings that have been tasked with keeping any who fall into a different reality from disturbing the peace within them." He tries to give me a reassuring look as the Watchers step into the alleyway. He turns to the Watchers.

The leading one regards Stephen for a moment, his golden eyes flicking to me as if scrutinizing my presence. Then, with a hiss like a whisper, it speaks.

"You have breached the fabric of reality, youngblood. You have taken many risks coming here." It slowly reaches up to its hood and removes it, revealing a blue skin with dark blue lines running in symmetrical lines. I take a step back as Stephen swiftly opens his notebook, snatching at the golden fountain pen in his breast pocket. He turns to a blank page.

"Do not fret, Promethean. We are not here to harm the boy. We are curious as to why he has come." The Watcher asks as he stares deeply into my eyes. Stephen starts as he glances back at me.

"Why have you come, youngblood?" The Watcher's eyes glow golden for a moment, and I suddenly desire to tell them everything. No, that can't be right. I shake my head from side to side, clearing my thoughts. I turn my attention to the Watcher, whose eyes widen and then fix an unnerving glare upon me.

"To think you have the power to resist my suggestion, truly you are something more than you know." Stephen lowers his stance and stares at me, his expression contemplative.

"Tell us why you are here, or we will have to resort to much more … forceful methods," he hisses. The others on either side of him reach into their cloaks, pulling out swords. Each is decorated with a ceremonial seal, seemingly archaic in design.

I take another step back, looking toward Stephen for support. I am met with an expectant glare as he stands his book in front of him, pen in hand. A brief moment of confusion passes through me as I wonder what he will do with that book to stop the Watchers before it is washed away by fear as I realize he also wants the answer. Looking past the Watchers,

I see that the street, previously bustling, is now devoid of people. With a shaky sigh, I realize there is no one to help me here.

"I am looking for someone," I offer weakly. The glare I am receiving increases in intensity, with only a slight lowering of the swords in the Watcher's hands.

"Who might that be?"

This time, Stephen inquires instead of the Watcher. My throat feels dry as I contemplate how much I should tell them. My paranoia comes from my lack of knowledge of who is allied with whom. I am broken from my internal debate when the Watcher in front pulls a rod from his cloak, his hand on the top of it. He grasps it, lightly tossing it up and catching it in the middle. A brief blue light pulses over the rod, and the rod extends into a trident.

"Youngblood, time is of the essence. We have sensed a disturbance within the balance of reality. We must correct it immediately, and if you do not answer us, we will be forced to kill you in the name of the balance." The Watcher hisses at me.

"My friend, he was taken from my school," I utter, unsure. Stephen raises an eyebrow.

"Your friend … was taken … so you come to the Second Reality?" he asks incredulously. He then starts laughing. I grit my teeth.

"He was taken by a group of soldiers. We were then attacked by someone who could stop time, and my teacher dropped me through a portal!" I growl. At this, the man stops laughing and looks deadly serious.

"He can manipulate time, you say? His name didn't happen to be Alexander, did it?" Stephen asks with a cruel smile working along his face. I take a step away from him and step into the alley's wall. I start to feel claustrophobic as Stephen takes a step around, seemingly to trap me against the wall.

"It appears, youngblood, that you have dealings with multiple Prometheans." As he says this, I feel the blood drain from my face. I finally registered that Alexander was referred to as a Promethean. Prometheus is not just the group that Alexander was in but rather a title given to members of the group as well. Stephen takes a step forward, a dark shadow eclipsing his face.

"Why don't you tell me just what Alexander was after in the First Reality." He takes another step to the side and brings his pen to his book. I catch a glimpse of the same gothic letter on the front of the journal that was upon Alexander's suit.

"You should start talking. It would be such a shame if you were to be erased," he says, a cruel smirk working its way to his face, creating a terrifying visage as his eyes betray a cold look I can barely discern in the darkness.

Suddenly a hiss of alarm comes from the Watchers as the one with the trident steps forward and slams the trident down.

"Tread carefully, Promethean. You may have the power to do just that, but we won't let it stand. He holds a place in the balance." Stephen grimaces and takes a step back.

"So, you wish to stand by someone whom you consider an unknown? How pretentious to believe you can make such decisions when you were just threatening him," Stephen claims with a dry chuckle.

Out of nowhere, I feel a sudden screaming pain in my arm, and I feel myself being knocked into the wall. I look down to see a small arrow-like object protruding from my shoulder.

"Aaaggghhh!" I scream, the pain growing worse with each breath. I suddenly realize I cannot move from the wall. I hear a clatter from down the hallway and see on the corner of the roof a man holding a crossbow loading another bolt into the weapon. Stephen frowns and takes a step toward the man.

"Now, why would you go and do that? I have some business with this boy here." He takes another step toward the man. The hallway suddenly feels a lot smaller, as if the very presence of Stephen is taking up most of it. The foreigner finishes loading another bolt and cradles the crossbow. An avaricious crazed smile crosses his face.

"I am here for the bounty on that one's head." He states as he raises the crossbow and fires at me. The bolt flashes toward me as I raise my good arm to shelter myself. I scrunch my eyes shut, anticipating the end to come. I hear a shuffle, then a metal clash.

I opened my eyes to see the bolt knocked to the ground, and the Watcher brandishing his trident in front of me in a defensive posture ready to intercept any other projectiles. I see Stephen begin to write in his book, but as that happens, more people are stepping into the hall, brandishing weapons. I hear Stephen sigh, clearly annoyed.

"I suppose you are all here for the bounty as well." It is more of a statement than a question. I observe the crowd, and one thing stands out. Each of them sports a golden pin belonging to the Syndicate group on their clothing. Stephen's eyes narrow; he must have noticed the same thing.

"Promethean, it would appear we have a common inconvenience. Come, let us take care of them, then we can settle our dispute with the youngblood." The Watchers all brandish their weapons, the swords in the other Watchers' arms beginning to glow an ominous blue as they step forward to their leader.

"You think you scare us? With the backing of Syndicate, we have nothing to fear!" shouts the same man with the crossbow.

"I see," Stephen says, gritting his teeth. "Damn you, Darius."

Bastian

"A contract, just like the old days," Namar says, grinning. My fists tighten, and I grit my teeth as I pummel the bars. "It looks like you cannot just leave after all."

"I took that last job to end it," I growl.

"Now look where you are." I turn my glare upon Namar's smug grin. "Stuck in Ashvale Keep, your only salvation a deal with the devil."

Namar's grin widens as I see him turn his head toward the bars to hide it.

"Damn it!" I curse under my breath as I smash my fist against the bar once more, lowering my head as I do so. I turn back to Namar to see him extending his arm toward me.

"It seems you have decided, so shall we get back to this? Just like the good old days." I roll my eyes and grind my teeth.

"This doesn't mean I am back in," I snarl as I thrust my arm forward, grabbing his.

"Whatever you say, killer," Namar says. His eyes flash a dim gray. A green bolt jumps from the bars, striking Namar and shocking us both. With a pained cry, we both fall back. Namar righted himself by taking a step backward.

"Wow ... That's a new one. I guess Ashvale has anti-magic within the keep." He pants as a green electric current cascades over his body. The awkward pause that follows after the shock is filled with another grotesque squelch. I hear Namar click his tongue in what I perceive to be an annoyance.

"I guess we will have to do it the hard way." Namar sighs as a sword flashes out of its sheath. The bars in front of Namar fall to the ground, leaving a small improvised doorway.

I gesture to Namar to go through first, and he gives me a dry look.

"You have the swords; you go first." A flash of recognition, and he reaches into his cloak. Producing a bundle of knives, he hands them over. I feel shocked. It has been years since I've seen them.

"Did you really think I would get you a contract without bringing your knives?"

Grabbing on to them gently, I ask, "How did you get them? I thought they were stolen by the turncoat, Carter." Looking at the ornate design on the daggers, I run my hands over the throwing knives, remembering the distinct silver notches, similar to the ones on the handle.

"He had a bounty placed upon him. In fact, it was one of the first-ever continental bounties." I raise my brow and fasten the belt around my waist; its weight feels eerily familiar.

"Continental bounties? Back up a second. What the hell has happened since I left?" I shake my head incredulously.

"Too much. When a continental bounty has been set, everyone within the reality seeks the person out, not just Syndicate members. We finally got him into a corner, but it took a lot of blood, and we couldn't kill him. Once I figured that out, I snatched these and removed myself from the equation." With a disappointed sigh, he steps out into the hallway. "The only scratch on my record too."

As I step through the bars, I hear another squelching sound. I shudder as Namar looks back at me, the ghost of a smile upon his face.

"Time to face the music. Let's go find out what little secret they've been hiding."

As we walk down the hallway, Namar gently pulls his second sword from its sheath. I palm one of the daggers from my belt. Getting to the end of the hallway, Namar peers around the corner, holding up a hand to stop me. I glance back to the empty cells.

Strange how few prisoners are here, especially with the crackdown starting when I left.

Namar motions forward as he edges around the corner. As I peer around, I am astonished to see a large rectangular room, divided into two floors. On the upper floor, a balcony overlooks the lower one, where we stand. A stone railing encircles the upper floor. Before us are several smaller doorways, similar to the one we just slipped out of, located symmetrically throughout the room, more than likely leading to other cells. At the far end of the room lies a huge unlit arch. At this distance, I can barely make out a darkened portcullis. As we step into the center of the room, I cannot help but shiver at the room's similarity to a gladiator pit.

A squelch comes from the darkness, and we turn toward the shadowed gate, weapons drawn. As we stare into the darkness, I see a shifting form, something unnatural. I narrow my eyes, trying to see further into the dark, but I am interrupted by a loud, gruff voice.

"Why are we here, Your Holiness?"

I turn to find the voice, and a movement on the upper level grabs my attention. A woman steps onto the balcony with Felgrand, still in his armor, and two other iron-clad soldiers following her. The woman is wearing a pristine white cloak, her face concealed by a hood.

"Patience, young proselyte. You will find out very soon. For now, direct your attention down to the room below," she replies in a soft regal voice. She gestures toward us, standing in the center of the room. As Felgrand scans the room, his glance immediately finds us in the center of the room. A look of recognition sweeps over his face, and his gaze steels as he sees the weapons in our hands.

"This is where those who could convert are sent?" Felgrand questions. Instead of answering, she moves toward the railing and places her hand on it. I flinch as the sound of metal grinding across stone fills the room.

I immediately turn toward the gate, my heart in my throat. I am relieved when the large gate does not seem to be rising. Instead, forms appear in the various hallways.

Namar and I instinctively move back as the forms step into the light to reveal more people. They appear run down and tired, their clothes in tatters. They shuffle into the room, glancing up toward the balcony, a strange hesitance on their faces. Then it strikes me as I see an old man shuffling forward from the darkness, his clothing riddled with holes. Upon his face is a look of pure horror as he shuffles toward the center of the room, glancing up at the attendees above. Anger fills my heart as I see the condition these people are in. I glare up at the woman in the white cloak, seeing a satisfied grin.

"No, proselyte. This is where we find those who can be converted," she finally replies with a sinister tone belying her regal voice.

"What?" Felgrand says, confused. She grasps a lever and pulls it, then steps back. The guards at her sides part for her, and I sense the confusion in the air as she replies, "This is also to make sure those with the Church are still devout followers." Felgrand turns his head to face her as he steps forward. A rumble shakes the room. Felgrand and the other guards fall to the floor, out of our vision as the quaking increases. The balcony falls away, crashing down on top of a few of the prisoners emerging from a room directly under it. I flinch as Felgrand stands up and looks at the girl above his massive sword, still attached to his back.

"What happened, High Priestess?" he shouts to the woman above as she reaches into her cloak producing a silver rod. She strikes it on the stone doorway, causing it to light up. It is some form of flare. I am bewildered a moment before I remember the Church has always frowned upon the use of modern-day things from the First Reality, often considering them anathema to the holy ways. Felgrand puts one hand on his sword, looking up at the priestess.

"Why do you have such a blasphemous item?" he snarls.

She laughs a dull dainty laugh as she casually tosses the flare toward the shadowed gate. I am speechless as I see the flare bounce against the gate, falling within and illuminating it. I see multiple scars and fractures across the dark metal. Bones are strewn across the floor, and the stone bears large scars, seemingly made by razor-sharp claws. The squelching sound resumes. This time, it sounds like it is just on the other side of the gate. When the sound picks up, the prisoners retreat to the opposite side of the hall. Some duck back into the little cell blocks from which they just emerged.

"To voluntarily give up the freedom they were just given," I mumble, setting my eyes back upon the priestess. "What horror would ever make someone choose captivity over freedom?" I demand. A knowing smile passes over the priestess's face.

"They know they will be judged and that their faith is false," she exclaims, bringing her arms together as if in prayer. A large tearing sound comes from the darkness, and liquid comes spraying out. I feebly hope the dark liquid isn't what I think it is. My hope is dashed by a scarlet river flowing into sight.

My shoulders lower, and I cock my head to the side. I see movement from the shadow just outside the dancing light flowing from the flare. Then it steps out, a creature straight out from my greatest nightmares.

As it steps into the light, more of its grotesque features come into sight. It has pale green skin, and its body looks gelatinous in nature. Spikes protrude through the skin, spreading over its back. They seem to move by themselves. It has two legs protruding from its hindquarters, which look almost humanoid, bent upwards and into a V-shape, giving it a distinct spider-like quality. It also has two humanoid arms bent outwards so its hands are angled toward its obscene body. On the arms are large talon-like claws. The feet are long, its curved talons gouging into the stone. The real outstanding image is the large bubble it has for a head, connected to the body by a long neck. Large dark hair came cascading down from the head, shrouding the face, but from in between the tresses, you could make out a huge mouth that had rows of jagged, sharp teeth. Though its large tresses, I can make out a lone black eye.

"What the hell is that?" Felgrand says, voicing my thoughts. The creature slams its hand down onto the flare, smashing the light out, shrouding it once more. However, I can still see the dark gleam in its lone eye.

"It is the Domme de Trofest," the priestess responds. Namar begins mumbling to himself. His head snaps up, fire in his eyes.

"Judge of the Faithful? What nonsense is that?" he growls.

"Be silent, you murderous heathen."

"Why is it here? Why have you thrown us to it?" Felgrand screams as he draws his sword, angling his body toward the gate as he glares aghast at the priestess.

"Because of the one you cut down back in the holy fields."

At this, Felgrand lowers his head, snapping it back up with a defiant look in his eyes.

"What about these two?" He nods to the two soldiers, who are picking themselves up from the rubble beside him.

"Each one here has broken the laws set upon them. They must pay for their sins." A brief pause as she seems to consider something. "On the other side of the cage, a door leads back out of this cell. Should you be allowed to move forward, you may rejoin the church. However, none have escaped the judgment before you."

"If none have ever escaped from here, you are just sending them to their deaths! This is no trial. It's an execution!" I scream at her.

Anger flashes across her face as she turns to me. "As a nonbeliever, you may call it what you will. However, the Judge of the Faithful will find the truth regardless. If you are a devout believer, step forward and kneel before Domme de Trofest. We shall see if you are worthy," she says, holding one hand to her heart, the other gesturing to the gate grandiosely. The two soldiers step forward toward the gate as Felgrand stands still, indecision on his face as his muscles tense.

"That is no Judge of the Faithful, ignorant witch," Namar hisses. All eyes turn to him at his disrespect for the woman. "That is a terrible being brought from the shadows of the deadlands. Do not be so presumptuous as to glorify such a monstrous being."

A gasp rings out from all corners of the room as the priestess drops her hand, placing one just inside the doorway.

"You are the presumptuous one. Do not lecture me about the Domme de Trofest!"

Namar growled. "You ungrateful bitch! You cannot lie to one who has had his family killed by one of these beasts!"

Shock flashes across the priestess's face, quickly replaced by a scowl. "Then you know far too much and cannot be allowed to speak against the Church's use of Domme de Trofest," she says with a smirk.

"Are you claiming what he says is true?" Felgrand shouts desperately, panic dancing in his eyes.

"Of course not!" she scoffs. "You have obviously lost your way, Felgrand; you are no longer a part of the Church."

After saying this, a pained expression runs across his face. He glances down at his blade. A few moments later, he growls.

"You are a deceiving imposter. You are no member of the Church!" he screams. Confused, I look at him and see a newfound fire burning in his gaze.

"What blaspehm—"

"If you were, I would be unable to hold this blade," Felgrand interrupts. "Only those blessed by the Church can wield it. If what you say is true—if I were not a part of the Church—I would no longer be able to wield my blade!" He takes a step forward, fixing a glare upon the priestess.

"Just who are you?" he demands. A calculating look dances across her face, and she smiles devilishly.

"Do not be fooled by this heathen before you! Kneel before the gateway and show your devotion! He only wishes to drag you from your place as true believers!" she screeches. She yanks her arm down, seemingly throwing a switch. The guards kneel in front of the gate as the sound of grinding metal once more rips through the room. This time, it is the portcullis rising. Each second feels like a year as I hear Namar throw a flurry of curses under his breath.

"I would stay and see who is worthy, but sadly, there are more pressing matters I must attend to. May we never meet again." She turns on her heel, disappearing back into the hallway.

I turn my attention back to the gate to see it clatter against the top of the arch. The darkness is menacingly silent. A full minute rolls by as we all brace for the monster to step forth. One of the soldiers looks up at the blackness, then turns to the other.

"Our faith must be sparing us from Domme de Trofest!" He turns to us, placing his back to the darkness. "The high priestess was right: you are all blasphemers!"

He looks to his fellow soldier, who begins to stand, only to start shaking and fall backward, trembling. The soldier scowls.

"You must not believe in your faith either!" he shouts at the guard. I stare into the shadows, trying to see what has spooked the other guard. Then I see it. The creature is standing up in the darkness, unmoving on its two spider-like legs right behind the soldier, looming over him as a reaper would his grain. I see one of the large talon claws rear back ever so slowly.

I cannot hear the soldier's rants or insults anymore as I see the monster behind him. I try to speak, to yell out to him, to save the man, but I cannot find my voice. The monstrosity behind him has robbed me of it. I swallow, trying to find my voice only to find it is as dry as a desert.

The monster moves, and in a heartbeat, the man gloating at the edge of the darkness is bisected. A brief look of shock is the only thing we see as a torrent of blood showers the other soldier, who has fallen back.

The beast pounces at a shocking speed for such a behemoth. Its large teeth flash as it rips into the blood-coated soldier. A shocked scream is replaced quickly by a bloody gurgle, followed by silence. The monster barely registers us as it feasts upon the poor soul, its teeth ripping flesh from the corpse, shredding the armor as it takes large, greedy bites.

"Do you think we can sneak past it?" I whisper to Namar. He nods as Felgrand looks at us expectantly.

We all shift as the beast seems to be content with the prey before him. As we take small steps toward the edges of the room, a man who has sheltered himself in the corner nearest the gate dashes forward, running as fast as he can toward the darkness. As he steps past the beast and into the large dark hallway, something shoots out and impales him, lifting him in the air. The man can only look shocked at what appears to be a large scorpion stinger protruding through his chest as he is held in the air. His arms fall limp as he expires from the grievous wound.

I swallow once more as I consider that the beast did not even turn its head to acknowledge the man's movement; it simply struck. I tighten my hands on my blades as I see the tail whip around erratically, throwing the body from it directly at Felgrand, who raises his sword, cutting through the body, sending its two halves around him like a stone divides a stream. Felgrand takes a step forward, clutching his sword with both hands.

"All right, you unholy beast, I shall avenge those you have snuffed out." His sword begins to glow as he says this. I step to his side.

"What do you think you are doing?" I hear Namar hiss behind me.

"Indeed, you should just leave here while you can. You seem to be a very worthy soul. I will only regret being unable to fight alongside you as brothers in spirit." Felgrand politely rejects.

"You spared me when you didn't have to. I am merely returning the favor by helping you put down this abomination." I smirk as I explain my actions. Out of the corner of my eye, I see Namar run a hand through his hair and huff with frustration.

"Why does my partner always have to be so goddamn nice?" He steps next to Felgrand as he flourishes his blade, a small smile working its way across his face. "At least the excitement never stops with you."

The beast throws the soldier's remains to the side, its body crashing into the wall. A sickening crack fills the air. The beast steps forward on all fours, its malevolent gaze bearing down on us as we stand before it.

"Be wary. Here it comes," Namar murmurs. The beast raises its head and screeches.

CHAPTER 4

THE CRUEL NATURE OF REALITY

Solaire

I stand there, momentarily stunned. The world seems to phase out from the cascading waves of pain in my shoulder. A soothing feeling comes over me as blue light engulfs my arm. I follow it back to the end of the trident from the Watcher.

"Be calm, youngblood. We shall deal with this swiftly," the Watcher says impassively. Someone in the crowd must have heard this as a roar of indignation shoots through the alley.

"Hah, you think only the four of you can stop us? We will merely kill you all too!" comes a shout from the rooftop hanging above the alleyway as a cheer runs through the crowd.

"*Sammen forsvare*," The Watcher encants softly. The other two Watchers rush forward to flank me on either side, creating a wall around my body.

"Watchers, step back and ensure the boy doesn't get hurt. It will be but a moment," Stephen orders as he steps to the center of the alleyway, twirling his pen rapidly in one of his hands.

"Promethean, I too have a name—"

"Save it, you two! Now die!" cries the rogue as he fires another bolt. This time, it goes straight for Stephen. He tilts his head to one side quickly, and the bolt sails past.

"Not very smart, are you?" I hear Stephen mumble, grabbing my attention as he raises his hand to his face. A thin line of blood has pooled on his cheek from the bolt. He runs his pen along the wound, and it takes up all the blood, seemingly to erase the wound.

"Don't let him finish. Attack!" the rogue cries, frantically loading another bolt.

The other rogues in the backstreet start charging down the path at us. I scramble for the bolt, trying to pry it from my body. I catch movement out of the corner of my eye. The thundering shoes crash ever closer as I turn to see the makeshift army only ten paces away from Stephen, still advancing.

"*Arta scrisa ...*"

Stephen begins scribbling as he recites the words, and I feel that same horrific feeling overwhelm me as his eyes begin to glow. The nearest rogue raises a sword as he prepares to cut down Stephen.

"Eviscerate!" he utters in no more than a whisper, although we can all clearly hear it. The single word seems to contain more power than all the might of the army before him as he raises his pen from the page and calmly shifts his posture toward me. Already taking a step toward me, the rogue swings the sword.

"Look out!" I cry. The rogue is now right before him, his body entering the light from the eclipsing shadows for the first time. Shocked, I see that his body is growing ashen as he steps forward, slowly flaking away. Just as the blade is about to strike, Stephen snaps his book shut with an audible clap, and as the tip of the blade crashes into Stephens's form, it explodes into a mass of gray powder. The rogue's arm crumbles away as a look of fear passes across his face. Then the rogue simply crumbles apart into dust. Turning my head, a small breeze flows down the hallway as the rest of the attackers join the first in a whirlwind of dust.

My throat is parched as I look back at Stephen, an impassive expression on his face as he steps closer to me. He has just reduced a significant force to nothing but ash. A bolt comes flying in between us, and Stephen slowly turns back to glare up at the man on the edge of the building, who, despite the distance, is clearly shaking.

"You monster! What did you do!" he cries desperately.

"It would appear I missed one." He opens the book again and brings his pen to the page swiftly, causing the rogue to jump and whimper as Stephen resumes writing.

"Please don't! Stop this. I will leave, and you will never see me again!" comes the desperate plea of the rogue from the rooftop. Stephen stops for a moment.

"How pathetic. Give one an army, and they will think they can do whatever they want." A brief pause as everyone holds their breath as he stops writing.

"They cannot." A cold look passes over his face as he starts writing again.

"*Arta scrisa.*" As he writes, the Watcher suddenly whirls his trident and slams it into the ground.

"*Parasi!*" Stephen calls out as the trident's crash echoes throughout the hallway.

"*Beskytte!*" cries the Watcher as a dome of blue water washes outward, just wide enough to cover the Watchers and me. I see the rogue turn to run as he crumbles away into dust. Stephen spins on his heel, seething anger plastered across his face.

"Noooo!" he screams. "Do you have any idea what it means to deny Prometheus?"

"Worry not, Promethean. You may still speak. However, the youngblood will not come to any harm," the Watcher retorts.

Stephen scowls. "You wish to make an enemy of me, of Prometheus?" Stephen says, threatening to open his book once more. The Watcher steps to the edge of the bubble, staring directly into Stephen's rage-filled eyes, not an ounce of fear as Stephen opens the book, putting his pen to the page.

"No, but I will not let you bring harm to one who has been asked only of the nature of their burden. Your previous display has showcased your power quite well, although you will not be able to affect us with it now." The ferocity in Stephen's eyes dulls to a frosty glare. Snapping his book shut, he takes a breath. The other two Watchers step up to either side of me. One grabs hold of me by my shoulders while the other grabs on to my arm with one hand. The other grasps on to the fletching of the bolt protruding from my arm. I yelp as I feel a sharp pain rack through me from the mere contact. The two Watchers share a glance and then rip the bolt from my shoulder, letting me drop lightly to the ground as I scream. As I kneel, I feel nauseated as dizziness flows through me.

"Very well." Stephen conceded as everyone shifts their attention to me.

"Now, I believe before we were so rudely interrupted that you had mentioned something about being dropped through a portal and looking for someone after being attacked by my ... colleague." He pauses, almost as if he can taste the word. "Yes, I suppose that is the most accurate depiction of our relationship."

Looking between the two intense glares, I debate how much I should share. My thoughts are broken by the head Watcher.

"Do not try to lie to us. I sense your desire to lead us astray," the Watcher says in a booming voice. Shocked, I glance into his yellow eyes, their eerie luminescence stealing any thoughts of concealing the truth. With a shaky sigh, I look back down to the ground.

"Yes ... we were attacked by people from a group that seems excessively militaristic. Then your *colleague* came out of nowhere and attacked us." I snarl at Stephen. He looks puzzled as he straightens his posture.

"Why, there had to be something he was looking for?" He ponders on it. As my eyes meet, his look of puzzlement turns to one of understanding.

"Your friend, the one who was taken, who was he?"

The Watcher speaks, raising his trident off the ground. "Now is not the time for you to learn, Promethean."

"So, you do make an enemy of Prometheus," he says, stepping back. A piercing screech echoes throughout the alleyway, sending the Watcher and me glancing around frantically to locate the source of the sound. I give him a quizzical look as he takes another step back, his back now pressed against the wall. As he makes contact with it, a portion of the wall above him begins to fade to white as a ghostly hand slowly reaches out and slams down on the wall as if it is trying to pull itself out.

"I will find out what he was looking for. As my colleague would say, you do nothing but buy yourself time, Watcher," he proclaims, his dark glare fixated upon me.

I feel a bead of sweat pooling on my head as another arm silently shoots out from the wall. It slowly drags with it a ghastly sight, an ethereal white being. From its semi-transparent body hangs long, flowing strands of clothing. Then comes its head—with a face that looks as if it has been recently unearthed after decomposing for some time. It is sunken and ruined. Its hair is pale orange, snaking out in all directions, flowing as if it were in water. I see the Watcher drop the butt of the trident to the ground, causing the water around us to spin rapidly and the light around us to disappear. The last thing I see before all light disappears is Stephen's piercing eyes as he speaks.

"We will meet again, boy. Next time, you won't have the protection of the Watchers, but even if you do, Prometheus will not be denied." He shakes his head slightly from side to side.

The voice rings in my ears as everything fades to black.

Bastian

The monster lets loose a deafening screech that pierces the air, causing many, including me, to bring their hands to their ears. I shut my eyes, trying to keep out the sudden grinding pain as after a quick rumbling sensation, I am thrust to the side. Slamming onto the ground, I roll into a crouch, looking back to where I am as a metallic grinding sound fills the air. In my previous location stands Namar, blades crossed, holding back one of the deadly razor-sharp claws.

A hiss comes from the creature as it stands on its hind legs, bearing its way down on Namar as it towers over him. Namar slips to his knees under the pressure with a grunt. The creature rears back, raising its other talon-covered appendage, its lone eye glaring out from between the tresses on its head.

I snap out of my stupor as I stand and start to run, grasping my knives. I rip them from their sheaths as the monster brings its claw down far faster than I could have imagined.

I'm not going to make it! I think as Felgrand meets the claw, bringing his longsword against it in a wide arc and thrusting against the appendage, putting the beast off balance and forcing it to take a step back, taking its weight off Namar for just an instant. The monster brings its dreadful claw back as I enter its immediate proximity, its lone eye fixated on me. It brings its claw across in a wide slicing motion. Dropping down into a slide, I feel a rush of air pass over my head as I slide toward the beast's legs. Barely registering the clash of the claw, I continue racing for Namar until I see him launch into Felgrand, sending them both rolling to the side.

Thinking quickly as the beast pivots its foot closest to me, raising it and bringing it down to crush me in a stomp, I drive my dagger into its other leg, earning a cry from the monster as its foot comes careening down toward me. I leverage my body, using the dagger to direct the movement of my slide around the foot as it smashes against the stone. As I pull my blade free, the beast kicks outward with its hind leg, lifting me into the air and sending me bouncing across the floor.

After recovering from the blow, I get to my knees. I see a rapid movement—the scorpion tail, whipping around frantically, trying to strike me.

"Shit!" I hiss under my breath as I dive to get behind the creature once more. I narrowly dodge the stinger, which lodges itself into the ground, burying the entire foot-long protuberance into the stone. I keep rolling across the floor until I am on the other side, then leap back to make some room as a sweeping claw comes slicing through the air at me. The claw passes right by my body, missing it by no more than a hair's length.

It tries to take another step forward, only to recoil as it stumbles back, restrained by its tail. The scorpion's tail flexes and whirls about, trying to dislodge itself from the stone floor.

"Its tail is stuck. Now is our chance!" I scream as it flails at me, trying to pull its tail free. The blades come so close to me as I take another step back, finally able to catch my breath for the first time since the monster rushed us. As I breathe, I feel something is wrong. A pungent smell permeates the air. Taking a strong whiff, I smell something sulfuric. I glance down at my dagger and see smoke lifting off the blade where I drove it into the hulking monstrosity. I glance back to the beast and see a fluorescent blue liquid running down the stab wound. As the blood slowly leaks down its leg, the trail first hits the floor as both Felgrand and

Namar rush at the beast from behind it. Once the blood hits the floor, I see a cloud of smoke rise, and a sinking feeling strikes my gut. As I see the other two raise their weapons, Felgrand is poised to cut through the stuck tail with Namar charging toward its body.

"Don't!" I warn the others—but too late. As Felgrand brings down his longsword, I see Namar's blade start to fall as well. The body of the beast bends over onto its arms, and it glares at me as Namar's blade slams into the creature's gelatinous body. A stuporous look passes over his face before he is shot backward, slamming across the ground on his back.

My horror-struck eyes dart back to Felgrand as the creature lunges from its kneeling position, leaping toward me, bringing its tail taut just as Felgrand's blade comes slashing through it, sending a spray of blood across Felgrand; severing the beast from its wedged appendage, as it flies toward me. A high-pitched screech fills the air as I dive to the side, bringing my knives in front of me as its claws race toward me.

I feel the clash as the claw grinds across the measly knives in my hands. As I fly through the air, redirected due to the force of the blade, I see the other claw raking across to bisect me. I eye the deadly appendage, seemingly moving in slow motion as it races to my side. Rolling my shoulder away from the beast, I leverage my knives to arch sideways, trying to bend from the path of the massive talon as it careens toward me. As I pivot my body higher, the force from the first appendage starts to overpower my grip on the blade, threatening to spin me over the claw. Looking over my shoulder, I see the blade moving to meet my new position. I grit my teeth as I perform a roundhouse kick in air, quickly twisting my body over my makeshift leverage point.

Flipping around in the air, I land behind the beast. Quickly turning around, I raise my blades in a defensive cross, only to find the beast driving its claws into the ground, catapulting toward the darkness.

On the verge of the tunnel, I spot one of the prisoners turning to face us, his eyes widening in horror as the monster shoots toward him. The massive body leans forward toward the poor soul as a startled scream escapes his mouth. It comes to a sudden chilling halt as the beast's body tears sideways with a sickening squelch.

As the beast races into the darkness, I see a lack of its previous victim, only a bloody stain on the wall, and I can only hope the man died before he was carried away in its death trap of a mouth.

As my narrow escape from death washes over me, I slip to my knees. A dull pain throbs at my side. At the same time, a moan of pain comes from across the room. I look down to see blood seeping through my turtleneck, staining it a dark crimson. Clenching my teeth, I scoff.

I should be better than this. The old me wouldn't have been caught by that creature's talon.

Inspecting the wound, I find I avoided the worst of the blow, receiving only an inch-long incision across my side. Putting pressure on the wound with a grunt, I turn to see Felgrand, moaning and clutching at his face as smoke rises from behind his fingers. He kneels on the floor, his massive blade at arm's length.

Namar reaches over and pulls Felgrand's arms away, and I can see the wound smoldering scarlet red as it continues to burn. He is struggling with the prone giant to keep his arms away from his face.

"It burns!" Felgrand moans, cradling his face.

"Yes, and rightly so! You are lucky you only received this much of his blood. Any worse, and you could have died!" Namar says, rearing his arm back and bringing his forearm down hard across Felgrand's face. A large slap is heard before I see Namar catapulted away from Felgrand by a kick.

Namar bounces twice before rolling to a crouch before he starts tearing at his leather bracer. A grinding sound fills the room as Felgrand stands up, dragging his sword.

"This is why I don't trust you thieves—you all betray trust at any chance you can, even when we rest from fighting such a demonic figure together." He steps forward as Namar stands up, dropping his bracer to the side.

"If I didn't know any better, I would say you have a problem with me, paladin," Namar growls, stepping over the bracer and staring up into the giant's eyes.

"Paladin?" I repeat, confused. Felgrand stares down at him in contempt.

"Figures you wouldn't know. The Crusades started after you left, Crusades in which those who did not believe in the Church were slaughtered, butchered by those who were considered paladins," Namar sneers.

"The Crusades were intended to save others, not kill them!" Felgrand cries.

"And look where that left you! Your church killed off hundreds, if not thousands!"

"We did it to kill demons. We were fighting for the greater good!" Felgrand bellows, tightening the grip on his sword.

"Really? You killed demons? Then why did I have to save your life just now?"

"Save my life? You call hitting me saving my life?" Felgrand says, waving his arms around in frustration.

"Just how many demons have you seen? The blood of that beast is corrosive. Anything it touches turns to jelly!" Namar says.

"So, what does that mean? I think you hit me because you can't stand me." Namar throws his arms up in exasperation.

"It means I removed the acid from your face the best way I could—wiping it off. Your cowering left me with but one method, and seeing you whine now, I don't regret it at all."

Felgrand looks past Namar at the bracer on the ground, and I hear a sharp intake of breath. Following his gaze, I see smoke rising off the bracer as part of it dissolves slowly. Silence fills the room as Felgrand studies Namar, huffing and turning away.

A scream pierces the silence.

"What now?" Namar says as we turn toward the source of the noise.

Scanning the room, we see the soldier bisected by Felgrand tearing flesh from the body of one of the prisoners. I look toward the other soldier and see it start twitching as it spasms on the floor. Raising an eyebrow, I glance over at Namar.

"Ever see anything like this?"

Namar unsheathes his sword as the body rises to its feet, facing us, then staring at the ground for a moment.

"Not in my lifetime," Namar says in a hushed voice. The revived soldier slowly raises its head. I try to swallow as its eyes make contact with ours. The eyes are still there. It's just that they convey no recognition, no thought—only hunger. Its soulless gaze is terrifying. I am broken out of my reverie as it lurches toward us, arms outstretched.

At an incomprehensible speed, Namar raises his sword and darts out with it, driving it through the breastplate on the soldier, shifting his weight as the body slumps down onto the blade.

"That wasn't so bad," Namar comments upon the being's anticlimactic demise. Then, the body on the blade jerks forward as its hands grasp at Namar, its teeth gnashing together, trying to bite him. Its hand grabs hold of his cloak, trying to pull him closer. I pull my knives, moving closer. Rearing one back, I let it fly. It zooms through the air, piercing the sweet spot between the links on the armor and the plating, just at the base of the neck. I see it jerk back, letting go of Namar as he kicks him free from the blade.

Stepping back, the new threat dashes back at Namar.

"Duck, rogue!" a voice boomed out from behind him as Namar drops to his knees. A massive blade flashes over him, decapitating the threat, its body tumbling past him.

Running up to the two of them, I rip my knife from the corpse. Glancing around the room, I look to see prisoners running back toward the hallways. More corpses rise and chase them, running and diving toward the screaming prisoners. As the screams of terror ring out in front of us, I hear similar hollow screams erupting from behind us. I turn to see more prisoners running out from the dark hallway. Turning around, I gaze upon a prisoner, who is pounced upon by another of the reanimated prisoners. A panicked yelp escapes from him as he grapples on the ground with the monster. It finally lands on top of him, edging closer as it gnashes its teeth, trying to bite into its victim. The prisoner looks up to us hopefully; however, upon taking his eyes from the assailant, it moves around the arm holding it back, and its jaws snap down upon the prisoner's neck, showering the both of them in blood.

A surprised gurgle escapes the mouth of the prisoner as his eyes lose their light. The prisoner stops thrashing, sits up, and looks around, its dull eyes searching for another victim before it spots us. Scrambling from its victim, it charges at us, wanton hunger deep in its eyes.

I smoothly pull a blade from my belt and let it fly. A dull thock resounds amidst the chaos as the blade buries up to the hilt into its head. The head snaps back, and the body tumbles forward, falling a mere five paces away. My attention, however, is elsewhere—specifically, on the body of the prisoner who has just had his throat torn out. I see his eyes cloud over, the dull irises growing darker and deader.

The body spasms as the face continues looking at me, a look of shock and fear still present as the body begins flailing on the floor. The body turns over as its face twists from frozen horror to the same hunger his murderer displayed.

"You have got to be fucking kidding me."

I stand rooted to my spot as the body of the prisoner thrashes toward us. I sense Namar turn to look at me as I let another blade fly before turning to look over my shoulder. Another muffled thud is followed by the sight of a stumbling body. I look Namar in the eyes.

"Zombies? This world has zombies now?" I ask in disbelief.

"Zombies? What in the blazes are those? These are undead, rogue." Felgrand's gruff voice admonishes. "I thought these were all gone and forgotten after the crusades."

"You don't get out much, do you, paladin? Zombies are the undead," Namar says. A roar of anger erupts from Felgrand as his sword flashes out to the side, bisecting one of the walking corpses.

"I was led to believe the undead were created by malevolent forces within this reality, not by the Church itself," he says, taking a step forward. "Have at it, you undead dogs!" he cries, beheading one of the zombies rushing at him.

I see Namar glance at me out of the corner of his eye, carrying an obvious question: *Should we help?* I nod as he rolls his eyes, stepping closer to me as I look around the room. As we move forward, the number of prisoners has been drastically reduced. Zombies are now chasing the few remaining prisoners, devouring those they capture. Others are charging at us with the same mindless hunger.

"Your kindness is going to get us killed one of these days," he hisses into my ear as he lunges forward, his sword flashing as the head flies off one of the charging zombies. Bending down, I rip my throwing knives from the corpses at my feet. I see Felgrand slay several more of the zombies in my periphery.

"We certainly won't last long by ourselves. The die has been cast. Time to follow through." I hear an exasperated sigh as Namar raises his swords once more.

"You are going to be the death of me, Bastian," Namar grumbles. We all square up to face the oncoming horde, their attention drawn by Felgrand's declaration. I remain silent as the great wave of the dead surges forward. Gritting my teeth, I let my blades fly. They land true, and the bodies fall back, disappearing into the mob. Already drawing my next pair, I hold them in a reverse grip.

"Think there's too many for that to work," Namar says sarcastically. I ignore him as the droves of the dead swarm closer.

"Less talking, more purging!" Felgrand's voice booms as he cleaves another with his massive sword.

Solaire

The first thing I notice as the roaring water drains away is blue light filtering through the whirling dome. As the water falls away, a light drizzle descends upon us. The room, if you could call it that, is amazing. Circular, its walls sloping inward, rising to a peak at the center of the room. Along the floor, five paths are lined with river stones. Placed halfway down the path are intricate stone lanterns holding an azure flame. Each path leads to a large open archway, in the style of an A-frame. Along the ground, beside the paths, grow plants of all kinds—ferns and bushes, all with vines creeping up the walls.

A flash of blue draws my attention to the floor. The gravel paths stop, and the stone trails form a circle around us. Upon the ground are shale pieces, evenly spaced, forming a pentagram, each point pointing down one of the paths. Looking closer, I notice a light blue wisp connecting each piece in the design to the next.

"Beautiful, isn't it?" comes the stoic voice of the Watcher. Looking up at him, I notice he is gazing over the plants. A light tap from his trident sends a light blue pulse through the plants and the budding flowers along the vine. As the pulse moves over the wildlife, they bloom while glowing the same luminescent blue.

"This is nature's last sanctuary. We refer to it as the Glade," the Watcher says proudly as he steps from the circle down the path in front of us. The other Watchers follow, leaving me on the floor.

Picking myself up, I hobble after him, slowly taking in the breathtaking room, clutching my arm and wincing in pain. The one with the trident stops at the entrance as the other two keep walking past him. As I get within a few paces of the Watcher, I look past him to see a small village with many Watchers walking around. The wildlife seems to be flourishing. Flowers and tall grasses are growing everywhere except along a single large stone road, which leads endlessly through the forest, where it curves around a tree at the end. A magnificent sunset bathes it all in its orange embrace.

"Be honored, youngblood. You are among the first to come to the Glade," the Watcher says, turning to me, his eyes fiercely examining.

"Why me? I haven't done anything special. I am not even supposed to be here," I proclaim, taking a step back.

"That's precisely why it was necessary to bring you here—to show you the meaning of the Glade and help you understand without the influence of those from more *unsightly* groups how significant your appearance truly is." Each word receives perfect articulation, flowing like water.

"What do you mean, 'significance'?"

Silently he steps off, following the well-tread stone path through the long grass. I look around, astonished, to see thatch houses with several villagers performing mundane tasks—farming, sweeping, digging—each stopping to look up at me as we pass. They all display a variation of a single emotion on their artistic blue faces: disgust. Their glares and scowls create an almost oppressive atmosphere.

As we step closer to the village, I can make out a group of children playing, kicking a wicker ball between each other. I glance around, seeing more members of this mysterious race scowling and snarling comments in a foreign language. My blood boils at the discrimination directed my way. I focus on the children if only to ignore the actions of those around us as we follow the stone path.

A female rushes forward, grabbing the arm of one of the children and wrenching him to her side, pointing at the other children before shouting at them.

"*Ga hjem!*" she says repeatedly, looking at me, a mixture of fear and anger on her face. My eyes fall upon the child, clutching for the ball that lies in the center of the road. The other two children dash off behind one of the huts. Approaching the ball in the middle of the road, the Watcher steps over it, and I slow to a halt. Almost absentmindedly, I reach down for the wicker ball, picking it up gingerly. Still crouched, I turn to the child by the mother's side and offer the ball to him. His eyes regard me curiously as he slowly reaches for the ball. A sudden movement and he is thrown backward. I hear the child yelp as he hits the ground. I look up to her, and I'm shocked as she steps forward, takes the ball from my hands, and smashes it onto the ground. I am lost for words as I rise to my feet.

The nerve of this woman.

"What the hell!" I scream, stepping toward the child. Something smashes into my side. A startled wheeze escapes my mouth as the breath is knocked from me. I stumble back, falling into the dust, rolling side over the side before coming to rest on the dusty path.

Taking a breath to compose myself, I look up to see a Watcher, with dark blue skin, an oceanic light blue mark flowing over his stomach. I'm astonished to see how similar his body structure is to that of a human. He wears shorts that look to be made from animal hide, but apart from that, he is naked. In his hands rests a large stone hammer. His body, muscular and defined, would be the envy of most bodybuilders.

Upon his neck, a white mark rises up to his chin, moving up to the left. I gasp as I gaze into his eyes. One of them is the standard yellow, the other a milky gray.

A cough racks my body as I slowly get up.

"No child should be treated like that." I snarled. The Watcher steps forward, fingering the hammer.

"*Folket ditt er ikke velkommen,*" he proclaims, stepping forward, raising the hammer once more. I raise my arms, ready to fight. I see the fire in his eyes.

"*Nok!*" a voice booms behind me, stopping the aggressor. Turning back, I see the elder Watcher with his trident extended.

"Youngblood, come here and continue along this path. Do not stop or look elsewhere than in front of you."

Keeping my eyes on the attacker, I take a tentative step back as a crowd begins to form behind him, their faces blending into a mix of blues and dark oranges as the receding sunlight falls upon them. Their glares set me on edge as I look back to the child, at the mother pulling him up before practically dragging him into the growing crowd. The child passes me one final longing glance before disappearing behind the legs of the others. Looking up, I can see her start to meld with the countless other faces, but not before casting one more look of disdain my way. I grind my teeth in a vain attempt to calm my seething anger.

With a sigh, I take another step back, my attention returning to the face at the center of that endless cesspool of hatred. Murmurs in the same foreign language come from the crowd in a mass of whispers. All the voices seem to spiral into a unified spiteful one.

"*Tch,*" he utters in disgust, spitting at my feet before turning around, ushering the crowd away. I bite my lip to prevent myself from decking that proud son of a bitch. Turning around, I feel the warm blood bead upon my lip as I walk, staring at the ground and its well-trodden trail to avoid smashing the next face sporting a disdainful look into the pavement.

"Why?" I barked out, almost involuntarily.

"Youngblood, the Watchers, our people, have been sought after by those seeking to keep us for their own petty whims. We are used as slaves and as pets. Humans with power have abused us in the past, seeking to own what is not theirs, what should never be owned." He speaks with passion, spitting out the word *human* with venom.

"And that justifies what happened?" I retort, which draws an irritated gaze from the Watcher, who looks over his shoulder while continuing onward.

"Many of the races have squandered that which is sacred, especially humans, and we have felt the consequences of their actions. We have always sought peace."

We come to a curve in the path as it angles toward a giant hollowed-out tree trunk.

"How can you not condemn their actions? How can any of those actions reflect peace?" I insist. He pauses briefly again, looking over his shoulder, a tired look hooding over his eyes.

"It is not that I condone these reactions, more so that I can justify their reasoning. Things have happened in the past, things that cannot—will not—happen again. After such faith is shaken, those who pursue peace can become jaded." As he speaks, resolve sparkles in his eyes. He digressed swiftly, turning back to the entrance. "Come, let me show you something."

Looking past the ornate wooden arch, I see a small circular glade resting with a gargantuan tree with hanging branches, each shouldering what appears to be millions of hanging leaves blossoming into a carpet of shining white petals. I stare, entranced at the brilliant white's contrast to its green background, moonlight bathing the tree.

"Beautiful," I whisper to myself.

"Yes, this is what the world was at one point. Beauty like this used to be commonplace. Yet now you look upon the last of its kind." He speaks softly from behind me. Turning around, I see him staring past me at the marvelous sight.

"Can't you just plant more?"

"This tree is not so simple. Certainly, it is not something that can be merely planted. This is a living tree. Quite literally, one may call it a lifeline. This tree keeps track of all life and helps govern nature itself." He steps closer to the tree, using his trident as a walking staff. "When there were more of them, life was abundant. Now we have only this one." He puts one hand onto the bark of the tree. "Nature was first defiled by humans. Then, when the Second Reality came into existence, we found this haven and moved here with what we could, rebuilding and hoping the tree would grow. You see, as long as nature is held within the balance and the realities remain kept, the tree will continue to grow. We created the Watchers to observe two realities from the sidelines, protecting them and intervening only when they are threatened." Raising his trident, he gently pulls down a branch filled with white flowers. Raising his other hand, he runs his hand over them, working his way to the end of the branch, still facing away from me.

"These leaves are special. Each one represents something living within one of the realities." He stills his hand, seemingly cradling something before bringing it out from among the hundreds of hanging flowers. Among them are some brown ones that appear to be dying.

"This morning, these leaves began turning brown. You see, when someone passes on, a leaf simply flies away into the wind. As people get older, the flowers begin to wilt, but they have never changed color." A sinking feeling rises in my gut as I sense where this conversation is headed.

"This morning, when you got here, they began changing."

He turns to look at me, his face stern. Dryness once again threatens to rob me of my voice.

"How do you know I caused it? Why does it have to be a human? Why does it have to be caused by one of the races you hate?" I scowl, my fingernails digging into the skin of my palms as I squeeze my eyes shut.

"Youngblood, do not misunderstand. These trees are tied to us in a way you could not fathom."

He lowers his arms to his sides, releasing the leaves. His gaze travels to the limbs hanging above him. "We *feel* what is happening to this tree, as we have felt what happened to all the others. We can feel that which ails it, and we can follow that feeling, and that feeling led us straight back to you."

His gaze snaps back to me with a predatory gleam. The sheer intensity makes me shuffle back a step.

"The role of the Head Watcher is to protect the tree of life. My name is Cu'jehi, and I am the Head Watcher. That is why you are here now, so that I may deem if you are a threat—not only to the tree of life but also to the boundary we have so carefully maintained for so long."

Not liking where this was going, I take a deep breath, and a dreadful feeling of helplessness sweeps over me.

"How could I ever threaten your carefully maintained balance?"

"By inviting death into these lands, by disrupting the natural order of things."

I growl as I feel my suppressed rage boil once more.

"I have known death. When I was younger, an earthquake ripped apart the foundation of the area where I lived. The gas mains tore apart." I pause, my vision beginning to blur as the scene flashes in my mind's eye.

"I was walking home from the store ... when I heard it. I felt it first, though, the explosion, after the shaking stopped. Uncertainty filled my gut, as I saw the flash from down the road. When something like that happens, you just know. I arrived at my house in time to find my parents dead, killed by the blast, my house in smoldering cinders. I pawed through them until I found her, my sister, bleeding out on the ground. I see her mangled leg first, her bright blue dress ..." I pause as I remember the happy smile on her face as she twirled for me earlier that day, showing it off, her pristine visage now replaced by the cruel depiction of her ruined body.

"I pulled her from the debris ... I had to hold her in my arms as I watched the light fade from her eyes. Those vivid blue eyes! I can still see them when I close my own, the fear on her face, the blood staining her cheek, her golden blonde hair. Do you really think that after that, I could want any more death?"

I shut my eyes as the image harasses me once more. As I hunch over, tears erupt from my eyes. A fugitive silence stalls the conversation.

"You told Stephen you came to find your friend, that your friend was taken. Why would you continue to pursue them into an entire world to which you have never been, especially one as barbaric as this one?"

"You want to know why I will travel worlds to save my friend, even come to this fucked-up bloodthirsty place? He was the one, the only one there, who arrived as I cradled her body in the rain. He was the one who took me in after my home was destroyed. After all, it was my fault she died. He gave me a home and a new family. He helped me through it. He saved me from myself!" I take a breath, attempting the impossible task of reining in my rage.

"Look, I know it was my fault. My phone died. I had no idea what to do, so I called for help. Do you know what it's like to call for help and get none?" I scream, looking up through the tears to see the same goddamn expression that so many others had given me: pity.

"Don't look at me with those goddamn compassionate eyes! I don't need your sympathy! I know I was too late! I know I could have—should have—done more! I was too late to save her!" I huff heavily, panting to catch my breath after my screams. The tears run hot, replacing those I wiped away as I take a moment to compose myself.

"I can't change that, but I have the chance to do the same for him—just like he saved me. So if you think I will give that up, you can go fuck yourself!"

"Would you still save him even if it endangered this?" he asks, his face almost begging.

"Why in the fucking world does that matter?" I scream, thrusting my arms outwards.

"Answer the question," he replies callously, slamming down the trident and straightening his back. He gazes down at me, that strange pleading look still in his eyes.

"Why would he even endanger this place? What could he possibly do?"

"Do not underestimate the ability a mere mortal can possess. I have already made that mistake once. If he is a threat, I will kill him," he responds, casting me a regret-filled look. My eyes snap wide open as the tears flow down my face. I have already stepped forward, my arm raising into a fist. Before I have even taken two steps, I see a metallic glint, and I suddenly find myself on the ground, glaring up at his remorseful expression as he holds the tip of the blade to my throat, drawing blood.

"What the fuck? Why, if you are someone who preaches peace, are you resorting to violence as the only solution?" I scream in frustration, edging my neck against the unmoving blade.

"As I said, I made that mistake before: I spared the last one who was a threat to the boundary, and he is why things are as they are now. That is the cruel nature of this reality." He steps back, dragging the blade from my chin. "Youngblood, just because you seem less likely to be a threat does not mean I trust you. Nor will I spare you if I find you to be one," he says, whisking the trident behind him.

"Do you really expect me to just give up because you say I cannot go? Simply because I *could* be a threat?"

He sighs, turning around once more, staring up through the trees and into the moonlight. The ethereal glow shimmers off the trees.

"You claim not to know how Second Reality works. So, let me make this simple for you. Those with no strength can only get in the way of those who do. Now, you may rest here for the night. Seek me out tomorrow. Take the trail that leads away from the one we took to get here." He walks forward, gesturing toward a small trail leading farther into the trees, visible through another ornate archway I have not noticed until now. "This will take you to my abode. From there, we can discuss your next moves. It has been a long evening. No matter what action you take next, you must rest."

With that, he walks forward, instantly disappearing into the trees.

Leaning back, I lie on the grass, my body feeling the strain of the day's events. I scoff.

I have to learn more about this world. I still have no idea what is happening or who is on whose side. Shaking my head, I roll onto my side. *I can deal with it tomorrow. At least the night here doesn't seem too cold,* I think as I let my eyes droop.

CHAPTER 5

TRIALS OF ENDURANCE

Bastian

A roar comes from Felgrand as he brings his massive blade down upon another of the undead, slicing it in two. Blood splashes against his armor as he spins on his heel, dragging his blade in a wide arc, a crazed look in his eye as he brings it down onto a turned prisoner.

"Come on, you undead savages!"

Grasping his blade with two hands, he pivots and brings it around, lopping the heads off two of the undead from behind him. The one he bisected crawls forward, grasping at his foot. Felgrand quickly raises his boot, bringing it down upon the undead, a sickening crunch as the offending limbs drop limply to the floor.

A snarling sound erupts from behind me. Namar dashes in front of me, his rapier flashing as he thrusts forward, nicking my cheek as the blade shoots past me, shocking me from my stupor.

"Man, you must have really grown rusty. Now is not the time to gawk at the crazy man. We will have plenty of time after we finish off our little group of fans," Namar quips.

My eyes run past the blade as it rushes past my face, following it to the undead creature behind me. The blade pierces his eye. It is one of the guards killed by the beast at the beginning of this pandemic, his blade still in its scabbard at his waist.

With renewed awareness, I snatch the blade from his corpse.

Shing.

I turn to face Namar. The ghost of a smile lights up his face.

"See? Now let's go join the big oaf."

Spinning on his heel, he pulls the blade from the beast's skull behind me, already moving before the clatter of the body behind me. As he turns, he brings both of his blades into a flurry of strikes, the first hitting and slicing the body of an undead minion, causing it to stumble, the second shooting forward like a spear into its skull. Another two are coming at him from both sides.

Namar already has the blade free from the first as he dashes to confront the one on his left, leaving himself open to the one behind him. I grasp the short sword, raising it up like a baseball bat and letting it swing as I run forward. I aim for the base of the neck. Letting the swing go, I feel a slight resistance before my blade continues through a wet splatter, hitting my arms as I hear the body collapse onto the floor with a thud.

A queasy feeling fills my stomach as I follow through with the swing, turning away from the body. I see two more stragglers coming from behind us. I reach into my belt, plucking another throwing knife. I let it fly into one of them. The ever-satisfying *thock* lets me know it hit home. I bring my blade up, swinging at just the right moment, as the zombie gets within range. The body vanishes as it tumbles to the ground. Running forward, I rip the throwing knife from the body and whirl around to see another getting closer. Turning on my heel, I let my knife fly from an over-the-shoulder throw. Time seems to slow as I watch the blade travel through the air toward where I perceive the zombie to be. Almost in sync, they arrive in the same spot. The body is thrown to the side, tumbling like a ragdoll.

Turning to the others, I see Namar dancing between the zombies, cutting down one while dodging the others, methodically cutting them down. I let another two blades fly, at two more zombies that start to crowd him.

Turning my attention to Felgrand, I see him still haphazardly swinging his massive blade, cleaving through as many as he can, bodies piling around him as the dead scamper closer. A quick glance around the room reveals only ten more reanimated corpses.

"I count ten!"

I let another blade fly, landing on the neck of another, barely missing its head. Taking advantage, Felgrand slams his blade down, cleaving it down the middle. Turning again, he swipes behind him, slashing the heads from two. But then, the blade becomes lodged in the third!

He quickly brings his boot down, crashing it into the chest of the zombie, pinning it to the ground such that the blade of his longsword became a spike standing tall through the writhing zombie. Felgrand thrusts his arm out. Plucking one of the dead from the air, he suspends it above the ground as he bats another away with the body. He thrusts the zombie in his hands into the blade's edge, its host snarling and grasping at the plated legs on top of him. With a cry, he grasps the massive blade with both hands as he turns overhead, his arms coming over his body as the blade leaves the body underneath him. I throw my last knife, watching as it lands in sync, smashing into the head of the one beneath Felgrand as he cleaves the zombie.

"That leaves four!" Felgrand's gruff voice calls out.

My attention flies to Namar as he ducks underneath the clutches of a zombie and rolls between the clutches of two more. His blade flashes out, striking the legs. One collapses as Namar backpedals away from the rest. I spot another coming from behind him. I dash forward.

"Namar, behind you!" I roar, taking the attention of two of the dead. The one with the severed leg and another come rushing at me. The one on the ground is clutching at the ground in an attempt to crawl.

Namar spins around, his blade flashing out, piercing the shoulder of the one behind him as the other blade comes across, relieving the zombie of its head. Seeing Namar turn to face the other, I turn my attention to my approaching threat. I bring the short sword down to cleave the undead in two. The blade becomes wedged in the shoulder of the undead.

"That leaves two!" I hear Namar yell as the undead creature on me pushes forward, driving the blade deeper into itself as it grasps for purchase on my body. Buckling, I fall to the ground, finding the undead climbing over me, its dull eyes as terrifying as the gnashing jaws getting closer.

Shit!

I curse myself for letting my skills deteriorate as they have. My eyes spot the other one scrambling closer. Struggling, I look for something, anything, as I feel the undead push closer. Spotting the hilt of one of my blades protruding from one of the bodies lying behind me, I scoot backward, using the undead I am holding back so I can slide backward.

I hear the sound of flesh splitting as more and more cool blood begins pouring on me. I glance back to the blade. Just a little more! I turn back the snarling constant, my heart throbbing in my throat.

I must get to it!

I hear the shuffling steps get closer and closer. Then I see it leap into the air toward me.

Namar is standing behind it, a look of fear on his face as he sees the beast come ever closer, sprinting over the bodies as he clutches his blades tighter. Abstract horror rakes me when I realize there is nothing I can do as I hold the sword up, slicing deeper into the mindless beast to keep at least one of them away from me. No way for Namar to get to me in time.

I grit my teeth as I see it rise in the air, seemingly in slow motion before it descends, wanton hunger on its face as it falls, its limbs clutching for me as it hurtles toward me. Closing my eyes, I resign myself to the impending doom.

Woosh.

Then a noise breaks the air. My eyes snap open to see Felgrand's large blade sail into the undead, sending it flying across the floor, clattering. I feel the weight of the one pinning me suddenly lift away. My attention switches back to the other undead, now being lifted from the blade in my arms by Felgrand, who merely tosses the undead over his shoulder at Namar, who doesn't even flinch as he spins, bringing his blade down upon the air-bound threat, killing it before it hits the floor.

I find Felgrand's large hand suddenly grabbing mine and hefting me to my feet before he gestures to my side.

"Then there was one."

I turn my eyes to it. Felgrand's blade erupts from it as it claws its way back to us, weighed down by the massive blade. I step forward, stopping in front of it as it grabs for me. I step down on its back, holding it in place as it snarls at me, blood pooling as it struggles to bite me, its lifeless eyes glaring up at me not in contempt but in hunger.

Bringing my sword up in a reverse grip, I glare at the unfortunate prisoner below my heel.

"You poor soul. None of them deserved this."

I bring the sword down, feeling the struggling stop. I bring my sword back up, releasing a deep sigh. As I step back from the undead, Felgrand reaches down, putting a foot on the corpse as he yanks his great sword free, tearing a large portion of the body with it.

"And now there are none."

It is a hollow voice I almost do not recognize as my own.

Solaire

I stir as I feel a warmth bask my body. As I open my eyes, I see the massive hanging tree looming over me, golden sunlight illuminating each petal, making them twinkle as if a golden sea. Bringing a hand to my head as I sit up, feeling sore from the ground, I remember what transpired the previous day.

With a sigh, I walk to the carved doorway Cu'jehi departed from the previous night. Glancing back at the entrance whence I emerged, I reach over to my side with a tender prod. A sharp pain flashes across my body, and I wince.

"That's right, and I am now in a fantasy story. I wish it was all a dream," I grumble, a grimace flowing to my face as I trek down the path. Lined with dimly glowing lanterns placed at even intervals along a trodden path, magnificent flora grow along it, bathed in warm sunlight coming from the second sun's rise. I hear the sound of a stream as I walk around a tree to be blinded by sunlight. Bringing my arm to my eyes, I make out a figure next to the stream, stepping closer to get out of the blinding sunlight.

"Hey—"

I stumble over a rock, launching myself forward. Out of the sunlight, the figure strikes faster than I can process. I find myself off the ground, flipping through the air before landing in the water. The impact has left me stunned, pain flowing throughout my body. A sudden pressure lands on my arms as cold water flows around me. Raising my head to keep it out of the water, I open my eyes to behold a magnificent sight: a Watcher, with light bluish-green skin and silver eyes, unlike many of the others. Her features are aristocratic and sharp, giving her a surreal beauty. A deep shade of blue, almost purple, makes her lips so distinguishable. Her features are encompassed by silver hair, just long enough to frame her face. On one side, her hair is curved, following her natural contour. On the other, it is swept back, meeting behind her head, where it is fastened to an ornate hairpin that was coming askew from her hair, leading me to believe there was a bun behind her head.

I expected to find the same look of disdain, but I see something else as the surprise drains from her expression. Instead of loathing, I see something else. Intrigue? My mind reeling from the difference, a sense of relief comes over me as I release a happy sigh that I can escape the blatant discrimination, if only for a moment.

Then I hear the end of a melodic sound. Snapping back to attention, I look back up to the Watcher. She seems to be expecting something, and in my relieved state, I must have missed it. Frowning, she growls her frustration, irritation staining her silver eyes.

"Answer me," she demands, her eyes never leaving mine. I try to sit up, moving my arm to support my body as I move my arm forward. In a swift movement, she lunges forward, kicking my arm to the side and pinning it with a foot on the elbow joint, splashing me with water. A cold sensation pricks my neck as I lie back, forced into the water.

"Do not move, stranger."

I open my eyes to see her kneeling over me with one leg pressing down on my left arm, my right pinned by her own hand, her other reaching to place something against my neck with a knee pressing down across my chest. What startles me is her free-flowing hair, I don't see the hairpin anymore. Following her arm to my neck, I see the end of the hairpin, and realize it must double as some sort of weapon. I take a shallow breath as she presses it against my neck a little harder. *Yep, definitely a blade.* She glares down at me expectantly, waiting for something.

"I am sorry. I didn't hear you. I was a little disoriented."

A twitch of her lip is the only reaction as she continues staring at me.

"I asked who you are and how you got here. This glade does not have many visitors," she responds curtly.

"My name is Solaire. I was brought here by the Watcher Cu'jehi. He told me to follow this path to his place, but I have gotten a bit lost." A shudder wracks my body as the water's cold bite adds to my anxiety about the situation.

"Very well. We shall see if you speak of the truth," she retorts. She leaps backward, using the knee on my chest as a springboard, landing gracefully on the riverbank. A slight throb remains from the unexpected pressure. I sit up in the water, eyeing her suspiciously.

"Well, now what?" I ask tentatively as I stand from the water. She gestures to a pair of barrels at the side of the river.

"You carry those and follow my directions." I raise an eyebrow.

"That's it? You will have me carry barrels, and then you will trust me?"

"No, that is to prevent you from using any magic and so you will not be behind me."

"What if I don't know any magic?" I ask offhandedly.

"As much as I would like to believe the words of a stranger, I do not know you. Now, move to the barrels."

Her grip tightens on the hairpin, which comes to a fine point at the end, a blade the size of a mere letter opener. She nods in the direction of the barrels. With a sigh, I trudge to the barrels. Seeing handles for each of them, I bend over, sneaking back a glance. She stands with her small blade held in front of her, now in a reverse grip. Grabbing the barrels, I tug up. Not expecting their hefty weight, I stumble forward.

"Your lack of grace is unbecoming. Be careful with my food."

I sigh. Clearly, things are not going as smoothly as I hoped.

"Step onto the path and keep going at a moderate pace unless you wish to find a blade betwixt your shoulders," she says in her even steely voice. With a roll of my eyes, I start my trek onto the path. A moment of silence passes as we keep walking. I see many beautiful bushes and trees, the bushes each bearing fruit of all different colors. Trees of all different kinds fill my vision.

"Take the right."

Her voice takes me out of my sightseeing. Looking back at the trail, I notice it is split in two, one headed toward a denser portion of the forest, this one looking the same as the one I walked the rest of the march, with the same agonizing silence filling the air.

"So, what is your name?" I ask, trying to break the silence. A moment passes without response. I sigh as I see the path continue with a small worn trail breaking off on the left side of the trail.

"Take the worn trail on your left."

A pool of distrust begins to build in my gut as my question goes unanswered. With growing concern, I decide to ask again, "Do you have a name?" I repeat, trying to hide my annoyance.

"I heard what you said before. As for my name, I cannot tell you yet. Names have a lot of power here."

"What? Then why did I have to tell you mine?" The concern is boiling into a new fear plaguing my mind.

Is she going to kill me?

"I forced you to tell me yours because it would give me an edge should you become a threat." I frown as the trees start thinning out and we move into a clearing. Turning around a tree, I can barely make out a hut through the trees.

Sensing the current conversation was ending, I decided to approach another question at the forefront of my mind.

"Why are you unlike the others?"

"How do you mean?" she casually answers.

"You don't have the same hate in your eyes," I say, taking a chance. We arrive at the front of the building, and I glance back, meeting her piercing silver eyes which stare into mine, her blade rising as she readies herself. She pauses for a second, her eyes falling to the ground before flashing back to me.

"I do not hate that which I do not know. I have never met a human, and while others may still hold hatred for those who have damaged us, I do not think others' actions should define who you are. That does *not* mean I will not be vigilant against *your* actions." She nods to the building as she moves around me.

"Place those at the base of the stairs and wait. We shall now see if you spoke the truth," she says regally, prancing around me to the stairs. Turning, I move to the edge of the stairs and set the barrels down, my arms feeling stringy from the weight. I rub them as I turn around to see my temporary charge. Looking around, I see she has vanished. Scanning the area left and right, I see no indication she is there. Turning back to the hut, I finally see it.

It is constructed out of wooden planks, forming a small staircase rising up to a landing. The walls are made from bamboo shoots, perfectly aligned, framing a wooden window and a door. The door itself is made from a bear pelt, stretched over the doorway and just long enough to drag on the floor. Looking up, I see the second sun coming up over the horizon, not as blinding as the first one, but the blue tint of the sun acts strangely, showering everything in a luminescent light, which at first appears very blue, but as the sun rises, more vivid oranges and yellows replace the blue glow that bathed everything. A hollow thud comes from the house, and I look back to see Cu'jehi stepping through the threshold, gazing thoughtfully as he slowly steps out onto the deck.

"You have come, but as I said, it is time to discuss your future." He stops at the top of the stairs.

"I don't have time for this. I need to go and save my friend now!" I growl, my irritation coming back full force.

"Need I remind you you will only be an inconvenience, unable to sway the tide of battle one way or the other as you are now." I grit my teeth as he continues. "While I cannot let you go now, I will let you go when you can protect yourself. Stay here until you can, and then I will direct you on your path."

"I need to go now!"

"If you go now, you will die!" Waving his trident around, a blue liquid flows down it to the blade. Creating a bubble around it, he swings it forward. "*Stromme!*"

A torrent of water smashes into me, shooting forward from the blade, sending me tumbling backward. Sputtering and wracked with pain, I crawl enough to let me glare up at him.

"If you think I am powerful, I am not, youngblood! There are those who would make what I just did seem like a pleasant dream! The Prometheans, you have seen their power, their reality-bending abilities! Do you really think they will just let you do as you wish? They want you. They need you! For whatever reason, you have knowledge they desire, and whatever it may be, they cannot have it."

"Why?" I ask as I get to my feet.

"They have caused so much harm in their pursuit, driven by their pride."

"Pursuit?"

"They formed for a single reason: to take power from a family with power and influence far greater than you can imagine. The Originals, those who found the Second Reality. They are what Prometheus has united to destroy."

"The devastation was so grand, it spread through the first reality, as well. Chernobyl, the world wars, the atomic bombs—all the result of clashes between Prometheus and the Originals."

A moment of awe passes as I realize my jaw is hanging open.

"What do you mean?"

"Simple, the beings that are pursuing you, the Prometheans, will not hesitate to lay waste to anything that gets in their way. I am offering to help you learn, so stay here, and we can get you ready so you may survive on your own."

"How do those events have anything to do with this?" I cry out in frustration.

"Those were all stories contrived to explain the events of the Second Reality to those from the first. After all, humans persecute those they do not understand." He looks past me with a pained look.

"Either way, my friend needs my help!" I reply.

His face is still unfocused, lost in thought. "Youngblood, where would you even start?"

"I have to find some person named Charles Haplas!" Cu'jehi flinches, and his eyes widen, snapping back to me.

"You said Haplas?"

"Yeah, so?"

"If that is the case, this has become more disastrous." He takes the first step down the staircase edging to the right side.

"What do you mean? Do you know him?"

"He is a member of a group directly opposed to Prometheus. Come, I will teach you how to fight and how to protect yourself. Only then can you stand even a chance of going to them."

"So, what would you have me do?"

"I shall teach you how to fight—or, at the very least, how to be an asset in one."

"Asset?" I repeat, puzzled.

"Yes, but worry not of that for now. First, we shall see if you have any talent with close-range combat," he says. His trident springs to life in his right hand, held lightly behind him as he descends to the next stair.

Reaching over the railing, he grabs at a rod and tosses it forward. I flinch as it strikes the ground in front of me with a metallic thud. I look back up at him as he takes another step, stopping at the final one.

"That is your weapon. Pick it up, and we will begin."

Bending down, I slowly reach and grab the end of the pole, dragging it to me as he takes the last step.

"Now what?" I ask as I hold the rod awkwardly.

"Now, youngblood, you fight," he says, dashing forward.

Surprised, I bring my rod up as he swings his down in a cleaving blow, smashing against mine. I buckle to a knee, only for a blow to my side to knock the wind out of me, sending me barreling into the ground. Cu'jehi lunges forward, the butt of the trident raised high, as if to impale me. Rolling to the side, I quickly get back on my feet, only to immediately raise my rod to block another smashing strike. Taking a step back, Cu'jehi sweeps my feet from under me. As I crash into the ground, my eyes shut for a moment as the rod is wrenched from my hands. I open my eyes to the bladed portion of the trident. Following it up once again, I see Cu'jehi holding my rod in his other hand. He slowly retracts the trident and offers the pole for me to grab. I grab it and pull myself up as he takes a step back.

"Again."

Solomon

"Nggg."

I groan as I come to, struggling to move my arms. Looking down on them, I see they are bound in metal shackles.

"What the hell?" I ask myself as I scan the room, seeing an ornate white door in front of me with large white bookshelves framing it on either side. Looking down, I appear to be seated in a wooden chair situated over a majestic carpet, with all kinds of royal blues with light green leaves, forming a whirlwind pattern across the floor. Trailing the wall to my right, I see the pristine bookshelf continue. Turning all the way around to look over my shoulder, I see one of the soldiers who attacked the school, standing with his arms clasped behind his back, staring forward at the door. Then I hear the click of the door as the handle turns and slowly opens.

My head whirls back in time to see a man enter, wearing a brown cloak, torn and ripped, draped over his body, sheltering his left side. On his right shoulder, it is held together with the same golden pin that I saw on the uniforms of the soldiers who grabbed me. His shoulder has a connection that looks to be a modern shoulder pad. His forearm is bare until it comes to a leather bracer on his wrist. Upon it are many bullets, neatly arranged. He wears dark gray fingerless leather gloves. An old red checkered flannel shirt, untucked over black pants. On his waist are two crisscrossing belts that hold many neatly aligned bullets along them. A holster on his hip catches my attention as the twinkle of a platinum revolver with a gold finish sparkles in the light. I cannot see the other hip due to the way the cloak rested on his person, but I assume it also has a pistol by the symmetrical style of the belts. Getting a good look at his face, I see it is a rugged kind of handsome—black ruffled hair unkempt, just long enough to cover his ears. It merges with sideburns, leading to a full beard and mustache. Tucked into the corner of his mouth is a cigarette, burning as the other corner is turned up in a smug smile.

He steps forward into the room, each step resounding in colossal booms. Looking down at his feet, I see leather boots. With a scoff, I look up at him.

"Now that we have Clint here, can someone please tell me where I am?"

A resounding smack fills the air as a blow descends upon my head. Shaking my head, I hear the man behind me step forward.

"Sir, I have brought him." The man behind me steps forward and salutes. A calculating look passes over the outlaw's face as he reaches up and takes hold of his cigarette, holding it in his mouth as a plume of smoke is breathed through his fingers.

"I can see that. Well done," he says, a gleeful crinkle on his face as I glare at him. "You may leave."

He finishes after a drag from the death stick, taking the cigarette from his mouth for the first time.

"Yes, sir! I will inform Darius of our success now," he says, breaking from his salute to step forward. The outlaw's smirk dies on his face as he says this. A single nod is his only reply as he takes a short step out of the soldier's way. As he steps toward the door, the outlaw clears his throat.

"What happened to the others from the retrieval squad?" he asks offhandedly, his gaze holding my own while he places the cigarette back between his lips. The soldier stops and looks back over his shoulder.

"They all stayed behind with a Promethean to buy me time to get here." A twinkle I am not sure I like enters the man's eyes.

"I see. So, they did their job well. And what of your journey? Has anyone seen you enter here?" he asks, his expression dour.

"No, sir. I took my time getting here to ensure I would not compromise the mission."

The reply catches me off guard. Better than voicing my obvious confusion over how long I have been unconscious, I simply observe the exchange.

"Perfect. Well done, soldier. Take your leave." he replies, taking the cigarette from his mouth with his left hand. The cloak lifts for the first time, allowing me to see the second revolver at his side, confirming my suspicions. The soldier nods and turns to the door, taking a step toward it. My gaze finds itself returning to the outlaw's eyes.

The man turns on his heel, his right hand gripping the revolver from the holster, and—*bang*—a gunshot rings out. The white door is spattered in crimson, and the soldier drops to the floor. I can only stare aghast at the sight.

"Sorry, soldier boy. Couldn't have you blabbing off to Darius about my own plans," he says as he flicks the cigarette from his fingers onto the corpse. As he turns back to me, my own terrified gaze meets the outlaw's calculating one. Taking two steps forward as he replaced his smoking pistol, he stops right in front of me, leaning forward as he places his left hand on my right shoulder, coming close enough to smell the burnt tobacco.

"What does Prometheus want with a greenhorn like you?" There is a pause as I stare defiantly into his eyes. "Fine, don't speak. I will find out everything in due time."

He stands, taking a step back as he motions to my left. I see a man in the corner toying with a large bowie knife, running it under the fingernails of one of his hands. The man has dark brown hair, cut short and parted on the right. He is lanky, covered by a dark orange leather jacket with dark brown highlights, and his cargo pants are dark green. He is leaning against the bookshelf, his gaze fixated on me despite the sharp blade so close to his hands. Pushing off from the wall, the man walks toward the outlaw.

"My dear friend here will help you find the courage to tell me everything I want to know." The outlaw turns and kicks the dead body before reaching for the stained door handle.

"Perhaps after some time alone with him, you will be willing to tell me why you are so sought-after."

He opens the door. A hand grips my left shoulder tightly, startling me and demanding my attention. The new man leans in close, his other hand holding the knife lazily, with two fingers supporting it as he holds it to the side. I see a mad gleam in his eyes as he playfully whirls his knife.

"Hey, mate, the name's Jack. We are going to be the *best of friends*." He lets out a short cackle, and the door clicks shut.

CHAPTER 6

PUSHED TO THE LIMIT

Solaire

"Again," comes the same cool, even voice.

As I pick myself up from the floor, gripping the dowel at my side, the bruises are already turning purple all over my arm. Panting heavily, I drag myself to my feet. After a moment, I charge him, raising my dowel for an overhead strike. Bringing it down, I feel it stop cold against his trident. A slight shuffle in the trident is the only warning I get as a kick collides with my side, knocking me off balance. With my dowel in my hand, the blows come raining down.

Left. I raise my dowel.

Crack.

Right.

Crack.

I barely make it in time. Then I see him draw his weapon back, shooting the end at me. Spinning to the side, I feel the air glide across my stomach, gleeful at my success at having dodged such a strike. Swinging my staff around like a bat, I meet the air. I lose sight of my opponent for an instant, and something hooks around my ankle. Dragged to the ground, I see the wooden dowel go bouncing away. Rolling toward the dowel, I feel the impact with the ground. Reaching my staff, I whirl around only to find nothing. Glancing left and right, I only now notice how close I am to the hut. Hearing footfalls on the wood, I turn just in time to see the butt end of the trident thrust into my chest. Spit mixed with blood flies out of my mouth as I hear a crack, and pain flares throughout my body as I bounce off the floor. I hear his feet hit the ground, followed by a sigh.

"You have improved, youngblood; however, you are still not proficient enough to keep up with those you may encounter here." Groaning, I sit up, ignoring the pain.

"Again ..."

I mumble, blood dripping onto the ground as I glare back up at his calm face, which shows no fatigue despite him throwing me on the ground countless times.

"No, youngblood, it seems combat is not your specialty."

"Then what would you have me do, might I ask?" I hiss, resulting in a baleful glare.

"No, I would have you focus upon a different way to help. Focus on helping those you know who can fight."

My mind flashes back to Bastian, seeing him fight the knights in that field with just a pair of scissors.

"What did you have in mind?" I ask tentatively.

"Healing. Considering how often you sustain injuries, it might hold personal interest for you."

"Healing? How am I supposed to do that? I do not have any medical equipment." I respond dejectedly, receiving a chuckle in response. I level a glare at him, meeting his glee-filled eyes. He takes a calming breath.

"Magic, youngblood. With magic."

"I don't know how to do magic. I fell here by accident! How can I learn magic?"

"You need only be taught."

I scoff.

"You say that as if it's easy to learn!"

"That's because some magic just so happens to be."

"Then why have the people of my world—"

"Your *reality*," he interrupts.

"Excuse me?"

"Reality. Not your *world* but your *reality*."

A SECOND LAYER OF REALITY

"Then explain the second sun!" I say, gesturing to the bluish sun in the sky.

"This reality is not only purer but offers many powerful techniques one may learn. As for our second sun, I could only guess." He shrugs.

"Regardless, why then, if magic is so easy to learn, do they not teach it in my *reality*?" I ask, squeezing my eyes shut in frustration.

"Simple. Not only are our realities vastly different, those who use magic in yours must learn to hide it. Surely, you remember history—the burnings, the beatings, the exiles. Perhaps the Salem Witch Trials?"

He listed while gesturing, as if he could see them. It all starts to click together. Looking down at my hands, swollen and bruised, a sick feeling churns in my stomach.

"How much of what I know is a lie?" I ask, dragging my eyes back to Cu'jehi's, receiving a disheartening sympathetic smile.

"More than you could ever imagine." Gritting my teeth, I dragged my battered left hand over my face in frustration.

"Fine, teach me," I mumble.

"Before I do, you must know about the costs of this magic."

"What do you mean, like frog legs and eyes of newt?" I said.

"Something like that." he chuckled in response. Stepping closer he continued. "There are four kinds of magic: ritualistic, arcane, demonic, and elemental. Ritualistic magic is based on sacrificing or tributing items to move the hands of fate. The more potent the offering, the more powerful the spell. It may help to think of Stephen's magic style to understand."

I raised my eyebrows. "Why his?"

"He used his blood as a tribute to power his spell."

"So, if I were to use my blood, could I also use his magic?" A scowl crosses Cu'jehi's face as he regards me.

"No, magic is not as easily taught or learned."

"Then how can I learn to heal?" I shout, drawing a glare.

"Patience, youngblood. Allow me to tell you about the other magics first."

"Why does that matter?" I growl.

"Knowing your enemy and what magic they use is important so you can identify the cost associated with such magic. That knowledge may be more important than fighting."

"Why would that matter?"

"Think, youngblood! If you know the costs incurred by any magic, then you can discern its weaknesses. Arcane magic is next. Arcane magics divest their costs from the user by taking part of the user and converting it into power. Some areas are inconsequential as taking energy to move further, while others can be as reality breaking as manipulating time." Remembering the eerie green of Alexander causes me to shudder as he takes a breath seeing the recognition play across my face.

"Arcane magic tends to be the most powerful, but usually at one of the steeper costs."

"What cost does Alexander pay?" I ask, remembering his brutal execution of the soldiers.

"I do not know, only that he guards it with the utmost secrecy. Knowing one's costs of magic is an immensely powerful thing." I nod, beginning to understand the advantage that such knowledge could give someone.

"The next is demonic magic, magic that is bestowed with one of the highest costs, the practitioner's soul in the most extreme cases usually by use of a contract of some form. The contract allows a being to use the magic of another or that of a transcendent being."

"Transcendent being?"

"Yes, but do not worry. For now, just consider them to be deities."

"What about holy magic?" I ask, wondering if all deities are included.

"How astute, youngblood." He nods in recognition. "Yes, ironically enough, holy magic is demonic magic, although I can assure you that practitioners of this magic will insist that it be referred to as holy magic. Another importance is that once you discover a transcendent being, a pledge can be all it takes to gain such magic. It is an agreement between two parties and can be revoked just as easily as it was bestowed.

"The final form of magic is elemental, the form that I practice and the one you will be learning. Elemental magic focuses on the balance of the elements. The cost of this magic is inconsequential compared to the others; however, you must be in tune with your element to fully use it at its greatest."

"What does that mean?"

"For instance, to utilize water magic as I do, you must be calm to properly control it. Not only that, but you must maintain the balance of all things. It is easier to apply your reality's physics to this. I believe it was Newton's third law?"

"To every reaction, there is an equal and opposite reaction." I droned out, surprised that such a thing can be pertinent in another reality. "What does that have to do with anything, though?"

"To use an element, you must take responsibility for the repercussions. For instance, flames burn the wielder as they do their target."

"What about your magic? What is the cost of yours?" I gesture to him, confused.

"There are two things regarding that: the first is the necessity of water but not from the environment. To use water that is not around you, to maintain the balance, you use the water within yourself." He holds up his hand as water pools into it, seemingly appearing before me.

"The cost of water magic is dehydrating yourself," he says as he lets the water fall to the ground.

"The other is understanding. Understanding the spell gives its caster more control and allows for the minimum consequences. If you fear a spell, you will only let it run amok. If you do not understand it, then there can be many consequences. Regardless, just as there are affinities to learning, there are affinities to magic. Some will be more geared toward other forms."

"Does that mean I will only be able to use one kind of magic?"

"No, youngblood, not by any means. It just means those you are proficient with will be far easier to use and carry fewer costs than others." Nodding in acceptance, I take a step closer.

"What is the magic you wish to teach me?"

"A simple spell. It is meant to heal the target, using water from your body as the medium."

"What would happen if we used water from external sources?" I ask, earning a raised eyebrow.

"Rather than elemental magic, this would be closer to arcane magic; while not necessarily a bad thing, the spell might do something other than what the caster intended."

"What do you mean?"

"It all stems from your understanding of your own spell. As everyone has their own spell, they also have their own understanding of what it will do." Reaching out, he takes my bruised hand with his calloused one. "*Helbrede*," he says softly.

"Take this simple healing spell. My understanding is that the water will wash over your injury, purifying it, healing the taint of injury." I can only watch in stunned silence as the water washes over my hand, fixing the bruises on my hand before the water even falls to the ground. "Understanding also lets us name spells to something that reflects how we are attuned. Therefore, two spells that function similarly may be differently named—just as your own spell will have its own unique name, effect, and cost."

"Does that mean if I believe that my spells should not have costs then they won't, and what if I don't want to have a name for a spell?"

"No, there is always a cost. As you discover it, you can only hope the cost is not too steep. As to the other question, to cast a spell, you need to speak its name to invoke the magic with your own words." Raising his trident, he waves his left hand over the end, and a bubble of water begins to form.

"Take the water from here and use it to remove the taint of your pain." Looking up from the bubble, I see uncertainty in his eyes.

"How am I supposed to do that?"

"Focus on moving the water over your injury. Imagine it flowing over your injuries and taking them away."

Picturing just that, I hesitantly bring my hand to the water as I scoop some of it into my palm, seeing it maintain its bubble-like form. I glance up to see Cu'jehi's stone-cut face, showing nothing but only eyeing the bubble.

"*Helbrede*," I utter, cupping a handful of water with one hand and washing over the other. I feel a cool, soothing sensation pass over my hand, but I do not see the wounds healing as they did before. Frowning in frustration, I pass my hand over the wounds once more.

"Do you feel any different?" The voice is calm as I glare at my hand. "Yes, the pain is gone, but the injuries are not. I did what you did, so why did it not work?"

"Your own magic will not work as mine does, youngblood. Besides, your first attempt at magic has succeeded, whereas most fail. But you lack the understanding, the reason *why* you cast your magic." I take a breath to speak, but I am stilled by a raised hand. "Do not tell me yet, youngblood. Take a while, find your inner peace, and then tell me."

He lets the water fall to the ground. Turning back to the hut, his trident collapses as he walks back up the stairs. Stopping at the top, he turns back to me.

"Come back when you have had time to discard your frustration and can tell me of not what you fight for but rather what you would *heal* for." He turns and disappears into the hut.

I shake my head, muttering, "But I do know what I heal for. Whatever. If I find that river again, I can practice using water to heal. Maybe I will get better if I do. I might be better at arcane magic anyway."

As I walk down the worn path, I recollect everything that has passed. My leisurely stroll is interrupted by the sound of arguing. Rushing ahead, I come to the river's edge to see the girl I saw before. She is facing the river, but standing behind her is the same Watcher who attacked me in the village. He is shouting something at her. Gritting my teeth, I eavesdrop on the conversation.

"I am an elite!" he roars. "Any female should be honored to be my mate!"

Without turning around, she replies in a calm voice, "Find one of the others from your flock of admirers."

"I am next in line to be Head Watcher—you should be honored that I would ask you!"

"Status has never impressed me, Ku'terik. There are those who find it very important. I assure you, they exist within your flock of devotees."

He reaches out and grabs her arm. "I do not want any of them. You alone have captured my attention, your unique beauty—"

Unable to restrain myself any longer, I step out from behind the tree. She wrenches her arm away from him, pivoting, causing him to stumble forward. A palm thrust to his torso makes him stumble backward.

"You will regret that!" He sneers as he steps forward, and I have decided enough is enough.

"Hey, you blue bastard!" I call out, snagging both their attention.

"You dare interrupt my conversation, feeble outcast!" he cries. The girl scoffs.

"If you are concerned for outcasts, you would do well to remember: for far too long *I* was treated as an outcast. Only *now* do you take any interest in me."

He turns over his shoulder to look at her.

"I will have what I want. When I become head of the Watchers, you will be mine." He walks toward me, meeting my scowl with a smug smile. As he steps closer, he hisses under his breath, "After I do, I will kill you, too, outsider."

My rage, roiling inside for so long, finally boils over. I thrust my head forward, smashing it into his. The smug smile is replaced by shock as he stumbles backward.

"That's for referring to her as a piece of property, asshole."

He straightens, a look of unadulterated rage settling on his face as he rushes at me, his movements slower than Cu'jehi's by many degrees. Throwing his fist forward, I see it and bring my left arm sweeping in front of me, knocking his aside. The anger on his face is replaced by surprise. I have no time to relish it as my body reacts by thrusting my own fist forward. My reward is the heavy smash of my fist against his face. He falls backward, his hands clutching his face, golden liquid flowing between his fingers as his eyes scream with rage.

"That's for blindsiding me earlier."

As I shake the pain out of my fingers, he thrusts his hand to his side, a sword flaring to life in his palm.

"I have had enough of your intrusion, outsider."

He steps forward menacingly, his off-weapon hand cradling his face. He steps forward, and I move back in perfect response. In my periphery, I see a blur: the girl leaping through the air, extending her leg, which crashes against Ku'terik's face. This sends him bouncing onto the path, his blade flying from his hand into the forest. We both stand there in a fighting stance as he sits up.

"You would dare side against your own for an outsider!" he screams.

"Begone, Ku'terik. Your actions bring shame upon yourself."

"Ai'hara, you will be mine." He scowls as he rises to his feet and walks away. Seeing him disappear between the trees, I look back to the woman who led me to Cu'jehi.

"Want to tell me what his problem is?"

She sighed before walking over to the river edge once more.

"Ku'terik has always felt himself to be somewhat of an elite amongst us. Despite our teachings, he has always thought of our race as superior to others, and since he has been named next Head of the Watch, he believes he is the most elite of us all." She speaks softly, but her anger is barely concealed. As I take a step closer, she does not move, merely stares into the water. Spotting a darkening spot on her arm with just a bead of gold pooling on it, I approach, unnerved by her apathy.

"Why does he get away with it?"

"As the next Head Watcher, he is too valuable," she says with contempt, "so much so, he can do whatever he wants with anyone."

Ai'hara wraps her arms around her body, rubbing the spot Ku'terik grabbed, golden ichor leaking from between her fingers. "Always trying to be better than everyone else." Her fingers grip harder, the skin darkening around them. Staying silent, I close the remaining step between us, approaching from behind. "He was—no, *is*—the reason I am an outcast," she continues. "He wanted so much to scorn me because I was different, claiming that I had no place here, that I was an abomination, nothing more." I can hear her teeth grinding as she continues looking down. I follow her gaze to see us both looking at her reflection. Her expression contorts to one of anger.

"Why does he want you then?"

She spins on her heel, burning her fierce expression into my mind. "He wants me because he cannot have me." She huffs. "All the others have been taught that to be mated with a Watcher is an honor, but I have seen the fate of such females: strong individuals turned into nothing more than trophies for those who claim strength." She brings her arm in front of her, tightening it into a fist. With a thrust of her hand to her side, she shakes her head, scattering her silver hair into the light breeze. "I will not be reduced to chattel! I am my own being!" she bellows, her aristocratic calm belied by her ferocity.

"I have seen the discrimination firsthand—"

I begin to say, but her frigid glare stops me cold.

"You think those mere moments are anything compared to what I have experienced? You understand nothing." She turns back to the stream, crossing her arms across her chest.

"You are right," I said, joining her, looking at my own reflection in the water. She cocked her head toward me quizzically. I continue looking into the water, at my own image.

"I don't know anything about what you have gone through, but I do know that if you do not fight for what you want, you'll only regret what remains available to you."

"Do you think me so ignorant I do not know this?"

"Not at all, but I know that right now, I am here, and I can help you fight."

As our eyes meet, I think I feel her anger downgrading to something less severe, like distrust.

"If you think this would cause me to fall for you, then you are sorely mistaken."

I raise my hand, trying to calm her down.

"No, I need help with my own fight, and I would like *you* to help me." I paused, seeing confusion etched on her face. "That guy is a prick."

She appears shocked, then returns her gaze to the river, and I swear I see the ghost of a smile touch her lips.

"Crass but certainly true. What kind of help do you need?"

"Saving a friend of mine, but before we get into that, let me help you."

"Help me?" Her eyes narrow as I reach out, taking her arm with one hand and placing the other one over it.

The word "*Helbrede*" comes to my voice as I stare at the bruised wound and stream of blood.

"You won't be able to heal without wa—" she begins, but she is stunned into silence by what happens next.

A small sheet of white ice spreads from my fingers to the edges of the wound, creeping over it. Her normally stoic expression is replaced by an almost slack-jawed expression as the ice starts cracking, large blue cracks appearing all over the patch. Each one makes a resounding *snap* before the entire sheet shatters. It shatters into a thin mist of snowflakes that scatter into the air as they break apart, seemingly disappearing. Inspecting the skin, we find that not only is the ice gone, but the wound has gone with it.

As I look up to see her stunned expression, she undoubtedly sees my own.

Bastian

Staring into the deceased face of the prisoner I have just killed, I am frozen in place. It feels so wrong as I look around me seeing the floor strewn with bodies. After an eternity, I feel a hand clamp down on my shoulder.

"Do not falter. Their blood is not on your hands."

I turn to look up into Felgrand's unwavering eyes. He turns to look down upon the same body I am contemplating.

"I know. This is why I left this place," I say almost too softly to hear, the harsh reality of what just happened hitting me as I look back down at the face of the prisoner I killed. It is contorted in a grotesque mask of agony and hunger. The mere sight makes my stomach flip, but for the life of me, I cannot turn from what I have done.

"You know this is nothing compared to what we have seen, to what we have done," Namar says smugly.

"Don't you think I know that?" I growl.

"Shut it, rogue. Let this one grieve. Fighting the undead will always be difficult. Take solace you have put them out of their misery. The fault for these atrocities lies with that heretic!" Felgrand says.

"Having trouble with your little religion there, mister crusader?" comes Namar's taunting voice.

"The Church would never be responsible for such atrocities! That was an imposter, and I will find them and make sure such events are exposed and those responsible judged justly," Felgrand bellows, his eyes burning with determination.

"Yeah, yeah, whatever you say, big guy." Namar scoffs as he steps in front of me, obscuring my view of the body. He pushes a pile of metallic items into my hands. "Look, you can be sad all you want after we get out of here and you help me, but right now, I need you to take these." Looking down, I see my throwing knives being piled into my hands. "You will need them. We are not out of the woods yet, killer."

He finishes by slapping my cheek, then steps back on the body of the fallen prisoner. I grit my teeth at his callous manner, but what really gets to me is that smug grin as he stands on the corpse.

"Have you no decency, no respect? Not even for the dead?" Felgrand cries, only to receive a scoff in response.

"Have you seen what happened here?" He gestures around the room, spreading his arms wide as I sheath my knives. Bodies are everywhere, from the massive mound that Felgrand has cleaved through to the blood smears leading to the crumbled body upon which he stands.

"How can I not see the death all around us, the death that we should have been able to stop?" Felgrand roars.

"Please … they died because they were not strong enough to protect themselves. We are the only ones here, and the reason is simple." Namar hops off the prisoner, landing gracefully next to it.

"We survived because only the strong can survive. The weak can only place their dreams onto those stronger than themselves because they are not strong enough to accomplish them alone." He closes his eyes, bringing his hands up in a shrug as he shakes his head slowly from side to side.

"Why, you …" Felgrand snarls as the giant reaches across, snatching Namar by his cloak at the base of his neck, dragging him closer and to the tips of his toes, his furious, passionate expression the opposite of Namar's smug, relaxed one.

"Wait," I mumble, the effort of speaking more taxing than I thought possible, but I manage to drag their attention to me. Felgrand's passion is replaced by confusion.

"You would ask that he get away with this?"

"No, but we will need him."

A scream echoes from the shadows into which the monster has escaped. Scowling, Felgrand throws Namar back as he grips his longsword with his other hand.

"Fine, I will join you to escape, but know I aim to avenge this atrocity and save all who can be saved. I do not aid you for this rogue," he huffs as Namar smoothes the ruffles on his cloak.

"Yeah, yeah, I know. Save it for when all this is over, big guy," Namar says.

Shing.

Metal springs forth as he again unsheaths both of his rapiers. I tighten the grip on my short sword. Turning back to the gate, we step forward, spotting the trail of luminescent neon green blood left behind by the beast.

"At least that trail will give us an idea of where they are," Namar says. We step into the low light, barely able to make out the stone brick hallway. Farther down the hallway, I can make out two iron torches on either side of the symmetrical hallway that seem to mark a widening area. Embers burn low inside braziers.

Creeping forward, I glance all around in the meager light, always looking back down to the trail of green blood. Reaching the torches, I look past them into another room. Inside this room, a bridge spans over a chasm with a large bonfire at one end, surrounded by a spiral staircase leading upward to another landing. From here, I can make out two archways, one on either side of the landing. Stepping to the edge of the entrance, I look down to see the trail of blood veering off to the right. Moving to the corner quietly, I slowly peek around the corner. My heart is hammering against my ribs as I grip my sword so tightly that somewhere in my mind, I know it must hurt, but I cannot bring myself to care.

The room opens up, leaving a small ledge in front of us. On the right, I can see the trail of blood leading into a destroyed section of the wall.

Pieces of stone litter the floor. Looking back to the cracked wall, I see the blood lead into the darkness, and I realize it must lead into a cave, which I hope leads elsewhere into this prison. I look left and see that, unlike the other side, a stone urn intricate in design, decorated with old hieroglyphics with a small flame burning atop of it. Aside from the antique urn, there is nothing of interest in that corner—until my eyes catch movement near the bottom of the urn.

There!

Poking out from around the urn's base, I see it, just a speck of white. The same color as the prisoners' garb. Putting my hand out, I gesture to the urn as I silently raise my sword. Sneaking forward on the balls of my feet, I get closer. My footfalls clatter upon the floor, causing unbearable anxiety.

Just a few more steps, and I will be at the urn.

I pause as I step into something wet. Glancing at the others, I see Namar wince before I hear a shuffling noise from behind the urn. Grabbing the sword with both hands, I hold it diagonally across my body.

With the element of surprise gone, I leap around the urn, brandishing my sword, only to see a haggard old man looking up in shock. He brings his hands up to cover himself, cowering against the urn. In the pale flames, I can see his salt-and-pepper hair, which falls to his shoulders, his long, scruffy beard caked with blood. I immediately spot a wound on his neck, a festering bite wound, and I can already guess what has happened, but what puzzles me is that the wound looks old, almost as if it is already scabbing over.

"Who are you, and how are you not one of them?" I ask quietly, unsure who else might be listening. Slowly, he meets my gaze, his fearful look remaining as he cradles his body. As he looks up at me and I see him more clearly, I notice how scrawny he is. His face is sunken and haggard. His eyes are beady and unfocused.

"Abner," he responds quietly and quickly as he turns away and curls into himself. He starts rocking in place, shuffling toward the edge farthest from me. I kneel next to him, getting him to look back at me, the fear coming back full force.

"How long have you been down here?" I ask, more calmly. His eyes seem to grow unfocused once more.

"Six ... no ... yeah ... no ... seven ...," he responds, shaking his head before settling back into shaking.

Hearing the footfalls behind me, I turn to see Namar and Felgrand walking closer. He looks up once more, shuffling away from Felgrand. I step in front of Felgrand, calmly placing a palm onto his chest plate, causing him to look down at me with a frown. Understanding, he takes a step back.

I look over to Abner as he stops shaking somewhat and returns to rocking back and forth while muttering something.

"Sorry, bud. It looks like you scared the poor lad with that huge cleaver, I don't blame him, though," Namar quips.

"I have heard about enough out of you, rogue."

I lean closer to hear what he is saying, a whisper I can barely make out as the others bicker.

"Stay in the light ... will be alright ... stay in the light ... be alright."

"So, if we stay in the light, we will be alright."

He looks up, shocked, before looking up to the urn above us, raising his emaciated hand, the veins and bones clearly visible beneath his pale skin, pointing to the flame on the urn.

"The one true light ... keeps back the fright," he utters, almost entranced by the flame dancing upon the urn. Looking back to the others, I hear them still hissing at each other. Rolling my eyes, I turn back to Abner, who has retreated himself once more.

"Do you know of a way out of here?" I ask softly, almost pleadingly. He nods slowly, pointing past me. Looking past the two, I see the bridge.

"The bridge?"

He shakes his head as his eyes burrow into my own. "Gate ... past gate ... don't be late ... raising means waking ..." he mumbles before shaking once more.

A shrill screech echoes throughout the halls, causing us all to turn back to the tunnel on the other side of the room.

"Why don't you leave?" I ask him quietly. He starts shaking and moves away from me. Standing up as I look upon his cowering form, I shake my head sadly. Feeling a hand clap down onto my shoulder, I turn to see Namar looking over his shoulder at me.

"Learn anything useful?"

I let out a frustrated sigh. "You would know if you actually listened."

"Hey, it's not my fault the big buffoon over here decided to distract me."

"Stop, you two," I hiss before Felgrand can retort. Pinching the bridge of my nose, I breathe deeply to calm myself. "Look, he mentioned there is a gate out of here. He speaks very little, but it seems the light keeps the monsters away. In either case, he pointed across the bridge."

"No offense, but are we really going to listen to this old man? He seems short a few marbles, if you know what I mean," Namar replies as he whirls his finger in the air.

"*Tch*, I'd trust this old man over you any day, rogue."

"I have a name. It is Namar. Come on, say it with me now."

"Shut it! We at least have to see what is over the bridge because going the way the monster did is not advisable," I say through clenched teeth.

"Sure, works for me—" "Agreed—" they say simultaneously.

With a sigh, I push past them, but before I get too far, Felgrand's gruff voice whispers, "One moment. I must do something first." He walks past us around the urn. I see him kneel as we lose sight of him. Namar walks to the edge of the bridge, peering over the railing, and my breath catches in my throat at the sight of Namar falling backward with a soft clatter as he continues staring at the banister. What seems to be an eternity passes as I run up to him, kneeling at his side, shaking him to make sure he is okay.

"What happened?"

"I know why that man didn't escape."

His normally jubilant voice is now a dull whisper, almost inaudible, but I can now see it. There, in the depths of his eyes, is the birth of an expression I have only seen once before: fear. Felgrand comes running around the urn to us as he moves past me, glancing at me as he moves to the banister. I see the energy leave him as his hold on the banister tightens.

"Oh, sweet, holy mother," Felgrand whispers.

"What?" I ask, moving from my stunned cohort to the edge slowly. I peer over, and my breath is robbed from me.

"No way …" I mumble at the sight. Over the edge lies a crevasse, but it is not the crevasse that shocked us so. It is all of them. There are droves of them, all piling and moving through each other as if they are worms. There must be millions of them, all of them donning the same scarlet-stained prisoners' garb.

"Guess we found where the undead are coming from," Namar's disheartened voice comes from behind us.

Solaire

"How did you do that?" Ai'hara's voice is shaky as my eyes meet hers.

Once full of certainty, they now betray fear. Her silver eyes widen as she takes a step back. I gave a weak shrug and a nervous smile.

"I just did what Cu'jehi told me to do."

"He didn't tell you how to do that."

"Does it matter how it happened? Your arm is better!"

She glances down at her arm before stepping closer, her hand snapping out. It catches my wrist, and I yelp in surprise.

"We have to go now," she orders, pulling me down the trail.

"What, why?"

"You used an elemental spell that should have utilized water. What you just used is frost, not water."

"What is the difference? Isn't ice a form of water?"

I feel the scowl break across my face as I can see the edge of the building through the trees.

"No, the frost is not the same as water. They are vastly different, to the extent that it would have made more sense for you to use no water than for ice to appear."

"Wait up, where are we going?" I step back and try to wrench my wrist from her grip. She stumbles for a second and casts a cold glare over her shoulder.

"To Cu'jehi. We must make haste," she says in a strained tone before yanking me forward toward a clearing in the trees.

Stepping into the clearing, I hear the clatter of metal and the grunts of effort. As we round the last tree, we are greeted by the sight of Cu'jehi and Ku'terik both, their weapons together. A scowl crosses my face as I see the racist bastard. I feel my lip twinge upward as Ku'terik is pushed back, his body flailing, the sword in his hands flapping wildly. His grace is all but lost as he stumbles backward. A quick blur from Cu'jehi's staff is all I see before he straightens and Ku'terik falls onto his back, growling.

"Enough," comes Cu'jehi's stoic response as he stands over the defeated assailant.

"I can still fight!" Cu'jehi looks past his fallen opponent, and his gaze lands on us. His focus moves from me to Ai'hara before a warm expression passes over him.

"Later. For now, it seems there is something more pressing."

A thousand words are conveyed between the two before I feel my arm yanked forward. I stumble forward, and Cu'jehi raises an eyebrow.

"Look, two strangers coming to interrupt—"

A pulse of pressure can be felt throughout the clearing, but it is gone as quickly as it appeared, effectively shutting him up. I drop to my knees and look around.

"What is that?" I look up to see Ai'hara's startled yet knowledgeable gaze as she regards me.

"His presence." She nods toward Cu'jehi. I am jostled from my shock when the heavy staff crashes onto the ground.

"What brings you both here?" the elder demands, giving me a welcoming gesture.

"He just tried to use your healing magic, and then something peculiar happened." As she speaks, my throat goes dry.

Ku'terik sneers. "So, he can't even get such a simple spell?"

"Silence yourself. What happened?" Cu'jehi responds, his trident slowly rising to rest in a ready stance.

"He went to heal me, and when he used your spell, ice formed on the wound briefly before shattering. After the ice broke, the wound was gone." The expression upon the Watcher's face grows pensive as he looks down, calculating how to respond.

"Ice magic is exceedingly rare. Having such an attunement with it that you unconsciously utilize it is incredible. However, for it to manifest now …"

"What does it matter if I use water or ice magic?"

"Ice magic has only ever been used in such a way by one other, one who has been feared by many and has been forgotten by even more. You see, ice magic is feared because of what its wielder wishes to do with it. You need only look past the golden fields of Ashvale to see the blight left behind."

"Why should ice magic be feared? If it is so powerful, can't it help me on my journey?"

"Ice magic in itself is not inherently evil, youngblood. However, the scars left upon the land will always remind us of the one to wield this ungodly power, the one who fought the entirety of Prometheus by himself. A true scourge that should never have existed."

His eyes now burn with righteous fury.

"Why would it matter what they did with their powers?" I reply.

"I will not have you become another blight upon this reality," Cu'jehi roars.

"I won't be a blight; I am here to save my friend, not destroy your messed-up little world!"

"I will not risk you becoming another monstrosity like he is!"

"I have to use everything I can to help save Solomon!" Cu'jehi's expression darkens, and an overwhelming pressure crashes down upon us once more. This time, I feel myself smash into the ground as Ai'hara falls to a knee as well.

"Solomon? As in Solomon Helgen?" Each word causes the pressure to increase as unrestrained rage breaks out across his face.

"Yeah, and what does it matter what his name is?"

"The Helgens are the family that has fought and destroyed most of the Second Reality! They are the family that helped bring the Second Reality into existence!"

"Not everyone with the same name is related to each other!"

"I know for a fact that Solomon is evil. I know for a fact that he will stop at nothing to destroy everything I have worked to protect, to salvage!"

"How can you possibly know that? How could you know him at all?"

"I know who he is because he is the plague that has been set upon the Second Reality. The only other one to utilize frost magic was Solomon Helgen!"

Solomon

I can't scream anymore even as he draws the blade across my arm once again. I barely get out a muffled whine as I glare up at him. Tears cascade from my eyes as I stare into his own merciless visage.

"Still going strong there, kiddo?"

He steps back, looking at the edge of his massive knife, casually stepping closer once more, bringing the blade to my once-white satin dress shirt, currently stained crimson. Giving me a once-over, he stops at my shirt. His hand thrusts forward, and I flinch before I feel a tug on my shirt.

"Relax, I ain't cuttin' you yet. That comes soon, but you can make it all go away." He wipes his blade off on one of the few clean portions of my ruined shirt before spreading his arms wide as he paces backward.

"All you have to do is tell me what I want to know." He spins around as he finishes, his psychotic display exaggerated by his bloodied hands, his leather jacket now stained a dark crimson.

"You look like shit." He points his blade at me as he leans on his back-left foot, standing in place.

"You're covered in more blood than I have ever seen. Your shirt is in ribbons!"

He chortles. Looking down, I see it is true: everything is ripped and torn, cuts of all different sizes littering my body. I sit in agony as I clench my teeth, the taste of blood staling each breath I take.

"I ... have ... no idea what you are talking about!"

I huff angrily, every few words requiring me to take a breath, fixing him with the harshest glare I can.

"Oh, how terrifyin'."

He brings his fingers in front of his face, waggling them mockingly. Then he lunges, driving the blade right through my left shoulder into the chair. I scream as he is suddenly in my face, still wearing that maniacal grin.

"You just keep wantin' to make this difficult." He sighs, almost remorsefully, as he steps back, leaving the blade in my shoulder but wiggling the hilt, resulting in an involuntary hiss.

"I am goin' to go talk to the boss. Then we'll see what you have to say," he says. As he turns back, stepping over the body of the deceased soldier, he opens the door. Reaching into his pocket, he fishes out a phone with his other hand. Turning back, our eyes meet, and I see the sadistic grin on his face.

"You will break, kiddo, no matter how strong ya look. 'Tis only a matter of time, and then you will tell me everything. I just have to push you to your limit."

CHAPTER 7

A STEP IN THE RIGHT DIRECTION

Bastian

Stepping back from the edge, I turn to the others.

"That's a whole lot of zombies," I murmur in disbelief.

"Yup, if we make any amount of noise, we will not have a lot of time to get out of here," Namar chides.

"They move as a herd. Should one notice us, the rest will follow," Felgrand observes. Namar steps forward, clapping Felgrand's iron-clad shoulder.

"Just got to stay quiet, big guy," he says, smirking as he steps onto the bridge. "Do what I do, and you will be fine."

A light growl follows from Felgrand as we step onto the bridge. Each step across the bridge feels like a shallow step into our own graves. Slowly but surely, we take each step, treading carefully with each shuffle. Turning back to where the man was, I see him peering out from behind the massive urn. The flame illuminates his terrified visage as he stares at us. Steeling ourselves we cross over the threshold to the other side. I hear soft chuckles from in front of me.

"Well, that wasn't too bad."

"Rogue, your optimism will be welcome once we find the way out. Until then, why don't you remain silent." Namar looks at expectantly at me, his arms crossed over his chest. I brush past him to the stairs and Namar scoffs. "Now what, genius?"

"Now, we go through that door," I whisper, already dreading every clack and metallic step we take. I see a faint light coming from the next room and the shadows dance upon the walls. I hold my arm for them to stop as I creep forward. Climbing to the top stair, I lie down, peering over the lip that the stairs provide into the doorway.

On the other side, I can make out a large metallic gate, with large bars closing off a gargantuan entrance. In the very center sits a metal door. The door itself has several sliding bolts locking it into place. Each of them is slanted in such a way that it slides down into a lock of some kind. Leading from the back of the bolts is a long length of wire leading up toward the ceiling, where I can barely make out the shapes of counterweights suspended from the ceiling. In the center of the room sits a large horizontal winch with a single large cord leading to join the others above. On the far side of the room is another darkened archway, the mirror image of the one across from it. I feel Namar climb silently beside me as Felgrand mumbles something unintelligible.

"What?" I turn toward him, his bulky body hilariously contorted to lie flat on the stairs.

"What do you see?" he asks quietly.

"A gate," comes Namar's dull response.

"A gate?"

"Yeah, although it seems locked by some kind of winch system." I stare intently, as I swear I see a flicker of movement in the shadow.

"You see that?" I hiss at Namar, his carefree attitude giving way to his usual.

"What?"

"Just a flicker, in the opposing archway. I swear I saw something," I mumble so softly, it is probably dismissed as a casual breath. I can feel it now, that feeling I always get when I am on a job with Namar—the excitement, the adrenaline. Then I see it again. This time it is more than a flicker. From the darkness emerges a man's head. A dark greasy mop, if the sheen from the light tells me anything, two beady eyes with bags gleaming underneath the mop. His prisoner's garb is torn in several places, as I can see from the white scraps that protrude from the darkness. He scans slowly back and forth before fixating on the gate. He turns around, motioning at something as he moves forward into the room. Then I see it.

There is no sound as I see something above the archway start to move. I would never have spotted it if the dulling neon green did not catch my attention. It is as if all oxygen was drained from the air; I can't speak, I can't even swallow. I go to move my arms, but I cannot move them. Above the archway, sitting on the ceiling, is the beast that we barely drove off the first time. It is just above the man, crawling slowly downward, stalking the man. Its every gargantuan limb, flattened against the stone wall, moving ever so deceptively.

I look back down at the prisoner. He has stepped out into the hallway and is now doing one last check. *Look up!* I want to scream, but it is as if everything in me is protesting. He looks overjoyed to see nothing as he takes another step into the room. He turns back to the shadows and gestures a come here motion, his entire body looking rejuvenated as if hope has entered into his being.

Back to the beast. I can see its razor teeth gleaming in the light cast from outside the bars. I shake my head slowly as if to deny it.

Not like this.

I cannot watch him die so close to the exit. As the beast gets closer, now at the very edge of the archway, its wickedly clawed right arm wraps around the ornate archway as its muscles tense—no doubt to pounce. All the blood drains from my face, however, when two more people step from the darkness, side by side, a woman and a man; both middle-aged but considering the bags under their eyes, that is an assumption at best. The woman has long blonde hair. From here, I can see the dried blood in it, staining its beauty, her face sunken as well. Her smooth face would be breathtaking were it not so grim. The man has sandy brown hair, fluffed in many different directions, a small beard sprouting from his chin. They are both garbed in the same torn prisoner clothing. The man's shirt has a huge gash across the shoulder, exposing a large scar of three lines as if he has been cut by the talons on the monstrosity.

"What's up there?" The eager whisper from behind me shakes me from my paralyzed shock.

"People." I speak so softly, I barely hear what I am saying.

"What?"

"There are people, and the monster is right above them," comes Namar's steely reply, the clatter of Felgrand's armor filling the air. Felgrand charges past me, grabbing the prisoners' attention as they take a step back at the sight of him. The beast leaps forward, effectively slashing into the prisoner in front before it throws him away over the ledge sending him screaming into darkness as snarls and growls fill the air. The other man pushes the woman to the ground as he runs back into the darkness behind him. The woman cowers on the floor as the beast casts a look at her. Before it can do anything, Felgrand's war cry catches its attention as he swings wide, catching only the air. He brings his blade up just in time to deflect the deadly talons.

Ring.

The sound of the metal rings out as the monstrosity lumbers backward with another swing. Its claw severs the cable with ease as it zooms for Felgrand. He steps back as the claw flies right past him, brushing the armor plating. Then, with a wicked thrust, Felgrand pierces the beast.

Screeeech.

The beast emits an ear-piercing shriek of pain as its acidic blood falls to the floor, with the cable flying to the ceiling. It swung wildly, its claws forcing Felgrand to leap back. He barely dodges a blur that shoots down from the ceiling, smashing the stone floor to rubble. The beast doesn't stop the swing as it turns with it, throwing itself into the very shadows that the other man ran into.

Getting up with a growl, I dash into the room to the girl as Felgrand runs past me to the edge of a cliff. I kneel down to the girl pulling her into a bridal carry as she just stares into the darkness where the monster ran, sheer terror the only emotion in her blue eyes.

"We have to go." Felgrand grabs my arm and pulls me toward the gate.

"No duh, holy boy," comes Namar's antagonistic response.

"We have to go now!" Felgrand roars as he runs to the gate, where Namar stands, trying to pry out the bolts. I run to the gate to the first of many clangs onto the floor. An ear-splitting cry echoes from the darkened hallway. Turning back as two more metallic pins crash against the floor, I see the first, a decaying arm grasping over the cliff's edge.

Snarls fill the air as over the edge tumbles a body, inhumanly contorting as it straightens itself, looking around the room, scanning for anything, anyone. Its flesh is a sickly pale tint of green, the eyes now just hollow dark pits in its grotesque face. Another metallic ping rings out, and the undead locks its eyes on us before letting out a deafening screech. Wincing, I see several hands start to grapple over the edge and several more bodies start flopping over it.

"Last one is almost out!" Namar cries as he struggles against the gate. Setting the girl down, I brandish my sword, stepping away from the gates. Namar looks back at me and does a double take, an action I catch in my periphery as the undead horde rushes forward, snarling and growling at us.

"I almost have it. Get over here!" he screams at me as both Felgrand and Namar struggle with the last bolt. Turning back, I cast a sad smile over my shoulder.

"Sorry, Namar—somebody's gotta keep them off of you. Don't forget to take the girl."

"Oh, no, you don't! You are going to carry this lady yourself. No way am I carrying your weight. You want to save someone, do it yourself," he shouts, his back to me as he pries at the bolt. The first of the dead leaps at me. I sidestep as it collapses onto the ground, snarling as it rights itself from its crooked form.

I have already swung before it could, swiftly snatching its head from its shoulders. It falls in a heap as several more leap forward. Slicing forward, I drop two of them as one of them glances off me.

"Why is this one so much harder to remove?" Felgrand's frustrated response drones from behind me as I slash and slice. At some point, it just becomes a whirl of death as they keep coming.

Slice, stab, thrust!

There is no end to them. For each one I cut down, two more come to take its place. Another wide swing removes three more heads as I take a step backward. My blade catches into the head of another, not deep enough as it pushes onto the blade. Rotating with him in a waltz-like motion instead of fighting the direction, I turn to match him, pulling the blade free from its skull. I turn with the momentum, my blade becoming a whirlwind of death, slashing through so many more of them before moving full circle to remove the upper head of the one I let fall behind me.

Rolling backward, several undead land in a heap behind me as they converge on my location. Crawling over each other, a light blue flicker to my side catches my attention as suddenly several of the undead catch fire, screaming and writhing before dropping to the ground. Shuffling from the corridor is the old man, his hands holding the last tatters of his clothing. Each torn into long tassels draped over his arm, the unforgettable flames of the urn burning the ends of each.

"When woke, burn the folk!" he cries frantically as he tosses one of the burning torches onto the pile of bodies. They screech louder, an inhuman sound that threatens to make my ears bleed from the intensity as the flames consume their bodies at an astounding rate, resulting in a large blue flame igniting them all. Each body touched by the flames stops almost as soon as it catches fire. The man took a step toward me, waving his remaining weapon at any of the undead that get anywhere near him.

They cower at the sight. Turning back to the main pile of undead, they all scramble away from the fire in the center of the room, but with each passing moment, the flames grow dimmer. The shadows begin to work their way closer to us, and the dead shuffle closer. The old man gets to my side, pushing me back as he stands at the edge of the bodies, tearing any unburned clothing he can and quickly holding it over the dissipating flames. As they catch fire, I take several steps backward.

"I got it!" Namar cries as I turn to see the door spring open. I scoop up the girl as I run through the door. Felgrand is already on the other side with Namar clutching one of the oversized pins, his other hand ready to swing the door closed.

Stopping in the doorway, I scream to the old man "Come on!"

Then something drops on top of the bodies, extinguishing the fire.

It is the beast! The beast now has azure blood oozing off of its body, its long tresses parting so we can see one malevolent eye. I feel a large hand clamp down on my shoulder, trying to drag me from the doorway, but I can't look away. The old man just stands there, in front of the beast. The makeshift torches in his hands flicker in the dimming light. He stares right back into the monster's eyes as it brings the talon up. The intensity the stare held gave me pause as it raises its talon-spiked paw, slowly, intentionally, as if it knows the man cannot get away. The man turns slowly, facing back to me as he tosses the torches to the sides, igniting several of the undead. The beast's eye focuses on me as I look between it and the decrepit man. A tinge of a smile plays across his face. Then, in one moment, it all fades as the talon crashes down upon the old man. The beast whirls back and forth, goring the body before tossing it at us. It is limp as it crashes against the bars of the gate. I have not even noticed the gate closed. Nor did I see Namar slip the pin back into the lock.

I set the girl down as I walk to the edge of the bars, looking down at the old man. He reaches out to me with a closed fist, and I see a sense of urgency on his face. I reach forward, grabbing his hand as he presses something metallic into mine, the urgency on his face replaced by relief as the first of the undead claws into him. I see him wince as he gives me a gentle smile. Then he is gone, ripped from my grip into the snarls. I glare at the beast as it haughtily stands among the undead, almost gleeful as the undead beat against the gate.

Looking down at my hand, I open my own clenched fist to see a small metal vial. It is silver, cool to the touch, and no bigger than a cigarette. Clenching it into my palm, I look up to see the beast rush toward the gates, slamming into the golden bars, hissing at us.

Solaire

"There is no way that is true. He is just a student!" I deny.

"He escaped from the Second Reality, gone for years without a trace. Most thought that he perished, but I knew better." Cu'jehi pauses, bringing his arms together, gripping his trident harder.

"A being that could desecrate so much of the land, he changed the very continent! Would you still aid such a being?" he continued.

"How do you know this is the same person?" I pleaded.

"There have been many atrocities over the years, but those that happened at the same time, the world wars, did you really think those were completely caused by humans?" I feel my brow contort in confusion.

"What are you trying to say?"

"All the incidents, all the most catastrophic events, were due to the battles he had here, with the very ones you have had the pleasure of meeting."

"Prometheus," I say. "Wait, how can battles in this reality have anything to do with significant events in mine?"

"Clashes strong enough in one reality are reflected across them all. The atomic bomb was nothing but a clash between Solomon and Prometheus, albeit one of the conclusive ones. It was still a battle here."

"Then why is that not known to us?" I challenge.

"There are those within your reality that change the flow of information so that magic is left out. As you likely know, the Salem Witch Trials publicized how magic is received."

"If he reshaped the continent through these battles, surely, the damage to these areas is not just one-sided," Ai'hara comments. I send her a grateful glance before redirecting my attention to Cu'jehi.

"Perhaps not all of it is him, but he covered most of the continent in ice. When it melted, it left much of it decrepit and devoid of the life it once had."

"But how—"

"Do you know what they call it now? The deadlands," he interrupts.

"He has killed so much as collateral, adding to the deaths he intended." I suck in a breath, ready to deny him, but then his rage subsides, and it is replaced with a calm, collected, steely gaze.

"Despite this, you still wish to save him, youngblood?"

"Yes."

"Despite what he has done?"

"Without a doubt, yes, I do."

"Why?" he pleads.

"Because he saved me when I was in my darkest days." The memory of the fire flashes through my head. Closing my eyes, I clench my hands into fists and grind my teeth.

"He was there for me when no one else was. Now, I suppose it's my turn to save him." Looking down at the ground, I clench my teeth as I see her in my arms once more. "You have to help me. I cannot let that happen to him!"

"That is not possible."

"What?"

"I cannot let you go."

"Is it because I am weak?"

"That was my initial reason, but now, I am afraid that you will be found by Prometheus."

"Not of me helping Solomon?"

"While I do not care for that monster, I know that the real threat to this reality is Prometheus." I shake my head from side to side.

"Why are you prepared to move against Solomon if he so magically reappeared but Prometheus has been left alone?"

"Prometheus has no concept of morality; therefore, they are not afraid to hurt others to get what they want. Despite this, Solomon is a greater threat because he is stronger than they are." I feel my eyes widen.

"Impossible!" cries a voice from the ground. Turning, I see Ku'terik.

"It is true."

"In either case, I still have to go," I repeat. Cu'jehi eyes me for a moment, then shuts his eyes.

"Very well. You may go see Haplas."

"What?" comes Ku'terik's reply.

"You are just going to let me go?" Dumbfounded, I cannot stop my response. A heavy sigh leaves the Watcher as he leans upon his trident, looking much more tired than he did moments ago.

"Yes, if you seek Haplas, he will judge you himself."

"What if I was lying to you?" I ask spitefully.

"You are not a liar, youngblood, at least not as proficient as the ones I have met. Even if you were, you have already met several influential members of the Second Reality, and none of us have recognized you, myself included—not to mention that I would have known with the flowers from the life tree."

"Then why did they want me? You say that they haven't recognized me."

"Prometheus wants you for the knowledge of Solomon, nothing more. After that, youngblood, they will terminate you."

"Then avoid Prometheus is all I have to do?"

"I do not trust your power, and I cannot be sure that you will not hurt the balance. Seeing as this is your first time within the Second Reality, I hardly believe that you have any current aces up your sleeve that will allow you to protect yourself outside of this glade. I will not allow any youngblood—even you—to venture out on a perilous quest in hate only to perish."

"Are you going to stop me? I don't have time to waste," I challenge, taking a combat stance.

"I had another idea." He straightens and leans his head back, his golden irises staring straight at me. "You will take Ai'hara with you."

"No, she is mine! She will stay here with me!" Ku'terik cries as he gets up from the ground.

"Remember, you may be my successor but only in name. I do not acknowledge the choice of the foolish council," Cu'jehi growls.

"You should bow before me!" Ku'terik cries as he steadies. He shoots forth like an arrow straight toward Cu'jehi, a blade forming in his hand. On a pivoting turn, the back of Cu'jehi's trident flashes, twirling as the blade takes Ku'terik's from his hand. Another flicker of movement, and the butt slams into his chest, picking him up from the ground. A stupefied look falls on his face as he falls backward.

"You have offended me for the last time with your arrogance." Cu'jehi turns toward us with a snap of his cloak. "Come, we must go to the transportation circle before the fools of the council try to hold you here."

"You want to help us?" I ask uncertainly.

"Of course, keeping you here with my people may very well be disastrous, especially should Prometheus continue searching for you. By helping you leave, I ensure they will not come here," he reasons as he breaks off into the trees to the right of the hut. I turn to Ai'hara, who has already stepped forward to follow. Shrugging to myself, I follow, eavesdropping on the two.

"You said the council appointed him your successor?" Ai'hara says in a trembling voice, filled with emotion compared to her usual flat tone.

"Indeed, those fools believed that by giving this all to a pureblood from two elders that he would lead them to greatness, disregarding the danger that he has become due to his arrogance," Cu'jehi says, scoffing.

"So you never supported them?" Ai'hara quivers as we break the tree line, emerging before the huge tree at which we first arrived.

"Of course not," he says, turning around as he steps onto the stone path leading to the center of the room.

"Now, come. I will send you to Iglagos, the City of Magic."

I finally speak up. "Why there?"

"That is where you will find Haplas. Seek out his group. The protectorate, they can help you find him." We stand in the center of the rocks as Cu'jehi slams his trident on the ground outside of the circle, water swirling around the blade, just like last time.

"Are you coming with us?"

"I cannot, youngblood. I have to stay here and prevent Ku'terik from endangering my people any more than he has."

"*Forræder!*" comes a hoarse cry from behind Cu'jehi. Looking past him, I see a mob of them all brandishing swords, and who is at the front of it?

"Speak of the devil," I mutter to myself, spying Ku'terik with a blade in his hand, a small dribble of blood on his lips.

"*Beskytte!*" comes the call as the trident once more crashes against the ground.

"The unwanted ones leave us!" cries one of the mob at the front, his celebration infecting others for a moment. Then, as if to match the dome of water sliding over the view, tinting our view of the event, everything changes. A shrill scream is heard, blood spilled across the ground, and I can only stare in shock.

"What have you done, Ku'terik?" Cu'jehi hisses, I follow his gaze and see why; standing at the front of the crowd, is Ku'terik, ripping his blade from the one who started to celebrate.

"What has to be done?" He looks down at the body emotionlessly.

"They have to be shown I am the one above the rest, and I will get what I want." He looks back up at Ai'hara, and I feel her shudder.

"I will come for you after I become the Head of the Watch." Cu'jehi stiffens.

"You are years too young to be talking like you will get to be Head of the Watch so easily," Cu'jehi says as the water rises, swirling around us faster with each moment.

"I think it is time for a change in management."

As he steps forward, I feel a searing sensation take over my body, over my right breast. Then it gets worse! The pain is so bad, I feel as if someone is tearing my chest open! I don't know what is happening, only that everything seems to stop as I feel a warm liquid start to pool in my chest.

"What is happening to him?" cries Ai'hara as I can see her kneeling over me.

That's strange. When did I get on the ground?

She reaches up, tearing the blade from her hair with practiced ease as she slices my shirt in two. Parting it, she gasps, followed by a mutter from Cu'jehi. I look down despite the pain, and my entire world seems to stop. There, in my chest, a letter S is carving itself into my body, the skin parting as if a knife were slicing into it. Then, slowly, it continues slicing a circle around the S. My screams pierce the air as the light fades, the water moving faster and faster. The roar tears away all sound as I see Ku'terik advancing toward a distracted Cu'jehi brandishing his sword. I try to move my arm, but I can barely raise it as everything goes dark.

Bastian

Clang.

The demon smashes against the gate, crushing several of the undead. It creeps back, striding through the hordes of undead, straining against the massive gate. It tramples forward again as I stare into its cruel eye. Its own growls and the thuds of each gallop overcome the snarls and hisses from the undead.

Clang.

The gate shakes, and I hear the metal groan as the beast looks up at the top of the gate, where a chunk of stone jostles free, falling onto the heads of the undead. Looking up, I feel the unsatisfied expression on my face as the gate holds back the beast. My eyes travel back to its only eye, and in it, I think I see a flicker of emotion: sadistic glee. It races back, faster this time as it prepares to charge again. A hand lightly touches my shoulder as I turn back to see the face of the girl. In the light, she is so much frailer than I first thought. Her face is sunken, and her eyes are surrounded with dark circles. Her legs are ready to buckle from simply standing. The only thing keeping her standing must have been the adrenaline from running from those monsters. She looks no older than eighteen. No one that young should have to endure this. Her white tunic has rips and tears along the arms and a pair of pants torn off at the left knee.

"I cannot believe this." I turn to Felgrand. Behind us is a rocky cliff, with dried moss and dead trees littering the edge. Over the cliff in the distance stand many more tall dead trees, with a gargantuan valley splitting the land in two. On the left side, a small trail of coal-colored stones leads down the mountainside. Standing at the edge are Felgrand and Namar, both staring around the wall that the prison walls are hiding.

I put the girl's arm around my shoulder as I walk her with me to the edge. Peeking around the corner, the first thing I see is the familiar golden fields that I first landed in. Following that, I see the walls of Ashvale. I let out a sigh of relief, seeing how close we were to the city. Only about two miles separated us from the city. In front of the walls stood a long stretch of the golden fields. The fields were separated by a roaring river that stretched several meters from shore to shore. One glance at the white rapids and jagged boulders is enough to see the current is unforgiving. The contrast on each side of the river was extreme. On our side, the ground was decayed and blackened. No plants grew and only large dead trees towered over the dead ground. Across the water is the bright golden brush of Ashvale fields.

"We are in the deadlands." As if to accompany Felgrand's statement, the snarls get louder as another slam echoes, and the metal groans in protest once more.

"All right, crew, that gate isn't going to hold forever, so we have to go, now!" Namar orders as he leaps over the cliffside to the path below, beginning to run along the trail.

"Show-off," I mutter as I pick the girl up in a bridal carry once again, running down the path as it turns into a hairpin curve leading to where Namar has landed. A scraping sound joins the next smash from the gate as Felgrand slides down the cliff with his long sword trailing into the cliff face behind him, acting as an anchor. An absurd groan shakes the air as a twisting crunch follows before a chorus of snarls pollutes the air.

A shocking explosion fills the air as something comes crashing down past us. I turn to peer over the edge to see the remains of the gate crash at the bottom of the mountain. The snarls grow louder as I see something shoot between Felgrand and me. It crashes against a boulder with a sickening crunch as it keeps tumbling down the hill, the blur now discernable as one of the undead. I see Felgrand turn up, raising his sword just in time as another flies into it. The mindless drone cleaves in two, shooting around him. I dash past Felgrand as he bats another out of the way. Namar surges past me as I hear the swing of his blade hissing through the air. Another of the snarls falls silent.

"All right, people! I am in back now. Felgrand, you keep front. Bastian, don't drop the girl! Whatever you do, don't look up!" Namar shouts. I hear his light footfall prancing behind me as Felgrand tramples past me with an expert wave of his sword, batting another from the air before it hits the ground.

A gasp from the girl in my arms causes me to look down, seeing her eyes widen in terror as she stares above. I see the sky darken for a moment. I don't look up. I don't have to. They start impacting all around us, like a worsening storm, the sickening crunches turning into a rumbling drumroll as we charge down the trail. A never-ending storm of bodies crashes all around us, the slashes Felgrand takes increasing with each new step.

Reaching the bottom of the mountain, we move away from the face of the cliff, huddling in a small circle as Namar and Felgrand cut down anything that moves toward us.

"Where now?" cries Felgrand as he cleaves through bodies, back and forth. Namar tries to look around but could not find the time as more and more undead began charging our position. I can see them fighting on both sides of me and hear their feet shuffling in the dirt. Clenching my teeth, I set the girl down, her hands clutching the front of my shirt.

She stares into my eyes, sheer terror causing them to go doe-eyed. I smile softly as I stare back, softly removing her grip from my clothes.

"Stay behind us."

Now soothed, she nods slowly, shifting her weight to stand on her own as I grasp the sword, walking forward, bringing it down, slicing through one that has started circling us.

"To the river! If we can cross it, we can get back to Ashvale!" I scream as I kick another down before beheading it as it scrambles back onto its feet. Seeing the horde begin to spread around us in a circling pattern, I strike down the increasing numbers, taking steps with each swing.

"I can't keep this up forever! Bastian, you remember how to use any of your magic?" Namar cries as he huffs. Grinding my teeth, I feel the bile rise into my throat. How could I ever forget that magic? It is why I left in the first place.

"I cannot use any of it!" I roar as I cut the head from another, throwing my knife into the face of the one behind it. It falls forward. Reaching forward, I snatch the blade before driving it into the head of another.

"I can use mine then!" Felgrand interjects as he whirls, sending bodies flying backward. He drops onto one knee as he pulls something out of his pocket. The undead kept rushing forward. Almost on him, I wheel around to save him, but I am too far! Namar shoots off to Felgrand's left, attracting the undead toward himself as he screams over his shoulder.

"Don't just stop killing! Let me know first, asshole!"

The response of a grunt of effort as he stabs another of the undead. I race forward, trying to drag the undead away from Felgrand and the girl, who is crawling across the ground toward him.

It is worse than in the prison, each moment a blur of stabbing and slashing. I have one throwing blade in my left hand, in a reverse grip. In my right is the short sword, caked an almost black crimson with the blood of the undead. Seconds seem to stretch into hours as the undead keep up their assault. I feel the exhaustion set in, aching to make me stop, but I can't—I must keep it up. I grind my teeth as I throw my knife into another undead racing between the midway point between Namar and me. It catches him in the face. The undead spin like a top, crashing onto the ground next to Felgrand. Turning back, I see three more undead are already upon me. Slashing wide, I take one out. I grab the second one, heaving it out of my way as I bring my sword onto the last one, lodging the blade in its head. A vice-like grip catches my other hand as I smash the pommel into the one on my arm. Lashing out to the side, I catch the other in the neck. It only stumbles as it descends upon me. Screaming, I stab it with my sword, holding the one at my side at bay.

The other let go of my arm just long enough for my hand to dart to my knives. A clean thud fills the air as I drive the knife into the head of the one to my side. Looking at the other one, I see it now as Namar struggles to hold back four on his own. The girl is screaming now. Odd, I didn't hear it before now. The undead are everywhere. More arms grab me as I fall to the ground.

"Smiting helix!"

A wave of golden light shoots out from Felgrand, colliding with all the undead in the clearing. The undead on me are blown away. One moment, I feel their grip digging into my skin. The next they are simply gone, reduced to ashes among the wind.

"About goddamn time!" Namar wheezes, a genuine smile on his face as he hunches over his arms resting on his knees.

"Rogue, I told you I would do it, and it is done, so do not worry."

"Don't worry? I must have missed something because I was pretty close to being dinner. In fact, I may have been better off using my own technique!"

"Then why didn't you?"

"I just got feeling back to my magic. That bolt really did a number on my abilities." I bent over to pick my other knife up, a sprinkle of dust lying on the burnt hilt. Frowning, I re-sheath the blade, the distant snarls coming ever closer.

"There are still more of those things?" Namar says, exasperated. A screech fills the air as a shadow passes over us before an explosion rocks the air.

"You have got to be fucking kidding me!" Namar huffs as he raises the sword in his left hand, bringing it above his head, holding it for a moment, waiting for the dust to clear. As the dust settles, standing in all its glory, the beast. It stands perched on its talons, the lone malevolent eye grinning as it stares right at Namar.

"You, beasty, have got to learn how to stay dead." The monster hisses as it leaps forward. At that moment, Namar thrust his blade into the ground. "*Chakraveer!*"

A rumble fills the ground as I see the hulking abomination lumber through the air. Then all at once, dark spots appear all around us. Nibs of black points, rising for just a moment, darting back into the darkness before they shoot upward, creating a forest of long blade-like pillars, each five meters tall with ends shaped like the blade Namar stabbed into the ground. A roar of pain fills the air as several spears enter the monstrosity, keeping it suspended in the air as it swipes at Namar.

"Come now. This won't hold them long," he huffs and gestures to a small path among the forest of blades. Several undead slam against the blades, driving themselves into them. Namar moves forward, taking his other sword and impaling it into the ground before removing the other one. Taking another step, he repeats the process as if he were walking with skis. Perching an eyebrow, I glance at him as I scoop up the girl.

"I have to have one of the blades in the ground to maintain the shadows," he grunts as he takes another step. More blade-like trees rising from the ground, sculpting a pathway to the water. The undead start to mount on top of each other, driving themselves onto the blades, reaching for the top of the wall.

Felgrand huffs. "They are going to climb over soon."

"They will indeed, but we can at least get closer to the water." Looking straight ahead to the river, I feel relief seeing we are so close. Only a few steps to the water as the forest of blades flickers before vanishing. I hear a shuffle turning back, and I see Namar being hoisted over Felgrand's shoulder.

"Run!" Everything behind us is released—the monster and the hordes of undead.

Splashing into the river, I stumble, cutting my legs on jagged rocks as I work my way through the water. It rose with every step, at the beginning only at my ankles, now at my thigh and rising higher. Reaching the middle the water rose to my waist. I can hear splashes behind me, and I look back.

The undead are swept away by the river, most stopping at the river's edge, spreading out along it as they seem deterred by the roaring rapids. Turning back, I see Felgrand already climbing out onto the other side, his longsword over his back with Namar in one arm and his dual rapiers in the other. Stepping out of the river I set the girl down onto the ground.

Screee.

The unholy sound pierces the air as the monster rushes forward, smashing undead aside, throwing them into the river, their snarls dying as they hit the water. The beast also stops on the river's edge, glaring at us with its monolithic eye.

"Why did it stop?"

"The water has kept the undead out for many years. It has to do with the purifying qualities of the water. That demon cannot get over either, else it would be purified just as those undead were." I watch the demon dip the front of its hand into the water, recoiling as steam rises from the water's surface as the monster hisses in anger.

"The monster will not be able to reach us now," Felgrand continues as I watch the monster wrap its talons around one of the undead at its side before raising its arm above its head.

"You have got to be fucking kidding me," I grumble as it pitches forward, throwing the undead over the river into the golden field, the body lost among the golden fronds.

"No!" Felgrand cries as the beast repeats the process, throwing another over the river onto our side, immediately grasping another to do it again.

Just as the demon raises its arm back, a distortion in the air forms. A swirling patch of orange that is slowly extending upwards, creating a crack in the air. It is spiraling in a helical pattern. Several flashes fill my vision, and I hear splashes and screams. Clearing my vision, I see several soldiers in the water, some swimming to our side and most to the other.

Gunfire erupts as the soldiers at the other end are attacked by the undead. Their screams echoed the gunshots as they fall. I see the remaining soldiers turn in the water, trying to swim back to the portal. Then time seems to stop as the demon grabs one of the undead and throws it at the opening in the air. Silence reigns as the body approaches the floating distortion. As the body touches the edge of the distortion, it disappears, and a flash of light erupts from the fissure.

A screech fills the air as the demon turns abruptly, trampling the undead around it as it races backward several strides before turning back around, decapitating several undead in its path. Then it charges, taking large strides as it nears the water. Leaping into the air, I feel my jaw drop as it arches toward the fissure in the air. It flies closer but starts to descend to the water. As if in slow motion, it starts to fall toward the soldiers in the water. They can only stare in horror as the beast falls. A howl of pain shoots through the air as it rips the soldiers to pieces as it leaps from the water once more into the portal. Everything sits still a moment before the distortion vanishes.

"Where did that portal go?" I ask one of the two huffing soldiers who were crawling onto our side of the river. A snarl comes from behind as I turn. An arm latches onto me, pulling me to the ground as another tears into the unexpecting soldiers next to us. Rolling over, I look right up into the dreadful dead eyes as it gnashes its teeth at me. Then the gun is pressed against its head, and I hear the hammer click back.

Bang.

The gunshot echoes as the body slumps over. There, standing in all his glory, is a man wearing a brown cloak cinched by the golden pin that signifies his affiliation with the Syndicate. He has a smoking revolver clutched by a leather glove and a phone pressed against his ear in the other, leather bracers on both of his wrists with a red flannel checkered shirt with a blood spatter across the front of it. He retrains the sight and shoots twice in succession.

Bang. Bang.

I watch the infected slump as the second shot hits the zombie in the head.

His companion stands up, a man in his later years if the graying stubble on his chin is anything to go by. On his head is a short buzzcut of receding bleach blonde hair. He is wearing simple camo fatigues with a rebreather over his mouth that led to an oxygen tank that is fixed on his back.

"Baron?" Namar inquires, tilting to get a better look at his face.

"Why did you kill him!" the soldier roars, raising his compact shotgun to aim at Baron, who keeps a straight face.

"These things are mindless beasts—zombies, if you will. Once bitten, it's over. I did him a favor. Now, since you and your soldiers so kindly showed up and fucked everything up, why don't you shut the fuck up and follow us." The soldier glares as he keeps his shotgun leveled.

"You think I believe that bull shit?" he screams, spittle flying out of his face, coating the inside of the rebreather.

"You just dropped from a portal into a river next to some zombies. Is it really that hard to believe?" Baron responded coolly.

"He is telling the truth," I speak up, still breathing hard, garnering the soldier's attention. His eyes widen.

"You are one of the kids that went missing from that school!"

"You know about that?"

"Did you stop the others?" Felgrand cries, interrupting me, only to be ignored.

"Namar, you sure got into a lot of trouble for such an easy task." Namar creaks his eyes open.

"Baron, what are you doing here?" He holds up a finger as he looks across the river.

"He knows something, Jack. There has to be some reason. Find out why they want him and do it fast. We are running out of time. Let him know I found some of his friends," he orders as he snaps the phone shut.

"What did you ask me?" he ponders as he places his revolver in its holster, replacing it with a cigarette, which he lights using a match struck upon the edge of his leather bracer. Looking closer, I see gritted edges on the insides of each of them.

"Why are you here?"

"Found out our boy here was captured, so I came to help, but I found that the town was attacked by these things." He kicks the body of the infected. He looks gleefully at us.

"What?!" Felgrand screams, falling to his knees.

"The town is overrun, and so, we are going to go in." Felgrand looks up hopefully.

"To save them?" Baron takes a long drag, releasing the smoke slowly, barely shifting to look down at Felgrand.

"If we find any survivors on the way, we can, but we need to find someone."

"Why does one person mean more than the rest?" Shock replaces the hope that shone within Felgrand's eyes. Baron ignores it as he turns on his heel, a slight smirk gracing his lips as he faces Namar.

"So, are you ready to go hunting for someone?"

"Who?"

"A kid who is bothering Darius, but I have some additional intel on this one I need to confirm before we complete the contract."

"As long as you both help me afterward, I am willing."

I sigh, looking at the city as plumes of smoke rise from behind the walls.

"Fine, but I will help the kid—not you, cowboy."

"First off, we have to go into this fresh hell and find out what he looks like, but before that ..." Baron trails off, whirling his gun trained on his target, the girl. She looks up in fright.

"Baron, what are you doing?" I scream as I step forward, only to be stopped cold by his glare.

"Murderer! Why do you do this?" Felgrand grips his longsword but Baron levels his other revolver at him.

"Now that you know everything you were just waiting to ambush us, weren't you?" Namar shifts his gaze between Baron and the girl, tense but uncertain.

"I don't quite follow you." Baron narrowed his eyes as he pulled back the hammer.

"Please." The girl rasps out, looking to me and Felgrand.

"She has been giving me a feeling of death since I got here. She is not an ordinary human," he explains as I turn to see her fearful expression freeze.

"She was in the prison with the damned, the stench is natural to cling to her!"

"Not like this, this feels like something that has already died."

"You are out of your min—"

112

Bang

The girl's head shuttered as a hole was left in it. Her body flops to the ground, with a smile on its face. For a moment, only the roaring river could be heard.

"You monster! You killed her!" Felgrand marched a step closer, but the click of the hammer stopped him. I fingered one of my knives, casting a glance at Namar, who shook his head lightly. Then a voice spoke up and we all stopped.

"What gave me away?" We all turned to the girl's corpse.

"There's no way ..." the clatter of Felgrand's sword barely registered.

"Gut feeling." Baron responded as he holstered his pistol.

"Dumb luck won't save you next time."

"It is a good thing we don't need it." Baron spat at the corpse.

"I hope you enjoy how I redecorated Ashvale. I know the Monarch will." It spoke, with a more malevolent tone. Then the body dissolved into darkness, leaving behind a decomposed skeleton, the wicked grin plastered on the skeleton's face.

"Quick, we have to hurry!" Baron instructs as he steps toward the golden sea of grain, casually flicking his cigarette onto the ground. I watch the soldier stamp it out as he follows him into the grain. I stand up to watch the others storm into the grains.

Only one thought enters my mind as I fall in step behind them, glancing one last time at the billowing smoke clouds ascending above the walls of Ashvale:

You had better be out of the city already, Solaire.

Solomon

Everything hurt, the smooth breeze floating through the room stifling the musty blood-soaked air. The light bears down upon my battered body. I cannot bear to look down at my crimson-stained dress shirt. Well, at least it was a dress shirt at one time. All I can do is stare at the door, waiting—waiting for something to come back through that door. The pain is so intense. I think I might lose my mind, and yet, I do not know why they hold me here. I have no idea why that other group wants me. Pain wracks my mind, snatching all reason and thought from it. Leaving me with only the silence.

The silence seems to stretch on, each beating second is pain. The only sense I have is overwhelming everything else, pain is my world. Then I hear it. It is soft, almost like a whisper, flitting across the wind. Glancing around, I look for it, then it comes again, too quiet to hear. I can't see anything, either.

"Who's there?" I exhale with all my strength, but it comes out as a pathetic sigh I can barely hear myself. A period of silence stretches on for what feels like an eternity. I must be losing my mind. The pain is driving me to lunacy. I shake my head, but then comes another murmur, this time ever slightly louder, and this time, I know it is real. Scanning the room, I see nothing different. Eyeing the body on the floor with intensity, I wonder if the soldier might still be alive. I swiftly discard the thought as I observe the bloody pool around it.

Then the sound of footsteps echoes from outside. I look up to see the door kicked open. In comes Jack, his carefree visage replaced with a deep grimace, an annoyed look staining his features as he stops in the doorway, quickly glancing around the room.

"You ready to tell me what I want to know?"

"I don't even know what you want!" I scream. He stomps toward me, sending a devastating boot down onto the back of the body.

"All right, kiddo, you are beginnin' to test my patience here." He pauses to grit his teeth, stopping in front of my chair.

"It seems like you have some friends comin' for yeh." He suddenly leans in, twisting the knife he left in my shoulder, eliciting a scream.

"Don' let that give you any hope, 'cause if you thin' that everythin's gonna work out, yeh haven't been payin' attention." He rips the blade from my shoulder. A soft whimper escapes me as I feebly glare at him from beneath my bangs.

"Yeh, already know what I can do." He reaches for another cloth, wiping the weapon down before discarding the cloth, carelessly dropping it to the floor. Pointing the knife at me, he grins.

"Tell me what I want tah know, or I am gonna drag yer friend in here next tah yah."

"It wouldn't help," I mumble.

"What?"

"It wouldn't help," I growl.

"Why is that? Do yeh not care 'bout yer friends?" He asks, his right eyebrow squirming up in amusement.

"I don't know anything! You say I have been here before, but I don't remember it! I don't remember anything!" I scream, spitting saliva and blood onto the floor. A blank look overtakes Jack's face for a moment as he lets the knife drop to his side. He starts pacing around me, to my left, nodding his head back and forth, until I lose sight of him from over my shoulder.

A sudden shuffle, and he is there over my right flank, his left hand clapping down on my injured shoulder, resulting in my startled yelp.

"Yeh don' remember? Then I guess I will just have to help yeh remember." He digs his fingers into my shoulder wound, causing me to grit my teeth through the fire igniting the pain.

"I know just how tah do it too." I see the knife flash past my right side, and I feel my heart hammering in my throat as he brings the hand with the knife down onto my chest, ripping my tattered shirt off.

"I will show yeh tah symbol that yeh used so long ago. In fact, I will make sure yeh neva forget it," he says gleefully into my ear. He brings the knife to my chest as he carves down my chest in a wavelike pattern. Searing pain envelops my chest as he suddenly begins making a large circle around his initial mark. I bellow in pain, the agony returning full force.

"What does Prometheus want with yeh?" he calls out over my screams, stopping for a moment, leaning back.

"I have no idea!" I spit at him. He stands up, dragging a palm across his face taking the saliva with it, a cruel challenging grin working its way to his face as he leans forward with the knife once more cleaving into my flesh.

"Perhaps all yeh need is a very painful reminder." My screams fill the air for another seeming eternity before he finally leans back.

"There. That should do it. Do you remember who yeh are? Maybe what they want from yeh?" he asks cruelly. Tears sear my vision as I shrink into the chair. A muffled sob escapes my lips. Staring down at my body for the first time, I see the cuts and scars all around my body, but the freshest one catches my attention, the giant S carved into my upper chest, a jagged circle encircling it.

"What is that?" He leans closer, bringing one hand to his ear mockingly.

"I don't know them. Why does it matter?" I gasp, entranced by the mark. It seems vaguely familiar, yet at the same time, I am confident I have never seen it before in my life.

"Remember yer little symbol? Remember yet how you used to carve this into your victims?" A tear makes it to my eye, a throbbing in the back of my head. I can hear them again, the faint whispers all around me. Glancing around, I frantically search the room for the source of these whispers. Turning back, I see Jack, leaning against one of the bookshelves with his arms crossed. My only thought is, *When did he get over there?*

"Do yeh remember now?"

"Don't you hear them?" I quiver as the voices seem to grow upset. He pushes himself off the bookshelf taking quick steps toward me.

"Hear what?" he asks, cocking his head to the side.

"The whispers, how can you not hear them?" I cry, wincing as the incoherent whispers grew louder as if to drown my response.

"Whispers? What are yeh babbling about, kiddo?" He looks confused, his eyebrows knitting together in frustration.

"Maybe ... maybe this is why they want yeh." Pausing, he toys with the edge of his massive blade. "I think they may have lied to me 'bout you."

"Huh?"

This intelligent response is all I can muster through the throbbing headache. The whispers die down to a tame hiss, seeming to permeate the air.

"Yeh are probably not the monster they say yeh are. They probably fed me those lies so they could make yeh a target." He shakes his head, burying it into one of his hands.

"Why do you even care?" I growl. He looks up from in between his fingers.

"We may be a group of killers and kidnappers, but we know at least to get rid o' Prometheus before their delusions ruin everything."

"Delusions?"

He drops his hands from his face and straightens his posture, pivoting on one foot as he begins to turn around.

"Look, kiddo, I am sorry for doing this to yeh, but they made yeh out to be a monster out of horror stories. Let me see what I can find. If I find out that yeh are not what they say, I will make things right myself. Let me know now if yer lyin' tah me. If I have tah find out the hard way, I will drag your friends in here next tah yeh and make what I did to yeh look like a paradise." He turns walking to the door, stepping around the body, opening the door, he steps out, sending one sympathetic look back at me as he closed the door. I cringed as he did so, not because of the door closing and me being alone in this godforsaken room. No, it is because of what I hear.

"*Fool.*" The whisper is barely audible, but I can hear what it said clearly this time as the whispering drones back to fill my ears as I scrunch my eyes, trying to shut them out.

CHAPTER 8

MORE QUESTIONS THAN ANSWERS

Solaire

We land on the ground, and I feel the smooth yet gritty texture of brick as the searing pain on my front contradicts it. My eyes focus, and I see large peaks of buildings, standing tall around me, each of them having blue shingles lining the roof. Each peak has a circular window adorned with various designs. Each window is set into dark oak paneling that continues to the ground.

I feel a shuffle next to me as a hand helps pull me to a sitting position. We are in the middle of a stone path in the center of a street stained crimson by the pool of blood around me, just large enough for two cars to fit side by side comfortably. On either side of the street, narrow alleyways run between the buildings. The street is deserted except for one man, who comes striding confidently toward us. His head is down, a scarlet red cowl draped over him, the hood pulled over his face so we could not see what lay underneath it. The cowl reaches down to join a tunic with a glowing stone over the center chest. His arms are at his sides as he continues marching toward us.

"Did you believe that you would be able to enter freely?"

He stops several feet from us, raising a hand, and a small spark springs to life on his fingers. It dances between each of them as he seems to be looking at us.

"He needs help!" Ai'hara screams as she helps me stand, blood seeping down my chest.

"Why would I help any associate of the Helgens?"

"How do you know that?" The man raises his hand and gestures toward me.

"That symbol is the family crest of the Helgens. What other proof do I need?" I feel Ai'hara pivot to the side with one of my arms around her shoulder.

"Who are you?"

"I am the vice-chair of security here—that is all you need to know. As for the help you wanted, you won't need it after I have incinerated you both." The spark springs into a flame in the palm of his palm as he takes a step forward. Ai'hara's grip on my hand tightens as the man takes another step.

"Burn."

He speaks calmly yet ferociously as he sweeps his hand forward. From the flame in his palm, a fireball shoots forth. As it careens toward us, Ai'hara moves, kicking the blood at our feet upward.

"*Vegg!*" she calls out as the blood forms a barrier, hissing as the fireball smashes against it. She pulls me not even a second later. Shooting off for the nearest alley on our left. A calm mumble is the only warning we receive as a hot blast brushes my back.

I feel myself grow dizzy as the world seems to spin. I can vaguely feel us turn direction down another corridor. I must be lying on Ai'hara now. It is so hard to keep my eyes open. Every time I blink, the same stone bricks are in the same places, but the surroundings are different. An alleyway. A street. I blink again. This time, I find myself leaning against something. I see Ai'hara desperately looking around. Shifting my head, I see a barred door sitting in the middle of a wall. Massive buildings box us in on either side. I feel her pick me up again and start to move away from the dead end. We stop very shortly after the first step. I strain my neck to look up. The pain is excruciating, but that is the least of our problems. Stepping calmly out from around the corner is the man, his hand enveloped with red flames, casting a menacing shadow across his cloak.

"Did you really think you could get away from me—in my own city, no less?"

"Why are you after us?" Ai'hara said in a disappointed manner.

"You should have never broken into this city, especially while brandishing a mark of the Helgens," he says, gesturing at my chest with his non-flaming hand.

"We don't know how this happened! He was fine one moment, and the next, it appeared."

"While it is fresh, I don't think I can trust you." He sighs as the flame on his hand grows bigger.

"Burn," he mutters as he swipes his arm at us. A sharp pain wracks my side as Ai'hara scratches across the wound. She lets go of my shoulder, dropping me as she whips her arm into the air. I see a small shower of crimson liquid tint the air.

"*Vegg*," she breathes out, bringing her arms in front of her chest. The blood in the air forms a small barrier as the flame engulfs it. The fire plumes outward but keeps going, slamming into her. A sharp intake of breath is all I hear as she bounces across the stone floor. A small whimper is the last sound I hear as she lies on the ground next to the gate.

"You surprised me the first time, but did you think that would work again?"

I hear his footsteps on the stone getting closer as my wound throbbed. Each step coincides with the painful throb of the wound. A shadow darkens my view of Ai'hara, and I turn my head to see the pursuer standing over me. He reaches forward, grabbing the scruff of my coat. He pulls me into a kneeling position, *slapping my check* once my vision clears.

"Why did you come here? How did you get this mark?" I shake my head.

"I don't know. I came here to find someone."

"Who?" He drags my head to look back up to him. I see a blur behind him on the building. A man, wearing a black suit of leather armor, a dark mask over his face. A twisted dagger gleams in his palm as he stares down at us.

"Someone by the name of Haplas," I mutter, looking past him, seeing another darkened hood poke over the roof.

"That scum?" He keeps looking into my eyes as his eyes scrunch up. "What are you looking at?"

The men on the roof leap to the next one. The man with the knife jumps, his blade in a reverse two-handed hold, ready to plunge into the back of the cloaked man. As the cloaked man turns to look up, he has already crossed much of the distance. He barely has time to bring his arm up when the blade plummets into his shoulder. A snarl erupts from the man as a flame shoots to his other hand.

"You will pay dearly for that." He stands up as the man takes off down the alley.

"Pyro blast!"

He hurls a huge flame forward from his hand. As I barely roll into the alleyway, the flame crashes into the stone brick wall with a blinding explosion. As the dust clears, the cloaked man reaches up to the blade embedded in his shoulder and grasps the handle. I watch it grow orange as the blade begins to turn into slag and sluff off onto the ground.

"Stay right here. It would appear I have pest problems to take care of," he growls. Bolting up, he starts pacing toward the dissipating smoke cloud. The embers in the air swirl toward the flame within the palm of his hand. As the smoke clears, I see the stone bricks blasted away as embers cling to the cracked stone. Rounding the corner, I can hear his footsteps echoing down the hallway.

Turning back to Ai'hara, I find another man in black standing over her. I take a breath in to speak only for a hand to clamp down over my mouth, forcing my head to turn and look behind me. I turn to see another woman dressed in similar armor, a single finger on her lips as she gestures back to Ai'hara.

The locked gate is wide open, and the man has her unconscious form next to him, one arm draped over his shoulder. He nods to me as he steps through the gate. The arm on my shoulder tightened as my arm is also draped over the woman's shoulder. She stands up with me on her arm as she walks me over to the gate. Stepping inside, she pulls the gate closed and slides the deadbolt locked.

We stand upon the top of the staircase at the end of a tunnel with torches adorning the sides resting close to the ceiling. A light shines from behind the stairs, and at the edge, there are bars that the water is flowing over. The stairs led down to a walkway that bordered a current of water. As we step down the stairs, I can't stop my curiosity.

"Who are you guys?"

"We are the Protectorate, and we don't really stand for random people getting picked on," comes the voice in front of me.

"That self-righteous prick and his destructive nature: he is going to destroy this place if he keeps attacking anyone who comes in that he hasn't vetted," spits the girl, shouldering me as we reach the bottom of the stairs. The man sits Ai'hara down next to a crate on the edge of the path. She has burns up her arms and soot covering her clothing and face.

"Who is that?"

"You don't know the prick? Good, keep it that way," the woman scoffs.

"Ignore her. The *prick* is Valin, the junior magistrate of the city."

"More of a local arsonist if you ask me," the woman grumbles.

"Where are we?"

"You are telling me you came here without a clue where you are?" I cautiously nod.

"Fuck, the kid's almost as bad as the prick."

A sidelong glance stills her.

"You have no idea what this place is, do you?" A slight shake of my head causes him to sigh as he stands up. He walks over to me. Taking me from the woman, he steps into the water. He drags me toward the edge, and I feel my jaw drop.

The water is cascading into a large lake below us. Throughout the air lay severed pieces of land, almost orbiting the waterfall. Stranger still are the giant blackened chains, each link as long as a car, buried deep within the ground. There are several, each of them leading up to the platform we are on, each chain taunt as if to keep us rooted to the ground.

"Welcome to Iglagos, the Chained City of the Magi."

Bastian

"Oh, God," I mumble. We now stand at the gates, looking in. Smoke billows from buildings up and down the street. Blood cakes the ground. The once-bustling market street now lies in ruins. Bodies are strewn in the streets. I see some survivors running across the street as undead chase after them. At the end of the street, a massive building lies in ruins. Several bodies lay among the rubble.

"Sorry, Felgrand, there doesn't seem much hope of saving anyone if it all looks like this." I sigh, reaching up and placing my hand on his shoulder.

"It can't be," Felgrand whispers. His eyes widen at the destruction, his tan skin paling at the sight.

"We cannot stay here. We have to go." Baron takes a step through the gate. Footsteps echo to our right, and we all turn, each of us brandishing arms. Baron raises one of his revolvers to the sound. A guard comes running from along the gate along with a cat-eared male in civilian clothing. The soldier with us raises his gun, aiming at the strange anomaly.

"Didn't know you let Perondine into your little safe haven," Baron remarks as the guard runs toward us. Baron puts his hand on the top of the man's gun, lowering it as the guard stepped closer. His armor bears many scratches and bloodstains. His shield is missing, and his helmet is dented in several places.

"Captain!" The soldier changes course as civilians run through the gate.

"What happened here?"

"They appeared out of nowhere! Demons, several of them! They were inside the gates before we knew what happened." Felgrand grasps his shoulders tightly, the armor indenting slightly.

"How?" Felgrand growls.

"They seem to walk out from the shadows. Sir, if you have to go anywhere, stick to the edges of the town. The undead are mostly within the main streets." Felgrand lets go, pushing him toward the gate.

"We will save who we can. Make sure anyone who makes it to the gate can make it out."

Walking down the alleyway the soldier ran from, we enter a small circular courtyard, with a tree in the center. An upturned table sits next to it. Spilled food and drink on the ground next to what can only be a bloodstain. I take a step forward, only to freeze as a voice rings out.

"Oh? You all seem to be running into the city, not out of it."

Startled, we turned, Baron's revolver already drawn. Following the barrel of the gun to a lone table among the chaos, sits a man and a woman, the man sipping from a teacup with a neatly folded suit jacket on the bench next to him. Next to the teacup lay a leather-bound notebook. Across the table sits a beautiful woman with scarlet shoulder-length hair. It has a natural wave, with one portion falling over her face and the other falling over her shoulder. She is wearing a black cocktail dress, and a black parasol leans against the table. She sat next to the man, observing me.

"You!" Baron hisses.

"Yes, me. What of it?" the man replies, taking another sip from his tea.

"Who is he?" Namar asks, fingering his blades. The man scoffs, looking sidelong at his companion, rolling his eyes.

"Your group really is quite disorganized. Perhaps I should just eviscerate Darius after all," he says offhandedly.

"This is Stephen Pendragon, the Writer of Prometheus." The man tilts his cup as if to toast Baron as he speaks before taking another sip.

"Yes, now that you know who I am, can I ask if Darius put a bounty out on a boy recently?" Silence greets him as he takes his pen in his other hand and writes something down in his notebook.

"He did. Now tell us what he looks like," Baron orders. Stephen stops writing as he looks up at Baron. He slowly set his teacup down on the ornate china plate, which matches the cup.

"What makes you think you are in any position to negotiate?"

"I have a gun leveled at your head, and I know I can shoot faster than you can write—not that you could stop an action of this magnitude without spilling a few drops," Baron says, a smug look making its way to his face as Stephen stiffens.

"How do you know that?"

"Tell us what you know, and I will let you in on my little secret."

Silence plagues the courtyard as Stephen's grip tightens on his pen in a frustrated manner, whitening his fingers as he slowly sets it down.

"Very well, I will tell you on one condition."

"Now, why do you think you get to negotiate?"

"I have the information as well as the means to kill you all. I only want to know something from him."

"Fine, what is it you want to know?" Stephen tilts his head, focusing on me.

"I want to know what Alexander wanted." My throat begins to close up at the prospect of Alexander showing up. *Could Stephen know about what happened at the school?*

"Why do you think this person has anything to do with Alexander?" Namar queries.

"He tells me that Alexander was there, and since then, I have not had any contact with him." I freeze. The world feels as if it is constricting. The only thing that Alexander could have been after is Solomon. That means the person who could have the bounty is Solaire!

"Why don't you ask your friend with the short sword?" comes the sultry voice of the girl, breaking me from my thoughts.

"What are you talking about?" Felgrand asks.

"He knows," she says with a voice as smooth as silk while calmly running her arm over to the parasol at the edge of the table.

"What does Bastian know?" Namar challenges.

"He knows who we speak of." I pause as all eyes turn to me. A stunned silence fills the air as I stand frozen, my thoughts scattered.

Crash.

The sound of a smashing window gathers our attention. Barreling toward us is an infected citizen! Baron raises his gun, firing a single shot.

Bang.

The lone shot echoes in the air for a moment. The woman stares straight into my eyes, hers a dull hazel.

"Care to tell us, Bastian?" she asks cloyingly.

"I don't have any idea what you are talking about," I stammer.

"Oh, but I think you do." Suddenly, the aggressive clink of Stephen's cup silences my protest.

"That's enough, Dahlia," Stephen states, standing up, picking up his neatly folded jacket, and laying it over his arm. Taking the notebook and pen, he begins scribbling as he steps toward us. Baron tenses, his revolver leveled at Stephen once more.

"I am going to have to stop you right there." Stephen pauses, not once looking at the notebook, instead focusing on me.

"No, you won't," he says confidently as he takes another step. Baron pulls back the hammer of the revolver.

"Last chance."

"The click of the hammer doesn't scare me. Although if you could have killed me, you would have done so by now," Stephen says as he closes the remaining distance between us. He tears a sheet from his journal and steps next to me. Putting his mouth to my ear, he whispers, and my eyes lock with Dahlia's piercing stare.

"I know you alone are the only link to get to what I want to know. Dahlia is many things, but she is never wrong when it comes to the connections souls have to one another. So when you find the boy in question, you will summon me with this." He whispers so quietly that it is almost as silent as air. I feel a folded note find its way into my hand.

"Why would I do that?" I whisper as he takes another step past me.

"A favor for a favor," he says as Dahlia's eyes widen in surprise, then dangerously narrow. The sound of paper tearing echoes behind me as I turn to see Stephen pivot, looking back at me as he drops a page to the floor.

"Where do you think you are going, Stephen?" Dahlia's conceited voice calls out.

"I have an errand to run, Dahlia. Now, won't you be a dear and find out what caused this little town's plight?" He speaks softly as the page begins to glow an ethereal green as he once more focuses on me.

"I have a feeling you will take my offer, *voiaj.*" he mutters before he vanishes in a green flash. Baron shifts his aim to Dahlia.

"How do you know Stephen?" A playful grin touches her lips.

"I should know him. I am a member of his little group, after all."

"You are a part of Prometheus?"

"Yes, and now I want to know what he said to you." A huge crash impacts the building to my left. The construct seems to groan in protest for a moment. Then a huge black mass bursts from the wooden wall, landing between the two groups. It writhes as it slowly begins to peel apart and disperse into the air, dissipating in mere moments.

From the hole in the wall steps a man in a lavish blue suit. He had a pitch-black tie on and a black ascot bearing the symbol of Prometheus.

"Dahlia, dear, I didn't expect to find you here. I am looking for Stephen. He mentioned finding someone of importance," he says in a British accent, with a sharp stress at the end of each word. Dahlia turns her head with a nod of acknowledgment.

"You just missed him, Colton. Speaking of, I need to know exactly what he told you," she says once more, flicking those eyes back to me.

"Did I now; and what does this boy have that intrigues you so?" I step back as the man circles toward Dahlia, stopping next to the table she sits at, one hand in his pocket, the other lazily at his side, covered in a black leather glove.

"I need to know what Stephen told him." Baron trains the revolver on the newcomer, pulling the trigger twice.

Bang. Bang.

"Rot," Colton grumbles as a miasma seems to settle in front of him. It ripples twice, and Baron scowls, ushering us backward. He turns the gun to Dahlia and pulls the trigger. The fog seems to extend over the table. I watch as the table seems to deconstruct before my eyes.

"Colton, you may kill any of them except for the boy," she orders. He smiles as a black orb flickers to life in his hands. Baron trains the pistol firing twice more as he pushes me behind him.

Bang. Bang.

The fog in front of Dahlia ripples, and the fog in front of Colton does as well.

"This is no mere fog. This is living decay, the likes of which you could never pierce," he says smugly, tilting his face upwards as if looking down upon us.

"Run," he says as he steps through the approaching fog. Baron steps back before turning and dashing past us for the edge of the wall just in front of me.

"Wither." A wave of the blackish-gray fog crashes into the wall in front of me. As I stumble, the tip of my sword enters the mist. I watch as it melts, twisting from the sword to the ground. Turning around, I pivot. Running past a staircase, I dash for the other side only for another wave of the deadly mist to hit the wall in front of us again, the unfortunate soldier stumbling right into it as he disintegrates in front of me. I skid to a stop as I dash up the steps. The clatter of the other footsteps are right behind me as we ascend the staircase. Reaching the top of the staircase, I rip open a wooden door. Entering a room, I turn to see supplies and another staircase leading up to the fort walls. Shrugging to myself, I run up the stairs. The bright light blinds me as I step into the sunlight. Once the initial glare dies down, I gasp.

The entire city lies in shambles, buildings burning in every street. Many more have collapsed. What was once a proud city now lies in ruin.

"Beautiful, isn't it?" a female voice comes from down the wall. A sharp intake of breath from Felgrand fills the air as we see the priestess standing in front of us, flanked by two soldiers clad in the same regal white holy garb.

"What have you done? Why have you betrayed the Church?" he demands, shaking with rage.

"For years, this church has operated under its own definition of righteous acts. I replaced the false prophet a while ago, and they have followed me since. I have seen how corrupted this church of yours really is. I am merely allowing the world to see the lies this group has put forward until the Monarch arises once more." Both guards flinch as they turn, a look of betrayal on both their faces.

"*Schuttle tur,*" she says gracefully as I watch the shadows at the feet of the soldiers shift. I feel my head turn as I hear Felgrand growl. The shadows both rise upwards, cleaving through the soldiers as the shadows reveal two more demons.

"Who are you? Who do you serve?" Felgrand agonizes as he draws his massive weapon. The woman tilts her head as she smiles. Reaching up to her veil, she rips it off, letting it fly in the wind. Reaching up, she grabs the upper portion of the cloak. It dissolves slowly, revealing a blackened set of armor. Two epaulets sit upon her shoulders, each with three protruding spikes.

Her posture is different now as well. Before, she tilted her shoulders forward and scrunched her neck almost in penance. Now, she stands tall, revealing no such weakness. Echoing footsteps can be heard from behind us as I look back to see Colton rounding the corner at the bottom of the stairs.

"We have to go now!" I yell, turning back to see her wave her hand as both beasts rush forward. Dashing forward, I slide under them as they swipe at me. Keeping my eyes on the beasts, I see Felgrand catch one on his massive blade. With a great yell, he throws the beast behind him, down the stairs, before charging forward.

The other flew through the air only to be gunned down by a slew of revolver fire. The revolvers repeatedly crack, sending a hail of bullets into the face of the flying demon. At the last moment, Baron dives to the side, rolling to his feet. He re-holsters one of the revolvers as he expertly reloads the other. I dash at the woman, grasping my destroyed sword. Her shadow begins bubbling once more, and I narrow my eyes, waiting for the moment the beast dives from it. As I approach, I watch it dive into the air, a wolf-like demon flying toward me. Slipping into a slide, I drive my weapon through the foot of the demon, pinning it to the ground as I continue past the woman, an insufferable grin on her face as she looks at me before casting a look down at her bubbling shadow. I dash forward, and see a descending staircase in front of me. Taking the first step, I look at the bottom only to find Dahlia grinning up at me from the bottom step.

"Going somewhere?" she asks innocently as I wheel around.

I see Colton reach the top of the opposite staircase. Between us stands the priestess surrounded by two more demons, one of which is pinned to the ground. As her shadow bubbles another demon shoots from it, dashing for Colton.

"All aspects fall to Prometheus. Nothing is above Prometheus, least of all this pretentious movement." A scoff, and then Colton, silently but clearly utters a word, as he keeps his eyes on the chaplain.

"Rot." The beast decays rapidly as it struggles to move forward in vain, breaking down with each lumbering movement it takes.

"Who are you really?" Colton implores as he eyes the woman in a relaxed manner.

"That would reveal the surprise, and I cannot do that just yet, Colton. For now you can call me the Summoner." Colton tenses as he hears her name. With a powerful thrust of his hand, a dark miasma flies toward the chaplain. The shadow at her feet bubbles for a moment as she falls backward, slipping into it as the deadly fog races over where she stood.

Looking past at Dahlia as she climbs the stairs, Baron grabs on to me with a shout.

"Grab onto me." I watch as the others all grab hold of his cloak. Suddenly there is a whirling tumble, and we fall onto dirt? Looking around, I find us on the middle of the path turning around. The path itself was an odd mix of gray gravel and orange sand, creating a dirt-like texture. I see the walls of Ashvale in the distance. The two figures stand upon the wall as a dark miasma begins eroding the walls, rotting away everything it brushes against.

"You did it, Baron!" Namar shouts as Baron collapses to the ground, spitting up blood.

People on the Wall

"I can still make them rot away if you would like, Dahlia?" Dahlia spins her umbrella as she speaks softly.

"Not yet, Colton, not yet. Stephen is here. While he is a part of Prometheus, I still don't know if taking out any factors is wise. If Stephen does have a plan for after we find Solomon, I shall reap his soul from his body. For now, let us find Solomon. We will have Mateo track them. After all, he is the best one for the job. Isn't that right, Mateo?"

As she finishes, she glances to the left of her at a glass window attached to the turret next to them. A figure starts to coalesce in the reflection, and the glass starts to bulge and distort as a Hispanic man steps from it, wearing a red tie and handkerchief also sporting the Prometheus P. Perched on his nose are a pair of rectangle-cut glasses, behind which sit a pair of cunning eyes.

She stares at the retreating group in front of her and Mateo speaks coolly. "It always surprises me that you can find me whenever I am around."

"It is impossible not to recognize your soul's distinct presence, Mateo."

"Very well. I shall follow them. If I find any important information, you will be the first to know, my lady." He bows ceremoniously and steps back into the window, the glass rippling back over his skin as he vanishes from the castle walls. Turning around, she spins her parasol and stares across the burning city. She grimaces.

"There seems to be another player to this game, one we have not seen yet." As she eyes one of the beasts it tears into a few guards down below within the courtyard. Colton steps forward and raises his hand, a dark miasma sprouting in his palm.

"Yes, the one who can escape the Church of the Righteous. It matters not, though," he says with a smile as he thrusts his palm forward, sending the miasma roaring toward the beast, consuming it and leaving everything around the beast to wither away and degrade. "They will rot like the rest."

"We must be careful, Colton. Stay here and rid us of these beasts. Better to kill them now than deal with their plague later." She turns as she spins her parasol and glances out toward the retreating crew.

"What makes you think you can order me around, Dahlia?" A challenging tone comes from Colton. With a whirl, Dahlia is facing Colton, her parasol shimmering and extending into a scythe, the blade pressed against Colton's neck. Colton is wearing a confident look on his face, betrayed by a lone bead of sweat trailing down the side of his face.

"Remember, Prometheus stands on the grounds of stopping Solomon and removing him before he can destroy our haven. I do not have to like you, nor do I have to trust you—just as I don't trust Stephen. However, the reason you should do what I say is that once Solomon is dead, I have no doubt that Prometheus will fall apart. I would like you to be on my side when this is all over," she finishes with a sultry smile as her body begins to shimmer and turn white and intangible. As she becomes a ghostly white figure, her ethereal beauty is captured. She lets out a screech as she floats into the air, flying into the dark clouds.

Solomon

"Do you think ignorance will keep me at bay?" I cringe as I press my chin into my chest, digging it into one of the cuts. The whispers coalesce to form one solid voice.

"Perhaps you thought the pain would make me go away." The voice hisses into my ear once more. Grinding my teeth, I can hear the voice as it almost seems to breathe into my ear.

"You know it won't work; I am here to stay."

"Who are you? Where are you?"

"Ah, those questions are much harder to answer. I am Solomon Helgen, the real Solomon, the one they fear."

"Why do they fear you?"

"They think of me as a monster. They think I will bring ruin to the world."

"What? Where are you?" I scan the room once more.

"You already know the answer to that question."

"No, I don't!"

"Ah, but you do, but if it helps you understand—or perhaps you cannot see past your own denial—Solomon, I am you."

"How could you be me?"

"In due time, you will find out what that means, but for now, you can assume I am another part of you and you are very much the person they claim you to be."

"No, it can't be. I am nothing like what they claim," I say, shaking my head side to side, my eyes scrunched shut.

"You will see in due time, and you will begin to live as they feared."

"You lie. How could I become such a monster?"

"I am no monster; I do what is right."

"Then why do they fear you?"

"That is not the right question. The real question is how long can you stop me?"

"If you are me, then why do I need to stop you?" His question unnerves me.

"When you understand what I want, you will not want to stop me. Nevertheless, even if you did, you would be unable to."

"What do you want?"

"*Telling you now would only jeopardize yourself.*"

"Just tell me already!" Silence fills the air.

"*I want to finish what I started, and you will help me.*" I feel the scowl on my face.

"I won't let you destroy everything."

"*There will come a time when you need me. When you see that I always worked in the best interest of everyone, then you will have your back to the wall and be forced to make the deal, and when you do, you will have to give up everything.*"

"I will not need to make a deal with you!"

"*As your resolve weakens, you will succumb to me. You will create the contract.*"

"I will never help you! I will never be the monster they paint you to be!"

"*I will be waiting, Solomon, and when you have had enough, I will be here.*" As the voice stops talking, I am left in silence as even the whispers have stopped.

"I can handle whatever happens." I snarl as the bracers dig into my arms.

Solaire

"The city is flying?" I ask, my mouth agape.

"Yes, a result of an influx of magic, the city begins to float. It took massive chains to keep the city in place. The magic has never dissipated either."

"Is that not normal?"

"Magic normally dissipates over time. This is the first instance of such an event happening. The city begins to float, and the ground below it becomes a lake."

The other chirps up.

"Anyway, what brings you here?"

"I was told that a group called the Protectorate can help me find someone." They both shift uncomfortably, passing a look between the two of them.

"Lucky you: we are the Protectorate. Now, who would you like to find?" he asks, taking a swig from a pocket flask, wincing as the liquid goes down his throat.

"I am told to find someone by the name of Haplas. Can you help me?" The man draws in a heavy breath and lets his shoulders drop. He deliberately looks at his companion as he sits silently. A conversation without words seems to take place when the facial expression on the girl's face morphs several times—from alarm to skepticism to disbelief to, finally, resignation.

"We know of him, yes. Who told you to find us?" the girl responds while wrapping the burn on Ai'hara's hand.

"Cu'jehi, Head of the Watch."

The man shoots forward from his relaxed state. "Cu'jehi, what about Durgess? Do you know where he is?" he demands. I shake my head.

"No, he stayed behind when some guy from Prometheus showed up."

"Prometheus? Shit, come on, get up. We have to get moving," he says, standing up.

"Where are we going?"

"Straight to Haplas'. If Prometheus is involved, we have to hurry." He moves over and picks Ai'hara up, slinging one arm over his shoulder. The girl moves forward, taking two pieces of paper from her cloak. The first she set upon Ai'hara's shoulder. I watch as it glows a dull orange before fixing to her clothing. She steps toward me, and I take a step back.

"What is that?" I ask, my suspicion growing.

"This is an anti-magic seal, developed for the sole purpose of giving those without magic a chance against those with it. It is also the only way we are taking you with us to see Charles Haplas." I frown as I let her put the tag on my arm. I feel a slight tingle but nothing out of the ordinary.

"Am I supposed to feel anything?" I ask.

"Wouldn't know. We don't have magic, so they don't work on us," the man says, stepping down the corridor.

"Do I get to know the names of our saviors?"

"I am Theron, and that is Yukio. The other guy is Bernard."

"You shouldn't tell him our names."

"It should be fine. Has the seal on him, anyways."

"You should take this seriously!" We approach a T-junction offering us a right path and a left one. Theron steps onto the left path.

"The kid looks like he is green as grass. He won't be able to do anything." I frown, then think about the other one, who distracted the flame-wielding man.

"Is this Bernard person going to be alright?"

Silence overtakes us, leaving only the heavy footfalls that echo throughout the sewer tunnel. I can make out a small ladder at the end of the tunnel.

"So, how did you guys find us?" I chirped up, trying to change the subject.

Yukio scoffs. "Luck."

"Don't listen to her. We heard the commotion on one of our routes to find supplies."

"So, luck," Yukio chimes in, earning a sidelong glance from Theron. He turns forward as we get to the base of the ladder, to which Yukio pushes past him, climbing the ladder swiftly. At the top, I see a metal grating. Quickly lifting the metal grating, she slips out of sight.

"Supplies?"

"Yeah, the magistrate cracks down on anything unregulated, and we move outside the law to make sure everyone stays safe. So you can imagine what lengths we have to go through to get what we need." He pulls Ai'hara over his shoulder as he begins climbing the ladder with one hand.

"She doesn't like me, does she?"

"She's had a tough life. Prometheus has taken a lot from her." He pauses at the last rung.

"She doesn't make many attachments, but you could say we are family. She is just worried about old Bernard." He disappears over the edge as I step on the first rung and begin climbing. Pulling myself over the edge, I find myself in a utility closet. The grinding of metal catches my attention as I see Theron drag the cover back over the ladder. Yukio stands at the door, peeking through it as she opens it only enough to allow a crack of light to hit her face. She looks back at us, waving us to follow her as she opens the door, peeking her head in before stepping into the light. Past her, I see another door opposite this one. It held a modern design on the white wood.

She moves to the door, producing a key from her pocket. As she places the key in the lock, the door creaks open slowly. She turns back to us, uncertainty filling her gaze as she reaches into her cloak, trading the key for a knife. She presses it open further, slowly stepping into the room. We follow in after her.

The room has a wooden floor with several small boards laid in an alternating pattern. A couch sits on one side of the room with a coffee table in front of it, next to a marble-finished fireplace. On the right side, there is a kitchenette with a long table. On the base of the floor sits a broken glass with a milky liquid. I hear the soft click of the door behind me as Theron closes it.

A gesture grabs my attention as Theron hands Ai'hara to me, pulling a tomahawk from his cloak, shushing me lightly as he did so. Looking past him, I see Yukio stop to look down at the floor, where the carpet has been stained red. Next to her stands a small dining table that could seat four.

My palms grow sweaty as I see Yukio press onward, opening another door as Theron moves to the kitchenette. The crunch of his shoes on the glass brings my attention to see him close his eyes in frustration. He takes a deep breath as he lowers his tomahawk.

"Aaaiiiiiiiiieeeee!"

A scream from the other room. Theron shoots off toward the door Yukio went through. I walk forward uncertainly. Seeing through the door, I see blood on the ground. I see Yukio walk out, guided by Theron, tears staining her mask-covered face. I set Ai'hara down on the couch as I move to look inside the room. Theron barred my way and only shook his head.

What did she see?

Moving around him, I peek inside to see what can only be described as a torture cell. A man lies splayed out on the floor while blood stains the floors and walls. A large battle ax lies next to him. Many slash marks mar the body. A butcher knife stands straight up from his chest. I turn around, walking back into the other room to see Yukio with her head down on the table. Theron is sitting next to her staring at the door, his eyes glazed over, one hand tightened into a fist. If he was not wearing gloves, I know his hand would have been white from the way it is trembling.

"All right, kid, time to start talking. Who were you trying to find?" Theron orders as I sit down across from him.

"I am looking for my friend Solomon." He looks at me, then down to the wound on my chest.

"I sincerely hope you don't mean Solomon Helgen," he pleads, pinching his temple.

"I do."

"Kiddo, we are into saving the world, not helping people who destroy it," he says, exasperated.

"Wait, we might need to," Yukio chimes in, sitting up, her eyes puffy and wet but her gaze intense.

"What are you talking about?"

"Solomon is the only way to take down Prometheus."

"It is too big a risk!"

"How many more people are we going to lose before we commit to something? How many more have to die?"

"Many more will die if we help Solomon."

"Why does everyone talk about Solomon as if he is a monster?" I interrupt.

"Kiddo, this city floats because of him. The dead lands exist because of him. What else besides a monster could do that?"

"Regardless, I have to save him. Prometheus is after him."

"They don't have him?" Theron's eyebrows rose.

"No, some people from Syndicate have him."

"Syndicate?" he repeated, his eyes narrowing. A weird sound begins to fill the air. A warbling sound as if a tape is rewinding. A dull green hue fills the room as we stand up. A neon green orb floats above the broken glass. Peering closer, it looks like a clock face. Several gears are behind it. The strange thing is that the hands on it are all moving backward.

"So, Darius still has him," a distorted voice rings out.

"What the fuck?" Yukio voices as the cup reassembles, the liquid pooling back into it. As it slowly rises, the orb suddenly expands creating a large ellipse of green that trailed into darkness. Peering left and right, both my allies have their weapons drawn and ready as the green fades, leaving that dreaded man with the glass of milk now at his lips. He slurps the drink and lets the glass drop again, his face scrunching up as he does so.

"Still terrible." He sighs as everyone tenses in the room. He glances around and spots Solaire.

"I would have had to spend a lot of valuable time to find out where the boy is," he says smugly.

"You bastards, you keep taking everyone from me. First, Colton; now you!" Yukio screams, running forward, raising her dagger.

"Noo!" Theron screams as he takes off after her.

"Stop." A transparent box forms around them both as they seem to stop.

"Thank you for telling me where to find Solomon." He turns to face me and freezes, a shocked look on his face as he eyes my bloody chest.

"It would appear your part in this isn't over." His eyes flash green for a moment.

"What?"

"Do you have any idea what that symbol means?"

"Seems like everyone else does, so why don't you tell me," I retort, causing him to chuckle.

"Now that we have no distractions, I am going to make you a deal. You come with me, and I leave the insignificant ants alone, or you can try to resist, and I kill them like the insects they are. Then I take you with me. Your choice." He says with a Cheshire grin spreading across his face.

CHAPTER 9

A RACE AGAINST TIME

Solaire

"Why should I come with you? You already know where Solomon is!" I growled.

"You don't really have a choice," Alexander says again as the green around the others darkened.

"The longer they are in that box, the less time they have." My eyes dart around the room, looking for any way out. I see the cloth cloak on Theron's back begin to shrivel.

"Well? Time is ticking, and I have places to be." He extends his arm to me, gesturing for me to join him. I grit my teeth, sneaking a look at Ai'hara's form on the couch. I scrunch my eyes shut and feel my lips purse in frustration as I take a step forward.

"*Incinerate!*" The wall behind Alexander is blasted to bits as a torpedo of flames shoots into the room. Alexander spins on his heel, stepping to the side. The flames scorch his side, distracting Alexander, his green box holding Yukio and Theron flickering away, allowing them to move for an instant. They both dive to the side. Theron drags me down with him as the flame sails over my head. Crashing into the wall of the fireplace, the stone melts as flames begin to spread through the room.

"It would seem insects just keep finding me." Alexander sighs as he runs his hand over the singed portion of his suit.

"Alexander, how did you get here?" Valin growls.

"You burned my favorite suit too." He huffs as Valin brings his hands together, a large flame building between them.

"It doesn't matter how you got here. It is time for you to go." Valin sneers, bringing a condescending smile to Alexander's face. He looks down at his feet as a deep rumble of laughter leaves him.

"You even have the audacity to order me around," he states, looking back up amused. I feel Theron pat my shoulder, dragging my attention away from the two adversaries. He nods behind me. I turn to see Yukio, shouldering Ai'hara quietly.

"You think you can stop me from doing what I want?" Alexander chirps mockingly.

"I know I can. I will kill you all and that boy working with Solomon," he growls, the flames in his hand glowing a pure white.

"I will have to stop you right there. I have need for the boy. Let me take the boy, and then you can carry on and finally roast the Protectorate like you wanted." We crawled on the floor toward the dining room.

"Not a chance in hell, Alexander."

"What even gives the delusion that you can stop me?"

"I know what you can stop with your time." The amusement dropped from Alexander's face as he snaps his hand upwards the small chain carrying the ornate pocket watch to his hand.

"Oh, and what would that be?"

"You can only stop physical objects, meaning you cannot stop this! *Pyro Blast!*" Valin roars with a thrust of his arms. The flames cascade forward.

"*Dilation.*" A green pulse flashes through the room, and everything seems to stop except for Alexander and the flames, which are moving forward at an entrancingly slow pace. Alexander looks down, shaking his head, stepping around the flame to the knife block, pulling one out. I tried to keep moving, only to feel as if every muscle in my body is being weighed down by millions of pounds.

"I commend you for understanding I can only stop objects of physical nature." He steps forward, admiring the blade, flipping it in his hands. Stopping right in front of him, he drives the knife into his chest. I watch his face slowly contort in pain, the blood slowly scattering into the air from the wound.

"You have no idea who you stand against," he says calmly as he strides toward me. Stopping in front of me, smirking past me at Theron, who still has a grip on my shoulder. He kicks forward, taking the arm from my shoulder.

"Now we see why you feel so different." He grips my shoulder, hauling me to my feet. Looking into his face, I see several gray hairs among his pristine black hair. I blink, and another strand is gray. Another pulse throughout the room, and everything returns to normal time.

Boom.

The flames collide with the other side of the room as Valin falls to his knees. I see him swing his hand toward us, letting a fire bellow toward us.

"*Burn!*" Alexander closes his eyes, frustrated as he dons a scowl.

"*Dilation.*" A box of green light forms around the flames and Valin as he reaches into his pocket, pulling out a neatly folded square of paper. He uses his one hand to unfold it. On the inside of the sheet is a large rune, encircled by several others.

"As much fun as it has been to show you the gap in our powers, it is time for us to go." He drops the sheet casually as a shuffle comes from behind us. I feel the grip lessen on my shirt as I find myself slamming against the floor, followed by a harsh stomp on my chest, making me lose my breath.

Shlick.

The sound of a blade entering flesh echoes as a warm drop lands on my face. Opening my eyes, I see Yukio holding her dagger, the end of it going right through Alexander's hand.

Pushing her back, she stumbles against the couch as he points his other hand at her.

"*Stop,*" he growls as a green pulse envelops her and Theron. He grips the dagger and pulls it out, letting blood drip across my face.

"You may think you have had a chance, that perhaps the sight of my blood is enough to give you hope." He leans closer to her, shifting his other foot such that it landed on the paper with the runes on it.

"*Upend.*" His eyes glow a deep green as the blood begins to flow upwards back into the wound as it seals itself shut. A shine grows from the sheet of paper.

"They say if it bleeds, you can kill it. I am here to tell you that no matter how much you can make me bleed, the outcome will always be the same." A pulse of green flashes, illuminating the room, stealing with it the green aura suspending the flames. The fire begins to creep faster and faster now that it is free from its stasis. The world flashes to white as I feel the heat approach my skin.

Bastian

I turn back, staring at the smoldering city of Ashvale. The screams still permeate the air, and I try to shut them out. We must have been about a mile from the city at this point. Despite this, I can still make out the shapes of the two Prometheans upon that wall, just standing there, as if observing us.

"We have to keep moving," Felgrand grumbles.

"Yeah, but where?" I ask, turning to the others. Felgrand stands staring at the city while Namar is leaning over Baron, one hand on his chest, the other holding up his head. A steady stream of blood pours from his lips. Each passing moment, the liquid lessens.

"We cannot go too far. He won't be able to make it," Namar speaks grimly before snapping his fingers, looking up at Felgrand.

"What?"

"Unless you have some sparkly magic to heal him?"

"I do not have any way to heal this man, no."

I contemplated. "Then, if my memory serves me, there are three places we can travel to: Iglagos to the west, Argentum to the north, or east to Winskar and find a small village there."

"Winskar? Fuck, no. That place is a big no-go."

"What, why not?"

"It has been transformed. It no longer is as it once was," Felgrand says remorsefully.

"What is it now?" I reply, intrigued.

Felgrand speaks up. "It has been tainted by plague and infection."

"With all the sickness, we call it something else now," Namar continues.

"What?"

"The Blight Lands." Namar speaks the name as if it is poison.

"Fine then, what about Iglagos?" I suggest.

"That might work," Felgrand says.

Namar scoffed. "I suppose if you want to be caught by their Magistrate."

"The Magistrate keeps unwanted entries to a minimum," Felgrand clarifies.

"How?" I inquired.

"Being a floating city, the most realistic way of arriving in the city is through a teleportation technique, and the Magistrate has a way of pinpointing where the arrival point in the city is," Namar explains.

"Rogue, you speak as if you can teleport us," Felgrand challenges.

"I can."

"You can teleport now?" I ask.

"Yep, I can take us where we need to go. All I need is a shadow."

Ring.

As he finishes, a phone rings. Glancing around, I see everyone confused.

Ring.

The sound came from Baron. I exchange looks with the others as I step forward, opening Baron's cloak, searching for a pocket.

Ring.

This time the inside of his coat lights up, and I find the pocket easily. Reaching in I feel the hilt of a knife as well as a phone. Pulling it out, I find an older flip phone. Quirking an eyebrow, I bring it up to show the others the unknown caller across the screen.

"Really?" I ask, getting a shrug from Namar. Shrugging to myself, I answer.

"Hello?"

"Who is this?" a voice responds.

"Sorry, bud. I have to know why you are calling the line, especially regarding whose phone this is."

"Yeh know whose phone that is?"

"I do. Now, who are you?"

"If yeh know who it is then yeh had bettah give it back."

"Baron will not hurt us. He is out of commission at the moment," I say, looking down at his unconscious body.

"What happened? What did yeh do to him?"

"Relax, we haven't done anything. We are looking for a place to help him heal. We were attacked. He had to use his magic to get us out." Silence drafts between us. I look at the phone to reassure myself that the call is still active. Putting it back to my ear, I hear a shuffle over the phone.

"I am at Argentum in the Bilge. Come here, and I can save him. Make sure yeh aren't followed."

Click.

The phone cuts to silence. Closing the phone, I put it into my pocket as I look at Namar.

"Looks like we will be heading to Argentum, a place called the Bilge. You know of it?" Namar smiles, a crooked line coming across his face.

"Oh, yeah. That's been our safe house for when things get bad. In fact, it is very close to the Syndicate's main halls." His smile turns to a scowl as he glares at Felgrand.

"What is it, rogue?"

"You had better keep yourself tame. This is where the Syndicate's operatives reside, and they will not be as lenient as I. So you had better keep to yourself, or you might find a dagger in your spine," Namar growls.

"Duly noted," Felgrand says, picking Baron up and tossing him over his shoulder. Namar unsheathes his left blade.

"Now hold on people, this—" He plunges his sword into the ground. "—is going to feel strange."

"What do you mean?" I ask, receiving a wolfish smile instead. I look down to see a blackness expand out from his sword, surrounding us. The black begins to crawl up my leg. A strange feeling of nothingness as it hungerly climbs higher, trying to consome me.

"Is this supposed to happen?" Felgrand cries out.

"Shadow walk." The darkness stops, and for a second, I think it is over before it lurches over us. I let out a yelp of surprise. An unsettling feeling of movement plagues the inside of the darkness and the light drains away.

A flickering light reveals Namar dusting himself off.

"What happened?" I ask, looking over the environment to find us in a library.

"This Bastian, is the Bilge." The library holds many ostentatious bookcases surrounding the room. Candles burn in a lantern next to a dark oak door. A dark red carpet sits on the floor. On the side of the room sits a small desk. In its seat is a man with a bloody knife. He stands up upon seeing us.

"It seems yeh made it." He walks past us to the door.

"Jack, what the hell is going on?" Namar asks.

"Grab Baron and leave the Crusader here."

"Why do I stay here?" Jack turns back, a wicked smile on his face.

"So, yeh don't get gutted in the hallway." I step forward, putting a hand on Felgrand as his face twists in rage.

"Just wait here. We won't be long. We will go get this sorted out, and then we can find my friend and help the people of Ashvale," I reassure as he slowly untenses.

"Fine," he says as we step from the room, Baron draped across Namar's shoulders. Stepping into the end of a darkened hallway, I notice several paintings adorning the walls, all of them depicting art from the Renaissance, if my memory serves well. The hallway travels farther. On my right is a white door. At the end of the hall are two small desks framing a set of double doors. I can also make out a lone door in the center of the hallway. I ran my hands along the wall as the door opens up, and a man in a dark cloak with a red bandana tied around his face steps through it. Jack nods to Namar, and the man steps forward, leading Namar through the door. I watch as it closes silently, leaving me with Jack.

"So, Bastian, is it?"

"Yeah, what of it?"

"Yeh was a part of Syndicate back in the day, right?"

"Correct," I say, gritting my teeth.

"What brought you back?"

"My friend was taken by some soldiers. I came back to find out where they took him." A dangerous glint enters Jack's eye.

"Why come here then?"

"Darius must have sanctioned it."

"What makes you say that?"

"It is a group of soldiers, and one of them had an emblem on his uniform. It is a Syndicate badge," I growl. Jack's smile is subdued as he points to the white door at the end of the hall.

"Darius mentioned setting a new addition in there." He steps forward, walking in front of me, reaching for the door. He stops, looking back.

"Whatevah is on the other side o' this door, it might not be pretty."

I push him to the side as I grasp the handle. "I have never been scared of not pretty," I hiss as I twist the handle opening the door. The first thing I smell is the scent of blood invading my nostrils. Then I see the corpse on the floor, the same uniform as the soldiers wore as they took Solomon!

"You believe me yet?" a gruff voice huffs, and I stumble forward. Unaware, I pass the threshold and I am not surprised by the sight inside. Strapped to a chair facing the door, is a man, his clothing blood-soaked in ribbons, barely clinging to his lacerated body. Nearly every portion of his skin has visible cuts. He looks up at me, and I gasp.

"Solomon," I whisper, aghast at his condition. His face is just as shocked as my own. In an instant, his shock turns to fury as I feel something crash into the back of my head, and I fall forward, everything fading to black. The last thing I hear is an unintelligible mumble. Then a sudden rush of cold sends me into nothingness.

Solomon

"You believe me yet?"

I barely cough out as I glare up toward the door. I feel my life will fade away as I find myself looking into the surprised face of Bastian.

"Solomon," he whispers no louder than a breeze. Then I see Jack walk in behind Bastian's still frame, his knife in hand, a manic smile on his face as he brings the butt of it into the air, hanging it over Bastian. I contort my face, nod my head, struggling to get his attention, but he seems to grow more confused as Jack brings his arm down.

Thud.

I see him slump to the floor. I feel the whispers return as the rage boils underneath my skin.

"He hurt your friend! Let me take control, Solomon!"

"I don't need you," I growl as I feel a burst of cold air around me. A crackling fills the air as I see a thin film of white substance creep up the chair, covering the armrests.

"It seems you do know more than you so innocently claimed. Guess your friend gets to stay." My attention snaps to Jack as he steps over Bastian walking to an identical chair to my own. He grips it, dragging it across the floor.

"What do you mean?" I shout.

"The ice crawling up your chair, the cold air in the room. You remember ... don't yeh?" He lets the chair thud against the floor in front of me as he bends over, picking Bastian up and setting him into it. He clicks the restraints together.

"I don't know what you are talking about!"

"The ice around yer chair says otherwise. So now that I know yeh is lying, I am going to kick this up a notch." His devilish smirk returns to his face as he whips his blade out, stepping in front of my sight of Bastian.

"Let me out. Let me kill him!" The voice rages, I wince, and Jack pauses.

"Since yeh won't tell me, back to the grind, I suppose." He spins the knife in his hands and takes another step closer.

"This won't hurt a bit." Jack spins on his heel, thrusting his blade forward. I hear the wet sound of it striking home, and a howl comes from Bastian as he wakes with a scream.

"Tell me what I want to know!" Jack screams, positioning himself behind the chair, his hand pressing the handle down into Bastian's shoulder.

"Let me have control, and he will die," the voice coolly reasons.

"No," I hiss.

"No?" Jack looks at me incredulously.

"Yeh, even have a wound in the same place! Guess friendship doesn't count for what it is worth anymore." Jack chuckles, ripping the knife from Bastian's shoulder.

"*You would let him kill your friend?*"

"Jack, why are you doing this?" Bastian grumbles.

"It's my job, buddy." Jack crouches, planting a hand on Bastian's shoulder, letting him look into his eye.

"Look, you don't have to do this!" Bastian pleads.

"Sadly, I do. The boss wants to know why Prometheus wants this boy, and, well, I have teh find out." Jack shrugs, spinning the knife in his hands.

"Listen, whatever Darius is af—"

He is interrupted by Jack's barking laugh.

"Yeh think that Darius has any control?" Bastian's face contorts with confusion.

"Darius hasn't been running the show for some time."

"What?"

"If yeh think Darius is ballsy enough to make such a move, then yer too gullible." The crackling of ice fills the room.

"*Just let me out, give me freedom, and your friend will not be harmed.*" A burst of air shoots out from me, freezing the floor.

"I don't need you!" I growl.

"Oh no! Fight it, Solomon!" Bastian screams.

"What are ye talkin' 'bout?" Jack questions.

"Shut it, you oaf. If he keeps pulsing like this, then they will know!"

"*Figures he would know,*" comes the voice in my head as the crackling continues. I see the carpet on the floor rip and tear as it froze from the intense cold.

"What do you mean?" I ask as a cold wave rushes through my body.

"*We have to leave here fast!*" the voice booms in me.

"Listen, Jack, I don't care what you do with me but get Solomon out of here!"

"Now why would—"

Crash.

The door slamming open interrupts him.

A Dark Chamber

Two flaming eyes snap open in the darkness. A large empty room devoid of all but a single ray of light that peeks through a crack in the ceiling. The ray lands at the bottom of a small staircase leading to a tall throne. A lone figure stands among the darkened throne as a figure steps through the gargantuan archway at the far end.

A dark guttural voice speaks. "Summoner, you have returned."

"Yes, Harbinger," a female voice says calmly.

"What of Ashvale?"

"It lies in ruins, as does everything else that would stand in his majesty's way." She steps forward, kneeling at the bottom of the staircase leading to the empty throne. A small pulse creaks the room as a small blue line trails along the floor, glowing among the cracks in the stone.

"It appears the key to his majesty's awakening is amongst us once more," the Harbinger speaks calmly.

"What should be done?"

"For now, we shall call upon the Pursuer." Large footsteps crash against the floor as the sound of grinding metal fills the throne room. A gargantuan figure steps into the lone beam of light, kneeling awkwardly toward the throne.

"Whaaaaaat," growls the behemoth.

"Find us the key, and with it his majesty will rise."

"Doooonnnneee." The behemoth hisses, rising to an impressive seven feet as its heavy footfalls crash against the stone floor.

Ai'hara

I awake with a dull throbbing in my arms. The abhorrent scent of smoldering flesh disturbingly fills the air. Opening my eyes, I feel the dissipating heat as I see a stocky body cradling a smaller one. Flames are dying out on the melted and burned surfaces of the room. In the kitchenette, Valin kneels, grasping at his own chest.

I hear a cry as I feel everything come clearer. Theron shifts, looking at me as he crawls over on his knees, cradling someone. His eyes are distraught, tears threatening to spill from them.

"Can you help her?" He gestures, leaning closer, showing me the badly burned body of a girl. Her mask is gone now, leaving burns across her face and body. Her arms are worse off. The skin is completely blackened and indiscernible from the black suit she is wearing. With that first glance, I can't help but question if she is alive. I see the slight rise of her chest, and my question is answered.

"Please, help her!"

"It's too late. It's a miracle she is alive," comes Valin's pained remark.

"Shut it, Valin. We can save her! This is a Watcher; they can heal people!" Theron shouts back, turning his gaze back to me.

"You can save her, right?" he asks, no, *pleads* with me. I nod, trying to shake away the rest of the daze. He gently but quickly puts the girl down, but due to his desperation he drops her on my lap. I feel a tug on my back as the anti-magic seal comes off.

"Water, I need water." Theron panics, rustling in his cloak, ripping frantically through his pockets. A few moments pass before he produces a simple flask. Holding it gingerly with his gigantic hands, he holds it out to me, his head bowed, his eyes peeking up at me expectantly. I reach out to take it with my own, mimicking the care he took with it. I open the flask, pouring water over the girl, eliciting a gasp from her.

"What are you doing?" Theron says, his eyes wide, watching the event.

"*Helbrede,*" I speak calmly as the water seems to caress the wounds, carrying the part of the water away from her as it rises toward my hands, moving up my arms. I bite back a scream as I feel my body begin to burn. My arms reignite as I see burns identical to hers move onto my own skin, marring it such that I can no longer move it. I look down at her expression and see it move from a pained one to a much more sedated version. A thud echoes across the room, drawing my attention to a closing orange orb. A man in a tattered suit drops to the floor. Standing up, he is wearing glasses. He is bald and has several beads of blood dripping onto the floor.

"Theron, what happened here?" he wheezes, spotting the big man next to me.

"Who the hell are you?" Valin growls.

"How did you get here, Jeffery?" Theron asks beside me.

"Had to give Alexander the run around in a twisted dimension." He spits blood onto the floor, leaning onto the table.

"Alexander? But he is the one who did this," Valin spits.

"What, how was I too late?" Jeffery growls, balling his fingers into a fist.

"You were equally responsible, Valin!" Theron growls.

"Fuck you. If it were not for your interference, I would have killed the boy before he was taken," Valin sneers.

"Taken, who has been taken?" Jeffery looks up, his face growing paler.

"Some kid by the name of Solaire." Jeffery looks ready to be sick as he surveys the room.

"Where is Haplas? Charles!" Jeffery calls out, hobbling farther into the room.

"You don't know?"

"Know what?" Jeffery spins, a maddened look in his eye.

"Jeffery ... Charles is dead. He was dead before we got here." Theron speaks softly, looking down, trying to avoid his gaze. All the fight seems to leave Jeffery as he slumps into a chair at the dining table.

"That's how he found out about where Solomon is." Valin looks up with an incredulous expression.

"Wait. Solomon Helgen has been found?" Everyone turns their attention to Jeffery as he sighs.

"Yes, but he got taken by Syndicate operatives before Alexander could get him."

"What now?" Theron asks as he struggles to stand.

"We have no time to find Darius to stop him from releasing the monster. Now we have to find a way to stop that monster instead." Straightening, he weaves his hands in a circle as a golden portal opens up before them. He stumbles forward, falling to one knee.

"We have to go. All of you, come with me."

Without a moment's hesitation, Theron picks up the girl as he moves toward the portal. Stepping into it, I awkwardly follow. Entering the portal, I find myself outside of an old monastery that looks to be partially destroyed. A forest has regrown onto it and around it, beautiful trees arching up, ripping apart the stone path lain on the ground. Heavy rain pelts everything around us, leaving only the darkened interior dry.

"I have a duty to protect this city. I cannot just leave!" Valin growls. I look back to see Jeffery give a noncommittal shrug as he takes in a deep, calming breath.

"If you do not come with me, then there will be no city to save!" Jeffery growls back as Valin struggles to his feet.

"Fine, but when this is over, I will raze you all to the ground," Valin pushes into Jeffery as he steps onto the cold stone.

Solaire

The world comes back to view as I find myself on a hardwood floor. Looking around, I find myself in a dark hallway, with a pair of double doors in front of me. Adorning the sides of the hallway are various fancy paintings and two small desks that were on either side of another door further down the hall on the right. At the opposite end sits a single white door.

"Get up, boy," Alexander says, lifting me to my feet. My legs shake, and every breath hurts. He nudges me toward the double doors in front of us. Touching the handle, I look back at him and see his face scrunch in annoyance as he pulls out his pocket watch. Snapping it to his hand, with a flick of his wrist he scowls.

"Time is of the essence, and I no longer have it to spare." I hear a mumble from within the room. I lean closer, then feel a shoe impact my back, kicking me through the door. Sliding across the floor into the room, I find myself at the feet of Darius, who looks down at me.

"You!" A look of fury crosses his face as he moves to kick me.

"Stop." A green pulse slams into Darius, stopping his motion. His eyes open wide in surprise.

"Ah, Alexander, impeccable timing. I was just asking our acquaintance why his little group seems to be making decisions without his input." Stephen's gaze slips toward me.

"I see you have also brought the one I was looking for, but seeing as you have shown up, he is no longer of any use to me," Stephen prattles.

"I would not go that far, Stephen. You see, I have learned some interesting things from this boy." Alexander steps farther into the room.

"What did you find out?"

"I found out that Solomon Helgen lives—and who has him now."

"Who has him? You speak as if he was captured," Stephen says, confused.

"It would appear he doesn't know about this world, or at the very least, he cannot remember it. Which leads me to you." He turns to Darius, the green glow fading from him as he stumbles backward.

"Where are you keeping Solomon Helgen?"

"What are you talking about? We don't have him," Darius shouts back.

"Then why is a group of your abduction squad interfering with my business?" Alexander queries as Darius turns pale.

"It would seem you lied," Stephen states, opening his notebook on top of the desk.

"No! It isn't me!" Darius screams.

"Then who is it?"

"That bastard Baron! He has been usurping my power for a while now."

"Do you know where he is?"

"No, but I can take you to him. Besides, I am one of you, now, right?"

"Take us to him. Then we can add you to the roster." Stephen smiles coolly as he stands up, stepping around the desk. Alexander looks down at me dismissively.

"O-of course," Darius stutters, hopping to the door.

"*Upend.*"

I feel a strange sensation as I start to move backward, falling upward until I am on my feet. A strange feeling of vertigo swims over me as I find myself standing next to Alexander once more.

"I have precious little time for delays. Take me to him." I look down the hall to see the door on the edge of the hallway open, with a man bracing himself against the door jamb.

"Baron, you traitorous bastard!" Darius shrieks. The man shifts, staring at us, raising a revolver shakily. He takes aim. Darius stops moving, but Alexander keeps walking. Each step is mockingly slow, like a predator that knows it has cornered its prey.

"Stop the pretense. I know you have Solomon—"

Bang.

The bullet fired from the pistol meets a pulse of green, slowing it to a stop just inches away from Alexander's face. Stephen pushes me forward, stumbling next to Alexander. His hand shoots out, catching me by the collar.

"You are leading this organization to hell! I won't let you bargain with these pretentious gods!" Baron screams, stumbling into the room.

"How do you expect to stop us with one foot in the grave?" Alexander taunts, nodding to the side as he steps forward.

"Darius, you get to follow them in."

I wrench my head around to see Darius ushered behind us by Stephen. I am dragged into the doorway and promptly slammed against it. I shoot a glare to a scowling Alexander, his attention drawn to the inside of the room. I observe the room, seeing two identical chairs across from each other. Solomon occupies the one opposite of us, and the other holds Bastian. Standing beside him, one hand resting upon the chair, is Baron. What troubles me the most is the revolver in his hand—trained upon the door and the body lying just in front of it.

"It didn't work the first time. What do you think will happen this time?" Alexander asks with a mocking sneer, taking a step inside and stopping just above the body. I recognize him. This is one of the soldiers who took Solomon.

"Solomon, are you all right!" I call out, earning another shove into the door as he looks up at me.

"What are you doing here?" Solomon asks, his body covered in dried blood.

"Which part of him seems okay to you?" Bastian asks, looking over his shoulder toward us. I hear a slight thud and look down to see Alexander retreat his boot from the corpse at his feet.

"It would seem you have already started cleaning up the loose ends."

"Baron, stand down!" Darius screams as he enters the doorway. His commanding tone somehow sounds like a plea at the same time.

"I will not stop for you! You are nothing more than a figurehead, another loose end!"

"That is wonderful. It saves me so much time. Since we are on the subject of tying up loose ends ..." Alexander reaches around, plucking Darius as he turns the corner, slamming him into the wall.

"Let me help you. You clearly think this organization is worthless under this miscreant, so why don't we come to a compromise. I'll finish him for you. Then, you get to lead the thugs the way you want, and I get the boy." Baron's face twitches as he pulls the trigger. Just as before, a green pulse shoots out to meet the bullet, stopping the bullet just shy of its target, just touching Darius's nose.

"If I want this scum dead, I could have seen to that long ago, although he has outlived his purpose," Alexander scoffs.

"What the hell! I brought you to him! The boy is here too! I thought you were going to let me join!" Alexander grins at Darius's feeble protest.

"When did you actually believe you were going to join us?" Alexander mocks.

"But Stephen said—" Darius begins, starting to blubber.

"Ah, forgive me. You must have misunderstood me. When I said I would let you join, I was merely speaking about joining the long list of casualties." Stephen speaks purposefully, as if savoring the despair in the atmosphere with each syllable.

"No ..." Darius says, his face growing ashen as he quakes in fear.

"Not only that, but with your recent performance with your merry band of thieves, did you honestly think we would still offer such a thing?" Alexander chuckles.

"Help me," Darius chokes out.

"*Consume.*" Just as before, Darius begins quaking as a green stream comes pouring into Alexander from Darius as he breaks down into dust that scatters onto the floor.

"Now that the trash is gone ..." Alexander turns and stops once more. Following his gaze, I find it stuck to Baron's revolver, now pressed against Solomon's neck, pointed down to travel through his entire torso.

"I know you can't stop this. You might be able to stop ordinary guns, him, or even me, but this bullet, this gun—I made it so you would not be able to stop it."

I hear the sound of Alexander grinding his teeth.

"You do not want to do that." Baron smirks, an arrogant crease along his pale face. He tightens the grip on the pistol.

"I think I do." He pulls the trigger.

Bang.

The shot echoes down the hall.

CHAPTER 10

CONSEQUENCES

Solaire

Solomon slumps back in his chair, limp, an ethereal glow illuminating his body. From where the bullet enters, a sky-blue crack spreads over his body as if he were a piece of cracked glass. His eyes are dull as he stares off in my direction. My vision swims, and I feel myself choking for air. I try to call out to him but my voice gets stuck in my throat. I fall to my knees. It is too much.

"You have no idea what you have just done," I hear Alexander snarl.

"I did what was necessary. Now no one can have him!" Baron brings the pistol back to Alexander.

"You just don't get it, do you?" Stephen speaks up, stomping past me.

"What don't I get?" A blue flash startles me as Solomon's eyes flick to the side. Staring directly at Baron, he moves, tearing through the shackles holding his hands. Striking out, his left arm darts underneath the raised revolver, pushing up the weapon and striking Baron's chest at the same time. Blood splatters as Solomon's arm pierces through Baron's ribs.

"That you didn't kill me. You have merely freed me," a callous voice whispers. Despite its low volume, we all hear it clearly. Baron drops the revolver, looking down at Solomon in shock.

"But how?" he asks, sputtering blood as he slumps to one knee. Solomon's vacant expression distorted with a blue warble flickering over his face. Then it expands, covering his whole body. A bluish figure, in the exact frame of Solomon's, stands up, stepping away from Solomon's cracked body. The form glides out of Solomon's body, leaving it behind like an empty husk. It stops, looking down at Baron's bewildered expression.

"The reason is simple." He slides closer, whispering into Baron's ear. Baron's eyes widen as a sharp crack fills the air, before looking up at the figure. Looking to the source of the sound, I see the body in the chair crumble in on itself, as if it were an empty shell for what it once held.

"Stop!" Alexander calls out, sending a pulse of green that covers them both.

"Stephen, do it now!" Alexander screams, pulling a blade out from his pocket and holding it out, pointing it behind him, his attention firmly set upon the new figure, which is slowly molding to a more defined shape. A blast of ice covers the floor, trailing over the arm and coating Baron's stomach.

"You should know by now, Alexander, that something like this will not stop me." The figure speaks calmly as Stephen gasps in pain. Looking back, I see Stephen pulling his arm from the blade in Alexander's hand. Grasping the pen in his other hand, he drives it into the very same wound. He winces as he pulls the fountain pen from the wound, then he quickly opens his notebook.

"It isn't meant to stop you, only to hold you. With your arm attached to Baron, you may not be stopped completely by the field, but your arm is." The figure chuckles as Baron's entire chest is coated in ice.

"Is that so? How did you ever come to that conclusion?"

"I know how my power works; do not pretend you know the limitations of my strength!" Alexander roars as the sound of scribbling fills the air. The figure looks down at its arm and frowns. Encased in ice, I see the figure strain as it tries to flex its muscle.

"*Shatter.*" He callously dismisses the word as if it were in passing, something so routine and so simple yet whose effects are anything but. Baron splinters as the ice over his chest cracks. First, a single large split from where his hand is. Then, it splinters again and again, rendering what was once a solid fixture of ice into hundreds of cracked pieces. Suddenly, the rest of the chest explodes in fragments as it falls away, leaving a gaping bloodless hole in Baron's chest. There he sits, suspended in time, the inside of his body frozen, looking like a part of a glacial freeze.

"Your attempt at a plan failed. What now, Alexander?"

The figure steps forward, its arm elongating into a single blade-like shape.

"*Arta scrisa: sigiliu!*" Stephen cries as he collapses to the ground. As he does, five runes fly from the page of his open notebook, flying toward the blue being. Four surround him while the fifth attempts to smash into his chest. The figure swings the blade arm, trying to cut the symbol in half. His blade impacts the rune at first but the rune slips over the blade, sliding along his arm and smashing into its shoulder.

"Is that it? Is that all you can do?" The figure swings its blade to the side as the remaining symbols smash into it, covering its body in ink that sloughs off to the ground. It takes another step forward, ice streaming along the ground from its feet, covering it in a near reflective blue ice. Alexander grasps his watch, holding it up. He spits at the figure.

"You will not beat us here, Solomon! *Dilation!*" he cries. Soon, a dark green box surrounds the figure.

"That's Solomon?"

"Yes," he says as the figure slowly morphs more into a replica of my friend, the very same who sat in the chair. His left arm, which holds the blade, is covered in a spiked shoulder piece of armor that runs down to his elbow. A lone rune glows an ominous red as the green from the box begins moving toward it. The figure speeds up with each moment inside the box. As he takes another victorious step, he positions himself beside Bastian's chair. The occupant looks up in shock.

"Solomon ..." he breathes out, causing the being to glance at him in curiosity. The sword arm flashes forward, and I hear a yelp of surprise.

"No!" Bastian looks up at the figure. I scream as the symbol on my chest begins to burn, a searing pain envelops the grooves carved into my flesh. The figure's attention snaps to me as Bastian falls forward from the chair. He looks upward, and I breathe a sigh of relief as Bastian stares up, stupefied.

The being speaks. "Do not be surprised. You stood for me while I was sealed, and for that, I have a debt to clear."

"You ..." the lookalike steps forward as the green fades, and Alexander also drops to one knee.

"What are you?" Alexander snarls at the being as it stops in front of him, raising his blade.

"I am Solomon Helgen, and you will die now."

Then the ink that sloughed to the floor shoots from the ground, bubbling around the blade as it evaporates into the air, leaving the blade unharmed.

"That is your attempt to stop me?" The being grunts in amusement as it stares impassively at Alexander. It brings the sword down, and then it happens. A shattering sound fills the air. The blade in his hand shatters apart, and so does the glossy veneer covering the doppelganger's skin. Beneath it is normal skin.

"What?" Solomon's eyes widen as he looks at the hand in shock, his body trembling as the icy skin begins to flake off.

"It took it long enough," Stephen chokes out along with a wet, gurgling laugh. At this, Solomon's shock turns to anger.

"What did you do!" he roars, rearing his other arm back, allowing a flash of cold. A spear forms in Solomon's arm. His face contorts into pure rage as he thrusts his blade toward Stephen's prone body. A silverish being shoots from the ice, a slim blade in hand, knocking the spear upwards.

Solomon's eyes narrow dangerously as the figure loses its silvery form, leaving a man wearing square glasses and a suit with a red tie. A distinct Hispanic gleam graces his face, with his small trimmed mustache. From his breast pocket sprouts a matching ascot bearing the Prometheus logo.

"It seems the seal worked," he says, tilting his head toward Stephen and Alexander. He casually places a palm onto Stephen's downed body.

"What seal?" Solomon growls, causing the new entry to chuckle.

"Did you really think we would fight you without some way to make you less powerful?"

"Where did you seal them?" He leans into the spear, dipping the saber ever so slightly.

"In a place you will never be able to reach. Forever your power will remain sealed within the Nexus."

"So, you used my power to further secure the locks upon Iglagos?"

"Now you will never be able to teleport there. You will be struck down before you have a chance," he sneers. A movement catches my eye as I see Alexander snake his hand into Stephen's limp one.

"You seem to be under the impression I am on your level."

"What are you talking about?"

"You seem to believe a seal of this magnitude is enough to stop me."

"What?" The grin seems to melt off his face.

"To any of you, I see how this would seal you completely, but to me ... this is but a limit," he says, flexing his other hand as blue begins to encase it.

"That's impossible!"

"No, this is just the vast difference in our strength. I may not be able to utilize all my abilities, but with these ... these will be enough to kill the rest of you." From the side of the room, a man brandishing a large knife leaps into the air.

"Solomon!" He turns, his arm whipping out, catching the arm holding the blade as he spins on one heel. Bringing the spear around, he thrusts it through the assailant's stomach.

"*Invert!*" The unnamed Promethean calls out from the floor as a silverish liquid engulfs the three Prometheans.

"You will not escape me forever. I will find you again, and next time, I will kill you all, whether I am at full power or not," he says as they sink into the floor, the ice cracking as they vanish from view.

"As for you ... I believe it is time for you to experience a fragment of what you did to me. Wouldn't you agree, Jack?" He turns to the body in his hands, a defiant look upon Jack's face.

"Do yer worst, yeh monstah," he spits, sending spittle onto Solomon's face.

"It's funny: until you felt so determined to hurt me, there was no possibility of me being able to do this to you." He thrusts the spear further into Jack's gut, drawing a cry of pain.

"So, I must thank you and your late boss. You both freed me, and for that, I will spare you from what is to come."

"Solomon, don't do it!" I scream, earning his piercing glare.

"You do know what this man did, right?"

161

"It doesn't matter. No one has to die." A weak gurgling chuckle comes from the man's throat.

"The kid's better than you will ever be." He grins at Solomon.

"Perhaps, but you will not be around to see it," he says to Jack.

"Stop!"

"I will not. He will die because if he does not, he will stand in my way again," he says as ice grows over Jack's right chest.

"You wanted to know what kind of monster they see in me?" The ice stops coating his right arm and his right chest.

"I suppose this is where you show me?" Jack says through chattering teeth.

"*Shatter.*" Jack's arm scatters apart into several pieces as he falls limp.

"It appears the seal has taken more from me than I could ever imagine," he says, letting Jack's unconscious body fall to the floor.

"Be grateful their seal stops me this much." He takes a step toward me. *Smash.*

The wall at the back of the room splinters to pieces as a man with a massive sword comes tumbling in with a shorter man, garbed in black.

"Namar, Felgrand! What happened?" Bastian moans as he brings himself to his knees. A heavy thud demands our attention as a gargantuan form enters the dusty entrance. The figure steps forward, revealing an eight-foot-tall behemoth with rounded shoulders, tapering down to a slim waist, then flaring out to powerful sculpted legs. Every bit of the body is covered in black scale-mail armor. The figure held a massive pommel in its hand. An eerie grinding fills the room as it drags a massive blade, much larger than the other man's, into the room. The figure brings the sword up with one hand, allowing me to see it stretch to an unreal size of six feet, pointing it into the room at Solomon.

"The ... key ... is ... here!" the figure snarls as the two who were thrown into the room shuffle to their feet.

Bastian

"Bastian, get to your feet, bud. This fucker showed up and started barreling through anything in its path!" Namar calls out, standing up straight, his swords poised for retaliation. Felgrand scrapes his own sword across the ground as he stands. I eye the being in front of me as it stands in the doorway, observing the room. A moment of silence strikes the room as I look back at Solomon's double. Our eyes meet, and he swiftly turns toward Solaire's groveling form. With each step, the glow on his chest burns brighter.

"Where do you think you are going?" I scream, hefting myself to my knees as Solomon continues a lumbering walk toward Solaire.

"Deal with that being, I have a seal to lift." The clashing of steel drags my attention to see Felgrand lock swords with the massive opponent. Namar runs to flank the beast on its right. The behemoth slams his free hand down on the edge of his blade, his gauntlet-covered hand forcing his blade forward, knocking Felgrand backward.

Namar weaved around him, stabbing forward under the giant's guard. His blade screams forward, impacting the heavy chest plate and merely gliding along it. I see the giant look down at him as if it were a god regarding a petulant child.

"You ... will ... not ... impede ... my ... pursuit," the giant's voice rumbles.

"Damn it all to hell!" I grit my teeth as I drive myself to stand, hobbling forward. I cast one last look to Solomon, our eyes catching once more, a smug smile set upon his face as he grips Solaire by his collar, dragging him from the room.

Turning forward, I have just enough time to register Namar's body careening past me into the far bookcases, his swords flying from his hands. The giant steps forward, its arms poised for a wide, sweeping strike. Pulling out two of my knives, I wait for the blade to descend.

The blade rockets forward, far faster than I imagined, and I barely bring my insignificant daggers into a hasty crisscross to catch the massive weapon. With the force of a freight train, it smashes against my defense. The blades nearly rip from my hands at the impact as they turn inwards.

I feel myself leave the ground. My eyes widen as I am shot backward through the doorway into the far wall.

I spit blood, and my body feels limp as I glare into the room to see the figure stride forward. Barely conscious, I can only look on as the lights begin to fade from the room. I almost miss Felgrand dash to confront the imposing foe, his war cry bringing everything into focus.

A powerful backhanded strike sends Felgrand to his knees. Felgrand shoots me a tired glance as the Pursuer's massive blade rears up, ready to strike him down. I feel my face contort painfully to warn him. At the last second, Felgrand spins, raising his blade in defiance.

Clang.

The sound echoes across the room as he is knocked back down, his sword flying from his grasp. Felgrand shoots upward again, once more with a roar. The figure strikes true: an armored knee flashes out, catching Felgrand in the stomach, sending him half a meter upward. The giant brings his blade's pommel down onto Felgrand, knocking him through the chair holding the ruined pieces of Solomon's fake body. I watch him roll out of sight as Namar comes limping into the hallway, only one rapier in hand.

The massive adversary stalks forward, picking up the chair I have been locked in. Each menacing step takes him closer to us. Namar turns on his heel as the echoing footsteps come closer. He thrusts outwards.

"I got you!" His blade rockets upwards. I see his target: the only vulnerable spot, the eye slits in the helmet. The giant parries it with the chair, sending Namar stumbling back. The giant steps into the hallway, glaring down at Namar as he leaps forward, thrusting for the same target.

I watch in shock as the giant uses the chair to bat him from the air, smashing it to pieces against him, sending Namar right through the doorway into the room where we entered. The giant steps into the hallway. Glancing down the hallway, he steps forward, ignoring me as I follow his gaze, everything growing hazier with each moment. I can barely make out the two shapes of Solomon and Solaire at the end of the hallway.

"So ... lo ... mon." the massive being growls as he steps toward them. Raising the sword in a threatening manner, he pauses for a moment.

"Give ... me ... the ... key," he grunts, taking another step forward.

"Perhaps you should leave things locked, as they should be." A bright blue covers the hazy forms of the two as the giant stops.

"I might have lost most of my abilities, but I can still do this." The big man charges at them, each footfall feeling as if an earthquake has begun.

"Too late," Solomon sings as a snap of his fingers fills the air in that distinct manner that only he can achieve. A shattering sound fills the air as I can no longer see the forms as the massive blade cleaves through where they stand.

"Aaaagggghhhh!" The roar shakes the building as everything finally fades to black.

Ai'hara

"I thought we were supposed to be finding something that could seal someone away, not coming to join the covenant," Valin complains.

I observe the old monastery. Despite how the stone has been overgrown and the building is falling apart, I feel it is more than that. As I look around, the stone path quickly gives way to a simple dirt trail that winds through the sparse trees. The trees stretch farther downhill. I blink, looking over the tree line, spotting a castle sitting in the distance.

"Is that Argentum?" I turn to see Jeffery step through the portal. He waves his hand, and the portal closes behind him.

"Yes, it is." Valin steps closer, gesturing toward the rundown building.

"Why are we here?" I step forward, unease filling my being. I look at the building. The front has two large arch-shaped doors that lay slightly opened inwards. Two large mural windows are positioned on either side. The one on the right has been shattered, and a tree leans on the building.

"We are looking for something that I left here." Jeffery steps forward leading the way.

At the top, resting above the door, sits a circular window. The window itself has eight tresses leading from the edges, all meeting at an apex in the center. The right side of the building has two broken windows pierced by large branches from the surrounding trees. A shift of movement in the window catches my eye, but looking closer, I see the branch swaying in the wind.

"What could possibly help us from this dump?" Theron questions.

"Something or someone?" I speak up, earning a confused look from Theron as he gestures to the building behind him.

"Does this look like anyone has been here?"

Valin speaks, glancing back as he does so. "Looks can be deceiving."

"Wise words, but there should not be anyone here." Jeffery hobbles forward, taking the lead, one hand clutching his wounds, motioning us to follow.

"Every minute counts," he urges as he approaches the open doors. I follow him, followed by the others. Jeffery stumbles as his foot catches a root growing through a long red carpet leading down the center of the room to a set of closed doors, much like the ones we just passed through. On either side of the room stand pillars supporting a second-floor terrace that overlooks the center of the room. To the right, a rotten staircase leads upwards, while the other side has a door farther down the corridor, near the corner.

Jeffery follows the path, each step an awkward hobble as he strides toward the door. Reaching the door, he pauses, catching his breath. Without looking back, Jeffery pushes the doors open, stumbling into a prayer room. Pews line the room, moving forward toward a pulpit in the center of the room with something resting upon it. A once-majestic tapestry, now worn and faded, hangs behind it. He stops, enthralled with the pew. I step closer, staring at the pulpit. The object in question is a box.

The box itself is coated in a golden sheen and is encrusted with many jewels of various kinds. The faint light in the room hits the box, causing it to glisten like treasure.

"Is that what we need?" Theron breathes, his voice barely audible from the shock.

"Yes, it is." He steps up to the pulpit, shuffling to the side so we can get closer. A shimmer catches my eye, upon closer inspection, I gasp. Inscribed on the golden exterior are millions of symbols. Each of them is so light and tiny, they can be mistaken for scratches. The characters themselves are a congregation of different runes and symbols; however, they are unique among themselves, none repeating itself across the box's surface. A small even crack runs along the edge of the box, as if it has been opened.

"You finally came for the box."

A flash of heat springs up behind me, making me jump. I wheel to see Valin glaring off to the side of the room, a fireball in his left hand.

"Jeffery, I thought you said this place was empty!" he roars. Trailing his gaze, I see a feminine figure sitting in the last pew, right against the pillar, barely visible due to the mottled gray cloak draped over her.

"It is supposed to be! No one should know what is here!" he retorts.

"I am greatly disappointed in you, Jeffery," She speaks softly, each word clearly audible despite the low timbre of her voice.

"Me, why?"

"You thought you could steal from me."

"I have done no such thing."

"Then tell me why one of my boxes lies on that pulpit?" She pulls her hood back, revealing a ponytail with long dark hair and firm feminine features. Upon her head lies a golden circlet.

"Who are you? Speak now, or I will incinerate you!" Valin orders. She stands from the pew.

He gasps as he stumbles backward. "Pandora."

"Wait. As in Pandora's box—that Pandora?" Theron rears back, paling.

She nods in affirmation. "One and the same."

I feel the color drain from my face as well. I kneel in her direction, my knees driving down into the ground, my face studying the stone floor.

"It would seem one of you remembers the ways of old," she says approvingly.

"I do not care who you are. We are going to stop Prometheus! We need this box to do it! So just crawl back to where you came from, and you won't get hurt!" Valin growls. I wince, looking up to meet her gaze, once carefree but becoming much colder.

"You have a lot of nerve, pyromancer. Tell me, why should I not simply lock you all into the box that you have sought?" The flame in Valin's hand roars into a mighty fireball.

"You won't be able to."

"Valin, cool it! We don't want to fight her." Theron's frightened voice breaks the tension as Jeffery steps forward.

"Even if you did, you wouldn't stand a chance," he says, glaring at Pandora.

"We need this to stop the plagues on this world." A laugh erupts from her.

"The very same evil that you yourself let out of that very box?" I look up at him, seeing a grim expression on Jeffery's face.

"What did she just say?" Theron sets down Yukio in the pew to his side before whipping around, grasping a handful of Jeffery's coat.

"You released the dark times upon us?"

"It was a mistake—"

"You broke into my storage. You took one of my boxes. You opened it because of one of your damned humanistic traits," Pandora scolds.

"Humanistic traits?" I chirp.

"He opened it out of curiosity— after I told everyone that to do so would condemn the world." She steps forward with a morose expression. A lone tear slips down the left side of her face, glittering in the light.

"Wait … did you say there is more than one box?" Valin inquires, to which she nods.

"We were lucky he released the one that he did. There are several worse beings than the one he brought forth." She speaks calmly, keeping her gaze on Jeffery. He raises his head with a defiant gleam in his eye.

"I intend to rectify my mistake," he growls, and she raises a hand, gesturing toward the box.

"And you plan to do so by using the very box you opened?"

"Of course! I will fix this!" he roars.

"Who did you release?" I question, looking between Pandora and Jeffery. He puts his head down, and his lip twitches a few times as he refuses to make eye contact with me.

"Who did you release, Durgess?" I ask.

"Tell them, or I will," Pandora orders.

"What difference does it make? It could have been any of the lost

mythical creatures from the fae to a god. I will seal him back, anyway."
Pandora's godlike aura pulses, and a wave of air rushes through the room.

"He is the one to release the bringer of calamities, the one who holds the key to the true king."

"What do you mean? Who is she talking about, Jeffery?" Valin demands, the flame blazing.

"She is talking about ..." He pauses, his lip twitching upward in disgust once more. Pandora scoffs.

"Strong in the shadows but craven in the light. How typical of a thief."

"I am no thief!" he roars. Pandora ignores him, addressing the rest of us.

"He released Solomon Helgen."

Solaire

The world shatters into shards of glass. Then we are in a courtyard. I am facing the same stone walls. Pillars support a walkway above us, which seems to overlook a garden in the middle. Tall bushes frame a walkway that surrounds the courtyard. A cough drags my attention to a tall cascading multi level fountain. Sitting on the edge, fingers laced together is a man wearing a two-piece suit with a purple tie. Around his neck lies a purple collar that puffs out, looking like a royal prince. I swallow hard. If things were consistent, every person wearing a suit so far would be part of Prometheus.

"I took a gamble, you know," he says, gesturing to the side, where the pristine grass is covered in blood. Differently clothed bodies lie strewn about. I count five from here. He looks up, and I see the symbol embossed upon his handkerchief, a spatter of blood across the front of his suit.

"What kind of gamble?" I ask as Solomon casually steps forward. He stands up, his arms spread wide to appear grandiose.

"I felt that spike of power, and I had the devil's instinct to rig all spatial distortions to land right here." The man made a circular gesture. "As you see, you were not the first. So, I patiently waited for you to show up."

"So, you saw what I did to Stephen and Alexander?" The smile runs away from his face as he cocks his head, eliciting Solomon to continue.

"They had someone emerge from the ice on the floor. If I am not mistaken, he used it as a medium to open a door." A dark look covers his face as he scowls to the side and mumbles something.

"You didn't know?" I ask, causing him to snap his head back to me.

"It doesn't matter. After I am through here, then I will have to talk about why they did appear." A wave of cold air hits me as a blade of ice forms in Solomon's hand.

"Solaire, step back. Let me take care of him really quick." The man perches an eyebrow as I comply, stepping behind the pillar into an empty hallway.

"Daring, are you not? Do you really think you can kill me?" Solomon sounds almost amused. "You don't know what happened to the last group, do you?"

"What are you talking about?" the Promethean inquires.

"I butchered your little group once with ease. What makes you think I can't kill you now?" Solomon speaks in a callous tone that makes me cringe.

"I am Carter Cúchulainn! I am above the rest! I am a god among men! I am a Promethean!" He bellows as he stomps forward. Solomon sighs as he dashes forward, bringing the blade down, intent on bisecting Carter. Carter raises his hand, angling it outwards with his palm outstretched as if he is going to catch the blade. At the last minute, the blade crashes against something. Sparks rain over them as Solomon's blade grinds off a hardened surface. Solomon swings again as Carter seems to dance around the swing and bat away the follow-up, another spray of sparks erupting from some unseen contact. Carter laughs, a dull laugh devoid of humor.

"You really aren't much without your powers, are you?"

Solomon growls as he steps back, a dull blue covering his being. Searing pain fills my chest as I crumble against the pillar I am hiding against. I look down to see the mark glowing a bright blue.

"I may not have all of my strength, but I am far from powerless."

Solomon raises his hand as he speaks. I scream as Solomon sweeps his arm forward, a wave of ice cascading toward Carter. He rolls to the side, using the fountain as cover, letting the ice shoot past him, where it collides with the wall on the far end, freezing it.

"It is apparent that you are not as powerless as I am led to believe," Carter says, nodding toward the frozen wall.

"That is exactly what they said." Solomon smiles as he leaps toward Carter. Carter brings his arm up, blocking the blow and pushing it to the side with his left hand. He thrusts his right forward. At an impossible angle, Solomon bends out of the way.

"Checkmate," Carter hisses as a rippling distortion appears in the air above Solomon's chest. From it, the tip of a spear emerges just before it shoots forward. Solomon sheds his skin like before, leaving the shell. He spins out the back of it, blade in hand. He turns it around in a reverse grip as the spear stabs through the upper torso of his former shell; after impact, spikes erupt from the torso of the figurine, shattering it to pieces.

Solomon continues his turning thrust. Carter slaps it away with his right hand as his left snatches the spear from the figurine's broken body. He jabs forward, and another surge of pain wracks my chest as Solomon skips backward, raising his left hand and pointing at him. A blue light springs to life on his index finger.

"*Bolt.*"

Carter stumbles as a blast of blue shoots into his chest. A sprout of blood erupts from his back as though he has been shot. He stumbles back a step. A small bloody hole coated in frost adorns his chest as he coughs once. Blood dribbles down his chin from the corner of his mouth.

"You think that will kill me!" He stumbles forward with another spear shooting into his other hand. A huge wet cough shakes his body and he spits blood onto the ground as he thrusts the spears forward. Another blade of ice forms in Solomon's right hand as he knocks the spears aside. He steps forward, stabbing them both into Carter's gut. Solomon brings his ear next to Carter's.

"You underestimated me." He twists the blade, causing Carter to twinge in pain before he drops his spears, catching Solomon in a bear hug.

"You think I am finished?" Carter screams as two more ripples surround Solomon. From each of them, a spearhead emerges. Solomon looks back in shock as they launch forward.

"Die!" Solomon turns back, and his expression of shock morphs into a cruel smile. He ducks and slides out from the legs of his body into a roll as the spears pierce through the figurine and into his own chest.

He falls backward as spines erupt from the spears protruding from his chest in a shower of gore. Shock permeates his face as he falls backward, the spears dissolving into nothing as his corpse settles, his head tilting to the side as he stills.

The burning pain subsides as Solomon strides over to me, an exhausted air about him. He winces as he sees the condition I am in.

"Damn you, Pandora," he growls, looking at the wound.

"Who is that?" I wheeze out, my vision blurry from unshed tears.

"The bitch who sealed me away. Apparently, she felt it necessary to curse me as well," he snarls.

"Curse?"

"When did that mark appear on you?"

"Yesterday, when I was at the Glade, I learned about magic from the Watchers."

He blinks at that. "The timing is right; however, when this is over, you must tell me how that happened."

"Sure, but what do you mean by the timing?" Solomon merely tugs his tattered clothes away from his chest, revealing many nasty cuts, but in the center, he bears the same mark as mine!

"They etched this into my chest as a torture method, and I would venture to guess that our bodies are linked. It seems using my powers strains your body as well as if I take damage. You seem to feel it too."

"But why?"

"More than likely to discourage my involvement in this reality by endangering you." I feel my face scrunch in confusion.

"Aren't you the bad guy?" He sighs exasperatedly as he kneels by my side, putting a hand on my shoulder.

"They all think I am the bad guy because I am the only one who has the guts to do what is necessary to save the world!" He jabs himself in the chest with his thumb.

"Save the world? Didn't you destroy this one?" Solomon scoffs.

"I fought against beings that were godlike. Collateral damage is unavoidable in such battles. That is why I have to save the world."

"Why haven't the others done anything?"

"They lack the mind to understand that the Second Reality is collateral to save the first." His words are full of conviction as he speaks like a charmer.

"Collateral? This whole world is collateral?" A gleam enters Solomon's eye.

"Yes, I will save it by collapsing the gateway between our worlds. Everything that has happened to your world is a result of this one. Can't you see it? The solution is to remove the danger of this one."

"You would be killing an entire reality's worth of people!"

"You may think that is evil and makes me the bad guy, but I am the only thing standing between what real evil is and our world." He snaps his hand, causing a familiar burn to enter my chest, causing me to wince as a box of ice forms around us.

"Where are we going?" I ask him warily.

"Iglagos—that is where they keep my power."

"Why would you go there? They told you where it is. It has to be a trap!" He nods.

"It most certainly is a trap."

"Then why do you need your power so bad?"

"That group, those Prometheans, will stop at nothing until they have either sealed me away or killed me. With how easily this fool found me, it will not be long before his royal pain-in-the-ass has his entourage come after me. Don't ask." Solomon gives me a pointed look as he snaps his fingers and the world shatters once more.

Bastian

"... up."

I am being shaken. Groggily I open my eyes. Everything is blurry as a figure steps into my view. A rumble echoes across the hallway.

"Wake up." He shakes me harder this time, looking back down the hallway.

"We have to go." Felgrand limps through the door frame, his longsword hanging off his back. I sit up, observing the room. A cry of pain erupts from nearby.

"What happened?" The hallway we sit in is intact; however, the end lies in ruins. Large scars within the boards trail down toward them, where the double doors lie carved into pieces.

"I think that big guy went after them but couldn't catch them." An explosion sounds from the room at the end of the hall. Namar tugs me to my feet.

"It seems that he is single-handedly ripping this place apart to find them." Reaching the end of the hallway, we stack up to the left side.

"Gggrrrr!" A loud growl penetrates the wall as a heavy thud crashes down upon the floor. Peering around the door, I see an office with the hulking behemoth in the center of it. His blade held out to his side, dripping with blood, his other hand braced at his side. My eyes dart around, detecting movement. There are three, each dressed in leather armor, scarlet bandanas across their faces. Each of them holds a sword and a wooden shield that appears to be made from the top of a barrel. Each of them is evenly spaced out, forming an encompassing hemisphere around the giant.

"Where ... is ... Solomon?" he grumbles. Each of the soldiers flinches before the one on the left dashes forward, raising his shield in front of him. With a war cry, the others follow. The giant waves his massive weapon in an almost unnoticeable wind-up. The soldier drops his shield to the side as he thrusts forward.

A shift of movement as the blade tears through his exposed arm in a blur. His blood sprays as his eyes widen, his blade clanging on the floor as he falls back. Next, the central soldier grasps his sword in a two-handed overhead swing. He never sees the left hand come up. It smashes into the side of his head, gripping it in a massive palm and dragging him down. With a spinning thrust downward, his head is smashed into the wooden floor, where his body goes limp.

The last soldier steps close, bringing his own sword down at the massive soldier's opening. The sound of metal meeting metal fills the air as the short sword slams down hard onto the exposed shoulder of the kneeling giant. A massive gauntlet flies up and clamps down on the hand that holds the sword against his armor. Several emotions fly over the soldier's face—shock, fear, and then despair—as the giant stands, picking the soldier up.

"Where ... is ... Solomon?" the giant repeats. The soldier scrunches his face as a loud cracking sound fills the air.

"Aaaggghhh!" he screams as his sword slips from his grip, falling into the floor.

"You won't get anything from me!" the man sneers, causing the giant to tilt its ironclad helmet. His massive sword shoots up. It rams right through the captured man, straight to the hilt. The man slumps forward onto the blade.

"You bastard!" a voice yells out from the left side of the room, dragging our attention to the first soldier to go down. Now with only one arm, he slowly picks himself up. The giant flicks his sword off to the right. The impaled body goes flying from it, slamming into the wall before crumpling into a grotesque pile.

The giant stomps toward the man. He stands tall, his shield crossed in front of him, clasping over his missing arm. The sword flashes up with the intent of crashing down on the man. A second passes, and the blade comes screaming downwards. The man steps sideways, bringing his shield to intercept the blow. The wooden shield does not even slow the blade down as it slices cleanly down the middle.

An armored leg shoots forward, smashing into his chest and sending him through the window behind him with a crash. He stalks forward, closer to the window, when a blue light pulses across his gauntlet.

The giant stops, looking down at his gauntlet intently. A blue orb coalesces over the glowing gauntlet before it shoots toward us. I duck against the wall, pressing myself to it with the others as a blue orb flashes past us down the corridor.

The massive figure barrels into the hallway, its massive sword anchoring it as he slides to the side, nearly ripping the floor cleanly in two. He goes shooting after the light, each massive stride leading him down the hallway in a massive bound, missing us completely. The imprint of his shoe is marked on the floor as his footsteps sound more distant. I let out a breath I have been holding as I turn to the others.

"We have to follow it," I declare, feeling my anger demanding action. Namar runs a hand through his hair before gesturing down the hall.

"Are you mad? We heard the results of what happened in that other room."

"The boy is right, rogue. If we do not follow it, then we cannot know what has gotten its attention."

"Syndicate is over, and this place has been destroyed," I speak up, patting Namar on the shoulder as I jog forward, following the boot indents in the floor. A single pair of footsteps follow me.

"God damn it!" Namar shouts before I hear another pair join in. I turn into the doorway where the behemoth went and see a grisly sight. Bodies litter the hallway; weapons lie broken and strewn about as the bodies of Syndicate's finest lie dead. A cleaved path through the hallway as more screams erupt from deeper down the hallway, where a pair of double doors sits in pieces, just like in the office. Dashing forward, I make it to the next set of doors and peek through just in time for a body to crash through a banister, slamming into the wall next to me.

The body embeds into the wall with dull eyes. I grit my teeth before stepping forward. Looking over the banister, I see the giant cleave through two more soldiers. It shoots forward, running its sword through another like a lance. Crashing through another door, I see the three remaining soldiers dash after it.

"Damn, this guy can run," Namar rasps as we run through the next door, entering a courtyard. The air grows colder, and I see a wall with a film of ice on it, the blue orb floating in front of it.

A triumphant roar echoes the courtyard as two more soldiers step between the massive being and the wall.

"Why are we not fighting it?" Felgrand questions, his own broadsword in his hands.

"Do you think we can take that thing down?" Namar questions, gesturing toward it as a soldier runs his blade down the armored back of the massive assailant.

"We have to try! We cannot let it do what it wants. Besides, it is after Solomon. If those two go toe to toe, I don't even want to think of the consequences the land could sustain." I shoot forward, pulling my knives from their holsters as the giant swings his blade, tossing the body from it into another rushing guard. He pivots on one foot bringing his sword up in a discrete manner as he turns to meet another soldier.

I jump, kicking off the soldier, knocking him back. He lets out a cry of anger as he falls to the ground. I bring my blades into a Cross block, catching the massive blade into the notch I make. I feel the crushing blow knock me down as I barely maneuver myself out of the path of the deadly blade. The blade cleaves the ground, slashing through stone as if it were paper. His helmet twitched as his attention fixated on me.

A twitch of his arm is the only warning as another swing comes at me. I hit the ground, feeling the air woosh above me.

"Who are you?" I cry out, my knives deflecting another large swing as he pushes closer to the wall.

"I ... am ... the ... Pursuer!" it roars, slashing sideways. He catches another soldier in the ribs, bringing the soldier down.

"I ... will ... get ... the key!" the behemoth bellows, grasping his blade with two hands for the first time. A dark glow covers the blade as he brings the sword around to meet one of the soldiers who has moved behind him. The man brings his sword up to block the blow. The massive cleaver doesn't stop for a moment. Passing through the short sword like butter, it screams forward, ripping the man in two.

A female soldier dashes forward, armed with two axes. She throws the first. It flies straight, knocking into the helmet of the massive being. The head moves an inch to the side as it turns to glare at the Syndicate soldier.

All of us dart forward in an attempt to overwhelm it. Our blades drawn, I see the wicked broadsword shoot forward. Namar ducks in front of the blow, his twin rapiers shrouded in darkness. He catches the massive sword in a cross-block, the darkness from each rapier coiling together. The giant's surprise is evident as he stops moving.

"You ... wield ... the ... shadows?" it grunts in confusion. His confusion turns into anger as the woman he is covering smashes her ax into the backside of his knee, causing it to buckle.

I jump, brandishing two daggers. I catch his neck, causing him no trouble as he supports my weight. The daggers scrape against the armor. I grit my teeth as I hold on. From the corner of my eye, the female warrior and Felgrand rush forward. The warrior slashes her ax against the giant's hand that holds his sword. The sword rattles against Namar's and rises, but another one smashes his own blade on its tip. The huge sword is knocked downwards, stabbing into the ground. Namar dashes, emerging under the giant's arm, and slashes against his other knee. A resounding screech echoes across the hall, and the giant falls to his other knee.

"Now!" Namar screams as he positions to hold the arm that holds the blade back, using the giant's body as a brace. Thudding footsteps bring my attention over the giant's shoulder.

Felgrand comes rushing forward. His sword is parallel to his face as he charges. A war scream booms as he jumps and he raises his shining blade above his head. He brings the massive blade downward, and a flash emanates from the glowing blade as the crash echoes across the room. The grinding of metal quickly becomes a twisting sound as everything goes silent as the head rolls forward.

Peering over his shoulder, I see that the massive blade has sunk into the breastplate of our captive. *It cut through the armor!* A smile graces my face as I look at Felgrand and meet his gaze. A triumphant smile contagiously spread to his own. I loosen my grip on the giant's neck before I look at the blade once more, and my heart sinks.

There is no blood on the blade, not even a single drop. I feel the shuffle of the armor before I see it. The giant's left arm strikes with the speed of a cobra sending a left hook into Felgrand's face, sending him flipping backward before clutching Felgrand's blade in his chest. I reach up, clutching my dagger, and drive it down onto the plated helmet. My blade scratches down the side of it harmlessly as sparks shower from its path. The sound of twisting metal fills the air once more as the giant shoots his head back, catching me in my own with a head butt.

I fall backward, my grip faltering as I slam into the ground. The giant is already moving. He twists to his left, and Felgrand's blade goes sailing into the Syndicate woman with the ax, spearing her to the ground. Her ax spins in the air toward the giant from the impact. His now empty hand snaps out, snatching the ax. Two soldiers stand atop of his blade poised, ready to stop him. The colossus turns to his right, swinging the weapon at the two standing atop his broadsword. One ducks, rolling toward the left, the other brings his blade to stop the ax. The blades collide and the smaller sword is pushed into the soldier's own neck..

The Pursuer wrenches his right arm forward, throwing Namar rolling in the dirt. As he comes to a stop on his knees, I get to my own as the now-free right arm draws the blade from the ground in front of him.

The soldier that rolled to dodge the ax gets up from the ground charging the giant's exposed left side, and I let out a cry of warning. The giant reaches across his body, clutching his massive claymore with two hands. He draws it across his body and slashes in a horizontal arc.

The soldier brings her remaining ax up in the nick of time. The massive blade strikes the short ax in the center, and for a moment, it stops. I smile at her reflexes as I grip my knives again, then an unholy sound drains what hope I have for her. The sound of metal shattering is the only warning I hear as the massive blade cleaves right through the soldier, but the blade doesn't stop there. The Pursuer follows through, pivoting on his heel. The blade comes careening toward me. I bring my knives up in a hasty reverse grip block. The force is too much as the blade catches my own. It carries my own across my body as I feel the cold hard steel slash across my chest.

Pain engulfs me as I lose my knives. They fly from my hands somewhere as I fall backward, blood spilling from a massive cut across my upper torso.

"You bastard!" Namar screams as I glance up, struggling to see past the Pursuer. He turns on a heel sending a wide arcing slash. As he sees who it is, he adjusts so that the flat of the blade slams into his chest. He tumbles across the floor several times, coming to a rest against the pillar to the left of the frozen wall. His blades are tumbling out of reach. The giant steps forward, his heavy footfalls echoing across the open pavilion.

I look around as the colossus steps closer to Namar, his blade once more at his side.

"Damn ..." I grumble out as I look around at everyone who has been defeated with such ease. Turning back to Namar, I see him give me a glance as he rests against the pillar, one arm over his chest, the other resting against the pillar. He gestures in a come-here movement. I cock my head as the giant nears him. He does it much more fervently this time. He nods to his blade that rests between us.

So, that is what he wants.

I raise my arm, trying to paw at the stone to turn, each movement agonizing as I pull my head from the ground. I reach for it, but I can't drag myself forward. It hurts to move. I look back up to the Pursuer. He is now only steps away!

I reach into my pocket, pulling two more of my knives. I grasp them in between the knuckles of my left hand, and I rear back. There is only one chance. This is it. I gulp as the Pursuer takes another step. I let the first fly and hold the second for just a moment longer. They both fly through the air. The first smacks its target. The helmet is knocked forward as the dull crash of metal echoes. He turns toward me, an irritatingly slow movement as the second blade is almost there! The blade nears the crack in the helmet. Then, just before it strikes, a metallic gauntlet rises up, knocking the blade to the ground, where it bounces once, landing right next to Namar.

"I ... will ... not ... be ... stopped!" he roars as he turns back to Namar. I watch the knife vanish into the shadows as Namar raises his hand, placing it against the ground in front of the Pursuer.

"Figured we couldn't stop you after that last display," he grunts, a smile gleaming on his face.

"What?"

"That is why we have to settle with something else ..." Namar trails off.

"Nonsense ... what ... goal?" The giant turns, taking a step toward the wall.

"Stalling you! *Chakraveer!*" The shadows surround the Pursuer as they billow before launching copies of the blade at him from various angles. Multiple blades screech against the armor as all but one fade into shadows after bouncing across his armor. The last blade arcs down after clattering uselessly against the Pursuer's armor.

The giant roars as his free hand snatches the dagger from its descent and rams it through Namar's shoulder, pinning him to a pillar. Namar lets loose a pained grunt as he grits his teeth.

"Just do it already!"

"You … are … of … the … shadow … your … time … is … far," the Pursuer grumbles as he turns to the frozen wall. One swipe opens it up and reveals an open courtyard with a broken fountain in the center. My eyes met Namar's own as he grasps the knife in his shoulder. A loud roar pierces the air as he scans back and forth.

"Gone!" the Pursuer screams, catching my attention. The first thing that catches my attention is the blood that covers the grass and in the center of it is a body. His face lies facing toward us. My breath hitches as I recognize the bloody face looking toward us.

"Well fuck me sideways," Namar growls. "Some bastard took my kill."

The body belonged to a Prometheus member, none other than the one that I fought before I left the Syndicate, the one that took my knives: Carter Cúchulainn. Carter was strewn out like a ragdoll, his face set in a lone trail of blood leading from his mouth down to his neck, a surprised look etched onto his face.

The Pursuer steps into the courtyard, marching toward the body. He stops at the fallen Promethean, staring down before snarling. His boot snaps out, catching the body underneath the jaw, sending it flying at the fountain. Carter's body smashes against the fountain, flopping downwards into the water with a splash. The Pursuer grasps his blade with two hands as he cleaves the fountain in two with a war cry.

It slowly slides apart as he clutches the massive sword with both hands. Holding it in front of his view for a moment, he stares into the blade as if looking for something. After a moment, his shoulders sag forward, and he brings the blade around and over in an overhead swing. A grunt of effort escapes him as a black line trails where his blade cut. As if the very air is cut, it drapes apart. A thin black line contrasts the bright sunny courtyard. The line bulges in the middle before expanding into a dark hemisphere. Pure blackness blocks out the light as he steps into it, snarling one last line.

"I ... failed ...your Majesty ... I ... will... not ... stop. The ... hunt ... continues." His broken speech is fixed as his form becomes one with the darkness. Then the makeshift door closes back into a black slit. It hovers in the air as it slowly gets smaller, eventually closing, leaving no sign of it being there at all.

CHAPTER 11

PREPARATION

Ai'hara

"You released Solomon Helgen?" I stand, stepping away from him as Jeffery looks down dejectedly. He pushes the glasses further onto his nose, raising his head, sighing.

"It was a job. I was paid to find the box."

"Told to find the box?" Pandora's question brings my attention back to her. Pandora's form flickers out of view. Then I hear a sudden sound of static and an intake of breath. I turn to see her standing right in front of Jeffery, staring right into his eyes.

"*Burn!*" Valin screams, punching out, his frame coated in flames, but she does not take her eyes from Jeffery. The flaming arm smashes against something in the air. A golden bubble glows around her. She raises her arms, bringing the palms to face each other, fingers curled inward. A blue line connects each digit to the others. She turns her hands, one clockwise and the other counterclockwise, as she shifts her hands so that the left one is moving to the bottom from the top.

Between her fingers, a shape is forming. As her hands stop moving, a miniature box is floating in between them. She gracefully plucks it up with the tips of her thumb and index finger. Valin stumbles backward, making room as she tosses it at him. He leaps backward, letting it fly over his face before it glows aquamarine. Then the box expands, absorbing

Valin into it, leaving only a surprised yelp as it falls to the ground. It clatters, falling against a stone where the glow dies down.

"As I was saying, you were instructed to find the box?"

"Yeah, I was." She waves her hand in the air, and suddenly we are in a hallway with shelves adorning the sides, the box we found resting on the pulpit standing proudly in the hallway behind Jeffery. The shelves go on for what could only be miles. On each shelf, there lie boxes, all plated in gold but with different gem patterns and symbols adorning them. On the right, I notice a gap between two of the boxes.

"Out of every one of the boxes I have here, how did you know to take that one?"

"Where are we?" Theron gasps, looking up and down the corridor.

"You are within a place many have only dreamed to reach, and of those, only a handful have managed to get inside." Pandora tilts her head, staring at Jeffery. He maintains his own look in retaliation.

"This is Pandora's vault."

"How did you bring us here and use those spells without an incantation?" I ask curiously. She smirks as she glances at me out of the corner of her eye.

"Any being that possesses the right understanding and power can forgo the incantation for a spell." Her face loses all its mirth as she looks back at Jeffery.

"Enough evading the question. Tell me how you knew to take this box."

"I was given the means to track it." Her eyes narrow.

"What do you mean?"

"My employer at the time gave me a gauntlet that let me summon a blue orb that would follow the source. I never knew how it worked, but it brought me right here. The gauntlet dissolved once I got the box though."

"How did you get inside?" she asks, her expression darkening with each word.

"They gave me an image of this room."

"No one could possibly know what this looks like," she growls.

"Someone did, and they were able to help me get here."

"Who is your employer?"

"He only spoke from the darkness and only gave me a title as his name."

"Who is it?"

"He claimed to be the Harbinger." With that, she takes a step back, her anger extinguished and concentration disrupted. The room flickers away, leaving us back in the church once more. Theron rolls his eyes.

"That isn't a name. That's a title."

"Who is this Harbinger?" I ask the obvious question.

"We don't have time for this," Jeffery growls. He jabs his finger toward Pandora. "We need to get this box, and we need to stop both Solomon and Prometheus. I do not care who this Harbinger is. I need to fix what I messed up." Her face contorts, restraining frustration, and she snaps her fingers. Theron flinches as a thud echoes beside us, and Valin is lying on the ground, the cube he was in now gone.

"The Harbinger knows that a box is empty. You have to hurry. Find Solomon and recapture him."

"Why should we do that? You locked me in a box. Can you not do the same to him?" Valin says in a rage.

"I cannot because I am limited to making a box for each being once, and the more powerful a being is, the longer it would take for me to use the construct to contain them—time I cannot spend away from the vault."

"Why not? If he is such a threat, we need your help."

"While that is true, the world would be in far more danger if any of the other beings are released."

"Fine, let us take the box, and then we will end this." Her eyes narrow once more.

"Do you take me to be a fool?" she growls as Jeffery reaches for the box on the pulpit. As his hand grasps it, the box turns intangible, letting his hand slide through it.

"We need this!" He turns a scowl, marring his face.

"The only way you get that box is if you give up the powers you used to take it in the first place." My eyes widen.

"Why do you need to do that if you can make the boxes intangible?"

"I can only do that to the boxes that I can see."

185

"What bullshit is this? You want to take the powers from someone that you are asking for help?" Valin says, exasperated.

"That is the deal so as to prevent any more beings from being released ever again." Jeffery runs a hand through his hair as he turns back and forth. Pacing, he turns suddenly and kicks the pulpit with a cry of anger. He turns, jabbing his finger at Pandora.

"Fine! But if we fail because I cannot use my powers, then this is on you!" he roars, causing a triumphant smirk to cross Pandora's face.

"Jeffery, this is but a taste of the rage I felt when the box was opened. Now I must return to the vault, grab the box, and it will take your powers." She points to the box. Its golden exterior glows brighter.

"You will get yours, Pandora," he growls, taking the box, the gold coursing over his arm as he lets out a bellowing scream before he stumbles to his knees, the box in his hands. Pandora nods her head at him.

"However, you are correct. In taking your powers, I have weakened you, so I will compensate for that." She walks to Yukio's unconscious body, bending down and placing her hand on her shoulder. A soft golden glow envelops her as Pandora stands once more, Theron already at Yukio's side as Pandora steps away.

"What did you do?" I ask warily. She looks as if she is about to speak when Theron gasps.

"Thank you!" Pandora nods to him as I see that the burn is now completely gone.

"You are welcome." She turns to Jeffery's prone figure.

"The contract has been completed. Now, fix your mistake," she orders as she flickers out of view.

"Wait!" he screams, but it is too late. She is gone.

"Fuck!" he screams, slamming his hand on the floor.

"What is the matter? We have the box." I shake my head, confused.

"Yes, but we do not know where to go. We don't know where Solomon is!" he retorts no sooner than a wave of pressure crashes upon me, forcing me to the ground. I fall first, and the others follow, smashing into the ground next to me.

"What is this?" Jeffery cries as he struggles to move, the cube clutched in his hand on the ground before him. I try to lift my arm or move my body, but it feels as if I am underneath a thousand pounds of water.

"Do not worry. You don't need to know where Solomon is." We all struggle to look at the doorway.

"Who are you?" Valin spits, his head an inch from the ground in defiance. I finally turn my head to see an unknown figure. Wearing a beige suit with a maroon tie, matching handkerchief and buttoned shirt underneath, he stands in the doorway for a moment, both hands clasped behind his back. His face has scales at its edges, and his sclera are black. The pupils themselves are milky white. He strides forward, walking in a strange manner, ignoring Valin, almost as if he is dancing. He would take a step with his left and bring his right foot to meet it before doing so again. He repeats this but leads with his right foot, bringing his left to meet his right.

"I asked you who you are!" A flame burns into light in his palm. The man continues walking, a smug expression on his face. He stops in front of Jeffery, his eyes leering down in what appears to be amusement.

"To think that you would know where to get one of her boxes." He brings his foot next to Jeffery's outstretched arm.

"Who I am is of no consequence to you," he says as he kneels closer to Jeffery, looking him in the eyes.

"You have no idea how happy it will make me to rub your failure in your face once more." Jeffery's eyes widen as he struggles on the floor.

"Mikhael, you bastard!"

"So you do remember me." He chuckles as he cocks his head to better see his face.

"*Burn.*"

The heat soars forward as the light reflects across the man's face. A look of mock surprise crosses his face as he leaps backward. The fireball brushes past his shoulder as the man raises his left hand to eye level. His face loses all mirth as he regards Valin, tilting his head to look down at him.

"You have no manners." Then he parts his lips, his tongue moving to the edge of his teeth as he looks down in pity. Then he snaps his fingers. "*Flux.*"

With that word, Valin cries out in agony as the ground around him splinters as he sinks into it. The even bricks splinter apart, crushed as Valin seems to press deeper into them.

"Stop!" I speak out against Mikhael, a condescending smile spreading across his scaled cheeks.

"Stop, but why?"

"You don't have to do this," I say softly. Mikhael's face softens contemplatively. Then it darkens just as swiftly.

"You all prance around so grandiloquently like you all have some form of righteous task to change the world," he spits.

"We do!" The man centers his look on Jeffery again, shaking his head lightly, his eyebrows rising in mock pity. He brings his foot onto Jeffery's hand, letting it sit there loosely.

"No, only those with power have the right to change the world." He leans forward, pressing his weight onto Jeffery's hand, grinding his heel. He grunts in pain as the cube clatters just out of his clutches. The man slowly reaches for the cube. Clutching it, he nods his head toward Jeffery.

"This is mine now," he replies, leering at Jeffery with sadistic glee. As he stands up, he twists his heel in one last imperious manner. He strides down the hallway, resuming his stride away from us.

"Where are you going?" Valin coughs from the gravel. The man stops, glancing over his shoulder.

"It really doesn't concern you, but if you want to see the show, then who am I to deny?" he says, turning around and walking to the doorway.

"Is this a game to you?" Theron snarls.

"No, but letting you see the shift of the world and watching the looks of despair as if you can do nothing? Now that ... that will make any other game feel inadequate," he calls out as he strides through the doorway.

"The show will start at Iglagos," He yells back at us. Then the pressure dissipates.

Solaire

The air is brisk as the inside of the courtyard shatters into a harsh green surrounding. Shaking my head, I glance around. Trees close around us as dense bushes guard the sight of anything else. Another wave of pain hits me, causing the world to shift uncomfortably. I step down, catching myself only to hear a crunch fill the air. I blink, looking down to see a patch of ice surrounding both Solomon's and my feet. Everything around us flashes frozen. Solomon steps forward, each footstep sliding over the ice.

"Where are we?" He keeps his attention focused on the tree line, stopping at the edge of the ice we landed on.

"We are almost at Iglagos."

"Why not just take us there?" He takes another step forward, ice rushing forward to meet where his foot would fall.

"Prometheus will be awaiting closer to the city itself. If I am correct, then the power supplied by the seal that holds my power will probably do more than just alert the city to intruders."

"Why does that matter? I came here to rescue you! Why not just leave?"

"Such a simplistic mindset. Do you really believe that this group will just let me go?"

"We could find somewhere to hide!" I reason, getting him to scoff.

"They found me when no one else could. There is nowhere to hide. Even if there is, they will destroy everything on their way to me."

"Then why go to Iglagos now?"

"Every moment more that we spend lets them collect themselves and get stronger. If I do not go now, then they will be ready for me when I do."

"You just killed one of them, though!"

"He was overconfident. Something that the others may not exhibit. Especially after they found out that I dispatched one of them."

"How can you talk about death so easily?"

"Death is a necessary part of life. That is a fact."

"You caused this one, though! I really want to believe that you are a good guy."

"A good guy? That you talk in such black-and-white terms offends me. There is no good and bad."

"What are you talking about?"

"I do what I do to secure a better tomorrow!"

"They tell me you wanted to destroy the Second Reality! How could that bring a better tomorrow?"

"Every day the First Reality, your reality, is plagued by events from the second one."

"Yeah, and you caused them!" He lets out a bark of laughter.

"Is that what they told you? I was attacked by them. Sure there are several that I have been a part of, but others? The nuclear strikes, the black plague—both disasters were caused by others that fought within the Second Reality." I stand there numb.

"What?" hearing it from others is something else, but from him, it is harder than before.

"Are you telling me that history is a lie?"

"History has always been—and always will be—written by the victors. The truth is merely a matter of perspective."

"What of those who will suffer from your destruction of the second reality?"

"Sacrifices have been made for lesser causes."

"A whole world is a worthy sacrifice?"

"If that is what it takes to ensure the survival of the first, then so be it."

"How can you disregard them like this?"

"I disregard no one! If I do not do this, then both realities will fall!"

"From what?"

"A being that believes itself to be king of everything."

"Then why fight? Why not work together?"

"Pride, fear, status. They live basing their position on what they hold dear to themselves. Everything I stand for is an affront to their way of life."

"So?"

"They would rather see the world burn than to see the world together, which is why I will help you see that the world can only be safe by making this sacrifice." He flicks his right arm to the side. My chest sears as a wave of ice shoots from his hand, forming a sword.

"No! I won't let you!"

"You think you have a choice?"

"I will stop this king, and I will stop you too! No one has to die!"

"What do you hope to do?" He stomps forward once more, bringing the blade above his head.

"Whatever I can!"

"Hah! You have learned for less than a day. You have no other power aside from what you have been taught by the Watchers. You have no weapons, and despite all this, you think you can stop anything?"

"I will find a way."

"I have the only way." He swings the blade, and I close my eyes, waiting for the pain. A moment passes, and I still feel nothing. I crack my right eye open to see the blade stop less than an inch from my left arm. It is so close, I feel the cold touch of the blade. Following the blade upward, I find myself looking into Solomon's eyes. Myriad emotions flow through them. He reaches forward, grabbing his right hand with his left, wrenching the blade away from me.

"Solaire!" he screams, dropping the blade.

"Run! I can only hold him back for so long!" he grunts out, falling to his knees. I step closer, and he flinches.

"Why stop me? I am going to get him to see things our way!" he screams, his voice lined with a darker distorted tone.

"Solaire, go!" I turn and run. The branches of trees and the low bushes claw at my skin as I run. A demonic scream rings throughout the air.

"I will find you; the only way is if I do this!" I break through the trees and stumble, losing my balance at the top of a hill. At the bottom sits a lazy stream with a small pond. Recovering, I hear trees shuffling behind me.

"I will protect you, Solaire! The world needs this!" His voice is much closer this time. I step to the side, onto a rock. It creaks, and I let out a yelp as the rock gives way. Tumbling down the hill, I land facing my own reflection in the pond. My chest burns, and a wave of ice forms on some of the trees several meters farther along the stream. Out of the trees steps Solomon. He glances to the left, searching for me. Seeing nothing, he turns to his right, spotting me. He strides toward me, each step painfully slow.

"I am not going to hurt you. I just want your help." I push my arms into the mud, trying to push myself up. I get halfway before they give out, leaving me to stand staring at my own reflection. Scratches all over my face, drying blood in streaks looking like dried tears. My glance lowers to my chest, observing the mark.

I grind my teeth together as the footsteps grow closer, and I find myself snarling at the reflection. This image, this mark, has corrupted the Solomon I knew. He is everything that they said he is. A flicker of movement catches my eye, and I see a man in a suit standing over me in the reflection. It is the man who came out of the reflection and saved Stephen and Alexander. The Promethean who helped Stephen and Alexander escape!

Gasping, I turn, looking behind me. I expect to find someone, but nobody is there. Confused, I look back at the reflection to see the man still standing behind me. Both arms clasped behind his back as he tilts his head curiously, as if to see what I am looking at. I look back, seeing nothing once more. Movement catches my eye, and my head snaps back to the water.

An arm shoots from the water gripping my neck. Choking, I am raised from the ground as the man steps from the water onto the edge of the pond.

"You!" Solomon snarls, stopping but a meter away. I see them both as the man nods curtly to Solomon.

"Yes, although I do not believe that we have been introduced. I am Mateo Guerrenzo. It's a pleasure." A satisfied smirk makes its way to his face as he continues holding me like a ragdoll.

"I don't care who you are. Just drop Solaire."

"Such an interesting choice of words. No matter, now we start the timer."

"What do you mean?" I choked out. He rolls his head to me.

"We will be waiting at Iglagos with your friend, Solomon." He turns back to Solomon. "Now you have the incentive to get there in a timely fashion. We both know that Alexander hates to be kept waiting, and I would be deeply saddened if anything happened to Solaire."

"You hurt him, and you die," Solomon growls, as Mateo's face scrunches up in confusion.

"Curious. You are intending to hurt him, are you not? So why does it matter if we do it?"

"I am—"

"Ahh, don't answer that."

Mateo raises a hand, interrupting him. Solomon growls, taking a step forward. The grip on my throat tightens.

"I wouldn't do that if I were you. If you really want Solaire back, then come die for us." The man leans back, and we fall toward the water. Cold air flows around us, but the rush of water never comes. I open my eyes to a world of white and the image of Solomon glaring down at us from the other side of a strange window.

Bastian

I sit up, the pain agonizing as I look down at my chest. My clothing is cleaved in two, a mass of blood trailing down my chest from the neatly parted skin. I wince as I try to stand, only for a hand to press down on my chest causing me to yelp.

"Don't move yet." It is Felgrand, he is kneeling over me. He places his other hand over the wound and focuses.

"*Rejuvenation.*" The skin grows warm and the pain dulls as his hand grows a blinding shade of gold. When the light dies down he collapses next to me.

"That should keep you from dying off on me." Looking down, I see the wound has sealed, leaving a dark red scar over my chest.

"What happened?" He grasps his left arm, the one that he placed over my cut, and works the iron gauntlet off. His skin is raw. Blood drips down his fingers as his skin appears flayed. He is gasping now.

"I took the wound and directed it toward myself. It put the damage from your cut onto my arm."

"You didn't have to do that!"

"I did. If we hope to have any chance at stopping Prometheus, then we need everyone we can get."

"How will you fight?"

"I can bear the pain."

"If you two are done lollygagging around, care to help me?" Namar's voice causes me to roll my eyes as I turn to him. Hanging limply from the wall, he gestures to the blade pinning him to it.

"You look like shit." I stand up, helping Felgrand to his own feet. I am surprised that I feel no pain at all, only mild exhaustion. My musings are interrupted by Namar grumbling. Felgrand has already reapplied his glove as we hobble over to him. We get to him and I reach for the blade. As I tug on it, nothing happens. I grip the pommel with both hands as I pull once more. The blade does not budge as Namar growls in pain.

"That hurts, you know!" I am nudged aside by Felgrand as he grabs the blade with his good hand.

"Before I release you, what did the Pursuer mean?"

"What are you talking about?"

"He tells me you are part of the shadow."

"How the hell am I supposed to know?" Felgrand's lip twitches, and he leans on the blade, causing Namar to yell out.

"Stop it!" I grab his shoulder, only for him to throw me off.

"I work with this rogue, but I do not trust him!" he roars, raising his hand, gesturing at the broken bodies of the Syndicate members.

"Look at them, none of them deserved this! I do not want to find out you are in league with a being that can do this so casually."

"You are right—they did not deserve this. That is why as soon as Prometheus has been dealt with, I am going to murder that knight." Felgrand tightens his grip on the blade.

"I will see to it that you do. That being took too much innocent life today."

"Aww, are you getting sympathetic toward Syndicate now?" Namar sneers. With a cry of pain, the blade is ripped out of his shoulder as Namar flops onto the ground.

"All life is still life." He slams his hand down onto Namar's shoulder, earning another cry of pain.

"You would do well to remember that. *Rejuvenation*." The golden glow flashes brightly as he takes back his hand. He steps back quickly, but I see a red tint to the palm of his hand. Inhaling heavily, I help Namar up.

"Surprising to see you all still alive." A voice sounds from behind us. We turn, glaring toward the fountain to see Alexander step out from the water, followed by Stephen.

"What the hell are you two doing here?" I see another man step from the water, standing next to Stephen. He is wearing a deep black suit with no tie but rather a white shawl with a white bow tie at the top of a matching black button-down shirt. He is scrawny and several inches shorter than both Stephen and Alexander. He has receding black hair with several spots of mottled gray hair in the mix. Atop his skinny face sits a pair of rounded glasses. He angles his eyes downward as if trying to avoid meeting anyone's gaze.

"Why tell you when we can show you," he says, a smug grin crossing his features. Stephen turns to the newcomer.

"Silas, get to work," he orders, tossing him toward Carter's body. Alexander steps in front of our view of them, his eyes growing green.

"On second thought, can't have you seeing the surprise just yet." He grins.

"*Upend.*" He waves his hand, and the rubble from the wall grows green. As it slowly lifts into the air, the wall rebuilds itself.

"If you want to see the surprise, then come to Iglagos. You may want to hurry as well." He taps his wrist where a watch would sit.

"The time before the show begins runs short. Wouldn't want to miss it now, would we?" His smug grin widens as the wall seals shut between us. I glare at the wall before Namar's voice breaks the silence.

"I hate that guy." I choke out a laugh as we collect our weapons. I see Felgrand stop above the woman, impaled by his sword. I walk up, standing beside him, looking down at her dull eyes as they stare lifelessly skyward.

"She fought hard; she did not deserve to be felled by this blade," he whispers morosely.

"No, but we have a chance to make up for that. We have to hurry; it will mean nothing if we do not get to Iglagos in time." I look at Namar as he sheaths his blades.

"I can take us halfway, but then we will have to run."

"Fine by me. As long as we can set things right. I will run forever."

Felgrand growls as he carefully slides the blade from the woman's corpse. He stands, placing the blade in its sheath on his back as Namar steps forward. He holds out his hands to each of us.

"Miraculously, yet another time we agree. If this keeps happening, you might convert me," he replies with a forced grin making its way to his face.

"That's the goal, rogue." He replies as we join hands and the world fades to black.

Ai'hara

"Damn, damn, damn it all!" Jeffery kicks the pew next to him.

"Pandora!" Theron calls out, only for silence to return.

"Just because Pandora is a deity does not mean that she is omniscient. Omniscience does not exist in the Second Reality. No being can know that much," I explain.

"How do you know that?"

"It is a Watcher's duty to know each of the threats that exist within my reality."

"Threats?"

"We have to go after him." I stride toward the door, ignoring his question.

"At the very least, we need to go to Iglagos to aid in the defense," Valin agreed.

"The path from here leads to the pass. If we get there first, we can stop him," Jeffery chimes in.

"Why does he even want the cube?" Yukio looks expectantly toward Jeffery, who merely shrugs.

"Pandora's boxes are mystic jails; they exist to capture things. With that box, he can capture any being he wishes. As to what he wants to contain, only time will tell."

"Do you feel anything from your magic, Jeffery?" I ask, gaining his attention.

"Nothing at all, so we must make haste," he laments, shaking his head as we step outside of the building. We dash into the forest, along the trail. A lone figure marches forward further down the road. The trees grow sparser as we continue, the crunch of shale underfoot as we fall in stride behind him.

"Up ahead is a beaten path that leads straight to the chasm. If we take it, we can beat him."

"How do you know this?"

"Did you really think that if I hid an object like one of Pandora's boxes that I would not learn something about the environment that I put it in?" He steps off the path, angling behind a boulder.

"Why do you know such a path?" I ask, getting him to turn back to me, a condescending smile on his face.

"The best trails are those not found on any map. If I needed to escape, I would be able to go straight to Iglagos. Away from prying eyes," he claims, sliding down a hill, clearing the tree line. We come across the edge of a cliff. At the bottom lies a dense forest. The path we walk on leads to a small ridge where most of the path has eroded away, leaving only a small ledge to stand on that disappears around the corner.

"Why Iglagos?"

"Iglagos is the most secure place in the Second Reality," Jeffery speaks as he edges along.

"Precisely."

"Can we get ahead of Mikhael?" Theron asks, and Jeffery nods before he slides around the corner. I step onto the corner and slide forward, the edge of my toes sitting over the edge of my perch.

"That's why we are taking this path."

"Why do we need to get ahead of him?" Yukio asks as I step down on a portion of rock that crumbles underfoot. Snatching out, I catch a jagged rock. Wincing as the rock slices into my hand, I heave myself to another foothold.

"I have a plan to get the box back."

"An ambush? I like the prospect. Any suggestions as to where?" Valin chirps in.

"Just over this ridge lies a chasm. A single rope bridge is the only way to cross for miles. We can stop him there."

"Perfect." I turn the corner and see the chasm, a wicked crag that divides the earth in two, like heaven and earth. A lone suspension bridge made of vines and wooden planks spans the gap. We step onto a small plateau spotted with boulders of different sizes. On the far side, a mountain looms over the widened area.

On either side of the bridge sit two larger boulders, one situated closer to the left side of the bridge, while the other sat several meters down the path. A lone worn path leads to the bridge. I hear the scuffle of the others as they emerge around the corner.

Jeffery limps ahead of us, pointing to several boulders around the mouth of the bridge.

"We have to hit him fast, and we have to hit him hard. Valin, it is your job to keep him on his toes with your flames."

"Why do you think you have the power to order me around?" Valin grumbles as Jeffery ignores him.

"Theron, you place a tag onto him to stall him." He turns to Yukio and me.

"You both have the most important roles; you have to grab the cube at any cost."

"What about you?" I ask, seeing him give a small smile.

"I get to be the live bait."

"What do you mean?"

"I will stand here and impede his path any way I can."

"Won't he know we are around if he sees you here?"

"I have a history with him, so leave that to me." I kneel behind a rock obscuring my view of the path as I stare at Jeffery.

"Now, we wait until he gets to the center of—"

His eyes widen as he stops speaking.

"Why, hello there, Jeffery. I would say it is a pleasant surprise seeing you again, but frankly, I knew you would try and stop me. Where are the others?" I hear the scuffing of his dress shoes on the shale path.

"Already on their way to Iglagos. Now give me the box," he chuckles.

"You know, Jeffery, some things don't change."

"Like what?"

"You were always a bad liar."

"*Flux.*" A snap echoes, and Jeffery crashes to the ground. The shuffle of shale crunches together, drowning out his cry. Mikhael dances forward, stooping down in front of Jeffery. I grip the blade holding my hair as I carefully slide it from its sheath.

"*Incinerate!*" A wall of flame collides with the ground blowing the two apart.

"How rude. You could have killed me with that," Valin growls as Mikhael dusts off his left shoulder.

"*Burn!*" He rolls to the side as another fireball explodes in a shower of shale.

"Where there is one, there are certainly more. So let's remove all the rocks the trash is hiding behind, yes?" He waves his hands out as he sidesteps another fireball.

"*Gravity collapse.*" He swings his arms together with a clap as the boulders all shift in the shale. They begin dragging forward.

"*Searing bolt!*" The boulder in front of me rushes forward, meeting the blaze as an explosion blasts against the boulder. The others slide forward, all shooting to collide with Valin. They all impact together into a makeshift mound.

A war cry brings my attention to Yukio as she bent to sweep Mikhael's feet out from under him. He skips over it, driving his knee into her face. I dash forward, leaping high like a tiger pouncing on its prey. Grasping the blade in both hands, I bring it down. He shifts at the last moment, pivoting so that my blade buries itself into his shoulder.

A grunt is all he responds with as he turns into the blow. Twisting the blade from my grasp, he delivers a powerful blow to my jaw. I rocket backward, sliding into the shale, momentarily stunned. I hear a deep groan as I see Theron impact the ground next to me. Landing on his stomach, he glares up at our adversary. I hop back to my feet only to crash back down as the pressure increases once more.

"I really expected more from you all, because frankly, this is pathetic." He reaches up to his shoulder, grasping my blade, eyeing me as he does so. He rips the blade from his shoulder with a slight twitch of his left eye. He holds the blade in front of his eyes as he inspects it, turning it over in the light.

"This is fine craftsmanship." He tosses it down to the ground. It bounces twice, landing in front of me.

"You can keep it." He walks forward, digging his hand into his pocket. He stops in front of Jeffery as he kneels down, pulling Pandora's box from his coat.

"You are so close too." He shakes his head in a mocking manner.

"*Pyroblast!*" The air grows hot, and the smell of burnt flesh fills the air. Then the boulders blast apart in a combination of fire and smoke. Molten chunks of rock shower the ground around us as Mikhael stands facing the cloud. He takes a step forward as the smoke clears, leaving a silhouette standing among the embers.

"Impressive, so you still stand, or is it that you just haven't died yet?" Another flame burst to life in the smoke, illuminating a ghastly sight, to which I gasp.

Standing in burnt tatters is Valin, his skin burnt red and black, on his chest a wicked stab wound from Alexander surrounded by darkened soot. His chest raises heavily with each breath he takes, sweat pouring down his body.

"Bravo. You survived, but you made a grave mistake." I can taste the condescending air around Mikhael.

"What mistake?" I ask.

"Why, my dear. He let me know the cost for his magic."

"How is that important?" Jeffery growls, causing Mikhael to wheel on his foot, a stupefied expression on his face.

"You have been in the Second Reality for how long, ten years? You don't know the power of one's cost?"

"How does it help?"

"It tells you their limitations." He raises a finger toward the billowing cloud, keeping his gaze on us. "He is simple. His magic, when used too much, breaks down the body, burning it as if he is succumbing to his own flames."

"He just blasted your rocks apart at point-blank range. How do you know he didn't burn from that?"

"Flames never burn one's wielder. It is the law of fire," I snarl.

"Of course, good on you, Watcher—that is correct."

"*Pyrocharge!*" Valin blasts forward, slamming into Mikhael's back.

"Nggh!" He is sent tumbling forward, and the pressure vanishes. In the next moment, we are all on our feet. Theron dashes forward, and I see the tag in his hand. He thrusts forward, smashing it into Mikhael's chest. He follows up with a punch to his jaw that sends him stumbling backward. I hop to Mikhael, kicking the box away from his hand and into Theron's own. He looks down at the box before making eye contact with me.

"Go to Iglagos! I will catch up!"

"No, we need the box!"

"None of us will make it if he keeps after us." With that, he turns on his heel, running back for the path we took. I hear a snarl as Mikhael stands slowly. Reaching down, he clutches the seal.

"You all think that you can take the box from me?" He tears it off, and we slam back into the ground. Blood collects in my mouth as the weight of the world bears down upon us. He steps forward, the ground beneath him crushing into dust, leaving him walking on fine sand. He takes another step forward, and the effect spreads.

"I will kill your friend, and then I will grind the rest of you into dust," he hisses as he shoots forward, the ground splintering to pieces with each stride he takes. Theron disappears around the edge as Mikhael pursues him.

"*Crush!*" he calls out as the wall splinters into pieces before him. He slows to a sedate walk as he disappears into his makeshift path. As soon as Mikhael turned the corner, the pressure on top of us is gone. I get up, corralling Yukio to the bridge as Jeffery loops Valin's seared arm around his shoulder, dragging him toward the bridge.

"Come on, we have to go." Wobbling over the bridge, we hear another explosion in the distance. I turn to see a large tree fall in the distance. Turning back, we cross the bridge. Reaching the other side, I set Yukio down. Jeffery leans Valin against the wooden post supporting the bridge.

"*Scorch.*" A snapping sound fills the air as the sulfuric smell of something burning catches my attention. I turn to see the side of the bridge falling free. He raises his hand, and with a flick, a wave of flames severs the ropes holding the other side of the bridge together. The bridge plummets into the void below.

"What are you doing?!" Yukio screams, grabbing Valin by the scruff of what remains of his collar as he snuffs out the flames with a wave of his hand.

"I am making sure that when Mikhael comes after us, he has to take another route."

"You assume he will fail," I observe, glaring at Valin's disrespect.

"I assume Theron will do his job. His job is to stall for us. Mikhael has been stalled. Therefore, he cannot fail, only provide longer avenues of success."

"You think he will be caught!" Yukio jabs her finger into his chest.

"Ah, yes, I do. He will be killed, and Mikhael will follow," he says casually as he straightens his cloak.

"If I did not need you, I would incinerate you and be done with it." Jeffery steps forward with his hands raised in an unaggressive manner.

"Let us make haste to Iglagos. At the very least, we should respect the sacrifice he did make." Yukio turns away, shaking her head as she walks in front of the group.

Solomon

I take back control in that moment. Peering into the water, I see Solaire staring back at me as Mateo gives me a satisfied grin. He throws Solaire from his neck, and he vanishes from the reflection. Mateo stares back at me as he adjusts his collar, popping it before he sweeps a hand through his fine hair. He turns on his heel so quickly, the tails of his suit snap up behind him as he too leaves the reflection.

I sink to my knees, staring at the water. I search the reflection for anything. For them to return, to see Solaire alive.

"Why do you care?" The voice echoes in the back of my mind once more.

"Shut up."

"We can save him and the world at the same time. We can stop the Monarch."

"I don't care! You almost made me kill him!"

"All pales—"

I thrust the sword into the water, slashing through the calm reflection, water splashing as ice spread from where the blade touched.

"No! My friends matter."

"They have them now. You need me."

I shake my head. Focusing on my reflection. "No, I don't need you, but you ... you need me."

I stand up, looking up the river I can make out the shape of a large chain rising through the air.

"You would forsake everything so you can stay in control?"

"I would die trying to save my friends, and if that means dying so you cannot hurt them, so be it."

"I can help you!" the voice hisses.

"I know, but the cost is too great." I begin walking.

"You will perish."

"Maybe so."

"They will kill him."

"I will offer my life in his place. That should be enough to sate them."

"If we die, the Monarch will rise!" the voice hisses.

"I don't care about the Monarch. I care about Solaire."

The voice goes silent as I duck under a tree. Peering forward, I see a massive chain holding down a piece of land. Atop it sit spires of buildings and stone walls.

"Perhaps I am too hasty," the voice resumes.*"Perhaps we must coexist and cooperate to fulfill our wishes."*

"You only suggest that because you are no longer in control." A smirk danced across my face.

"Be that as it may. We will fail in both of our endeavors at this rate."

"What do you have in mind?"

"There is a way we can each maintain a hold of half of the mind."

"That helps us how?"

"It would be a momentary truce. A way to ensure that you do not die on your little quest to save your friend and take down Prometheus as well."

"Why should I trust you?"

"*Because if you do not, you leave your friend in the hands of Prometheus, a group far more sadistic than I am.*" I pause, pursing my lips.

"What do we have to do?"

"*We shall make a contract, one that will set my powers onto your own until this event is over.*"

"What would the terms be?"

"*Why do you ask?*"

"It is foolish to accept a contract without the terms being listed."

"*I will control the movements of the body, the actions, the reactions, and the killing. However, during the time that Solaire is held by Prometheus I will only advise. All actions will be yours to command.*"

"What do you get out of this?"

"*After your friend has been saved from Prometheus, or you relinquish your control, I will take and perform the necessary action of destroying the connection between the realities.*" I frown as I stop at the edge of the hill. Looking down, I see two people sitting at the edge of the water—a man standing next to a woman, who is carrying a parasol. The woman is spinning the parasol as she looks in this direction. The man is merely looking up toward the floating city.

"Why, hello, Solomon. Have you come to die for me?" the woman calls out in a sultry manner. The man turns, and I see the purple handkerchief.

"*Do you accept the terms of this contract?*"

"I am sorry you might not know who we are." She speaks quickly, standing up.

"I do," I hissed to the voice in my mind.

"I am Dahlia, and this is Colton," she speaks confidently. The ground cracks as frost begins to build in the air around me.

"*By the power I have, I grant you this contract.*" I feel power rush through me as a pulse of ice rushes across the ground, freezing everything in my immediate vicinity.

"*Let us lay waste to them now.*" I feel a blade form in my right hand as I advance.

"I could not agree more."

CHAPTER 12

IGLAGOS

Solaire

I tumble onto the ground, stunned. White walls surround me, forming an oddly twisting polygon-shaped hallway. On many of the faces sit window-like shapes, showing different views of the world.

"Welcome to the mirror world," Mateo gestures around as he walks up one of the white walls as if it were the floor.

"Here, gravity doesn't exist. At least not by conventional means." He turns away, observing one of the panes as I shoot down the hall away from him. I hear a heavy sigh as I turn down a corridor. I catch my own shoe, nearly tripping. I start falling toward the wall only to fall onto it. Perplexed, I look back to the floor and see it is now a wall, as if gravity has shifted.

"Where are you going to go?" he asks, his footsteps echoing behind me. The hallway split in two at the end. Hurling myself forward, I curve around the right corner, looking back as I feel an impact. Falling backward, I look forward only to see Mateo staring down at me, both hands in his pockets.

"The mirror world is an extension of myself. I can loop any passage, I can maneuver any path. All of them lead back to me. So again, where are you going?" He shrugs, looking around at the mirrors. My eyes catch the one on the surface to my right. I dive for it, only to slam against it. A warm liquid trickles down my face as I cradle my aching forehead.

"I suppose I should have mentioned it, although you have learned the lesson. Only I can interact with reflections here." He kneels down, lifting my head with his left hand.

"Man, you really hurt yourself there." He shakes his head disappointedly.

"Why don't you just kill me. After all, Solomon is walking right into your trap anyway." He chuckles, his eyes betraying the laugh.

"You seem to have it all wrong. We are not villains, and Solomon is certainly not a hero."

"Why should I believe you? You kidnapped me!"

"Such a two-dimensional outlook. Do you actually believe that this world is black and white, that you and your friends, even Solomon, are the protagonists of this story? That perhaps you all have some form of deity watching over you?" Mateo scoffs.

"What are you talking about? Why are you speaking as if you are the good guys?" I inquired.

"I wish that I could say we are protecting the reality, but we are by no means the heroes. The truth is that no one knows what will happen if Solomon separates the two realities. It doesn't matter what happens, if the realities merge or if they are separated. We were brought together in our like-mindedness so that Solomon cannot create that boundary. It is the change that scares us, the unpredictable nature of what could come to pass. Each and every one of us fights to prevent that."

"You don't have to kill him! We can do this another way!"

"Hah! The last time we sealed Solomon, this happened. We failed, he got out, and now he walks among us. Marching to regain his power once more."

"You guys put the seal on him back at Syndicate's base, though."

"That is nothing but a supplementary aid. He is currently sealed twice. Both of which are powering Iglagos."

"Powering?"

"His powers are what suspend the city above. If he takes them back, he will kill everyone in that city."

"What?"

"If you believe that his powers before are monstrous, then you will

be horrified to see what he can do when he is at full strength," Mateo
scowls. "That is why we have to stop him. He will destroy the world if we
can't stop him."

"He only wants to protect the First Reality!"

"That is what he told us too, but have you seen the state of the other
reality? It has been tried before, the merging of realities. The Salem Witch
Trials, the pursuit of Dracula, the incredible hunter Van Helsing? All of
them are consequences of the world's interaction. If that was ineffective
then, now, when your world is divided most, what hope is there to invite
new beings?"

"That doesn't mean that he cannot do it! We can find a way to save
both worlds and keep them apart!"

"Wake up! He is going to destroy everything the world has to offer—
and he will kill everyone who gets in his way. You have already seen the
lengths he will go to, those men back in Argentum: Baron and Darius.
Those are both the start. What do you think will happen if any of your
friends stood in his way, or better yet, if you stood in his way?"

"He wouldn't …"

I trail off, the image of Solomon standing before me, his blade rising,
flashes through my mind.

"So, you have already seen it, the lengths he will go to in order to
accomplish what he wants."

"He wasn't in his right mind; something is trying to control him!"

"Every magic has a cost—the more powerful, the steeper the cost.
Perhaps for him, it is his sanity."

"Then we have to save him!"

"Precisely, we have to save him from himself; that is why I didn't kill
you. We need you to help us save him."

"You want to help him?"

"At the very least we need to stop him. We cannot let him destroy so
many lives in the light of insanity." He outstretches his hand, offering it
to me.

"Come on, we can focus on how to save him after we stop him." I
bring my hand, shaking as it rose to meet his own. Then I notice it. To

my horror, the skin on my arm grows black, flaying before me. The skin peels back, and a torrent of pain engulfs my arm.

An almost unnoticeable slight sting stung my cheek, and I stop moving. Mateo's eyes grow cautious. Bringing my other hand to my face, I swipe it, and it comes away with blood.

"What?" I hold my hand between us as my chest burns as another needle springs from my arm. A clean cut forms on my forearm just above the blackened skin, blood slithering out at a slow pace. Fear grips my heart as I see Mateo turn on his heel, dashing toward one of the mirrors behind him.

Solomon

"I need to be the one to finish it, Colton," Dahlia says, spinning her parasol. Colton matches me, watching me intently as I march closer.

"Yes, I will be sure to not kill him outright. I want to have fun first anyway." I tighten the grip on my sword.

"Where is he?" I demand.

"Where is who?" Colton taunts.

"Where is Solaire?"

"I have no idea who that is." A black aura forms around his arms, reaching to his fists. I swing the blade forward with a disturbing ease. He steps back as the blade narrowly misses him. He steps closer, winding a left cross up. I snake the blade back aiming for his neck. He brings his forearm up into the path of the blade. My sword smacks against his forearm, a dull thud. Without a moment's pause, he punches forward. Skipping back, I dodge the dark aura as his fist whizzes over me. My eyes meet his, and a satisfied look upon his face tells me he knows what he is doing.

"Confused?" He stands, straightening his back, a haughty smile on his face, admiring the back of his forearm. A small cut parts the fabric where my blade met his sleeve. I narrow my eyes, glaring at him as I look down at my blade. The blade's edge was rounded to the shape of Colton's arm.

"Your blade will not be able to cut me." I swing the blade, ignoring him. He raises his hand, catching the blade.

"I told you, it doesn't matter what you do." He tightens his grip on the leather gloves catching the reflection from the sun. The blade clatters in his hands for a moment. Then it shatters, showering pieces of ice around him. He lunges forward, his hand balling into a fist. I raise my forearm to meet his strike. Immediately, a burning sensation fills my arm and I throw his arm away. I skip backward, gaining room as he stops, stepping backward as he once again dusts himself off.

I look down at my arm.

"What?" The place where his arm touched mine started to rot, the skin peeling away to show putrid pink flesh. The sight itself is enough to make my stomach lurch.

"He is destroying the blade as he touches it. That is why you cannot harm him. As for your wound, this will be most troublesome if he lands anything more than a glancing blow," the inner voice rings out. A refreshing cool feeling rushes over my arm as ice grows over the wound before cracking. It shatters into a vibrant display of ice flakes, leaving no wound on my arm.

"An instantaneous healing ability. I wonder what the cost for such a technique is."

"Cost?" I question the voice in my head.

"Do not worry about the cost. For now, focus on him," the voice in my mind speaks to me calmly as Colton continues speaking.

"You don't seem to know the cost, so it probably is more considerable than even I can comprehend. Impressive, though. Even after being sealed, as you are, you have quite the skill set. However, merely healing your wounds will not be enough."

"He's right. What should I do?" I mumble to myself.

"Talking to yourself, are we? You must really be nuts."

"Try this." A series of images flashes in my mind. Grinning, I step forward.

"Let's do it." I thrust my hand to the side and feel the familiar weight of a blade.

"Oh, still have confidence?" The wind picks up, furrowing his jacket, letting it billow behind him, his hair waving with the breeze. I run forward, swinging my blade like a club, trying to tear his head from his shoulders. He shakes his head as he catches the blade.

"This is the definition of insanity." I take my other hand from the blade and bring it back. I feel the shiver as power builds up in my reared-back fist. I bring it forward. I aim for this chest, trying to strike him. My fist whizzes through the air. His other hand snaps out, catching my arm by the wrist.

"I will admit, you almost caught me by surprise—almost." He smiles as my sword falls apart once more. The dreadful aching spread across my wrist. I twist my fist so the palm faces up.

"*Bolt.*" I flick my fingers, and the power flies, smashing into Colton. He flies backward, tumbling across the ground. He bounces twice as he comes to a stop, facing the ground on his hands and knees. I can't stop the smirk that makes its way to my face as he glares up at me.

He slowly stands up, and I get a look at his chest, where the magic had hit him. His dress shirt now sports a large tear; wrinkles spread throughout what is left of the shirt desperately clung together against his chest, framing a reddened patch of skin. Upon various patches of the shirt lie white clumps of ice, which slowly slough off onto the ground.

"Stop playing around. We need to finish this as fast as we can." Dahlia steps forward, snapping her parasol closed. She swings it to the side, and it flickers into a long scythe with a curved blade.

"I can handle this, Dahlia," he growls.

"Evidently, you cannot." She turns a sidelong glance at him, staring at his ripped dress shirt. He scoffs as he faces me.

"Looks like your time is up." I bite my lip as I feel a chill in both of my palms. Two blades shimmered into existence next to each other, the one in my left hand twinging in pain as I quickly studied my wrist. Already a small patch of ice is spreading over it, and the pain is dissipating.

"No, you both are the ones who are going to die."

"How cute, you think that you can win against us."

"You don't seem to understand what Prometheus is; we have been brought together to kill you. We will not fail in such a mission."

"Didn't you say that you weren't trying to kill me?"

"No, you see we each have our own agenda; and I must be the one to kill you to fulfill mine." Dahlia shoots forward, her scythe reared back to cleave me in two. I cross my blades in front of me, and they clatter together. I lean toward her, sliding one of my blades slowly out of the deadlock as I inched closer. Then she smiles widely, a crazed look entering her eyes. I lose my balance as I suddenly fall forward. A whoosh is the only warning I get as I snap my head to the left as the scythe grazes my cheek.

"What?" I barely have time to contemplate as Colton emerges from around her, his fist wound back as he slams a punch into my diaphragm, sending me rolling backward. The air escapes me as I slam onto my back. I breathe in and immediately roll to the side as the scythe slams into the ground where I am. Making room, I stand back, eyeing Dahlia's scythe. The disturbing smile on her face makes me feel as if I am missing something.

"Did you miss it?" she asks tauntingly. I nod, convinced my blade had held hers.

"Care to share?" She shakes her head as she lunges again.

"No, but I can show you." I narrow my eyes as I bring my right arm closer to me, my left rising to meet her blade. The smashing clang rings through the air. My sword barely holds as a crack spreads over the base of the blade. I growl as I push my other blade into it, pushing hers away. I eye the blade lock. Her blade flickers, becoming a duller color, almost intangible as I lose my balance just like before. Then the scythe slowly works its way through my blades, physically flowing through them as if they are rocks in water. I rock to my left as the blade scratches my right arm, sending an agonizing pulse through me.

"Do you understand yet?" She grins as she runs her hand along the back of her scythe.

"You will die because you cannot stop my blade." An ominous feeling fills my being.

"*Rot.*" Colton's voice rings out and I roll to the side, barely dodging a dark miasma. I see Colton dive under a swipe from Dahlia.

"Do not kill him," she hisses at him as she brings the blade back, her face scrunched in fury. He straightens, turning his back to me.

"I just want to rot off a limb or two. Make things easier," he says.

211

Her face adopts a stoic look. "You will only incapacitate him. I need him intact when I kill him."

"I am not liking the tone you are taking with me." I see my opportunity, and I take it, dashing forward at his exposed side, closing the distance. He does not turn, and I thrust my sword forward, intent on stabbing Colton. He snaps his hand out, a mere flicker due to his speed. He catches my blade between his fingers. I watch it disperse in a matter of seconds, dissolving into nothing.

"Has no one told you of how rude it is to interrupt others?" He cocks his head toward me. I catch a glint of steel, and I try to pull the handle of the sword from his hand. Dahlia stands behind Colton, her scythe poised to swing.

She wouldn't, I thought. As if to answer me, a devilish glint in her eye sparkles. She swings the blade in a wide sweep from behind him. I let go of my blade, falling back as Colton chuckles.

"Letting go of one's blade is bad luck." He feels a disturbance and turns his head. His smirk falls into shock when he sees the guillotine catch the light. Then, it passes through him. His head topples off, landing in the grass. His body stands tall for a moment. Shaking in the breeze, she rears back and kicks it. I watch it bounce to my feet, the expression of shock etched into his face.

"Serves him right after I gave him such an opportunity too," she scowls, looking down at the severed head.

"Why did you kill him?" She tilts her head coyly.

"Why, that's easy: he didn't do what I instructed." She twirls the scythe as she kicks the head to the side.

"You are a monster."

"No, once you are dead, I will release a monster."

"*Run*," the voice in my head echoes. I don't need another warning. I turn, sprinting away from her. "*Go to the massive chains. Scale them to Iglagos.*" I grit my teeth as I shift my sprint to the one in my sight.

"Do you think running will help?" her voice calls out tauntingly. A shrill cry fills the air, and I turn back. I let out a shocked gasp as I see Dahlia's body shift, the entire being flashing to a yellowish-white transparent body. Her skin seemingly mummifies with her hair and tattered clothing flipping out as if moved by an unnoticeable breeze. I stumble awkwardly forward, slamming my fingers into the ground. I feel the soil embed itself underneath my fingernails as I propel myself forward.

I shake my head as she shoots forward, a screeching whistle on the wind as she flies closer. A sickly foreboding sense fills my head as I shoot down into a roll. A ghastly form whizzes over my head. I come to rest on my knees as the ghastly figure floats to a halt, scythe in hand, positioned right between me and the chain. Then she speaks, her once-soothing voice a shrill hissing across the air.

"Did you think I would let you get to Iglagos? That I would let you get your power back?" Her body phases back to her human form, letting her drop a few inches to the ground. She pulls her scythe back, holding it behind her with one arm, the blade curving wickedly behind her back in the sunlight, the staff coming up over her shoulder.

"Solomon, what did you do?" a familiar voice echoes behind me. I turn around, and the world seems to stop. Standing above Colton's severed head is Solaire, with Mateo flanking him and a prone figure hunched over on the ground next to them. I register Solaire staring at me in abstract horror, angling his attention to my hand. Following his gaze, my eyes lock onto the blade in my hands. I turn back to him, a sense of dread filling my being.

"This isn't what it looks like," I reason as Mateo put his hand on Solaire's shoulder.

"Don't you dare touch him!" I scream as Solaire looks up morosely.

"This is why we cannot let him keep going. He kills indiscriminately. He has to be stopped."

"Don't listen to him!"

"I ... I ... you can't keep killing. I am sorry, Solomon." Solaire chokes, tears running down his cheeks. I feel my lips curl back in anger as my jaw muscles hike upwards. Mateo reaches into his coat, pulling something forth. Slipping out of his jacket is a jagged ritualistic dagger. The hilt holds a single ruby at the pommel. He reaches out, placing the blade to Solaire's chest.

"This is the only way." Confusion and fear bubble together in my heart as I step forward, only to feel the breeze pick up.

"What do you mean?" Turning, I barely bring my blade up to stop the scythe, but just as before it slides through mine, flying to cut me down. I lean to the side and the blade nicks my cheek as she flies by, landing in front of Solaire.

The refreshing cool encases my cheek as I feel the wound shatter away. Then it happens on Solaire's mirroring cheek—a small scratch appears where I felt mine. I grind my teeth as I feel that the entirety of the world is bearing down upon me. Something feels off. The world begins to spin, causing me to drop to my knees as I feel my bodily control slipping away.

"It would seem it is time to change our contract. I will not allow myself to perish just yet."

Solaire
Moments before

Inside the great hall of mirrors, the searing pain makes me wince as more and more of the strange wounds appear on my body. I clutch at my arm as the skin begins to flake away, leaving a sickly black patch of flesh.

"What happened to him?" I fearfully look up from my disfigured arm to see Mateo reappear, holding on to a frail-looking man. He appears to be in his late thirties, with wiry old glasses perched on his nose. His dark hair has receded, leaving a small tuft on top of his head. He wears a tan trench coat, opened so that I see a wrinkled matching suit underneath. A once-white yellowed button provides the background for a faded orange tie. In his breast pocket sits a matching orange handkerchief bearing the Promethean symbol.

"I don't know, Silas, but need to fix him," Mateo urges Silas. He stumbles to his knees next to me, his trench coat fanning out around him as he looks at me with tired eyes. He raises his hands, his head lazily lolling to the side as he slowly brings it to mine. Just as he is about to touch my hand, he snatches out in a show of speed, grasping my own in an unexpectedly tight grip.

"*Bringer's light,*" he drawls, glowing a golden orange hue. A warm fuzzy feeling dances over my arm. I look down to see nothing short of a miracle. The decrepit flesh seems to shift and tremble as it slowly trails into streaks that speed over my arm, crossing my shoulders to my chest. I gawk as they move to my other arm, flowing to the hand that Silas is grasping so tightly, it hurts. The injury moves away from my arm to his own, his face flinching as the wound stops where the mirror would be.

I snap back to my arm and see only clean, healthy skin. He slumps back, leaving me to admire the clean skin where the injury was situated. I look back to Mateo, hoping to catch his eye. He is bracing himself against the strange wall, peering into one of the mirrors.

"What the hell is happening over there? Where are the others?" He snarls at the image. I hiss as a large gash runs down my arm.

"What the hell?" Silas murmurs. My attention is dragged to Mateo, who is sucking down air.

"There is no way, it can't be ..." he says, trailing off.

"What?"

"We have to go now!" he growls, looking back at the reflection. He latches his arms on to both Silas and me, dragging us to the mirror. Without a word he leaps into it. A cold sensation floods over me before it is replaced by a moderate warmth. I open my eyes, and terror rushes through me. On the ground in front of me is a severed head staring back up at me in abstract surprise.

"Do you see what he has done? Do you see why he must be stopped?" Mateo hisses into my ear. I look up when I hear the ring of steel. Solomon stands, his back to me, and I can only shake my head in disappointment.

"Solomon, what did you do?" He turns, facing me as he drives off another pursuit from the woman. She lands in between us.

He suddenly bends over, clutching his head with a cry of pain. I step forward for a hand to clamp down onto my shoulder. I turn to look at Mateo. He shakes his head as he reaches into his jacket.

"I have a way to stop him, but you will have to trust me." Uncertain,

I nod my head as he produces a butterfly dagger from his pocket. He presses it to my face.

"What are you doing?" I ask as fear grips me with the cold of the blade against my cheek.

"Watch. This is how we stop him."

"By using me as a hostage?" Solomon stands slowly, taking a thundering step forward. I hiss as the steel, pressed deeper into my skin, carves a path for a small trail of blood to slide down my cheek. He stops though as a small mark appears on his face, a single slice on the side of his cheek mirroring my own.

"Any damage we inflict upon you is also inflicted upon him." He moves the dagger back, angling it toward my chest.

"I thought you were going to help me save him?"

"I did say that, didn't I?" His features curl into a pensive expression, and he shrugs. "I guess I lied."

"What?" He leans in closer.

"We never planned on helping him, only on killing him, and you are the perfect way to do so." The muscles tense and his arm shifts as I close my eyes. A moment passes without the pressing pain of a dagger in my chest. I wait a moment more, then open my eyes to meet the end of a wicked staff made from darkened steel, an ornamentation of skulls running down to meet the hands of the crazed woman. Her dark hair spills out in a chaotic disorder, a single curled strand following the curve of her nose. His face sets in fury as she glares at my chest, then at Mateo.

"Why did you stop me?" I look down to see the blade just barely hovering above my chest, above my heart.

"I need to be the one to kill him, remember?" A cold sensation on my neck makes me flinch to the side. Against my neck, reaching back to Mateo's weapon, is the curved blade of her scythe.

"Then do it." Anticipation loses way to distaste and she scoffs as the blade is removed. With a twirl, she places it onto her shoulder, turning to face Solomon. She takes her other hand, flipping the rogue strand of hair over her shoulder.

"I do not feel Solomon's soul within him. I do not think reaping him would accomplish what is needed." She eyes me for a moment before flicking her attention back to Mateo

"The boy is safe, for now. At least until I cleave you in two. I wonder if he will split in half just like you will," she says, directing the comment to Solomon.

A look of absolute fury forms on Solomon's face, and Dahlia steps backward closer to us. My chest burns once more as a shroud of fog surrounds Solomon's being. It trails down into his palm, where it coalesces into a single flowing blue orb. He thrusts his hand forward, and the ball flies, impacting against the ground between us. The air grows frigid and rumbles from the impact. Then a massive set of spikes erupts from the ground creating a wall between us and Solomon. The wall is turquoise, made of many crystals that are melded together. From the wall an eerie fog emanates, obscuring the sun's glow.

"A barrier? Mateo, if you would be so kind?" She strides forward, her heels clicking against the hard dirt, the scythe whirling behind her, the blade curving up wickedly, gleaming in the sunlight.

Mateo shoves me to the ground. I land on my arms and knees as he strides forward, straightening his ruffled coat. He raises his hand toward the wall and snaps his fingers.

"*Safaron.*" The bluish hue of the wall flickers as Dahlia steps closer to the wall. Then the portion of the wall falls away as a tunnel forms through the ice, allowing us to see Solomon's figure standing at the base of the giant chain. He glances back at Dahlia.

"You say that you have to be the one to kill me? Let's see you try it once I descend from Iglagos," he shouts as he runs up the chain.

"Why ... why do you have to kill him?" Mateo turns to look at me, a dark bruise forming over his chest.

"Why? It is because he and his family are the ones who endanger everyone. Besides, it is only natural for those with power to exercise it. We are merely preventing him from abusing his own." A blinding flash forms on our right. Then, out of the light, Stephen falls, followed by Alexander landing next to Silas. More footsteps echo from the light. My eyes widen as his face becomes visible.

"You ..." I trail off as they all stare down at me.

Ai'hara

We trek for hours through the rocky terrain until the massive floating city appears. Valin walks in front, each trudge painful as the exhaustion sets in upon him. I feel no better. Scrapes, cuts, and burns litter my body as we make our way over the shale path. I see one of the massive chains descending from Iglagos anchored near us as Valin aims for it.

"Why are we heading to that chain?" I inquire.

"The chains act as staircases in. They all lead to the same spot. Once there, we can seal off the city."

"Seal the city? What does that have anything to do with Solomon Helgen?" Valin steps onto the massive chain, testing the metal as he takes another step.

"The city is my main concern. Once the city is secured, we can focus on Solomon. There is no doubt in my mind he is coming here. Besides, if we can lock him outside of the city with Prometheus, perhaps two of my problems will solve themselves," Valin says.

"Regardless, we have to get to the city. We can decide our next move once we get inside," Jeffery directs as a blast of blue catches my attention, just as an icy blue spire shoots from the ground below in the distance.

"We have to hurry. They have already engaged." I feel the familiar clatter of stone under my foot, signaling our arrival across the massive chain.

"This way!" Valin enters through an ancient stone doorway. The stones layer to make a rectangular doorway. Moving through it, we find ourselves in a giant circular room. Countless doors of the same stature provide entry at evenly spaced intervals around the room. In the center sits a massive stone staircase. Each step seems to be a massive circle with a smaller one on top of it. At the very top of the altar-like staircase lies a spiraling staircase. Each step is a transparent white, shining in a dull blue light emanating from blue crystalline structures emerging from the ceiling. The aura the room put off is peaceful, yet deceivingly so. A familiar feeling of magic hangs in the air, stagnant as if making each breath seem stale.

"Now that we are inside …" Valin says, ushering the others into the magnificent room. He steps to the side of the door as he reaches into his pocket, producing a small silver vial from his cloak. He holds it up to the wall. A small yellow crystal lies next to the entrance, buried in the stone. A beam of light connected with the vial makes it turn a fantastic gold.

A deep rumbling echoes as the crystal next to the door glows a bright orange, the color spreads out across the wall, running between the cracks in the stone, and moving up toward the ceiling. As it spreads, the blue crystals on the ceiling transition to orange as the color seeps into them. Atop a spiral staircase in the center of the room, is a small dark orb, that seems to devour the light around it.

"What is that?" Valin arches an eyebrow as he steps past me, squinting his eyes to get a closer look.

"I have no idea," he sputters, intrigued. Then, all at once, a massive blade thrusts from the sphere, leaving a massive black streak in the air before it crashes downward, smashing into the top of the pillar, raising a cloud of dust and debris. The sword then slowly tucks back into the darkness, leaving the massive black streak in the air.

An unease settles upon us as I bring my blade into a ready stance. I feel the heat spring from Valin as he coaxes a flame into his hand, the skin growing red under the heat of his own power. The black streak splits open, startling us.

From the black void steps a being clad in armor, a massive greatsword at his side as he looks around the room.

"How did he get here?" Durgess hisses as he steps back.

"It shouldn't be possible. None of the alarms went off ..." Valin says, trailing off.

"What about the security thing you just did?" Yukio growls.

"He shouldn't even be able to get here now." Valin stands stupefied as the flame flickers to a dull glow in his palm. The figure continues scanning back and forth as if it is searching for something. Then its gaze lands on us, and I stiffen. It lingers painfully for a moment before it goes back to searching. It moves around the top of the pillar as it keeps twisting its head back and forth.

A dense drop of the temperature is the only giveaway as a blue bolt comes flying from one of the tunnels on the other side of the room. It smashes into the figure, sending it flying from its perch at the top of the altar. The massive figure sails through the air as it plummets down the staircase, landing in a great crash as stone and sand are sent exploding up in a cloud, obscuring the huge body.

My eyes escape the fascinating display, looking back toward the tunnel-like doorway the bolt flew from as the figure emerges, swaying his arms in smug victory. I see the body take a breath as the figure steps into the light.

"I am very grateful that you would do me such a favor as locking out those who try to fight me before I recover." I feel my eyebrows come together as Valin growls.

"Solomon," he hisses under his breath. The flame reignites in a furious display. Solomon merely steps forward toward the stairs as he starts ascending them with a blue orb in one of his hands. He casually tosses it back and forth as he takes each measured step up the stairs leading to the other staircase.

"I trust you can stall my pursuer for me?" he asks rhetorically as he tosses the ball down onto the stairs. It shimmers as it blasts to the sides, freezing everything between the two walls, creating a massive barrier between him and us. Cruel laughter erupts in the hall, and I bite my lip as I glare at his form moving on the other side of the ice. A growl erupts from the other side of the room, and the Pursuer stands. Shaking its head back and forth, its gaze rests on us. Brandishing its massive sword, it takes a menacing step toward us, the crunch echoing throughout the hallway.

"I don't suppose that you would ignore us and continue?" Jeffery suggests as a fireball flies past him, smashing into the Pursuer's armor, sending him reeling back in an explosion of soot and smoke. I follow it to Valin's smoldering outstretched hand.

"Intruders will be struck down—first him, then Solomon." A roar echoes through the room as the Pursuer steps from the smoke, blade screeching against the stone of the floor.

A SECOND LAYER OF REALITY

Solomon

I hear the blast and see the red flash through the ice as I ascend the stairs. I can't help but let a small grin cross my face.

"Of course that pretentious lawman would strike out against the Pursuer."

I reach the spiral staircase as another impact rattles the ice wall. I pause to see the figures on the other side of the wall.

"You have to help them!" my other side voices its concern.

"I am obligated to do nothing," I say callously as I ascend the spiral stairs. The sound of fighting fills the air. I round the top of the staircase as I feel the other side bellowing at me.

"You coward, get down there!"

"It would only be a swift death for you if I did. I can only do that with my power." The other voice falls silent as I enter a large circular room with gigantic crystal growths on the sides. In the center floats a gargantuan shard of aquamarine. Layers upon layers of brilliant crystals line the floor between me and the giant shard. A small gap to my left trails around the edge of the room to a ladder leading upwards to a catwalk, jutting toward the massive crystal.

I look back to the aquamarine, and I feel the connection to it. A pull inside myself. I know instantly that this is where my power is stored. I feel the static in my skin from the proximity.

I do not even realize I have moved until I am at the top of the ladder, and I have taken my first step onto the catwalk out toward the crystal. I stop right before it, and I reach out slowly as if to caress the outside of the crystal that seems to be calling to me. I stop just before I touch it. Something is wrong. A chill flies up my spine, as I feel like I am being watched.

A wondrously harmonic voice speaks from behind me. "I wondered how long it would be until I see you again." I don't need to turn to know who it is. However, the young soul inside me does. I internally scoff as I turn. There she stands regally, her hands clasped behind her back.

"Pandora, to what do I owe the pleasure?"

Ai'hara

"Damn." Valin curses as his hand smolders. The thudding footsteps resume as the Pursuer steps from the fresh cloud of cinders.

"Why did you do that?" I hiss at him.

"Intruders are not allowed within Iglagos."

"Enough with your rules. He is after Solomon. You should have let them fight instead!" Jeffery scolds.

"I cannot let them run amok; the city can be destroyed over such an action." A rumbling growl ends the conversation as we all turn toward the Pursuer. He stands, straightening his back. Lifting his massive blade with one hand, he directs the tip to point at us.

"Impudent … obstacles … will … be … removed."

"Wonderful!" Yukio exclaims, raising her hands swiftly and bringing them down, exasperated. She jabs a finger at Valin. "This is your fault."

The subtle shift of metal is my cue to turn back to the newest attacker. My fingers are already clutching my hairpin knife. Another short fireball springs to life.

"Don't attack blindly!" Jeffery screams as the flame leaves his hands and rockets toward the behemoth. A quick swipe cleaves the small combustion in two. The flame hovers for a moment as it swirls around the blade, coiling around it like a helix. It whirls into a point at the base of the hilt. A red symbol floats above the blade, clearly visible in the glowing light provided by the crystals within the room. It slowly floats toward the surface of the armor, where it blends into a sea of symbols similar to it.

"What is that?" I ask out loud to myself.

"Now … your flames of that caliber will do nothing," Valid scoffs at Jeffery's response, as the flames flicker to life in his hand once more. He swipes his hand, throwing the small fireball at the Pursuer. As the flames draws closer, the giant makes no attempt to move. Just as the flames are about to smash into him, the new symbol on his armor flashes a golden hue. I blink, and then the flames are gone, dispersed as if it has been repelled.

"What happened?" Valin gasps.

"You just had to throw your fire at it, hoping it would solve the issue!"

Yukio huffs, unsheathing her ax from the side sling within her cloak. The Pursuer lets a deep breath out, causing a steady stream of steam to float out through the mouth guard on the imposing helmet. Through the smoke, I can see two narrow red dots through the shadow cast by the helmet. I stare at the helm, fixating on the small red dots. They come into my vision, and I flinch as they come into clarity. Two scarlet red eyes with slitted pupils staring right back at me. Then he charges toward us at a dead sprint, his eyes flicking between each of us before finding me once more.

"*Incinerate!*" A torrent of flames slams into our adversary, causing him to stumble slightly as the flame is stopped for a moment. Then the rune glows a deep red before the flames are snuffed out into another cloud of smoke.

From the smoke, his massive blade emerges. He leaps with it, high into the air, swinging down his sword as he descends, his hands firmly grasping the pommel.

"Move!" Yukio shouts as we break apart. Not a second too soon did we separate. He lands, thrusting his sword deep into the stone. Shards of rock scattered from the impact. He jostles the sword, trying to pry it from the ground.

"I have you now!" Yukio screams as she rolls forward, her ax clutched with both hands. The Pursuer takes one hand from his blade and swipes a wide hook. Yukio slides under the blade, then leaps up, bringing the ax down hard in an overhand strike.

Crash.

The blade clatters against the armor almost playfully.

The Pursuer regards her with a tilt of his head before the arm travels back, smashing across her face with a devastating right hook. She bounces away, but I don't have time to see where she lands as the Pursuer brings both arms to the sword and with one last massive lurch, tears the blade from the stone. In an instant, his overbearing shadow envelops me. I roll to my left as the swoosh of the blade echoes in my ears, the cold breeze batting my shoulder. I stand as the giant pivots. His blade continues around in a full circle. Once more facing the blade but with no time to move, I bring my puny blade in front of me in a final attempt to stop his. A slight impact rings on my arms as a massive clang echoes throughout the hall. The knife has done it! I gasp as my hair knife bites into the massive blade, cleaving into the metal, leaving an inch-long trail before it stops.

A growl brings me from my stupor. Then a massive hand finds its way to my neck, snatching me off the ground in a choking grasp. I wince as the pressure increases as he raises me to look into the eyes of his mask. I snarl as I tear my knife from his weapon, before driving it forward. A shriek pierces the air as he flinches backward and the blade is torn from my grasp.

There in his neck is the knife. The knife had pierced his armor! Hope fills my being for a moment as the room grows darker.

"Take this, you overgrown hulk!" Valin screams as he places his hand on the Pursuer's shoulder. "*Pyro blast!*"

A short burst of intense flames sends me dropping to the ground. He doesn't stop, though. A hiss of pain escapes Valin's lips as he licks the top one, a bead of sweat creeping onto his brow.

"*Pyro helix!*" He punches forward, sending an ocean of flames much larger than the last. The heat forces me to shield my eyes with one of my hands. The blazing flames course onwards, smashing into the Pursuer.

A massive tunneling crater littered with flames spans across the room. Small cinders dance in the air. A howl of pain draws my attention back to Valin as he clutches his arm. It has grown ashen at this point. Cracks have formed in the skin, spreading up his arm. He leans away from them as they crawl up his forearm. The skin begins to flake away, leaving a burnt arm in its wake. Then the arm falls limply to his side.

I turn my attention back to the blazing trail from the onslaught of flames. A massive trench has been dug by the flames. Across it, the stone has melted. In the trench lies small fires, matched by an equal number of small streaming smoke clouds. Farther down the path lies a metallic object. Smoke rises from it as I make out the jagged edge of the Pursuer's blade, the body nowhere to be seen. At the back of the trench, a massive fire is burning, smoke making an obscuring cloud.

"That should do it," Valin huffs as he cradles his arm. Jeffery steps forward closer to me as he holds his hand out. I look at it in confusion.

"The blade, may I see it?" I scowl as I step backward.

"Why?

"By all accounts, you should be dead. That blade should not have stopped his guillotine from removing your head," he insists.

The images drift throughout my mind. I reluctantly hold the blade out. He takes it gingerly and steps back, looking over the small weapon.

"Fascinating. How did you come across this?"

"What is it?" Yukio asks, limping over to him.

"I got it from the Head of the Watch."

"This is amazing. The number of these left is exceedingly low."

"What is it?" Yukio huffs.

"This girl." Jeffery scoffs, rolling his eyes. "This is orichalcum."

"Orichalcum? The metal from Atlantis?"

"Not quite. You see, this metal is found here. This metal contains a property that makes it incredibly useful."

"And that is?"

"It is a metal that has anti-magic components. To see it in a sculpted form is amazing let alone the form of a blade."

"Anti-magic components?"

"It can pierce any magical construct, cut through any object imbued with magic."

"So, that means the massive sword is magical?"

"Of course, it is the conduit for absorbing Valin's flames." He holds it out in the palm of his hand, gingerly offering it to me. I reach for it, grasping it from his hands.

"Take good care—"

His words are cut off as something rips him from my contact. He is sent tumbling away from us, speared by a giant object. I don't have to see it to know.

"You have got to be kidding me!" Yukio screams as we turn to see the Pursuer standing in the trench. His armor is melted and scorched on the right side. His left side is merely blackened by soot as the red symbol stands out among them. His left arm is extended as if he has thrown something. I look for his sword in vain, but I already knew where it is. It has speared Jeffery. The behemoth straightens as it stomps forward.

"Death!" It growls as its red eyes glare at us.

Bastian

A deep rumble silences us as we reach the clearing. Moving out of the dark curtain of shadows, on top of the floating city, I am blinded by the sunlight as it reflects from the top of the buildings.

"I still can't believe how close you got us." I turn around to see Namar stumble out of the shadow. Felgrand steps forward, tripping as he catches himself with the trunk of a nearby tree. A rumble brings my attention down the cliff we stand on to a growing spire of ice.

"Shit, they must have already gotten here," I mutter as I help Namar up.

"We have to get down there." He slides down the edge as I dash down, landing on the ground, my breath hitched in my throat. Standing in front of me are the members of Prometheus. My eyes loiter over them; all our eyes—Stephen's, Alexander's, Mateo's, Silas', Dahlia's, and mine—linger on the one standing next to the prone form of Solaire.

"Aren't you supposed to be dead?" He turns to face me, pats his chest, and ruffles his coat.

"Not nearly as dead as you are led to believe," he smirks as he holds his hand out, and a spear falls into it. I hear the shuffle of dirt as the others land next to me.

"Dahlia, let me handle these three. Two of them have a little grudge against me." She looks back before shrugging. Flicking her scythe to the side, it flashes into a parasol that she rests upon her shoulders.

"Carter!" Namar shouts in rage as he unsheathes his swords.

"Shall we dance?" he speaks while whirling his spear. I reach into my coat, producing my daggers as my shoulders dip. Exhaustion permeates my body. A bright glow emits from behind us. I turn to witness a band of energy come crashing down near the chain. The energy forms a barrier between us and the city. The wall continues curving with the city as it is enveloped in a dome of bluish energy. Then it fades away.

Felgrand reaches for where the wall sat. Hesitantly, he brings his hand forward, but suddenly stops.

"Why did you stop?"

"I didn't. That barrier is still here." The smashing footfalls behind us are the only sign as I spin, barely blocking a thrust from Carter's spear.

"Don't turn your back on me!" Namar shoots forward, his sword colliding with the spear driving him back a step as I right myself.

"Would not dream of it," he growls as his other sword darts around the spear. Carter's left hand leaves the spear, and meets the tip of Namar's blade. It halts as sparks drift from the edge of Carter's hand. Dark tangible ripples swirl in the air around his hand.

"Ferocious, but you lack the stamina to fight me for long." He skips backward, cackling as Felgrand's longsword swings over Namar's head.

"You fall today, heathen."

"Big words coming from someone excommunicated by their own church." he sneers, giving me the chance to throw one of my blades as I pull another dagger from my coat. Namar rockets forward again, one sword high and one sword low, the thrown knife shooting past his head. Carter holds his left hand in the blade's path as he lowers his spear into a defensive stance, with part of it behind his back. The blade strikes his hand, and the air ripples as if a droplet of water had splashed against the palm of his hand before the knife sank into it.

"You really will have to do better than that if you want even a chance." Namar's swords shoots out in a scissoring motion. A quick hand gesture and a ripple to Carter's left shoots a spear, forcing Namar to stumble out of the way. Then the spear in Carter's hands shoots forward. Thinking fast, Namar drops to his knees, turning his back to Carter in a poor attempt to maintain his balance.

That is all the time he needs. Carter steps closer, using his other arm to grab near the spearhead crossing his hands over each other. I leap into the air, trying to land on him. He spins around, bringing the spear through his guard around his neck. With a twist of his hip, he sends Namar flipping into the dome.

Snap.

It is the only sound I hear as two ripples in the air telegraph the spears. I cross my arms in front of me, the blades facing out as they shoot toward me. I knock back the spears, which bounce in the air before falling though more ripples. Felgrand grunts as he brings his blade careening downwards. Carter scoots backward, a spearhead deflecting the blade. Then, with a twirl, the butt of the spear crashes into Felgrand's face.

He stumbles back, waving the sword in front of him. I hit the ground. Groaning, I pull myself up to Carter, ducking under the blow. Then, he uses his blade to push the longsword further, sending Felgrand reeling to the side.

Another blow to his face sends him staggering closer to the wall. Carter twirls like an elegant dancer. He readies his spear, then thrusts. The spear is barely deflected by the massive long sword, exhaustion clearly creeping onto Felgrand's face as the spearhead slices the corner of his armor. I throw another blade as I pull my last knife.

Carter merely moves his back as the blade shoots right past him. He turns to me, sending his boot into Felgrand's face, sending him colliding with the wall. I shoot forward as I bring my knives down onto his spear. He grins from ear to ear as he looks into my eyes over the deadlock.

"Two are down. You are winded. Your options are limited." He pauses as his eyes glaze for a moment. "Let me make this more interesting."

He backs up, letting me stumble forward. The butt of the spear smashes into my ribs. I stumble back as he snaps his fingers. Seven spears fall around us, spearing the ground around the dome wall. Locking us in.

"Now you have nowhere to go. What will you do now?" I growl as I shoot forward. He bats my blades aside and kicks me backward. He gives a dismissive wave with his hand, and the air in front of him ripples.

"You can have this back now." My eyes widen as my throwing knife comes whirling from the distortion in the air. Smashing into my arm, I turn like a top, landing next to Felgrand. I glare up at the gleeful Promethean. I back up as he steps forward.

"It's just like before." He takes another step, bending his body to look down on me.

"What is?" I crawl back further, my eyes darting for a way out.

"Why this, of course." He opens his arms, gesturing to the area around us. "You have lost again. You have no means of escape as you did last time."

He grins sardonically as he takes another lording step. I back into the wall, and then suddenly, a flash of light shoots from my pocket. He steps back suddenly as the feeling of a wall behind me falls away, and I tumble backward. I look up, and I reach for the others. Carter's eyes flash in anger as he steps forward. With a flourish, he stabs the spear forward, and I fall backward, anticipating pain. The spear stops just short of my chest, the blue of the dome glowing as the spear rests against it.

"Hide there all you want. When this wall comes down, you will fall just like you did now," he sneers as he straightens, and with a snap of his fingers, the spears surrounding him fall away into the very distortions whence they came. He turns away as I help the others to their feet. Reaching up, I grasp the knife in my side. With a cry of pain and a swift tug, the blade is in my hands as I gesture to the chain.

"Better start climbing," Namar groans as Felgrand huffs in annoyance.

"For once, I am beginning to see why the rogue behaves the way he does."

Ai'hara

He is on us in an instant. A reckless charge angles toward Durgess' body—specifically, his sword.

"This is our chance!" I scream as I grip the blade. I move into his path, crouching, feeling the muscles in my legs coil, ready to spring.

"*Combustion!*"

A fireball flies to the side, angled at the ground in front of the Pursuer. It meets the ground just in front of the massive leg. The ground lost where he would step, the Pursuer stumbles. He slows considerably as the flames on the ground are absorbed into the armor. Yukio slides behind him, her ax flashing out, screeching against the backs of the knees. Down the Pursuer falls, his massive knee digging up the charred, ruined stone.

I spring forward, launching myself. I feel the muscles in my leg tear from the stress put onto it as I fly at the Pursuer. I drive my dagger into his shoulder, the blade sinking to the hilt. I feel my lips turn up into a satisfied grin. Then pain envelops my wrist. The Pursuer's massive hand closes around my own as he starts squeezing tighter. I feel my wrist crack as he tightens his grip.

"Let go of her!" Yukio screams as she leaps at him from behind, the ax brandished between both hands in an overhead strike. She soars in the air, descending rapidly. The Pursuer doesn't even look. His other arm goes flying back as he comes to a stand. The back of the massive gauntlet smashes into her face and sends her flying. She slams into the wall of ice. Shards and dust kick up as the impact echoes around the room. Distracted, I don't see Valin move.

"*Scorching hellfire!*"

Valin's fist smashes into the Pursuer's helmet. Flames explode, knocking him off balance, blackening the side of the helmet. He lets go of my arm, and I kick forward. Planting both feet into his chest, I pull my blade free as I flip backward. A small growl erupts from the Pursuer. Landing away from the massive attacker, Valin brings his injured arm back, and flames coalesce around it. The heat starts to build in the room. Soon, a sweltering heat washes over me as Valin's arm turns bright orange. A droplet of liquid drops from his arm. I watch as the floor melts away as the liquid splashes on the stone floor. Then, his arm turns a bright white.

The Pursuer rights himself and walks forward, holding his left arm in front of his body as an improvised shield. He marches forward, his other arm flexing as the fingers hooked into a claw-like posture.

"Let the very flames of hell consume you! *Pyroclasm!*" Valin screams as he punches forward. A flood of white fire slams into the Pursuer, enveloping him. The trail of flames smashes into the wall of ice far behind him. The flames explode in a massive torrent, raining molten slag as the ice holds for a moment before it melts away.

A massive trench of flames and billowing smoke obscures the room. I hear Valin hit the floor as he is gasping, holding his shoulder. His blackened arm smokes as it hangs limply at his side. A light breeze flows through the room as I approach, cradling my wrist. Then his arm cracks up to the shoulder. The breeze whirls once more, and then his arm simply falls to dust on the wind.

"That should be it," Valin mutters barely audibly as he puts all his weight on his knee. I walk up, eyeing the smoke for any sign of movement. Still several meters away, the flames from the trench threaten to burn me from even this distance. I wince as cinders kiss my skin as they float past my face.

"Now on to Solomon," he says, gasping as we both stare into the smoke billowing up from the trench.

Solomon

"It has been a while, Solomon," Pandora greets me, her voice smooth as water.

"Yes, and now I can finally be whole again," I say, stepping forward confidently, my eyes set upon the crystalized core.

"That is not the answer."

I look over my shoulder at her. "Yes, it is."

"No, I have come because we have to continue to protect you, protect the world from what you house." She reaches forward, grabbing onto my shoulder.

"What I house?"

"Yes." She pauses thoughtfully, searching for the words as she stands there, the pieces gradually fit together.

"You did not do what I think you did—"

"Solomon, I am sorry. It was the only way." I throw her hand from my shoulder.

"You tell me I am key to sealing him away, that I am what is holding him back. I figured that meant he is imprisoned in your vault with me as a source of power," I say, jabbing my finger toward her.

"Solomon, he is too strong for the vault. That is why I hid you away, why I let you stay in the box. So that you could be safe."

"Sealing him inside me is safe?"

"Not you, in your shadow." I flinch before looking down at it. It seems to writhe and bubble a moment as it slowly forms back into itself.

"That is why it is important to keep you safe. Should you fall he will escape."

"All the more reason to fight now, before they find even more to stand against me," I growl.

"No, think about this. I can take and hide you away."

"Where? You can't use the box again. Hiding is but a half measure.

They will find me, and then it will be up to me to stop them when they are ready."

"I can hide you in the vault. You will be safe there." She reaches out, her fingers extending outward. I look down at the ground, grinding my teeth as I look between her and the hovering crystal. Then I reach out to the side that would decide everything.

CHAPTER 13

THE FALL

Bastian

"Damn, that is a long climb," Namar says, leaning against the edge of the stone inlet. Felgrand pushes past him stepping to the stone doorway. He jerks as he slams into something solid. He lurches back, clutching his nose.

"We cannot progress," Felgrand growls. Namar scoffs as he shuffles his way to the door.

"Stop miming around. Let's go." He bats Felgrand out of the way. Stepping forward, holding his hand forward, he looks back at me when his hand stops moving forward.

"Well, I'll be. It feels like there is a wall here." Felgrand slams his hand into the wall.

"Of course, there is." Namar rolls his eyes.

"How did you get us into the dome?" I shrug as I look down at my pocket.

"My pocket glowed, and then it felt like the wall fell away." I look back up at him as he crosses his arms.

"Well, don't just stand there. Check your pocket!" he says. As I reach in, my eyes widen as something cool and metallic slides in between the fingers. Pulling it out, I see the small vial.

"What is that?"

"This is the vial from the old man at Ashvale Keep." The scenes

233

from when he was taken by the undead replay in my mind. Namar steps forward, swiping it from my hand.

"Now, why would he have something that could let us into here?" he asks, spinning on his heel as he steps closer, sticking his hand out. A moment later, the vial grows silver as a warm light bathes the hallway.

"Really?" Namar shakes his head slightly, looking over his shoulder at me.

"I don't know how, but somehow your good intentions once again unbelievably found us the answer," he scoffs, turning into the tunnel as we follow the path. A giant rumble shakes the ground we are standing on. We all make eye contact. Wordlessly, we all sprint into the next room to find the most bizarre sight. A massive wall of ice branches across from one side of the room to the other, a massive trench running parallel to it with flames snaking across the room. A giant trail of smoke seems to bisect the room. Running through the barrier of ice, I see two figures. One is an exotic-looking Watcher; the other, a man in a burnt and tattered cloak. His arm is burnt off at the shoulder. He is clutching the stump as he kneels at the start of the trench.

"Damn, looks like you guys had all the fun without us," Namar quips, causing the girl to turn around with surprise. She holds a small knife in front of her.

"Are you both all right?" I ask, ignoring Namar.

"How did you get in here?" the man asks, looking back at us as he reaches up with his good hand to pull back his hood.

"We got in here with this." Namar flips the vial in the air and catches it. Then he tenses as the man's hood falls backward.

"You!" Namar screams as I see the movement. I pull one of my knives, rear back, and throw it.

Ai'hara

I am unprepared for the band of people to rush in. I whirl, startled by the racket behind me. Two of smaller stature, I instantly pinpoint their badges from Syndicate, but what are they doing here? Then the tall one in back, roughly three-fourths the size of the Pursuer, but his armor is that of one of the churches. When the one with two swords starts speaking, I can't hear anything. The world is deafened, I now realize, probably from Valin's massive attack.

Then everything turns for the worse when I see them take an accusing step toward Valin. The muffled shout comes clearer with each moment. They speak for a moment, a heated exchange before one of them shouts.

"You!" Then the other throws a knife. It barely misses my head as I prepare to charge my attackers.

Clang.

I freeze as the metallic clang fills the air. My head turns ever so slowly as I see it. From the smoke the Pursuer steps once more. A roar splits the air as his leg lashes out from the cover of the smoke, slamming into Valin, sending him bouncing backward. The Pursuer leaps forward, the smoke clinging to him as he lands, driving his knee into Valin's chest.

Crack.

A sickening sound fills the air as his head bounces up to meet the Pursuer's metallic fist. He smashes the ground and lies still.

"Valin!" I scream as the massive adversary stands up. The smoke finally dissipates, and we see his form. His armor is melted, having lost any of the royal designs it once bore. I see the places where the metal has melted and cooled as it now has beads of dried metal on the plating, which is now smooth instead of rigid. Soot now covers his entire being. A lone cinder skids across the smooth chest plate, moving over to his left side. Then I notice his left arm is missing. The armor has melted, leaving a sizable gap between the plating exposing his flesh. His helmet remains blackened but for the most part intact as the red eyes glare mercilessly at us. A whistle from behind me catches my attention.

"Shit, you did that to him and he is still going?" the one with two swords says.

"Yes, I don't know what it will take to bring him down."

"Looks like we have our work cut out for us. My name's Namar, the guy with the knives is Bastian and the big dolt is Felgrand."

"Roooaaarrr!"

The Pursuer charges, barreling at me. I raise my arms as he bashes his arm into me, the dagger in my arms slicing right through the plate on his gauntlet. I tumble back, losing hold of the knife. It clatters away as I look up to see the Pursuer continue charging toward the new group. They each pull their weapons.

Felgrand darts forward, swiping his blade in a broad stroke.

Clang.

The blade smashes against the gauntlet as the Pursuer pushes it out of his way before delivering a fist to Felgrand's face, sending him stumbling backward. Bastian got inside his guard, hopping over the kick aimed his way. He drives his knives into the exposed flesh on his left side. With a roar, the giant's arm grips the boy's chest. He throws him straight into Namar. He continues running past him, and I see what he is aiming for as his hand closes around the handle of his great sword. Namar sprints two steps behind him as the Pursuer turns, rotating his hand on the blade. He flicks the handle, sending Durgess's body slamming against him, and Namar rolling back into a twisted pile. The Pursuer turns his head to me and starts advancing, his blade held out to the side, the wicked point glittering from the light of the crystals up high.

Five meters away, he leaps, raising his blade, intent on bringing it down on my prone figure. I raise my arms in a mock defense as he nears. I scowl at him as I see the eyes glare down at me. I close my eyes just as he begins his descent.

Clang.

I open them to see Felgrand standing over me, his blade held sideways, braced with his other hand farther down the blade. Despite this, the impact drives him to his knees.

"Now is not the time to give up," he grunts underneath the pressure of the blade. He rises, angling his blade to the side, allowing the Pursuer's to slide off. He rises with a roar. His bellow grows louder as he rises until he is cut short by the massive boot crashing into his face. He lands next to me. I share a glance as we both look up at the Pursuer.

"Ants ... die," he grunts out as he crosses the massive blade over his body, ready to bisect the both of us. He swings as I try to shuffle backward. The shadow underneath the Pursuer shifts as two blades shoot up into its path. Namar slowly moves up from the darkness as he skids backward from the force of the swing.

"You are … one with … the shadow."

"I think you have someone else," Namar grunts as he strains against the bigger blade. Bastian flips onto his left side, stabbing his knives into the left side once more. He shifts his weight driving a hard knee into the behemoth's helmet. The giant stumbles backward, his sword leaving the deadlock. Namar pushes forward as he spins, allowing the blades to whirl outwards. The Pursuer drives his elbow into Bastian's face. He lets go of the blades as he falls to the ground.

He then lunges forward with the added momentum. His blades screeched off the armor, leaving faint scars in the melted metal. He skips backward to avoid a sweeping retaliation from the massive adversary.

"This walking excuse for a marshmallow is quite strong. How did he get that?" He points his blade out at the giant's neck, where the first cut landed. The Pursuer recovers as he moves toward Bastian's recovering form.

"Shit!" he screams, running forward as the blade comes careening down. He dives, both swords held in a cross in front of him. A metallic scream fills the air as the blade impacts on the side where Bastian lies. Bastian rolls to a crouch away from the massive blade.

"My knife—it bounced away when I hit him last. It cuts right through his armor!" I gasp, pawing around for the blade. Bastian stops near me, glancing around. Another crash of metal on metal rings out, and I look up, seeing Namar once more locking blades with the Pursuer as Felgrand charges in from the side. I look back down on the ground, searching for the blade as the barbaric sounds ring throughout the room.

"Found it!" Bastian screams as he holds the knife up to me. A crashing thud makes us both turn to see Felgrand on the ground underneath the Pursuer's foot as Namar is being crushed downwards by the massive blade. Bastian grasps the blade as he rears his hand back and lets the blade fly.

It soars through the air, end over end. We stand transfixed as it approaches the Pursuer as he leans on the blade, driving Namar's further downward. Then the blade makes its impact, impaling to the hilt, right in the base of the neck. The Pursuer flinches, backing off just enough for Namar to move. He capitalizes. He slides from underneath, the massive blade letting him stumble forward. At that moment, I see Felgrand kick upwards, sending him off balance as Namar dives forward between the Pursuer's massive legs. He twists as he passes through the Pursuer's legs, kicking into the backs of the Pursuer's knees. The Pursuer falls forwards. He does not get far, though, as Felgrand rises and tackles the Pursuer, sending him flying backward.

The behemoth rolls in a feat of unbelievable agility, landing on his feet, his blade screeching against the stone. He stands, reversing his hand on the hilt of the sword. He beats it against his chest once before he stabs the sword downwards.

"Now what?" A symbol on his chest lights up, the very same that absorbed Valin's attacks. Then a small spark flickers in front of him. He reaches out to it, placing his hand on it as a fireball coalesces in front of him. It fumbles and folds on itself as it grows bigger. I get to my feet, ready to dodge as the flame grows larger and larger until it suddenly stops. Forming a perfect sphere, it levitates in the air, a white spot of intense heat that I feel on my skin from where I stand.

"What the fuck! He can use fire magic too?" Namar screams as he shifts, ready to dodge. Then the fire bursts outwards, spreading to reach everything we can see. My vision fills with white light as the sea of flames bathes us in the light.

I lose sight of Namar first as his shadow is obliterated by the blinding light.

The light is so intense! I close my eyes. A moment passes, and then the room rocks as the explosion goes off. I am blasted backward as lumps of searing objects slam into my body, launching me backward.

I open my eyes, trying to see into the poor lighting from before. The remnants of a barrier stand erected in the middle of the room. Smoke lifts off of it as cinders dance through the air. I look around, noticing all of us—Namar, Bastian, and Felgrand—all lying on the ground, nursing wounds from the impact of whatever barrier stands in the flame's path. Each looks stupefied gazing upon the Pursuer's figure. I see a small chunk near my hand. I reach out, grabbing it. It is cold to the touch, so I drop it.

Suddenly, a blue lance flies from the corner of my periphery, smashing into the Pursuer. He tumbles to the side as light snowflakes flit through the air.

I trace the bolt back, and in the tunnel born by Valin's flames, he stands—a figure coated in a suit of cobalt armor, a helmet featuring swirling spirals coming from it. The design reminds me of a crown.

"I would like to see you face me now." He steps forward, taking off the helmet. I gasp.

"Solomon!" the Pursuer growls as he stands back on his two legs. Solomon merely holds his hand out to his side as a sliver of ice runs upwards between his hand. He grasps it, and it starts to twist and morph. As the Pursuer takes a step forward, the room rumbles.

"What … is that?" I ask. Then I see a shard of the ice start to rise.

Solaire

One by one, they step forward as a green glow emanates from the ground in front of us. Dahlia standing next to Colton's corpse, Mateo behind me with Silas leaning on the ground holding his arm that now bears my wounds. With a flash of green, three more people stand on the grass.

"So nice to see you again, Solaire," that prideful voice rings out, and I knew who it was before the light had even cleared. My suspicions are correct as Alexander's smug smirk fills my vision. Then the second steps from the light, allowing it to die down leaving the third. Holding a notebook in hand, clutching his pen was Stephen but behind him, striding toward us was someone who couldn't possibly be here. The last time I saw him, he was a corpse. Yet here he is, fighting the others. I see Bastian barely make it into the dome as he dodges a thrust from his spear. I flinch as his eyes land on me.

"How are you not dead Carter?"

"Who knows?" he smirks, and Stephen looks down at Colton's lifeless head.

"Silas, heal this man. We will need him when we fight Solomon."

Silas shuffles over to the body, a lost look in his eyes as he looks at the remnants.

"I cannot heal this. I can only heal things that are in one piece," he says softly. Carter scoffs.

"Typical worthless trash. I wonder why they even let you into our group."

"Carter, enough." Stephen's voice is dull and heavy, so unlike his tone when I met him. "Alexander, if you would be so kind."

Alexander steps forward, his smirk waning as he waves his hand.

"*Upend.*" The body stands up and rejoins its head before it tumbles to the ground. Alexander glares down at the body.

"Why did he not revive"? he scowls as he looks at the body on the ground.

"Silas, now try." He puts his hands next to Colton's head, and a golden glow emanates from them, bathing Colton's head in a bright glow before the light fades. He shakes his head before whipping his head to an annoyed Alexander.

"Well? Time is of the essence." Alexander taps his foot as Silas turns back, reaching back, the golden light enveloping Colton's head once more before it dies down. Tears slip down Silas's cheeks.

"It's not working!" he whimpers as he assumes a fetal position. Carter lunges forward, dragging Silas up and forcing him to look into his eyes.

"Why? You useless piece of trash, tell me why it is not working!"

"It's like he doesn't have a soul anymore." I see Alexander straighten as he takes a step back, his hand roughly running through his kempt hair as he turns around.

"What are we waiting for? Let's kill the boy and then go and kill Solomon!" Dahlia screeches, a manic smile crossing her face.

"This boy is linked to Solomon. Are you not the one who wanted to kill Solomon with your own scythe?" Mateo steps forward, raising his hands in a plaintive gesture. The manic smile drops as she takes several deep breaths.

"You're right. The death and the blood around me are … intoxicating." She speaks with half-lidded eyes as she licks her fingers.

"Dahlia!" Stephen growls. He is pinching his nose as he steps forward, each step calm and precise despite the creasing brow on his forehead. The force with each step belies his calm visage.

"You took his soul, didn't you?" he says as he steps closer to her. She steps forward, anger replacing her pleased look.

"And if I did?"

"Dahlia, need I remind you why those in the Second Reality fear sharing their names? You will answer me," he says, his voice restrained as his pen shoots into his hand. An uncertain look passes through her eyes as she stands back.

"You can't hurt me. You don't even know my name."

"You truly believe me to be naive, don't you?" She says nothing as he stops in front of her face.

Alexander speaks from behind her. "Stephen, stand down. Now is not the time."

"No, now is the perfect time. I think everyone here needs to remember: I am the one who created Prometheus. I am the leader." I see the eerie glow of his eyes shine off the pale complexion of Dahlia's face.

"Fine, I killed him. I reaped his soul because he was in my way. He would not let me kill Solomon." She sneers as she gets back into Stephen's face. I scoff, and all eyes are on me. A look of warning passes Dahlia's face as she glares at me.

"You killed him because he would have killed Solomon first."

She lunges, swinging her parasol. I flinch as her parasol flickers into the scythe. The blade flashes forward.

"*Stop.*"

A green tinge surrounds the edge of the blade mere inches from my skin.

"Is that true, Dahlia?"

"So what? He didn't listen to me! I should be the one to kill him!" Alexander cocks his head and shakes it.

"You killed him? Do you know how important we each are to take him down?"

"So what? We can do it without one of us."

Slap.

Dahlia's face snaps to the side as Stephen shakes with anger.

"Do you have any idea how long it took me to find all of you?" Blood runs down his fingertips dripping onto the pen as he shakes violently. A wave of pressure slams me down to the ground as everyone else straightens.

"Whoa, whoa … let's save the breakdown of our little group for after Solomon is dead."

"Mikhael!" Dahlia growls as we all turn to see him. I blink as my eyes land upon him. His clothing is disheveled. Rips, smudges, and scorch marks mar his suit.

"What the hell happened to you?" Carter scoffs as he takes in his appearance.

"I discovered something that could have produced a variable that would not be able to be accounted for."

"Did you deal with it?" Stephen asks. Mikhael reaches into his coat producing a small box with intricate golden designs covering the outside. A red splatter covers the edge as he looks down at the cube in his hands.

"Yes, yes, I did." I swallow as I realize it is blood covering the box. A loud buzz fills the air, and we look around, trying to find the source.

"What is that?"

"Where is it coming from?"

"There!" Mateo points to the sky, and true enough, the top portion of the dome becomes visible as it dissolves into the air. The buzzing grows louder as it descends, until it slams into the ground kicking up dust.

"It appears the dome has fallen."

"Whatever, let's get to killing! Start with the boy. Then we kill Solomon."

"Dahlia, you will do no such thing," Stephen orders.

"And why not, because you say so? You have no power over me." She lets go of the scythe as she brings her arm back. It turns a ghostly white as the muscles tense across her body.

"I am only going to say this once more, Dahlia. Stop it now."

"I don't care what you have to say! He is dead!" She lurches forward as her arm torpedoes for my chest, fingers extended like knives

"*Dahlia von Volaire,*" he hisses into the air, and she stops. Her fingers brush my chest as they flicker back to normal. Her face loses its manic gleam as her eyes palpitate with fear. Her face becomes ashen as she turns over her shoulder.

"What ... did you just say?"

"Did you really think you may join this organization only because I found you? That I would gather the strongest souls possible without some form of leverage? I know each of your names."

"How did you find out?"

"It doesn't matter. Just know that if you continue, you will cease to exist." She steps back, grabbing the handle of her scythe; it flickers back to a parasol before the green tint dissipates, letting her lift it back to her shoulder.

Clap.

Mikhael gathers our attention as he steps forward.

"Well, this is fun and all, but I am getting bored, and I think it is impolite of Solomon to keep us waiting. Shall I call them down to us?"

Carter sneers. "What could you possibly do?"

"You really have to get off your high horse. You already died once. Let us not see it happen again," Alexander chides. Before he can retort, Mikhael speaks once more.

"Alexander, I trust that you will cover the cost?" Alexander raises an eyebrow as he slowly nods.

"Great. Then without further ado, let the fun begin," he says out as the air grows heavy around him. A grin breaks out across his face as he turns toward the city holding out one hand, his palm facing upwards.

"*Influx.*" The city vibrates for a moment. Then Mikhael turns his hand downwards. For a second nothing happens.

Crack.

The ground underneath Mikhael cracks and splinters as he is slowly pushed into the ground.

"Here comes the fun part." He grunts as he drops to one knee, smashing the stone to bits as his knees drop on it. Then it moves. In the corner of my eye, my heart catches in my throat at the inexplicably terrifying sight of the city starting to move downward.

"Fall from the sky," Mikhael grumbles, a tired grin on his face as he struggles to kneel. Then the city plummets, the chains ripping from the city, leaving suspended chunks of stone in the air as the city rushes down to the lake. The city slams into the lake, splintering into pieces. Stone smashes against stone, buildings collapse like towers of cards. A shockwave of dust shoots past us, blinding and ruffling me as the gust mashes against me. I grit my teeth as debris lacerates my skin. All is silent as the pile of rubble lies before us.

"This can't be happening," I mumble to myself as I stare out across the former city.

"You killed them all!" With a flick of her wrist, Dahlia turns her parasol into a scythe once more. She stops and scoffs. "So, he killed himself?"

I look and nearly vomit at what I see. Where Mikhael was, all that remains is a red splatter. Blood, tons of it, covers the ground. A heavy sigh draws my attention to Alexander, who shakes his head with disappointment as he looks down at his suit, stained by the shockwave of dust.

"Of course, this is what he meant."

A green glow covers Alexander as the stain leaves his clothing. One of the strands of his hair turns gray as the green leaves him. He raises his arm toward the bloody mess that was Mikhael.

"*Upend.*" The blood reassembles, grotesquely coalescing into Mikhael's form.

"That was … unpleasant." he says as he straightens his coat. "Perhaps I overdid it?"

"Not at all," Alexander says, stepping forward over a loose stone. "This will not have ended him."

"He just dropped a city on Solomon! You took my prey!" Dahlia roars.

"Hush now, Dahlia. Solomon is still alive," Stephen chirps up causing Dahlia to turn on her heel, a wild mixture of rage and disbelief settling across her face..

"How could anyone survive that?" She roars as an explosion sends spires of ice erupting through the ground. She turns slowly, almost fearfully, to peek at the source. Tall spires of ice spring from the ground as debris flies to each side. The stone wall in front of us shakes with each spire that juts from the ground, each one making loose bricks tumble onto the loose piles of stone.

The next spire shoots through the wall, smashing it to pieces as a figure steps through the settling dust.

"Did you really think that would faze me?" Solomon's voice echoes in a condescending tone. Alexander smiles as he puts one of his hands into his pocket.

"No, we just wanted to get you down here. We were getting impatient."

"Good, because now I am going to kill you." A harsh cackle echoes out from Dahlia as she stomps toward me.

"I am so excited! I can't wait to spill your blood. But first ..."

She spins, swinging her umbrella away as she bends, shoving her crazed eyes into my face. An insane grin spreads across her face before it took on a disturbing glean.

"Stay away from him!" Solomon calls out.

"So, you do care for him," she speaks out, turning away from me, bringing one finger up to her lip. She lifts her arm and I see a flicker before a scythe slashes down across me, from my right cheek down my chest to my opposite hip.

Cough.

Warm blood gushes across me as I slump backward. My arm is already clutching at the massive wound on my chest, desperately trying to close it. As I slip backward, the world grows frigid as Solomon's face is covered by his hair.

"What the hell are you doing?" Stephen screams as he steps toward Dahlia. My vision swims as I fumble on the ground to look up toward the both of them, alternating my heavy eyes from them to Solomon. Solomon doesn't even twitch this time. No blood runs down his chest. No scar weaves across his body, either.

"It doesn't seem to matter! Nothing happened to Solomon anyway! I am simply taking care of another liability."

"For the first time, I had hope." Solomon takes a step forward.

Carter scoffs. "Such a foolish belief to have hope against us."

"For the first time, I felt there may have been another way."

Dahlia sneers. "What are you talking about? Have you lost your mind?"

"It appears I was wrong ..." Solomon says, trailing off.

"Would you care to enlighten us as to what you are wrong about?" Solomon stops in front of me, looking down at the body.

"Before we kill you," Carter chirps up.

"He is the first one I actually cared about."

"Don't worry about that. When you die, both of you will be together again," Dahlia says.

"I am going to scatter your body into the wind," Solomon hisses as a pillar of ice forms at his feet before shooting upward as he grasps it with his arm. "I am going to make sure you pay for what you did."

"Ha, and how are you going to do that?"

"I am sorry, Solaire. It appears I cannot keep my promise, after all. I am going to devastate this reality," he says as he rips the ice from the ground as it shapes into a large dagger.

"We will discuss this after he is dead, Dahlia," Stephen chides as he snaps his book open.

A crackling sound fills the air, and the argument stops. All eyes turn toward Solomon, his body glowing an eerie blue. He exhales, and a stream of frozen breath lingers in the air.

"Forest of the Borealis!"

Solomon stabs the dagger into the ground, and skinny spears smash through the ground, erupting through destroyed buildings and gigantic boulders alike as they spread outwards in a random sequence. The spears erupt in a treelike manner with spiny branches shooting forward from them, creating a beautiful forest of deadly barbs. The ground trembles as spikes rise all around me, separating the Prometheans as they fan out. Stones rain around me as they create a nook for me to lie in.

CHAPTER 14

PROMETHEUS

Solomon

The dust settles as the forest of frozen spikes holds up the torn earth. Shards of buildings create a labyrinth of walls around me. My footsteps echo out as I step forward. I stand turning between the various shards. No sight of any of the Prometheans.

"Come out, Prometheus! You are joined together to kill me, so are you too cowardly to do so?" I cry. As I turn at the sound of a woosh, a cold static goes down my arm.

Chink.

I turn and step back as the point of the spear is level with my eye, stuck within a pillar of ice not an inch away from my skin. I look past the pillar and the flash-frozen spear. Carter steps out, a scowl set on his face as a spear ripples into his left hand.

"Didn't I already kill you?" A smile graces his lips as he waves the comment off.

"You surprised me, and I suppose you could say I got a second chance," he says, twirling his spear as he marches forward. A compulsion to lift my arm fills me. Confused, I do so, then the same chilling sensation fills me as I observe the ice spread on the ground. It shoots upwards, splitting into a jagged edge. Carter stops, watching cautiously.

I turn back to the ice to see it shifting, forming on its own. It becomes much more shapely, the edges gradually getting sharper. Then I realize what is happening. The bottom has morphed further. It is molding into a weapon! The bottom has become a large spear-like head, a small rectangular pointed tip jutting out from the edges of a doubled-sided ax, each side different. One is a smaller blade—pike-like in nature with a small grip between the blades. Across from the blade a massive cleaver runs over about a third of the length of the shaft with only the head of it attached at the end of the spear. On the other end, a massive jagged blade with three one-sided barbs leads back to the center of the handle.

"Take it!"

I reach out hesitantly as I grasp the shaft. Uncertainly, I give it a small tug. Small icicles break off as the blade rackets in its frozen stand. I tug once more, and it breaks free with a small clatter. The remaining icicles break off into the wind. I look at the blade incredulously, expecting it to be heavier. I twirl it mindlessly, and I blink. I never had the ability to twirl such a thing. Especially not one like this.

"Fancy blade!" Carter grunts as a ripple appears next to his head. A spear shoots out as he charges me. I flinch backward, but my arm moves on its own. Twirling the blade in a brilliant display, I knock the projectile from the air. I spin with momentum as I move forward. Right over left, I hold the hybrid weapon as I feel the back of the weapon smash into something. I whirl, seeing the spear's blade knocked back. I raise the edge with the barbs and slash downwards. Carter snaps the center of his spear upwards. A resounding crack fills the air as I drive him to his knees.

His arms rattle as he struggles to hold the spear and by proxy my blade from him. I reach up and press my palm to the flat of the blade, driving his guard downwards as I lean onto the blade. Carter grunts as sweat runs down his brow. A ripple swirls next to his head, and I shoot my head to the left to dodge another spear.

A hollow hiss erupts from behind me, causing me to duck. A firm swipe of wind bathes the back of my neck as I kick forward, sending Carter rolling in the rubble. I turn to see Dahlia falling through the air. I swish my blade out, the curved back catching her blade as I twist to the side, letting it glide past me. I cross my arms over each other, gripping the staff, and I whirl it, bringing the spearhead into her chest.

A look of shock passes over her face as her body shimmers a ghostly white, then her body decays as it turns into wisps of intangible smoke, her flesh melting away, leaving a horrible nightmare in its place. Her hair snakes out like flayed pieces of kelp floating in water.

Her face grows monstrous as she lets out an ear-piercing screech. I grip my hand to my ear to block out the screech, as I slash with my blade. It tears free from her chest, cleanly passing through her body, her ghoulish flesh parting for the blade as a sea around a rock.

She moves with the blade as it tears from her chest. She recoils as she raises her blade in an overly telegraphed attack. She swings in a poor overhand slash, one hand on the blade.

Clang.

The large hand guard already moving intercepts the blade. Her hideous face scrunches in a scowl as we stand in the deadlock.

"Carter, you almost killed me!" she snarls as she presses down harder on my blade.

"A phantasmal being such as her will not be wounded by physical attacks. Try this."

I pause as a plan is spoken telepathically into my head. A subtle shift, and I refocus on the scythe as it grows translucent as well. First the tip slowly slides into my own blade. My eyes widen as it begins picking up speed.

"Burst!" A ball of ice floats up, blasting frigid air between us. I feel the ice coat my fingers as ice grows on her rotten flesh. Another piercing screech fills the air as the ghost flies back. Landing on both feet, the ghastly features dissipate back into the beautiful woman she once was. A newfound burn adorns her chest where the ice had impacted her. A footfall behind me alerts me to Carter's presence as he speaks up.

"Don't leave yourself open, or he will take you down in a second."

"I don't need you to tell me that," Dahlia says.

"Do you say that because you have an idea of what I can do or because I have already killed you once?" I reply.

"This won't go like last time," Carter huffs, his spear returning to his hand.

"Oh, you are right. This time you won't be given a second chance."

I stand between them. Dahlia is in front of me, Carter in the back. A cool rush flies up my arm as the air solidifies around my hand. I barely register the dull pain in my arm as I thrust my arm in front of me.

"*Bolt.*" The frost leaves my arm charging toward Carter as I twist. Another shriek alerts me that Dahlia is in pursuit. Carter thrusts forward, and I knock the spear aside. Two ripples appear in the air, one on either side of Carter's head as I run down his spear. The spears shoot forward, and I snap my weapon up. In a whirling motion, I knock one upwards and the other downwards as I keep pushing forward.

I snap a leg out, catching him in the chest once more, knocking him backward. A premonition of danger makes me duck just as the scythe flies over my head. I swipe the blade with my left arm as the cold grows on my right. A twinge of pain echoes in my hand as the blade swipes through her body. My hand comes up.

"*Burst.*" The frost blast makes her screech as she drifts back. But I am not done. I keep turning, gripping my spear in a reverse grip just under the double-bladed edge. I turn back to see Carter righting himself. I rear my arm back, and his eyes widen as I let the spear fly.

It soars through the air. He thrusts his arms out to his sides as ripples open in the air, but nothing comes out. I look down to the ground. Counting, I look up triumphantly.

"That's seven. I know the legend of Cúchulainn; you don't have any more." His eyes grow wide as he steps back. Slipping on a loose shingle, he slowly falls, the spearhead speeding toward him.

"*Stop.*" I curse silently as the spear, encased in green, stops in the air. I turn to see Alexander step out to my side.

"You didn't think we would just let you kill us off one by one, did you?" he smirks as he looks down at the rubble. Taking cautious steps, he steps down from the broken archway onto the crumbled battleground we stand upon. Stepping off just in front of the flailing Dahlia I release my weapon and snap forward. Smashing my fist into Carter's chest, I am rewarded with a gagged yelp as he rockets back, smashing into a pile of rubble. His head tilts backward from the blow. A moment of nothing until he juts his head forward and spits. Viscous blood splatters across the floor. He sneers as he reaches to the side, letting his hand rest on one of his spears that have settled next to where he lies, and his fingers curl around the handle as he struggles to get up but cannot.

"*Upend.*"

I whip around to see a smug Alexander wave his hand to the right, seemingly gesturing to Dahlia. A green aura envelops her as the ice on her chest creeps away. I blink, and Alexander's hair grows whiter.

Dahlia dashes forward as Alexander leisurely stands, clutching his watch in one hand. I lean back as the scythe's blade whizzes past my face. I kick forward, and Dahlia flickers into her ghostlike form.

I thrust a punch upwards, letting the cold feeling take over. A wail of pain lights up the air as she flinches backward, ice coating her face. Then the same green glow envelops her. My eyes dart back to the smug Alexander. I feel the scowl seat on my face before I stamp my foot down. Letting the cold sting overtake me, I yell.

"*Labyrinth!*" I take pride in the shock that shoots across his face as ice splits the ground. A large wall of ice sprouts between us, the sight of him replaced with the ugly sight of my sadistic face.

Bastian

I creep over to the fallen Watcher through the smashed stone and crushed crystals. She lies next to a small stream, running just barely out of reach of her fingertips.

I wonder if she is reaching for water because of her magic?

Kneeling next to her, I place my palm onto her back and feel the shallow rise as her lungs fill with air.

I turn her over, and her hand lashes out. Snatching my wrist, I lean in, placing a finger to my lips. She snarls, and as she moves, a wince follows.

"Are you all right?" I ask, reaching out to her.

"Yes ..." she lies, batting my hand away. She flinches with the movement and shuts her eyes. When she reopens them, she reaches out and takes my hand. A heavy footfall to my left, and I have a knife ready to throw, only to sigh in relief as it is Felgrand.

"Bastian, it would appear we are lucky. The room split open like an egg, letting the rubble fall around us for the most part." I look around, noticing the bowl shape of rubble enclosing us, plumes of dust floating across the sky like impending clouds.

"You should learn how to be quiet, crusader," Namar says as he steps over a large crystal.

"I am no crusader," he retorts, only to be ignored as Namar steps forward, nodding off to another fallen figure.

"Oi, this one over here is alright too." I look over to see Yukio, lying with chunks of crystal on top of her. She moans in pain as she tries to push a stone pillar off of her leg.

"Here, help me out, Felgrand," Namar orders.

"So, you have grown a heart now, rogue?"

"Shut it, Namar, and you too, Felgrand. Antagonize each other after we get out of here." They grasp the pillar and with one heave lift the edge of it. Namar looks over expectantly at me.

"Help out anytime!" he grunts, his forehead turning red from exertion. I scramble forward, grabbing Yukio's hands. I tug, easily sliding her among the rubble. She hisses in pain as her leg slides forward.

"She seems all right!"

"You are lucky as we all are," Felgrand says as he steps back, lifting his mighty sword from among the stones.

"Luck doesn't really have anything to do with it. I think Solomon knew exactly where to be, Felgrand," I say casually. "You assume he is the one responsible for that?"

Namar looks up at my question as he dusts off his swords.

"He is not," a ghostly voice says, breaking our peace. We stand, searching for the speaker. I narrow my eyes as a flicker of blue light catches my attention. A wisp of blue energy floats closer. It is met by another that lifts from the dust, soon to be joined by another and another. They slowly join, forming a greater orb.

"What now?" Namar groans, already sliding his sword from its sheath.

"Fear not, for I have not come to hurt you." The orb expands outwards and shrinks to reveal a beautiful woman.

"Lady Pandora!" Ai'hara gasps as she comes into view, her

once-pristine clothing now dirtied and a small gash running across her stomach, a golden hue staining her clothing.

"Prometheus is responsible for this."

"Of course they are."

"Why have you come?" Namar stands cautiously, ready for the worst. Pandora waves her hand to the side, and the wall of debris flattens, letting us see a small clearing overtaken by ice.

"Through here, you will find a boy. He is no longer among the living. I need you all to remedy this."

"My lady, I do not know how to bring someone back." I look down, disappointed in myself.

"Nor do I," Felgrand says solemnly.

"There is no need to fear that. One of Prometheus has the ability to cure any wound, even those inflicted upon the soul. But for that, the price is steep. A soul for a soul."

"A wound upon the soul?" Namar repeats curiously.

"Yes, a wound caused by the reaper's scythe."

"You must be talking of Dahlia."

"Indeed, I am."

"Now you want us to help you, but why in the world should we do that?" Namar says, leaning back against an awkwardly leaning wall. A crash in the distance distracts me for just a moment as Pandora responds.

"Solomon has crossed a line that he should not have, and should he fall today, he will release a plague much darker than Prometheus could ever be."

"Why would the boy matter, then?"

"He matters because of his connection to Solomon."

"Connection?" I ask.

"We care why?" Namar says.

"Namar!" I chide. We are hushed when Pandora raises her hand.

"Because, Namar, your contract will come into default should he fall." Namar straightens as she speaks.

"Contract, what contract?" I question.

"Rogue, have you taken another job?" Felgrand growls.

"Shut it, Felgrand. You? What do you know of my contract?"

"Enough to know that you cannot afford to let that pass." Then as quickly as she appeared, she vanishes as the blue wisps break apart.

"What is that?" I ask as Namar pushes past me toward the opening. I glare at his back as I pick up Yukio and drape her arm over my shoulder.

"We have no time to waste," he replies without looking back.

Solomon

"How did it come to this?" I mutter to myself as I run a hand over my grin. It feels fake, as if it and the bloodlust are not my own, yet they drive me forward all the same. It feels fake, as if it is not my own. A blur of movement in the reflection draws my attention to Mateo running toward me from the side. With a knife held in a reverse grip, he lunges. I turn, bringing my arms to defend, but nobody is there. A sharp pain erupts from my back as I feel a hand come clawing to my jaw, wrenching my head to the side. He brings his face next to my ear. I feel the hot, heavy breath across my ear.

"You seem to have forgotten about your reflection." I drive my elbow backward, scoring a hit. I hiss as his blade withdraws. I turn, rearing back a punch as I do so. Seeing his smug face, I step forward, my fist flashing toward his confident smile.

Crack.

I wince as pain shoots through my hand. His image cracks as the wall of ice splinters underneath my face. He leans to the side, tauntingly observing the cracks in the image. He looks to the side and smirks as his lips move. I can't hear him, but I can only imagine as his eyes begin to glow.

I turn around, peering at the reflective walls around me. A small gap appears in the wall in front of me. My eyes widen as one of Carter's spears flashes through it. I lean to the side, letting it race past me. In the reflection, I stutter as another portal opens up, accepting the spear.

My eyes dart back and forth as I search for the spear. I catch a glimpse of it as another opens up. I duck under it, cursing under my breath as it races into another portal. This time, I feel the spear slice into my skin. A thin line as it shoots toward another portal.

"*Shatter!*" I grip my fist tight as a shockwave erupts from me. The ice blows apart. Not a trace left of them, the first sight I see is Carter bent down, one hand on his knee as Silas kneels next to him, both hands on Carter's chest, a golden glow emanating from them.

He is healing him! I scowl as I draw upon the cold once more. This time I feel a searing pain in my arm. I glance down as ice shoots out of my hand. Blood drips from the tip of the edge as it grows into a savage looking bolas. More of my blood runs down the weapon. I growl as I let it fly.

"*Stop.*" I am ready as I rear my arm back. The searing pain continues as I swing it forward, letting three more fly.

"*Dilation!*" A green box encapsulates the projectiles. I glare over my shoulder to see Alexander leaning against a wall. His face looks years older.

"Forget about the projectiles. Stop Solomon!" Dahlia screams from behind me.

"Don't try to tell me how to use my power!" he grunts. His concentration must have slipped because the green flickers and the weapons fly forward.

"Damn it!" I turn, weaving to the side as I do, narrowly dodging the blade again. My arm thrusts out, a snaking trail of ice floating through the air, glittering as it flies.

I catch Dahlia by the neck. A piercing wail erupts from her as she struggles.

"Ahhh!" I move closer to her, closing the space as I press the staff of her weapon against her. She pulls her arm, holding the scythe backward, dragging the blade to me. My hand finds the handle, stopping it. I feel the pain of the cold as it creeps over the handle and her side.

She screams once more as she thrashes against me, her body flickering a ghostly white. When her body flickers she slips through mine, her arms thrashing through my own. I peer past her to see Silas being held by Carter as a human shield. His body is pinned by the bola. He flinches as his clothes are soaked by the blood.

I take my arm from her side, raising it beside me. I straighten my fingers. A light icy sheen crawls up them.

"*Now, take your revenge.*"

I feel my smirk grow bigger as the voice resounds through my head. My hand shoots forward of its own volition, and a green glow flashes onto my hand. It drags to a halt. I look past my hand to a rapidly aging Alexander. His hand spreads out with his other gripping it by the wrist as he angles it toward me. I tilt my head as I crank it back to Dahlia. I turn my head slowly, almost mockingly, toward my frozen hand. Anger shoots through me.

She has to die! But as surely as it comes, rage gives way to innovation, and an idea forms in my head.

I feel the crawling cold slither up my fingers as the points of digits grow small points.

Oh, yes. This could work.

The tips grow longer, forming a set of spikes that inch forward.

So close. Yes, they are close now.

I see them about to escape the greenish hew in the air. Then a massive weight lands on me. I fall to the ground, my knee smashing against the stone. I lose my grip, and Dahlia tumbles away. Turning ghostlike, she darts to the side. I turn to see Mikhael stumble out from a piece of stone, his clothing ripped and torn, dust covering each bit of his body, effectively standing between Dahlia and me.

"Took me a while to get out, but that's all right—they did their job."

He limps forward and holds up his hand, opening his fingers.

"Look what I have." All the blood in my body runs cold as I look upon the box that was previously my prison.

Solaire

When I awake, a cold, lifeless feeling clings to my body. The entire area is gray and dull, no walls or ceiling as the space seems to stretch on for miles. I shiver as the cold intensifies.

"So, I guess I am dead?" I whisper to myself. Silence permeates the air as I pick myself up. I dust my legs off before I give myself a hug to keep myself warm.

"Better to keep moving now that I am dead. Maybe there will be something around here."

"Yes and no."

I stop my eyes from going wide as a female voice reaches my ears. I spin to find a woman with unspeakable beauty in a dress, a regal air about her. My eyes fixate on a wound in the middle of her chest.

"Are you a ghost?"

"No, and neither are you."

"Aren't I dead?"

"As I said, yes and no."

"What does that mean?"

"It means you will not be here for long."

"How do you know that?"

"When you wake up, you will have to do something important."

I scoff. "Really, and what is that?"

"If you want Solomon to live past this day, you will help him escape once you wake up."

"Let's say I do wake up! How will I do anything?" She waves her hand to the side, and an image of Solomon with a spear in his side conjures on a thin blanket of mist.

"Remove the stakes holding him down, and then the rest will fall into place."

"Fine, but how am I supposed to get close enough, let alone remove the spear?"

She extends her hand with a closed fist. She turns her hand over and opens her fingers. In her hands sits a beautiful pure-white crystal, in a precise octagonal cut.

"With this." I reach out tenderly, carefully taking the gem from her palm.

"What is it?" I roll it around in my hand lightly.

"Crush it once you wake up, and you will have your chance." I feel the cold recede a little bit.

Bastian

We edge into the clearing, seeing the mighty battle in front of us. We crouch as Felgrand feels Solaire's neck. He shakes his head slightly.

257

"She is right: no life in the boy." I feel as if a massive load slams down onto me, a heavy disappointment permeates the air.

Then everything stops as Mikhael steps out from behind a large slab of stone. He speaks distantly, a victorious smile on his face as he stares Solomon down. He reaches into his jacket and produces something that makes my blood run cold: one of Pandora's boxes and on the top is a splash of crimson.

Solomon gasps. "How did you get that box?"

"I let others find it for me," Mikhael replies.

"Where is he?" Yukio screams, stumbling forward. I catch her wrist as Mikhael turns our way.

"Oh, it's the others I speak of." He opens his arms in an inviting gesture.

"Where is Theron?" she demands, swiping forward as I hold her against my shoulder.

"Who, your friend?" A glance to the side as his lips purse, holding back a malicious grin. "Let's just say he probably isn't doing so well."

He laughs in response.

"You bastard!" A cold wind sweeps through the air.

"Stop right there!" Mikhael turns, grasping the box as he holds it toward Solomon, and the wind dies down.

"How did you get one of her boxes?"

"She gave it to me."

"Liar. She would never give one of them to you!"

"So what if I am lying. What matters is that I have the box now." The ground cracks as frost spreads outward from the ground underneath Solomon.

"You think I fear being sealed again?" A mask of frost begins forming over his face.

"I know you do." He tosses the cube forward. Almost immediately, ice shoots forward, each a curving fang protruding from the ground, each one racing for a member of Prometheus.

"*Stop.*" A pulse of green stops the talon aimed at Alexander. Dahlia raises her scythe, bringing it down and catching the arcing ice in the crook of the blade. Carter steps to the side, slapping the ice projectile away. He flips his spear around and throws it forward as Mateo holds up a piece of the shattered ice. Mateo places the ice in the spears path. The spear enters the reflective surface unimpeded, vanishing from view.

Shlick.

The spear strikes Solomon in the back. He stumbles forward as a pulse of frigid air slams into the environment. Frost grows on the damaged remains of the walls around us. Snowflakes flicker around the growing circle of frozen ground surrounding Solomon. I run to Silas's downed form. Stopping at his side I lean over him, seeing his pained expression.

"You have to help!"

"I don't have to do anything! Prometheus and the others—they use me! Now I am dying in the dirt for their stupid reasons," he groans as he holds his chest, his scarlet blood soaking his weathered shirt.

"If you are dying, you can do one last thing," I plead. He grits his teeth as he shakily pushes his glasses up, pinching the bridge of his nose.

"What is it?" he says, groaning painfully.

"You can help him, right?" I motion Felgrand over. He brings Solaire's limp body.

"Why should I help him?" Silas growls.

"Listen: Pandora told us that he is necessary," Ai'hara speaks up.

"I see it. The way they torment you. It is just like what happened to him." I gesture toward Solaire.

"So? If I do this, I die." I grab Silas by the collar.

"Don't you see? You are already dying! Why don't you use your last breaths as a way to save him?" He sighs and coughs once.

"To give up my life for someone I don't know? I want to keep living!" he growls at me, a small trail of blood spilling down his lips. I hold his gaze as he winces and another trail of blood drops from his lips.

"No one wants to die, but at least you can save him before you do." He rolls his eyes as he reaches out and places his palm on Solaire's neck.

"He doesn't have a soul; I cannot help him."

"Pandora—she said you could help him." He looks up, shocked, before a ghostly smirk touches his pale cheeks.

"I should have guessed that she would know." A sickly wet cough erupts from him as he spits out blood. He looks down at it morosely.

"Please, you have to! At least give him a chance. Your time may be up, but you can right things now."

"Fine, I can do it, but he better help set things right." He reaches out and glares up at me. "And kid, you better fuck Prometheus up."

"Thank you."

"Don't thank me yet. You better hold your end."

"I don't even know your name."

"Silas. Don't forget me, yeah?" A wild grin spreads over my face as a silver glow dances across Silas's fingers.

"Name's Bastian, and I won't. Any of the others you want dead first?"

"I would want nothing more than to see that arrogant bastard Alexander die."

"I will do it twice just for you," comes my reply, spoken as his fingers touch Solaire's forehead.

Solomon

"Do you feel it?"

The voice is back again. I twist my head trying to ignore it, but something is off. I feel something more, something foreign. I reach for the spear in my gut and tug. A solemn cold fills my injury.

"Let it spread. Let that feeling take over."

The voice is intoxicating as it feels so right to let the feeling spread. Silas begins screaming, and I see it spread. Ice begins creeping over him, a thin sheet that spreads like a virus. Then it dawns on me: the spread of the ice is what I feel. I watch it encase him, his face frozen in agony as the others crowd around him.

"Now, just as all things must do, magic or otherwise, let it shatter, and with it their illusion of immortality."

"Shatter." I utter the word so cruelly, so lacking in life that I barely wince as I hear a cry pierce the air.

"How did it come to this?"

CHAPTER 15

POSTPONING THE INEVITABLE

Bastian

"No!" I gasp as I lean onto Silas clutching at his frozen cloak. A moment of horrific silence steals the air. Then a large crack splits his face.

"No!" Several other cracks start spreading over Silas' body. Then he begins to shatter, cracking and splitting. I feel myself slip through him as he is rendered into mere shards in the air as they shred themselves, splitting smaller and smaller. I look over at Ai'hara as I hold the particles between my fingers. My hands shake feebly as I open them up to her contorted face and the remainder scatter into the wind.

I turn to Solomon, rage consuming me as I feel myself shake.

"You killed him!" He looks at me, confusion spreading across his face. "Bastian?"

"He is the only one who could save him!" His brow furrows as he looks past me.

"What are you talking about?"

"He was the only one who could bring Solaire back!"

"What ... no ... you're lying!" he screams as his face twists in anger. A ring of ice, bending around his arm like a reactive quake, makes its way down his arm, which grips his head. The ripple splits and folds in on itself as it moves over his skin. The ice becomes square as it reassembles over his skin and breaks apart repeatedly.

"Why would I lie to you? I am the one who helped keep you secret for years! I lied to Solaire for you!"

"You lied for me?"

"Did you really think that with everyone looking for you that you just managed to slip under the radar?"

"What do you mean?"

"You surviving in the First Reality was a part of the plan that Pandora created."

"Pandora did this?"

"She assigned me and Durgess as your keepers. After your other half was sealed away."

"You all lied to me?"

"We lied for you!"

"Then why Durgess, why you?"

"Durgess was tasked as a way to repent for releasing you."

"And you?"

"This was my out from Syndicate. A small price to pay for my freedom."

"So you became my friend because it was your job?"

"No! I became your friend naturally. I was just supposed to help keep you safe!"

"Regardless, Solaire is gone!"

"Now he is! Silas could have saved him!"

"Silas? Silas! Now you know their names! Those monsters want me dead, and you are over there befriending them?" I lean forward.

"He told me as he prepared to save him! Then you killed him!" I spit with venom.

"You don't know that he could have saved him."

"Pandora told me he could!" His eyes snap open, and he stares in shock.

"You can't be telling the truth ... I killed her." He lets out a howl as a spear pierces his side. The blade is narrow at first before it springs outward, sending five more spearheads just like it, erupting from the impact point in his chest. I flinch as they each shoot from his chest. He coughs out blood as he slumps to one knee.

Solomon

The sun begins to dip on the horizon as I grip the spear in my side. Blood trickles down my chin as I feel it slip past my lips. With a grind of my teeth and a harsh yank, I tear it from me. Tossing it onto the ground, I glare at Carter.

"Not so easy this time, is it?" he gloats as if he were a child winning for the first time. I go to stand, but then lose feeling in my legs.

"*Stop.*" I shoot an angry glare at an amused Alexander. "What can I say? I like seeing you on your knees."

"It is a shame, though, about your friend. He is right: Silas could have saved him," Alexander smirks, his pocket watch clutched in a frail aging hand. Grief washes over me as I lower my head.

"Enough about that. You killed the Lady?" I raise my head to see Ai'hara screaming at me.

"Shut it!" A pulse of green, and Ai'hara is suspended.

"The nerve—and after I got to see you wallow in despair too. What a way to ruin it. Dahlia, if you would." He rises, a sneer on his face.

A sense of danger, and I snap my head to the right, my hand flying first. Then the crushing pressure comes down upon it. Just before it stops Dahlia's blade, my hand crashes to the ground. The scythe draws closer. Inches, centimeters, millimeters. Then it stops as my left hand catches the blade right in front of my eye. I follow the blade back to an irate Dahlia. Ice creeps along the edge of the blade as I nudge it away from my face.

I feel my stance wobble as my feet come free, but my hand stops as the green box surrounds both the blade and my arm. Heavy footfalls stomp behind me, and then Carter's spear flies over my shoulder, slamming into the green box. I gasp as the blade distorts in the air approaching my hand. I desperately try to wrench my hand out of the way, but I can't. I wince as the point pierces my hand, sliding its blade halfway through it.

Dahlia smirks as she releases her scythe and dances to the spear. Grabbing it, she smiles at me before it falls away into a rage-filled sneer, her lips furrowing outward. She thrust the spear forward into my other hand, staking them both to the ground. I cry as she steps backward, catching the handle of the suspended scythe.

"Now it is time to reap you of your soul."

"*Stop!*" The green aura freezes around Dahlia's arms.

"What are you doing, Alexander!" she screeches, her face twisting in anger.

"I cannot let you reap the soul of such a powerful being."

"And why not? He would die all the same!" Carter steps forward, holding his hand out as if he wants to hold Alexander's response. Alexander shakes his head condescendingly.

"To reap a soul means to consume it and to take whatever is there into your own."

"Dahlia! You didn't tell me of this!" Mateo roars as Dahlia purses her lips.

"It does not matter so long as he dies!" she hisses.

"You speak of Solomon's power as if it is anything less than godly."

"It doesn't matter. We can fight like petulant children after he is dead," Stephen says authoritatively.

Solaire

I awake with a startled gasp as the cold clutch on me sweeps away in a silver warmth. I woke to see Bastian kneeling, one hand on my stomach as he stares to the side. I look over to see Solomon kneeling between the Prometheus members, barely holding them off. I sit up, the hand on top of me sliding off as Bastian turns, shocked.

"How are you—"

I silence him by holding up my hand as the others turn to see me. Namar's face lights up in joy as he sees me awake.

"Kid, you are something else."

"You are still quite strong."

I look over to Ai'hara. A light grin graces her lips as relief passes over her carefully cultivated features.

I turn back to Solomon to see Stephen walking forward, stopping just in front of him. Standing up, the others look on in shock as they prepare to catch me. I wobble before I take a step forward. I am stopped as Felgrand grabs my arm with his massive hand.

"What are you doing?" I glance down at the crystal in my hand as I clutch it tighter in my fist.

"Saving my friend." I shake him from my arm and squeeze my fist tighter. I feel the crystal crunch in between my fingers, and dust flows from between them. It lightly swirls around me as I begin to feel light.

"What is happening to you?" Ai'hara asks, pointing one finger at me. I follow it to my hand—which is now dispersing away into the air, like dust. I scramble, clutching onto my wrist as I panic, flailing about as my hand splinters into the air. I grasp the stump of my hand as the rest of my body dissolves into the air. I feel myself scatter, each piece of me floating into the wind as I float in the air at the ashen expressions of the two friends. Namar squares his jaw as he stabs one of his blades into the ground angrily.

"... No," Bastian breathed out as he collapsed onto his knees.

"That idiot went and killed himself!" I go to move my arm, and I feel the muscles move, and a strange conscious knowledge of where each piece of me is in the air. I turn around and on a whim, move toward Solomon. Gliding through the air, a chill rises up my spine as I drift forward, the chill moving through each cell of my body.

I slither around them, stopping beside Solomon to look at the members of Prometheus argue. I glare at Alexander and he straightens as if he feels my gaze. He looks right at me, and his eyes linger for a moment, and I feel my hands move in front of me in my mock defensive stance. The air makes me feel cold to the bone. Then I look back to Solomon's pierced hands. I kneel beside him, preparing myself. This will be a one-chance ordeal.

Solomon

I wrestle against the spear pinning my hands to the ground.

"You may have the conviction, but you lack the strength to beat us," Stephen speaks as he steps regally from another piece of rubble, his hands clasped behind his back, neatly holding his book, inching closer with each shuffle.

"I have the strength and the cause. It is you who have no cause!" I spit, meeting the dignified and satisfied looks among the Prometheans.

"We merely want to stop you from destroying this world," he reasons, taking another step.

"I would not destroy the world; I would be saving it!"

"Hah! You speak of grandeur, but we have seen what you can do. You have reformed the very land we stand on. Your very power brought upon the ice ages, devastating the other reality. You have caused more hurt to both realities than any other being ever has or ever could. So, tell me, despite all that, how could you possibly save the world?" Alexander shakes his head lightly as he waves his hand over a piece of wood that glows green as it forms into a neat chair, upon which he sits.

"I would sever it in two. I would separate your reality and the other."

"What good could ever come from separating us from the other reality if you could even achieve such a thing?"

"I would use my power at the heart of this world to freeze the trickle of magic that leaks into the other world. I now have the power; I just need to get there." Alexander leans forward in the chair and sneers at me.

"You will never get to ruin our reality."

"You just don't get it, do you?" Stephen steps forward. I cannot help but glare as he kneels down to look me in the eyes.

"What are you talking about?" He leans forward, bringing his lips next to my ear and whispers.

"I could have killed you at any time." He leans back, a devious smile on his face as he taps his notebook lightly.

"It would not have been hard."

"Then why do this? Why let me live?" I scream in surprise.

"What is he talking about, Stephen?" Alexander straightens. A faux look of surprise washes over Stephen's face.

"Nothing. He is merely trying to drive us apart."

"Bullshit! You told him something just now."

"I merely told him that this is inevitable. It could have happened at any time. His running is merely a cog in the machine."

"Machine? Are you saying that you planned this?" Dahlia screeches.

"Dahlia, do be quiet. Let Stephen speak for himself." Stephen merely regards the ground as he stares intently. I look down and flinch backward as my shadow begins to writhe and bulge, spreading and contracting in grotesque ways. Pain wracks my body.

"Time is of the essence ... Mikhael ... if you will?"

"Fuck you, Stephen." Mikhael steps backward, making some room. Stephen nods his head as his lips purse into a thoughtful frown.

"It would seem that my leadership over you all is waning. Perhaps we need another demonstration of why I lead you all?"

"Oh, do shut up. We followed you to kill Solomon—nothing more," Carter spits.

"It is in your best interest Carter, to not insult those who are stronger than you," Alexander chides as Stephen turns to face me once more.

"In either case, I do believe that this is goodbye, Solomon" he says assuredly as he withdraws his notebook.

"Hey, where's the kid's body?" Stephen's eyes widen as he shoots around, eyes frantically searching for Solaire's body.

Solaire

They all turn around to look for me, and I take this moment to reach forward. Particles assemble into the air as my hands form around the spear's handle. The particles continue upwards as I pull the spear from Solomon's hand, which snaps up to clutch Stephen's own. Blood pools across his hand as it bubbles through the wound, a forlorn look of surprise on Stephen's face as he struggles to get away. I marvel at my body as it slowly but surely comes together once more.

"I have you now." A murderous grin plasters onto Solomon's face as a soft clink echoes at our feet, and we all look down. It is the box!

"Noooo!" Solomon screams as a golden light bathes the three of us. The last thing I see as I stumble back is Mikhael's gleeful expression as he lowers his arm. Then we are left in a void. Everything we can see is white as fog surrounds us.

"It would appear we will get to see each other for a while longer, Solomon," Stephen says cruelly.

"You speak as if you are not worried."

"I am not afraid of you Solomon." A heavy sigh leaves Stephen as he shrugs his shoulders.

"Then you will die braver than most," Solomon retorts as a sliver of ice extends upwards from the ground.

"Not just yet, not just yet. My machinations are just beginning," he says as his eyes begin to glow and he grips his pen tighter.

Bastian

"Ah-ha! We did it!" Mikhael cheers as he turns around, smiling.

"Will you let me go now, Alexander?" Dahlia snarls. The green glow flickers before vanishing.

"Sure, there is no need to hold you back now." Dahlia snatches her scythe as she grabs it with both hands, ready to swing it at Alexander.

"Are you sure it is wise to fight me Dahlia?" he taunts. I stand up, keeping my eyes on them as they all stiffen. I hold my hand up so the others will stay.

"I don't care about that! I care far more for how the kid is alive, let alone appearing out of thin air!" Mikhael roars, gesturing toward the cube. I step to the side behind one of the pillars, breaking the line of sight.

"Yeah, what happened? He just vanished, and then he reappears from thin air!" Mateo questions. I edge along the cover of a broken wall, crossing to the other side. I peek around to see the back of Alexander's chair. He shuffles, straightening, placing both legs on the ground. I look across to the next wall. I just need to get past the gap. The next piece of cover is a stone wall, partially covered in crystals.

"Just like that bitch, Pandora," Carter scoffs. As Carter speaks, I dash for it as quietly as I can. Without turning back, I stop. Closing my eyes, I hold my breath to still my beating heart.

"Enough. In Stephen's absence, I shall lead us." I peer around the next corner to see Alexander stand up. I see the cube just a couple steps from me. I edge out a little bit, looking between them as they all turn to Alexander.

"Why do you get that choice?"

"Do you really wish to test me?" he says, straightening his back as his eyes glow a dull green.

"You have used enough of your time. I don't think you can stop us with what you have left."

"I have plenty to spare for the likes of you." I inch farther along, my hand stretching out as I eye the group.

So close, so close.

"Namar!" I snarl. As Mikhael turns to me, my hand falls to the ground, its weight tripled. They all turn to face me, their visages ranging from anger to outright hatred. They step forward as one.

"You will not lay even a finger on that cube," Mikhael taunts. I tear a blade from my holster and let it fly. With a flick, the first sails forward, a blur to all. I launch a second immediately after.

Shink.

The blade strikes Mikhael, and my arm can move again. I reach forward.

"Flux!"

I am suddenly forced back, my fingers barely kissing the box's exterior as Mikhael mirrors me. The second blade skids on the ground. I curse as it misses. Then my eyes widen as the shadow that Pandora's box casts grows darker and a blade pokes through it pushing the box to me.

"Stop!"

The blade stops in the air, but the box soars toward me. I catch it in my hands as I bounce across the ground. I roll to the side to dodge Dahlia's scythe, then dart to the others. Weaving between the standing ruins, I feel them shatter and break the debris as the Prometheans pursue me, destroying everything in their way.

"Run, run as fast as you can! We will get that box!" Alexander booms as I reach the others. I turn back to see a spear whiz past my face, and Carter stepping through a toppled arch, Dahlia following after him.

I tighten my hold on the box as particles begin to rise from it. I huddle closer together as boulders are sent flying from behind us, and more of the Prometheans step out. I curse lightly as I see a Promethean at every one of the entrances to the ruin.

The particles collate and form a figure.

"Lady Pandora!" Ai'hara gasps, bowing slightly. I keep an eye on the adversaries as they all come to a stop.

"I thought you died."

"For someone such as me to perish takes quite a bit more than Solomon could ever accomplish."

Alexander sighs. "To what do I owe the pleasure, Pandora?"

"I will not let you have the box so easily, Alexander." She stretches her arm out in front of us protectively, and a sigil on the ground beneath us lights up. Markings spread until they rest just under our feet.

"What are you doing?" Mateo screams as he stares at the radiant brightness. The light grows before it flashes in a blinding hew of green.

The glow dies down as we land in shallow waters. I crack my eyes as I feel the rocks dig into my flesh, the current passing through my clothes. I look down at the ground to see dirt and stones. A pleasant temperature settles upon us. The sound of running water distracts me, and I look over to see a large shallow river running next to us.

"Where the fuck is this?" Namar's unsurprising outburst rings out.

"Well, something seems to live here—or did," I explain, eyeing the broken wicker basket.

"What do you mean?" Felgrand asks, following my gaze. Ai'hara takes in a sharp breath of air.

"This stream! I know where we are!"

"Well, then, speak up. Where are we, most insightful one?" Namar prods.

"We are in the Glade!"

"The Glade? Never heard of it!"

"This is where the Watchers reside."

"You mean something is actually looking up for once?"

"Don't jinx us yet, Namar." We sit down near the river as I hold out the cube in the fading sunlight.

"So now what?"

"We rest, and at first light, we have Cu'jehi help us," Ai'hara says confidently, a newfound strength behind her gaze.

In the Rubble

"Where did you take them?" Dahlia roars as she swings her scythe to decapitate Pandora.

Clang.

The blade meets Pandora's outstretched hand, and a look of shock passes over Dahlia's face.

"My spirit is resolute. Your blade cannot touch me." She turns a hue of silver as wisps begin to trail from her body, disappearing into the air.

"Stop!" An aged Alexander steps forward, his body leaning over as his age rapidly increases. The wisps and Pandora stop midair, still clutching the scythe.

"You may exist outside of space, but not of time. Being outside one makes you vulnerable to the other." Gravel crunches under Mateo's heel as a curious expression works across his face.

"Why did the box work? I know that each being can only be imprisoned once. Why was Solomon imprisoned?" A shadow looms over Alexander's face as he contemplates Mateo.

"A group of people is not the same, even if one of them has been imprisoned before."

"Now, Pandora—"

"I will not speak of where they are." Cut off by Pandora, Alexander's lip twitched downward and shot forward, leering into her face, switching his gaze from one of her eyes to the other.

"You may not now, but all in due time … all in due time, Lady Pandora," he says as his eyes flash a wicked green. "You only postpone the inevitable."

CHAPTER 16

THE MONARCH

Solaire

"So long as I don't injure you until I have a kill shot then I don't have to worry about it." Solomon proclaims as ice spreading up from the ground forms the distinctive shape of Solomon's halberd.

"Oh, is that all?" Stephen's lip curls upwards. His hand scribbles as Solomon snatches the halberd from the ice. Dashing forward, Solomon calls to me.

"Solaire, find somewhere to hide!"

"There is nowhere you can hide from me." He skips backward to dodge Solomon's blade. I scramble away, running into the mist.

"*Arta scrisa.*" I dive behind one of the boulders, and I can hear Solomon swinging his weapon once more.

"*Circ.*" I keep running as the word echoes after me. The mist thickens and then for a moment I can only see white. Then it lessens and I see two figures ahead. It is Solomon and Stephen.

How did I get back here?

"Anywhere you run will take you back here." Solomon stabs forward and Stephen knocks the blade away with his book.

"Your book is able to stop a blade?"

"Of course, it is, after all it is something of a contract with a god."

"Which god?" Stephen chuckles, ignoring him as he scribbles once more.

"Arta scrisa aplatiza." Solomon smashes into the ground.

"Bolt!" Solomon flicks his fingers forward and from them an icicle launches at Stephen.

"You cannot hurt me with that," Stephen scoffs, getting Solomon to growl in response before he smashes his polearm into the ground, sending a wave of ice at Stephen. A flash of green light and the ice parts. Solomon slashes downward, missing Stephen by no more than a hair's length.

"Arta scrisa aplatiza."

Solomon hits the ground again; coughing violently, he spits up blood. Stephen lurks forward. He scribbles again and again. Solomon's grunts of pain fill the air as he smashes into the ground repeatedly.

"Have you had enough yet?"

"When I get my hands on on you ..." Solomon trails off, blood dribbling down his chin. Stephen steps closer, stopping right in front of him.

"I really want to kill you right now." His foot lashes out, catching Solomon beneath his chin. *I can't take it anymore. I have to separate them.*

"Stop it!" A powerful gust rushes forward. Stephen skips backward as the ground freezes and a small barrier erects itself between Solomon and Stephen. Stephen glares at Solomon.

"So, you still have fight in you, or perhaps ..." He pauses, his gaze slipping to me. "It was you."

"Stay away from him." Stephen crunches forward along the ice angling to me.

"Run Solaire!" Solomon screams, as Stephen writes once more in his book. The air leaves my lungs as fear shakes my being. My feet won't move.

"Arta Scrisa." I fall to my knees as he stalks forward, a predatory gleam in his eyes. Then he utters the spell that terrifies me.

"Eviscerate." The fight leaves me as tears slip down my cheek.

"I am so sorry Solomon," I whisper.

"Say your goodbyes, Solomon."

"You bastard! Solaire, I won't let you die!" I smile sadly as I see the skin on my hand grow ashen.

"It's okay, just save yourself."

"No!" I feel weird and I look down at my hands. An icy crevasse begins crawling up it.

"What is this?" I look up at Solomon, his hand stretching out toward me. His fingers glow a frosty blue.

"How intriguing, you actually found a way to stop it," Stephen mocks with a forlorn look of disgust. "Yet you used your power to save your friend."

"Of course, I would. He reminded me, what it means to be myself."

"It really is a shame that I will be killing you soon." He scribbles in his book once more. The wall of ice next to Solomon explodes and he flinches as ice peppers his body as he is thrown backwards.

"You should know your place, Helgen!" Stephen ferociously brings the pen down to the page again. Just as before the land moves. Solomon struggles to stand as he is battered again.

"*Bolt!*" An icy beam fires from Solomon's hand. The shaky beam heads straight for Stephen, a condescending grin on his face.

"Useless!" A flourish of his pen, almost as if checking a box from a list and the beam scatters, breaking into snowflakes.

"You cannot touch me with power like this."

'I have to do something!'

A cry rings out as Solomon is buffeted by stone once more.

"Stop it, you monster!" I run forward screaming at him.

"Ah Solaire, I had almost gotten carried away to the point I had forgotten about you"

"I told you I won't let him die!" A quick glance from Stephen and then a quick note.

"Silence you," Solomon cries out as he smashes into the ground.

"Solaire, I don't know why, but my magic doesn't seem to affect you as it should. You are special between your unnatural connection with Solomon and your resistance to my magic."

"How can you use your magic so freely? I thought you needed blood?" Solomon calls out, dragging Stephen's attention from me.

"Now, you begin to see, the cost you all saw me pay, was nothing but a front." He shakes his head condescendingly. "Blood was never needed.

Even now the greater purpose of Prometheus escapes you. As you can see, I am far stronger than I have let on."

"What are you saying?" Stephen turns to me, a wicked satisfaction playing across his face before he turns stomping over to Solomon.

"I never built Prometheus with the sole idea of defeating you, Solomon. I need them so that I can take down a bigger foe." He pauses and Solomon turns his attention to the ground, where his writhing shadow lies.

"That's right, the Monarch." Stephen spoke as if to confirm his suspicion.

"There can only ever be one Monarch, and I will take him down. His crown will be mine. Therefore, I cannot kill you just yet. I do need to kill you, but I need to do it with the rest of Prometheus there to aid me, and be in a location his army cannot interfere."

"That is why you needed the box. You wanted to get us within one of Pandora's cells and die within it."

"Correct, and now all I need is to get the rest of Prometheus here and then once you are dead, the Monarch will be soon after." Anger boils under my skin.

"Why do all this for that? What does becoming the Monarch give you?"

"The right to rule, plain and simple. Although, that does remind me. I need you as well, Solaire." He takes a step closer to me and Solomon struggles against the boulders containing him.

"Why is everyone so fixated on me?"

"I wrote your name in my book." I flinch.

"What do you mean?"

"You were supposed to find me in some way."

"I am here now," I state, my confusion evident.

"You were written to seek me out, and then your friend was intended to help you do so."

"Maybe you didn't do it right."

"There is no way I messed up! I have done this for years!" he roars, stomping forward. I stumble and trip as I back up.

"You have immunity to my magic, and if you are immune to other magic, then perhaps you will be instrumental in the downfall of the Monarch."

"How do you know that I am immune to magic? I was teleported and dragged through mirrors by your team!"

"Then you had better hope that you are immune to more than just my magic." He stops in front of me and reaches out.

"Stay away from me!" The air rushes around me, carrying shards of ice, forcing Stephen to step back from the initial gust. He grunts and a scarlet bead slips down his cheek as he hardens his gaze. Two fingers trail the drop, letting him stare down at the liquid on his hand. Solomon scowls as he pants.

"You still have strength?" Stephen queries disinterested. A quick swipe of his pen and Solomon crashes into the ground once more.

"Why are you doing this?" I scream, scooting back.

"The why is easy, the only question is how long are you going to impede me."

"I would rather see you fail before I lift a finger to help you." I spit.

"All you are doing is angering me. I will be the Monarch, either you can help me now and I will spare you, or you and all your friends can perish once I hold the crown." He reaches forward as his arm glows an eerie green.

Bastian

Following the strange river was easy enough but odd scratches and broken branches litter the path. As we approach a clearing a foreboding sense fills my heart. Hobbling into the small village a strange wooden crucifix stands tall in the center of the village, a body strung up on it. A gasp escapes Ai'hara as she dashes past me.

"Cu'jehi!" Ai'hara cries running forward to the cross, stopping at the base of it. The labored rise and fall of his chest is the only indication that he is not dead.

"Who is he?" I put my hand on her shoulder, gaining her attention.

"He is the Head of the Watchers." Then a voice comes from behind us.

"Former head." We turn to see a Watcher with one good eye, staring down at us from a hastily made wicker throne.

"I really do not have the energy to keep fighting. Give it a rest yeah?" Namar pants, slowly drawing his sword once more.

"Ku'terik, what have you done?"

"I have taken my rightful place." From the huts several Watchers emerge.

"You can't do this! What about those who follow the way?" Ai'hara snarls.

"They were taken care of first, and now you will be mine."

"Never." She turns to the other Watchers. "You all have to help us; he is abandoning the ways of old!"

"They won't listen to you. Everyone listen closely! She has brought us human scum! She is the one who has breached the old ways. She loses all rights and should be mine. Help me teach these intruders their place!" Several more Watchers emerge on either side of the throne and step forward with various weapons in their hands.

"It appears we don't have a choice," Felgrand sighs as he pulls his longsword from his sheath.

"You are mad, "Ku'terik!"

"I am not mad! Mad is waiting for the world to change. Mad is following old beliefs. Mad is not taking what is rightfully mine."

"Rightfully yours?" Namar scoffs, shaking his head as his blade bounces uncertainly with each breath.

"Aye, he seems to have lost his mind," Felgrand continues.

"Quiet! I will have your heads for that!" Ku'terik roars, a stone sword coming to life in his hands. Ai'hara scans the crowd.

"Why are the others standing with you? Where are those who support Cu'jehi?"

"Simple, I got rid of them."

"A coup in your own city, and the others follow. You are all sheep!" Felgrand scoffs.

"How could they sit by and allow you to do this?" I scream.

"They would not have, if a human was not invited here. Humans are the scum of this reality. Multiplying and colonizing everything, like ants."

"Not all of us are like that!" I retaliate, the dull throb in my bones falling way to the anticipation. I slip Pandora's box into my pocket and draw my knives.

"Don't try arguing with him, he won't change his mind. I suppose it is better if we just fight," Namar spits, and several of the Watchers step forward brandishing axes, spades, sickles.

The first charges at Ai'hara and she lashes out kicking the attacker, causing him to skid backwards.

"Look, she has attacked one of her own," Ku'terik scoffs, stepping backwards.

"He attacked me!" Ai'hara screams out as I lean forward to duck under a swipe of a Watcher's ax. I dart upwards, my blade angled for her neck.

"Don't kill them!" Ai'hara calls out and at the last minute I pivot to smash my fist into the Watcher's face. I turn her around and throw the assailant into the encroaching mob.

I glance around to see Felgrand shrug one off and send him sprawling across the ground courtesy of a boot.

"Why not?"

"They are my people!" Out of the corner of my eye a female with a sickle strikes out at Namar. Namar turns, a sinister glint catching his eye as he strikes her down, bifurcating her with a casual slash. Golden ichor splashes him, as he turns coldly to the rest of the shocked crowd, who begin to mumble amongst themselves.

"See, humans are monsters!" One of the crowd shouts out.

"Look how he didn't hesitate to kill her," another murmurs.

"This is why we have to follow Ku'terik," one proclaims as Ku'terik nods in acknowledgement.

"Do you really think that I am going to just let you go after you attack me?" Namar scoffs.

"Rogue, they are people too."

"I don't care what they are." He turns to the ground, his lip twinging uncontrollably. His eyes bore into each face amongst the crowd. "You have the gall to attack us, and then when we fight back you call us monsters? You are nothing more than sheep brought to a slaughter."

"Do not fear!" Ku'terik shouts out, as all eyes shift to him. "Attack at once and they shall fall!" The Watchers stop for a moment, glancing amongst each other. Turning in unison to us, they all rush forward, like a sea cascading against a mighty stone. We hold. I duck and weave amongst the mortal instruments they have employed as weapons. I lash out every chance I get, scoring superficial wounds that only anger the onslaught of enemies.

A heavy bellow comes from behind me. I skip to the side and send a glance behind me to see Felgrand succumb, slipping to his knees as the Watchers pin him to the ground and discard his weapon. Namar fares much better, until a hammer shoots out, smashing him across the face. He spits blood as he turns slowly, his blades falling from his hands as he too tumbles to the ground.

"Don't fall with those pathetic mongrels. Just surrender now and I promise to make you love me Ai'hara," I scowl, kicking another Watcher from my way, as I start to march toward this arrogant wannabe.

A screech distracts me for just a moment and a sickle nicks my cheek. I lean to dodge a second swing before I barrel forward, leading with a shoulder, to knock the wind out of the Watcher.

Ai'hara shoots forward, sliding underneath the Watcher I smashed into just a moment after. She stands up and sprints at Ku'terik, her hair pin clenched in her palm.

"I don't want to hurt what is mine," Ku'terik sneers, as he raises his blade.

"I belong to no one!" Her hair pin intercepts his blade. The blade holds for but a moment before her hair pin carves through his. I see the spark of surprise on his face. In the split second it takes for her weapon to cleave through half of his, a hand snakes forward, catching her wrist. He looks down on her smugly as he pulls his blade from hers.

She punches forward, clocking his head to the side. He turns and brings the blade across in a wide arc. She tries to dodge but he still has a grasp on her wrist. He swings and scores a shallow gash on her chest. He smirks condescendingly as he raises the blade once more.

"You, see? You are weak!" Ku'terik roars as the blade cuts into her side again.

"Get away from her!" I lunge forward, ducking under one of his lackies and slam my fist into another that steps into my path.

"She is mine, but I suppose I can kill you first." He drops Ai'hara to the ground, where she cradles her wound, scuffling away from this prick.

He swings his sword. My dagger clashes with it, chipping his partially cleaved blade. I bring my other blade up and dart it forward. The blade slams into his chest. His fist comes up smashing into my face. He grabs on to my shirt, hoisting me up as I pant from the effort.

"Look at you, so tired after just one action." My face wrinkles in disgust as anger crawls beneath my skin. His sword clatters onto the gravel below as he smashes his fist into my face once more. *Damn, if only I hadn't fought so much, I would not be so tired!*

Blood swims around my tongue as he uses one hand to grab the edge of my jacket.

"Now what was so important that you pocketed it?" He reaches into my jacket, pulling out the box. A neatly folded sheet of paper slips from my pocket as he does so. The page slowly twirls in the air as it descends. The scuffle seems to halt as all eyes spectate the page. It hits the ground and unfolds. A single bead of sweat trails down my cheek. *How do I still have that blasted paper he gave me!*

"A paper bearing the image of Prometheus?" Ku'terik muses.

"Why do you have that?" Namar glares at the paper. The unique design of the gothic letter surrounded by a seven-pointed star. It glows green as a flash of light blinds me for an instant. In that instant I reach forward grasping the blade in Ku'terik's chest, bringing my foot up to his stomach. I springboard away, tearing the blade from his skin. His howl pierces the air as I tumble back. The light dies down to reveal a figure. In the place of the paper stands Stephen, clutching his book, his hand outstretched as if he was reaching for someone.

"Where am I?" He turns on his heel, surprise marring his face. His gaze scans until it finds the box.

"Now things make more sense."

"Stephen, why are you here? How did you escape Pandora's box?" I snarl glaring up at him. Stephen scoffs as he looks around.

"I didn't, all I did was change from one of her boxes to another," Ku'terik scoffs.

"More human scum." Stephen turns, one of his eyebrows fishing upwards. I scan and see everyone else has stopped.

"Me scum? You seem to have it backwards; you are all just insects before Prometheus."

"Prometheus? The name rings a bell, but ultimately you are just a different variant of scum. Leave now before I kill you!" Ku'terik stomps up to Stephen, his blade once more in his hand. The box is clutched in the other. Stephen chuckles.

"Kill me, and just who are you?"

"I am Ku'terik, and I am the head of the Watch!" He swings his sword at Stephen.

"You have lofty goals for someone I have never heard of." Stephen leans back letting the blade pass by harmlessly, then he juts out his leg smashing Ku'terik backwards. The box and blade land at Stephen's feet. With a swift kick the box bounces over to me. I look up confused as Stephen opens his book.

"I really don't have the patience to deal with another pretentious leader like you."

"Help me!" Ku'terik looks behind him when not a soul moves. The other Watchers all stand back, glaring down at him and beginning to step back as a whole.

"You look pathetic," Felgrand sneers.

"It seems that they are in agreement as well," Stephen berates.

"You filthy wretches! I am an elite! You should be begging me to lead you!" The crowd parts as Cu'jehi is helped forward.

"For your transgressions against us, Ku'terik, you must pay the price."

"You!"

"Even I must agree you are quite pathetic." Cu'jehi shakes his head.

"*Arta Scrisa: Eviscerate.*" Stephen whirls and his gaze stops on me, and I flinch. I dare not move a muscle as my eyes train on the pen pressed to the paper in his book. He seems to ponder for a moment as the pen lightly scrapes against the notebook's surface. Then with a sudden moment he snaps the book closed.

"Now that we have everything in order, let's get the rest of Prometheus here," Ai'hara scoffs at Stephen.

"Summon others, to the Glade? That is impossible."

"The Glade is nothing more than a prison of Pandora's." Cu'jehi flinches at that. Ai'hara stands up.

"You don't know what you are talking about!"

"This is just another of Pandora's boxes, the only difference is that you have contracted with her and have the ability to leave this one. Things cannot simply enter and leave freely. I however have a different way around it."

"How?" Cu'jehi's shaken voice utters in a crushed tone.

"Loopholes, loopholes. Reflections are not objects by themselves but once they are present the object must exist as well." Stephen reaches into his pocket and pulls forth a chrome marble. The surface is reflective in nature. He holds it up in the light, admiring it. His attention shifts to me.

"If I were you, I would open the box." A wretched cackle escapes him as the marble drops from his hand. It smashes on the ground, the pieces exploding into large shards that shift into a metallic liquid that forms a pool in front of him. I reach down, placing my hand onto the magical prison as he simply stares in a content, victorious manner.

With Prometheus

"You will never get anything from me!" Pandora growls, causing Alexander to sigh as his hands glow green once more.

"Never is a long time. Now that I have recovered the time I have lost, I am willing to keep this going as long as I need. Let me allow you to stew upon that for a moment or two."

"Alexander." Mateo steps forward meeting Alexander as he steps away from Pandora.

"What is it?"

"It would seem that Stephen has summoned us." Mateo holds out his palm where a chrome droplet the size of his palm lay. He turns his palm and a small stream pours from it; however, the droplet remains fixed to his palm and never reduces in size as the metallic stream spreads across the ground forming a reflective surface.

"I don't seem to need you anymore." He looks over at Pandora and her spiteful defiance.

"Perfect." Dahlia gleefully skips forward and with a quick slice parts Pandora's head from her body.

"You fool! Now we work on borrowed time!" Alexander shoves Dahlia toward the expanding liquid.

"She was useless to us." Alexander grabs Dahlia by her shoulders and shakes her.

"Now she will recover faster!" He throws her to the slick puddle where she slowly sinks into it.

"I cannot wait to kill you, Alexander."

"You are more than welcome to try once Solomon is dead," Alexander sneers, stepping onto the reflective liquid.

Bastian

I scowl while opening the box. A brief shine of light blinds me as two forms appear. Solomon and Solaire appear side-by-side. Solaire looks no worse for wear; however, Solomon is much worse.

Solomon's armor, once pristine, is now ripped and torn. Large gashes adorn the icy blue metal, not showing any damage to his skin. He turns his head side to side before his eyes focus on a massive tree grove on the opposite side of the clearing.

"After so long, the boundary is within my grasp ..." Solomon laughs almost maniacally. "I have to thank you for this Prometheus."

He marches away from us like a devotee to his cause. Each step increases his energy for the next. Then he stops as a green glow envelops his person.

"I would not be thanking us just yet. Just because you see the goal at the end of the line doesn't mean you will be able to reach it." I wheel to see standing next to Stephen are Mikhael and Alexander with his damned smile. I move to stand only for a pressure to push me back down.

"Why don't you all sit there and observe. This is why we exist," Mikhael ridicules as they move past us.

"But first let me remove some of our spectators!" Alexander grins as a transparent clock face fills the sky. The hands both stand on twelve.

"What are you doing?"

"Just removing some of the complacent souls that amount to nothing and giving me the time I need for this battle."

"Stop!" Ai'hara cries out.

"*Consume the meek.*" The clock begins to tick backwards as cries can be heard from the Watchers. They grow older as a green light captures the crowd. Cu'jehi sneers through a pained expression as he is enveloped in the green light. They cry in fear as they swiftly turn to dust.

"You monster!" Ai'hara weeps as she watches those she knows become dust.

"I prefer the term self-serving."

Solomon

"*Remember why you do this.*" The other me speaks clearly. "*You do this to protect your friends.*"

"Here I thought that you had wanted to remove the boundary, but you are just standing still," Alexander mocks as Carter dashes forward with Dahlia flying just behind him.

"*They will keep coming to stop us, to stop you from making sure your friends are safe. The only solution is to remove the problem. Now show them that you will do anything for your friends.*" The voice in my head eggs me on as I feel my body begin to move.

"It doesn't matter if you can move if I land the first hit!" Carter shouts as he thrusts his spear. I lean backwards, leaving behind a shell of my body to be speared.

"*Arte scrisa: bombard.*" I leap backwards as boulders smash into the ground I stood upon. I hear a hiss behind me, and my eyes widen as I duck, frost whirling around my fingers as I feel them harden into a makeshift blade. Dahlia looks on in surprise as I impale her onto my arm. I leave her stranded in the air as pain registers on her face. I turn back to dodge another attack from Carter. Rolling on the ground, he stabs down trying to pin me to the dirt underneath me. I roll to a crouch as he descends from a leap intent on impaling me. I quickly rise, my left arm darting upwards and grabbing his wrist. His shock is momentary as he begins to wrench out of my grip. I see Mikhael dashing forward from behind him. Out of the corner of my eye I spot Dahlia float overhead, her scythe gripped in between both hands, ready to behead me, but my onslaught has just begun.

"*Burst,*" I utter confidently, hearing Dahlia scream as she is torn in half. At the same time I pull Carter closer, his spear nicking my cheek as I pierce Carter's chest with my arm. He coughs in surprise and Mikhael curls his fingers as if ready to throw a punch. I close my fingers that had just pierced through the corpse on my shoulder, letting a swell of power pool between them.

"*Bolt.*" I let the magic fly. I watch it smash into Mikhael and he falls like a stone, collapsing onto the dirt face first. I stand, tearing my arm from Carter, letting his body flop onto the ground like the trash it is. I meet Stephen's calculating gaze mirrored by Alexander's maniacal one.

"What now?" I pant as I stand up straight. Alexander shakes his head.

"Don't you think that was a little too easy?" The bodies all split apart into a reflective ooze. Then a searing pain grazes my cheek when one of Carter's spears comes flying past me.

"What!" I turn to see Mateo stepping out of the ooze with pristine versions of Dahlia, Mikhael, and Carter. Carter smirks before he dashes forward, several ripples forming in the air around him as he pushes, Dahlia taking off just behind him.

I attempt to raise my hand in the air as a spear comes rushing into my palm, only to find I cannot move it.

"Damn you, Alexander!" I pull myself upwards using the immobile spear as a grip only for it to shatter, letting me fall toward Carter's spears. I push both hands in front of me, crossing them. Ice forms a shield to take the impact of the spear sending me flying back.

I blink as I find myself slowing down midair. Then Dahlia flies over

Carter, blade already slashing. I feel myself turn intangible letting myself fall out of the shell. Her blade cuts clean through the statue.

"*Razor hail!*" The statue explodes, sending razor-sharp glass at both of my assailants, where it pelts the ground.

"This seems a lot harder for you now that we are all working together," Alexander mirthlessly scorns.

"*Frozen Armor!*" I shift to a different idea, as ice encases my body.

"*Arte Scrisa: Eviscerate!*" My armor shatters to dust as Carter charges once more. I form two blades as I duck under his weapon, only to be forced to jump backward, as Dahlia slashes downward covering his side.

My swords break as soon as they form, and I stop in midair once more. Once again, I slip through a shell of my body.

"That doesn't work on me."

"No but this does, *Influx.*" I find myself catapulted toward Carter's blade. Shocked, I smash my arm into the ground trying to pull myself to a halt. Dahlia leaps in the air bringing her scythe to bisect me.

I feel my feet drag on the ground before I lose feeling in my lower body. Then I smash into the ground as gravity doubles. I bring both arms together and ice jets out from the ground on either side of me forming a barrier that just catches the scythe. The magic lets go of me as I roll forward toward the end of the barrier I made. As I crawl along the ground, I notice a strange image of a spear in my reflection.

"Shit!" I barely lean to the side as Carter's spear comes shooting through the reflective surface and then I roll backwards just in time to dodge another reflected spear.

The dome shatters and I barely dodge the suspended weapon above me. I dive at a surprised Carter. I ball one of my fists as cold energy gathers inside of it, only to find myself stopping just inches out of range before I am rocketed forward smashing into Mikhael's fist.

"*Crush.*" He grins as he spits blood. An unimaginable weight smashes upon my chest, sending me rocketing backwards, blood splashing across the ground as I too come to lie in a heap.

"*This is pathetic … you won't save your friends at this rate.*" The voice taunts me. I look up to see Prometheus encircling my prone body, each moving in with the intent to finish me.

"*Just freeze everything, then destroy the tree!*" I look up as Carter charges. "Fine, you all leave me no choice!" I scream, as I feel a build up of power.

"Yes, your only choice is death!" His eyes grow wide as he sees mine glow an ethereal azure.

"*Blizzard!*" The cry calls upon freezing winds that buffet the others sending them back, but Carter, who is caught right in front of me, is frozen solid. I sneer as the shock is stilled into his sculpture. Finally, I got one of them. "*Shatter.*"

He splits to pieces, his spear landing on the ground as I turn toward the tree, a triumphant grin on my face.

"*Stop.*" I slow to a stop as a green glow encases my body. Alexander shakes his head from side to side stepping forward.

"I hope you didn't forget about me," he speaks in a tantalizing manner.

"Damn it, not now!" I curse.

Bastian

"Bastian, we need to help him!" Felgrand screams from the rapidly chilling dirt.

"I know! What would you have me do!?"

"Your magic! It is time! Use it!" Namar yells and Alexander perks up at this.

"I suppose that is right, I have not seen you utilize any magic since this hunt has begun." Alexander nods sagely.

"I can't control it," I hiss at them.

"If you don't do something, then we are all going to die!" Namar huffs.

"Namar, everything could go wrong if I do this," I plead.

"Bastian, everything already has." I meet his gaze and I see the last emotion I thought I would ever see on his face: desperation. I grit my teeth together as I turn myself over to lay on my back.

"Fine, but you had better not regret this." I inhale deeply, before I stand up, putting myself in between Stephen and Solomon. Alexander steps back, curiosity scarcely suppressed.

"Please show me. I want to see everything you hope for come crashing down as I strip the time from Solomon." His eyes grow green as he observes. I raise my hand, my fingers equally spaced as I glance at Namar. He nods back and I turn to stare into Alexander's curious stare.

"Whatever happens, it is on you." I let my wrist roll back and forth as I feel the magic build up in my body. The pressure builds and I shudder thinking about what could happen.

"*Syrda,*" I utter, turning my wrist in a full circle. A resounding crack fills the air as that unwelcome feeling takes over my body. The green glow around Solomon fades causing Alexander to gasp. He looks frantically at his hands, as he extends them repeatedly before glaring at me.

"What have you done!?" he screams, his cool confidence melting into an abstract combination of horror and disbelief.

"Alexander, what is wrong?" Stephen's eyes narrow as he asks.

"I can't feel it anymore! My connection to the sands of time!" I smirk as blood dribbles from between my lips.

"Perhaps they are sealed away or even just momentarily inactive. I don't know."

"You will not win just because I cannot use my abilities. I am but one of many Prometheans," Alexander growls.

"We have Solomon, we won't lose," I counter, feeling some sense of victory for once.

A yelp from behind startles me and I turn to see Solomon grasping at something. A dark protrusion from his shadow had pierced his stomach.

"Namar!" I look over, my anger quickly quelled by the confusion marring his face.

"It wasn't me …" he trails off. I turn back as a squelch demands my attention. The shadow bubbles upward as it seemingly comes alive. The sludge-like ooze grows higher as it bubbles upwards surrounding Solomon.

His eyes glaze over, and a deep blue aura amasses around him. He glares down at the shadow and spits.

"I will not be done in by the likes of you! I have come too far! I am so close!" His eyes glow as well as he booms.

"Absolute zero!" The distinct sound of ice twisting fills the air as snowflakes dance around Solomon. A blast of blue and the bubbling shadows are covered in a bluish-white sheet.

"I will not be stopped when I am so close to saving the world! So close to saving it from ruin!" A hand curls around the icy spike impaling him from his shadow. He flexes and it snaps, leaving the tip of the spear in his chest. He turns, marching forward only to stop as a dull boom fills the air. Solomon timidly turns his gaze downward, then the ice shatters and the dark bubbling shadows shoot upwards engulfing him. A muffled scream dies shortly after it starts as the shadows drag Solomon's form down into the ground, leaving a large, darkened circle where he once stood.

The shadow bulges upward in a grotesque manner, branching out in a strange way, leaving the silhouette of a man. The darkness slides from his form leaving in his place a regal figure. A dark shroud billows around his gigantic form. He stands at an imposing height of six foot five, taller than Felgrand, with dark brown hair supporting a rustic crown. Two bangs frame his head, which would have been symmetric had a massive scar not bisected the left side of his face, leaving a jagged crag down to his lips.

His face betrays age despite having a youthful composition, his eyes containing an analytical coldness to them as they dart around his surroundings. His posture is that of someone of a higher class than everyone else. From the shroud of darkness, I catch a glimpse of black metal. My breath hitches in my throat. *It was the same as the kind the Pursuer wore!*

"Who are you, and what did you do to Solomon?"

"This is the Monarch," Stephen declares, as a bead of sweat pooled on his forehead.

"So, I am still remembered?" He quirks an eyebrow.

"Yes, and we will have your crown," Stephen speaks confidently as he steps forward.

"Stephen, you knew about this didn't you?" Alexander scowls, taking a step backwards.

"Of course, I did, this is why I gathered you all here, after all I could have taken Solomon down on my own," Stephen says as he writes in his book.

"You bastard! I didn't want this!" Mateo screams, and Dahlia brandishes her scythe.

"I will kill you, Stephen."

"Well too bad, the Monarch is here now, so first you have to kill him," Stephen smirks victoriously.

"You play a dangerous game, Stephen," Alexander speaks, sending him a sideways glare.

"Despite knowing who I am, you dare challenge me?"

"*Pillars.*" Large masses of earth rise from the ground on either side of the Monarch. He casually glances between both, before his eyes land upon Mikhael.

"Your magic has quite the cost." The ground underneath Mikhael cracks as sweat rushes down his face. He smiles tiredly.

"Costs that can be reversed are not really costs." The Monarch quirks a brow.

"*Flux.*" The two massive pillars smash together onto the bored adversary, crushing and grinding together into a massive ball of dirt and stone. I turn to see the bloody mess of Mikhael's crushed body. Alexander scoffs as he looks at the face on his watch.

"I truly despise having to save you every time you utilize your magic to any relevant extent."

"Alexander, just do it," Stephen orders and Alexander grips his watch tighter, marching past me.

"I believe that I have had just about enough of you ordering me around!" His eyes grow green as he marches toward Stephen.

"What insolence." The Monarch's voice rings out, causing us to shoot our attention to the rock, just in time to see a torrent of darkness tear the earth asunder. The Monarch stands a frown spreading across his face.

"You actually thought that you could stop me with that?" he scoffs, as he shakes his head. He raises his arm and a dark slag forms on the edge of his fingers.

"*Arte Scrisa: Frezera,*" Stephen cries, desperately scribbling in his book.

"Intriguing, I can't move my arm," the Monarch utters, observing his arm.

"No, you can't—" he stops as several concentric circular patterns appear around his arm.

"Magic that stops an object. Not well known and very powerful, but your cost is steep."

"Stop your prattling, your time is almost up," Alexander interjects.

"Pretentious words coming from one who can barely hold me back," the Monarch sneers as his arm inches forward, a wicked grin crossing his face.

"Stephen, you had better hurry!" Alexander growls as his eyes glow a dull shade of green. "I still can't use my magic!"

Arte Scrisa Erasure! Stephen writes the last few words and his pen drops from the page. A wide pulse shakes the air as the pulse seems to stop as it strikes the Monarch. He looks down at his arm clad in the dark armor. He raises his eyebrows as he observes it.

"It's over for you now!" Stephen's face takes an insane grin as he steps past Alexander, who takes two steps backwards.

"What do you mean?" the Monarch questions as he continues studying his arm.

"You don't feel it? I just erased you from existence! You won't have even a digit left once it is done! Your crown will be mine!"

"You think that foolish god, Ionidulos's power will get rid of me? Especially when contracted by one such as yourself?"

"What?" Stephen pauses as he takes a closer look. "Why aren't you disappearing?"

"I really thought that I had eliminated all of those foolish enough to pursue contracts. I guess I was wrong." The Monarch steps forward tearing his arm free from the immobilizing magic.

"You … you are a monster! Stay away from me!" Stephen backs up, as he begins writing once more.

"No, I think that I will put an end to your nonsense now." He waves his hand and Stephen's shadow bulges before it expands, engulfing him, and dragging him into the ground leaving nothing in its place. The Monarch takes a step closer, and I grab one of my knives and hold it at the ready. He eyes me with forlorn disgust.

"What do you hope to do with that?"

"I won't let you take Namar!" His passive look morphes into fury.

"You dare tell me what I can and cannot do!" A sharp pain registers in my chest and I cough, spilling blood on the ground. I glance down to see a spear of darkness erupting from my chest.

"You bastard!" Namar screams, rising to his feet.

"Namar, let's gut this monster!" Felgrand smashes his foot down flipping his longsword to his hands, his face contorting into a twist of rage.

"Once again, Felgrand, I cannot agree more!"

"A holy knight and one who bears a contract with me, working together? Blasphemous!" Namar flinches as they both charge.

"I will never serve you," Namar screams, and the Monarch simply smiles in return.

"You speak as if you have a choice, but don't worry, I will have you watch as I slaughter your friends before I bring your contract in default." He raises his left hand as a dark flame encompasses his palm.

Just as Namar and Felgrand swing their weapons, the ground shifts and cleaves in two, leaving a large void to separate them from the Monarch. I see the surprise on the Monarch's face as the space between our land and the Monarch is increased. I feel a presence behind me. I struggle to lean back and see Pandora floating lightly behind me.

"Pandora, to think the witch herself would come crawling out of her vault for peasants like these." The fire extinguishes from his hands.

"It appears that I made it in time," she speaks calmly as she keeps a focus on the Monarch.

"Why did you stop us!" Namar bellows.

"Their value has not become apparent to you yet." She waves her hand, and a dark circle surrounds us, leaving us to look at the Monarch through a murky distortion.

"You even take the one who has a contract with me." The Monarch's twisted reflection scowls.

"You have more important things to worry about than him." The

Monarch straightens as Dahlia dashes at him from behind, her scythe poised to strike. A quick backhand sends her flying backwards.

"Mateo, Alexander, help me kill him!"

"No, I don't think I will," Alexander replies as he steps closer to Mateo.

"What do you mean, no?"

"Goodbye, Dahlia," Alexander smirks, ignoring her as Mateo bows in a grandiose manner. He lets a reflective orb fall from his hand he has extended out to his side.

"Mateo, you worthless traitor! You were supposed to be on my side!" Dahlia screeches.

"I suppose that was true, but I prefer to stay on the side of the one who will not heedlessly backstab me." She flinches and scowls.

"He does have a point," Alexander points out, with a condescending grin.

"You insufferably arrogant boy!"

"Now, there is no reason for such language."

"Dahlia, I only have the power to bring back one more soul. All you have to do is kill them, and when I return you can go free too," Mateo reasons, with a placating smile.

"Fine, but if you don't, I will find a way to take your soul." She glares as they sink into the reflection.

"Oh Dahlia, you won't need us to come back. He is only saying that as a pleasantry. You have wasted enough of our time. Now you can use what pathetic little you have left to try and fight the Monarch." Alexander's cocky smirk is the last sight we see as Dahlia begins to tremble.

"Now that you understand that you have been left for dead, do you not see?" the Monarch lectures.

"I will kill you!" Dahlia roars bearing her scythe down toward the Monarch. The Monarch shakes his head in a frustrated manner.

"Me, what makes you believe I even have the patience to fight you?"

"What?" Dahlia gasps as he waves his hand in front of his body as a mass of darkness rises from the ground. A black bulge grows to head height, where it thins and wanes, forming into a humanoid shape. It takes the form of a man standing with his two hands resting upon the pommel of a sword, the tip digging into the soil. His flaming eyes bore through the white exterior of a bull skull, the bleached bone contrasting the armor he wore. His dark cloak encloses his armor, making it seem like a solid shade of black. The armor itself is made from long fibers that cross over each other, gleaming like steel. His double-edged, evenly serrated blade reflects the sunlight.

"No, I think that my Arbiter will be more than enough for you." He turns away.

"Where do you think you are going? You are stuck here inside this box." Dahlia runs a hand through her hair as she berates the Monarch.

"Silence you wench!" the Arbiter speaks for the first time: a dark hollow tone, betraying anger and agony with each reverberation of his unholy voice.

"Darkness can never be contained with just a box. Arbiter, finish her."

"As for you Pandora, hiding away your little champions will only serve to irritate me. I won't bother searching, but that doesn't mean that my agents will not." With a dismissive gesture a geyser of darkness erupts from the ground, eclipsing his figure before it slips back into it leaving an empty void.

The area around us flickers and we find ourselves falling into a blur of green and brown with no sign of Pandora.

"Rest here and recover, the Monarch will not wait forever. I will call when it is time." Pandora's voice echoes around us.

I feel Solaire cradle my limp body as I succumb to the sleepy haziness.

Solaire

I cradle Bastian as I kneel into the gravelly dirt beneath my heel. Great trees stand around us. Ferns with great leaves and the rustle of grasses surround us. Through the leaves on the trees and those of the ferns, you could see great mountains sitting around us. A tear slips down my face. Bastians face is stark white, a massive scarlet stain creeping through the makeshift press. I move, dragging a shell shocked Ai'hara to him, tears stream down her cheeks as she barely registers Bastian's body. I place her hand on the wound and her eyes refocus. In a lethargic manner, she casts a healing spell.

A hand snags my collar bringing me eye-to-eye with Namar.

"This is your fault! I should have just killed you and collected the bounty!" He shakes me, spit splashing against my face. Felgrand stares on passively.

"You think I don't know that? Bastian wasn't supposed to get hurt! Solomon gave me everything! He was my friend! He wasn't supposed to be the monster they all made him out to be!" Felgrand brings a hand down onto Namar's shoulder. A solemn shake of his head and Namar lets me drop to the ground.

"Stop your crying, the Monarch has risen and now my contract can be called upon."

"Who is this Monarch and what contract do you have with him?" Felgrand pipes up as another wave of tears assault my vision. I turn to see him glance at the blade in his hand.

"The shadows I use … I contract them through a deity. I never knew what it was until after I had formed my contract. All I knew was their name: Croatoan. After I made the contract, he appeared before me."

"Who did?"

"The Arbiter."

"The Arbiter, the guy that the Monarch summoned?" I ask, remembering his terrifying appearance.

"Yeah, and he told me that when the Monarch rose, that I would be called to serve. I am sure it is only a matter of time before I am ordered to do so. We have to stop him before he can enact the contract!" He grabs my collar again bringing me up to his face.

"I don't care how sad you are! You got me into this mess, and you will help me get out of it. You and Bastian will help me find a way to bring the Monarch down. I will not be used as a pawn of his, contract be damned," he sneers.

"He will help, rogue, but first we have to recover," Namar scowls as he finally looks around.

"Where are we even?" Namar huffs out, while stretching his arms before letting them flop back down against his side. Looking up for the first time I see the reddened dirt and through the trees I see large mountains forming a bowl around us.

"These trees … this soil." I start.

"You know it?" Felgrand asks, his eyes warily darting around.

"Yeah, these are only common to California."

"California." Ai'hara briefly tastes the foreign words as she continues to pass water over Bastian's wound, barely paying attention. "What a strange name."

"At least we can have a moment to rest now that we are finally safe," Namar sighs, sliding down against one of the trees around us and placing his swords at his side.

"You are just going to relax then, rogue?" Felgrand jeers.

"Ah, forget it. I have had a long day, being stabbed, and beaten around by Prometheus and Solomon. I can't really do anything while Bastian heals so I might as well take it easy. Everything hurts, so unless you need me, good night." He smiles in a victorious yet strained manner and flops onto his side.

"The nerve … angry one moment and carefree the next," Felgrand trails off as he removes his hands from Bastian and sits back as well.

"He is stable, at least, I have done what I can," Ai'hara responds sitting back, looking me in the eye.

"Thank you." She nods and stares up at the sky before frowning. "I cannot help but feel anxious, there is more to come."

The First Reality

He stands overlooking the smoldering corpse of the monster. A hideous beast that bled acidic blood and had wretched claws. Everything it killed turned into a zombie-like beast.

"This thing took a lot of men to bring down," he speaks to no one in particular, despite the mob of soldiers behind him.

"Director!" A voice echoes out as another man runs forward, a lab coat whirling as he rushes to meet him.

"Yes?"

"The contagion, we can't stop it! We must do something! It has already reached the city!"

"Everyone, sterilization protocol! We lift off in five!" he calls out.

"What about the city?" A phone rings and the man in charge pulls it out.

"Simple, if we cannot stop the infection, we remove any traces of it." He presses the button on his phone and brings it to his ear, his shoes clacking against the ground as he steps away.

"Sir, another anomaly has been detected." The man turns back, lingering on the charred remains of the monster that had come through the first one.

"Where?"

"Near the Mammoth Mountains, California."

"I want a team isolating the area, I am on the way. If anything tries to leave the isolation, and seems otherworldly in any way, I want you to put it down with extreme prejudice. Do I make myself clear?" He steps forward, over the body of one of the turned that his men had eliminated just minutes before.

Printed in the United States
by Baker & Taylor Publisher Services